A DOUBLE-BARREL BLAST
OF WESTERN ACTION!
ONE LOW PRICE!

COME A-SMOKIN'

"Suppose we talk about how we hooked up with each other?" Marratt said.

"No mystery about that," the tall man said. "I picked you up out of the slop of the road during that storm we had here the other night. Been doing the best I can to take care of you—"

"For a price of course." Marratt's lips turned bitter. "Get your cards on the table—how much you been hoping to stand me up for?"

The tall man, eyeing him incredulously, snorted. "Do you take me for a total fool?"

"I'm going to take you for a target in about ten seconds!"

HORSES, WOMEN & GUNS

The marshal slammed Final across the face with his pistol, the ungiving impact spinning Jim sideways. Trying to stay on his feet, half blind and bloody, Jim hit the keg.

The marshal kicked Final's gun loose. He said, standing over him, "You'll pack no iron in this town!"

Final, pushing himself up, got dizzily onto his feet. His mind bitterly told him to let well enough alone, but this bullypuss treatment on top of everything was more than he could stomach.

"You don't think I'll take this lying down, do you?" he growled.

COME A-SMOKIN'/
HORSES, WOMEN AND GUNS

NELSON NYE

LEISURE BOOKS NEW YORK CITY

For Nick Gardea—
Chihuahua was never like this!

A LEISURE BOOK®

August 1994

Published by

Dorchester Publishing Co., Inc.
276 Fifth Avenue
New York, NY 10001

Printed in the United States of America.

COME
A-SMOKIN'

He was tall, whip lean and freckled with dust-streaked sunburnt features whose expression of drugged indifference masked a turmoil as explosive and deadly as the crust that covers a slumbering volcano. The last bite of stolen food had gone through his stomach three days ago and, though stolen money clanked in the pockets of the bedraggled stolen clothes he wore, the stolen freedom which had kept him going had been reckoned too precious to be risked through contact with the cupidity motivating others of his kind.

He cursed through cracked and beard stubbled

lips as he peered from the fronds of a scraggly mesquite at a huddle of houses racked against the far slope. He had no idea what town this was or how near it might be to the Mexican border; only the encroaching proximity of starvation had pressured him into considering it at all. But he had reached the point where forced realization warned he hadn't much choice if he would continue to live.

He was two weeks out of Yuma; roughly a hundred and eighty miles east of it and God only knew how many miles south. He was still afoot, had no papers or weapons, and his name was Grete Marratt —which probably wouldn't mean much without you'd been concerned or had followed the trial in the Prescott, Phoenix or Tucson papers. In that case, unless you were connected with law enforcement or preferred to make your living from what you could catch in bounties, you'd be a heap inclined to give him all the room he wanted. According to the records Grete Marratt was a killer.

He had certainly rubbed out one man. Deliberately, coldbloodedly and with obvious malice aforethought, he had gunned him down on the main street of Prescott. The prosecution had produced thirty-seven independent witnesses. There had never been the slightest doubt about the outcome; but as a case it had caused an inordinate amount of jaw wag-

4

ging because the fellow Marratt killed had been a Deputy U. S. Marshal.

Hugh Clagg, the deceased, had been a stranger in that section whereas Marratt had been well known, a rancher who had lived his entire thirty-two years in the region 'adjacent to Prescott. He'd been generally respected and had never been in serious trouble.

Clagg had been sent to look into a payroll stage robbery in which two sacks of mail had been taken. Subsequent investigation had thoroughly disproved any possibility of Marratt's having been involved in the case Clagg was working on. No connection had been found between the marshal and Marratt; so far as could be learned they had never exchanged two words up to the time of the shooting. Marratt had said something then but had spoken so guardedly no one else could repeat the few words he had used.

He wouldn't talk when arrested. What he felt, what he thought, was locked away secure behind a poker-face stare. "Think whatever you want—I've got nothing to say." He had stuck to that attitude all during the trial. Not even his friends could get any more out of him. And now, once again, he was on the loose; an escaped convict for whom men were watching the whole length of the border.

Another man might have laughed, at least been grimly amused at the concept of all those alerted tin-packers hunkered back of cocked rifles along a line he hadn't any intention of crossing.

Marratt never gave the matter a thought. He was far too engrossed with this business of survival, with staying alive till he could track down Clagg's partner, the three-fingered man with the uptilted nose and the jagged knife scar across his left temple. These were the things which were important to Marratt; these, with his need to stay out of the law's hands until this business was done with.

He was not a patient man but he could exercise patience. He had no flair for getting a gun out of leather but, once he had one focused, he could call his shots. The sight of blood turned his stomach but he had worlds of determination; it had survived five years of Yuma and would continue unabated until Clagg's partner joined the marshal.

Bella Loma wasn't much of a place, Marratt saw, even for Arizona. No more than the proverbial jog in the road, it contained four saloons, a big general store, a blacksmith shop, an assayer's office, a public corral with feed lot attached, three rooming houses, a crib, no homes and a packing-crate post office which, according to the sign crudely chalked on its door, was only open for business on Saturday nights. There was also a restaurant, if you cared to flatter the Lone Star Grub with the title.

6

It was lamp-lighting time when Marratt limped into the place and sagged onto a stool at the fly-blown counter. A blowsy, redfaced blonde with a once-white apron stretched across buxom breasts took his order and foghorned it over to the sallow-cheeked oldster bent above the greasy stove. There were half a dozen customers mingling conversation with the clatter of pans and dishes and though he propped both elbows on the oilcloth, hands cupping his face to mask all he could of his profile, Marratt kept his ears skinned for any mention of his name.

Planking the food he had ordered in front of him, the redfaced blonde drifted down to the other end to shoot the breeze with a corpulent drummer. Marratt ate with a cautious care, chewing slowly, hearing no mention of himself in the talk around him. One by one the others finished and straggled off to pursuits more personal, the drummer being the last to depart after fixing up a tentative date with the hasher. The cook filled a plate and took a stool at the counter. The blonde picked over some of the stuff on the stove, finally hung up her apron and went out the back door.

The cook swabbed his plate out, picked up Marratt's cup and drew him another coffee. "Never figured you'd come back," he said, setting the smoking beverage in front of him.

Marratt sat perfectly still for the space of one

heartbeat, then went on with his chewing, not looking at the man but very conscious of his inspection.

He didn't know what to say hardly, but it began to be apparent he was going to have to say something. The cook hadn't budged and he was still looking at him. Marratt grunted. "Don't they always?"

"I didn't look for you to. I always figured you had a heap too much savvy."

Marratt pushed a crust of bread around the trough of his plate. He put his teeth to work on it while he thoughtfully assayed the cook's words for significance. "Meaning, I guess, you didn't reckon pride—"

"Pride!" The old man snorted. "What did pride ever get your pappy? If it's pride fetched you back you're a goddam fool!"

Scowling with outrage he snatched up his plate and three-four other dirty dishes and dumped them, back of the stove, on the double-barreled two-foot stack in the sink. Taking up a broom he started sweeping the place out. "Pride!" he muttered, swinging the broom with a venomous vigor. But when he reached the counter he glared at Marratt again. "What the hell you fixing to do?"

"I think," Marratt said, "you've mixed me up with someone else."

"You better not try handing that line to Wineglass!"

Marratt swallowed the rest of his coffee. He

8

dropped a silver dollar beside his plate and let his eyes play over the cook's scowling face. "Just who do you happen to have me pegged for?"

The old man took a good long look at him. "You've changed some, I'll admit it; but not enough to pull any wool over Wineglass. You look just about the way old Jake did at your age—a lot more like him than you did fifteen years ago. And them whiskers you're growing is a plumb waste of time."

Marratt shook his head. Hoof sound and laughter pounded past on the street outside and he saw the old man stiffen, swivel a quick glance toward the windows. When he brought his face back there was no doubting his sincerity. "Go out the back way, Luke, and mebbe you can get out of town without any of that bunch seein' you."

"But I tell you—"

"Would you involve a defenseless old man in your feuding? Don't argue, you featherheaded dimwit—git goin'!" he rasped harshly, and shoved Marratt doorward.

Marratt stepped out of light into thick felted darkness.

It was commencing to rain. He heard the patter of it round him as the cook slammed the door shut, and a low ground wind carried the smell of it strongly through the additional odors of wet sand and cedar.

Hunching his shoulders, Marratt turned up his collar, knowing the need to get away from this place. There might be no more back of the old man's talk than a desire to hooraw what he took for a down-and-outer, but a fugitive couldn't afford that chance.

He had seen beforehand the very real risks he must expect to encounter if he were forced to approach or go into some town and had planned his escape with these risks well in mind. The Mexican border was hardly a stone's throw south of Yuma but Marratt was not fooled by that mirage of safety. Nor was he tempted into trying one of the several other routes a really clever man might have elected to travel. He had chosen the impossible and gone straight east into the wastes of the desert, convinced this was the only direction no intelligent man would expect him to head for.

He had gone through the Wellton Hills and braved the peaks of the Copper Mountains, the Mohawks and the Eagle Tanks, skirting the northern slopes of the Craters and Saucedas, finally floundering his way across the crags of the Sand Tanks to come into Bella Loma from the south. He had never before been in this part of the country and had reckoned himself reasonably safe from meeting anyone who might know him; he could hardly have expected to be taken for another.

Nor was he satisfied he had been. He found it

easier to believe that old cook had been hoorawing him; but whatever the reason behind that old man's talk and actions it plainly behooved Marratt to get the hell away from here as speedily as possible.

He had three sure things in his favor. Before coming into this town at all he'd made sure it had no telegraph. Outlying regions could not be warned to be on the watch for him. The night would conceal his movements and this cold drizzle should wipe out his tracks before morning. So, no matter what was back of that old coot's talk or what he might now be doing about it, the way to escape was still open.

On the debit side of the ledger, however, was the encroaching result of that food he had just taken into his overtaxed half-starved system. The effects were already becoming apparent in the unwonted inertia that was blurring his perceptions. He felt a terrible desire to crawl into some covert and sleep the clock around. He had to fight this with all his resistance. He knew his mind wasn't working with its accustomed precision; the wheels of his thinking had slowed to a snail's pace and it was all he could do to keep his eyes open.

He tipped back his head and let the cold rain beat into his face and it helped some, but the orange shine of those lamp-lighted windows exerted a tremendous attraction; he wheeled with a frightened curse when he found himself clomping toward them. *Get yourself in hand, you goddam fool!*

He broke into a shambling run and the rain-slicked gumbo underfoot sent him sprawling. A kind of panic got into him. He clawed himself upright and hurled a curse into the windy, rain-lashed night and stood glaring about him. Like an animal at bay, he thought bitterly; and started walking. Before he had covered fifty feet of puddled ground the desire to lie down was at work on him again and the lights of a boarding house loomed squarely ahead of him. A dollar a night, said the sign beneath the lantern to the left of the door. He had his hand on the knob when something hammered his right side and flung him halfway around.

He sagged against the wall, squeezing the knob of that door with all the strength he had in him, raking the wet blackness of the street with frantic eyes.

You don't question the shock of lead ripping into you; there's no other feeling like it. Marratt knew he had been shot and was trying to spot the shooter when he realized what a beautiful target he presented crouched beneath that goddam lantern.

He was reaching for it, whirling, when the second shot beat dust from the weathered facing of the doorframe. He flung the lantern into the mud of the road, dropping prone to the boards of the porch as he did so.

The third shot howled above Marratt's head and he heard it plow through the porch rail. That gave him the angle and he caught one brief glimpse of a short and broad shape vanishing around the corner of one of those across-the-street saloons.

He staggered onto his feet, trying to understand the psychology of a community which gave no attention to the racket of gunfire. Not a window had gone up, not a door had been flung open. Nor could he think of any reason for this attempt on the life of a total stranger unless some truth lurked behind that damn cook's jawing and he had again been mistaken for somebody else.

It didn't make sense but he wasn't going to argue. He wasn't going to wait around for any further hints. The quicker he got out of this town the better he'd be suited.

But in the rainswept murk the numbness in his side produced by the shock of the bushwhacker's bullet began to wear away and pain sledged through him in nauseating waves. The second time he stumbled he latched hold of a tree to steady himself and flung a wondering glance across his left shoulder at the line of racked horses hitched before the saloons.

Bad, however, as he was tempted to try for one, common sense assured him that to show himself now in the light from those windows could too easy turn out to be the same thing as suicide.

Shanks' mare was rough but an unarmed man could find a lot of things rougher.

CHAPTER 2

He was more used up than he had realized. He had no idea of how long he had been walking or how far he might have come. It all looked the same. Darkness garbed the land with impenetrable curtains and when he stopped, as he sometimes did to listen, there was nothing to be heard beyond the drone of the rain and the gusty slapping of the fitful wind.

Crossing those mountains had taken a lot out of him and this hole in his side wasn't helping matters any. He was chilled to the marrow and unutterably weary. The weight of his sopping store clothes seemed to add an immeasurable burden to the intolerable performance of hoisting one foot and putting it down before the other. It was too remindful of pulling cows out of bog holes.

He lost all count of the times he fell down. It would be simpler, he thought, just to stay down; but always something seemed to prod him onto his feet. If the goddam ground would only stay where it belonged he thought he might be able to keep going, at least until he found some kind of shelter to crawl into.

But everything seemed to conspire against him. When the ground wasn't standing on end to defy him, the whole frilling world was reeling round in a circle and the next thing he'd know he'd be down in the muck again, swearing and puking like a pulque drunk squaw.

Getting up was the hardest but, some way, he always made it. Then he'd stand there awhile trying to get his bearings, swinging his head from side to side like a bull until someone would jeer: Grete Marratt, you fool, you've reached the end of your rope.

Every time he heard that his stubborn jaws would clamp together and he would go splashing on through the rainswept murk, stumbling and staggering, talking like he was out of his head. *Howl, damn you!* he'd swear at the wind. *Howl your fool guts*

15

out and see what that gets you! You ain't stopping Grete Marratt, you son of a bitch!

There wasn't nobody going to stop Marratt; not, by God, this side of Clagg's partner.

Once he thought he heard buggy wheels, the plop-plopping of hoofs. That was crazy, of course, and he had sense enough to know it. No one but a moron or a fugitive was going to be wandering around in this downpour.

And then he got to thinking he saw the mist-blurred shining of some faroff lamp and he was like some ship-wrecked sailor with his eyes glued on that held-out hope of sanctuary, convinced that he could reach it if the locoed damn thing would have the sense to stay put and not go frisking all over the whole horizon.

Just went to show how wild a mind could get. Like Marratt imagining he saw the gaunt outlines of some kind of shack when any nump would know you couldn't see ten foot ahead of you through these sheeted gusts of wind-driven rain. He seemed to have lost the light now, but he was still floundering toward the shape of that shack when the goddam slop reared up out of the road and slapped him hell west and crooked.

The next impression Marratt had was of hearing those phantom hoofbeats again and the squish-squash-squish of buggy wheels. But when he finally got his mind to where it could pin down the truth he couldn't hear nothing but the slog of the rain. He remembered being on his face again and, centuries later, of hands pawing at him—or maybe it was buzzards. He was too damn tired to look.

When he did open his eyes it wasn't night any more and he reckoned he was out of his head for sure. He appeared to be lying on some sort of a bed in a long narrow room before a burned-down fire that was still throwing warmth. Or maybe it was the sun coming in that west window that had chased the night's damp chill from his marrow. If this were hell he was satisfied. One thing was certain: He'd never been here before.

It wasn't until much later that he began to wonder if he'd made it to the shack—the goddam shack that wasn't there. He reopened one eye cautiously. Somebody'd built the fire up. It was dark beyond the window now and there was a lighted lamp in a wall bracket, turned low but giving the room a yellow radiance brightened and made friendly by the dancing snap and crackle of the burning logs in the fireplace.

He opened the other eye and saw a tumbler of water and a white crockery pitcher placed handy on a chair that he could reach by putting a hand out. By these signs he understood that someone was

17

taking care of him because he sure as hell hadn't done all this himself. It was kind of nice to think that anyone would bother—was, that is, till he recollected who he was.

Realization suddenly hit him with all the shock of a knee in the groin. It slammed the floodgates of memory wide open. He flung back the blankets someone had put over him and, thoroughly aroused now, was fixing to swing his feet to the floor when pain exploded across his right side with all the breath-gagging nausea of being kicked by a mule.

He sank back white-lipped and trembling and felt cold sweat crack through the pores of his body. That damned bushwhacker's bullet! Alarm spread through him, narrowing his stare as the dangerous implications of his plight unreeled before him. Every instinct of the fugitive warned him to get out of here.

He forced himself to remain perfectly still but he could not control the feverish tumult of his thoughts. He'd been taken in and cared for but you couldn't pin hope on that; even now his unknown benefactor might be summoning a sheriff. How much time had elapsed since he'd been shot in Bella Loma? How much ground had he covered since turning his back on Bella Loma's lights? Where was he now? Where was the person who had fetched him here and how long had that person been gone from the house?

A look at the logs in the fireplace assured him the

man hadn't been out of the room long, not over ten or fifteen minutes. He remembered the horse hoofs and buggy wheels then and knew that his Samaritan could not have been a woman for no woman could have lifted him and he sure hadn't gotten here under his own steam.

He'd better try to get up, pain or no pain.

It was only then he discovered he had been undressed. Stripped naked, by God! And no clothes in sight!

That gave him a turn and brought the sweat out again. There was a bandage strapped tight about his ribs but you couldn't go wandering around in a bandage!

He stifled a groan and got an arm beneath his head, hoping it might enable him to locate his clothes. He couldn't see the whole place but he saw enough to know he was in a ranch house and that he was on some kind of couch in what probably passed for the living room.

It didn't seem to have been lived in for a hell of a long while.

Dust lay over everything. Cobwebs hung from the raftered wooden ceiling and were draped from the meager moth-eaten furnishings; webs that hadn't been made yesterday, dark and thick with musty dust.

And then the memory of his nakedness prodded

19

him again and, very carefully, he rolled over and got one foot down solid on the uncarpeted floor preparatory to rising.

With both hands braced firmly under him he reckoned he could anyways get into a sitting position before his hurt side slugged him into a faint. He could damn well try, and he was going to. Because any gent that would take a fellow's clothes away from him—

He didn't finish the thought because just then he put his hands down and one of them connected with the barrel of a pistol. It was laying on the couch, had been tucked in beneath the blanket. A .45 and fully loaded except, of course, for the single chamber on which the hammer rested.

The weight of that pistol in his hand did wonders for Marratt. It made him feel about seven feet tall and gave him enough gumption to bear the pain of getting onto his feet.

White-cheeked and dizzy, he had just got the blanket wrapped around his middle and was fixing to hunt the house for clothes when he heard the approaching crunch of boots in the gravel outside the room's west door.

Marratt turned, braced the gun against his hip and waited.

The person who opened the door had his left arm piled with groceries. He looked to be crowding sixty; a tall grizzled man in a black alpaca with a black San An tugged low above eyes that flicked toward the couch, fanned outward a little and came swiveling around until they picked up Marratt.

He gave no evidence of being disconcerted. "Expect you're feeling some better," he commented, booting the door shut and fetching his parcels on over to the table. "How's the appetite?"

"Suppose we talk about you."

"Pretty dull subject." The tall man offered a fleeting smile. "You can put that gun down, Luke; I won't bite you."

Marratt said: "Start talking!"

The tall man eyed him a moment longer. But when the hammer clicked back under Marratt's thumb he shrugged and said drily, "All right. What about?"

"About how we got hooked up with each other."

"No mystery about that. I picked you out of the slop of the road during that storm we had here the other night. Been doing the best I can to take care of you—"

"For a price, of course," Marratt's lips turned bitter. He felt weak with standing but he'd got over his dizziness and his mind was at work in some very odd corners. "Get your cards on the table—how much you been hoping to stand me up for?"

Anger darkened the other's cheeks. Then he pushed it away and said coldly to Marratt, "I was

21

hoping the years had taught you something but I guess you haven't changed much, Usher."

"We'll speak of that later. Right now I want to know who you are, what's your angle and why you stuck me in this empty house. I want to know where it is and—"

The tall man, eyeing him incredulously, snorted. "Do you take me for a total fool?"

"I'm going to take you for a target in about ten seconds!"

"All right. I'm Doc Frailey, as you damned well know. Night before last I found you lying unconscious outside the gate. I fetched you here because it was handy, because you happen to own it and because I wasn't at all sure you'd be wanting folks to know you'd come back."

"Any particular reason I wouldn't want them to know it?"

"You're the best judge of that."

"Been away quite a spell, have I?"

Frailey, scowling, finally shrugged and said drily, "Fifteen years."

"And you were able to remember—"

"You took care of that part!"

Marratt said, fishing: "Run out on a bill, did I?"

"Some might be tempted to put it that way."

They considered each other for a couple of moments. Frailey said impatiently: "I didn't come here to play games, Usher. Put up that—"

"I'm not playing games. I'm trying to get to the bottom of what's going on here; you're not the first to remember me, Frailey."

"I suspicioned as much when I got a look at your side. What the hell did you expect, coming back to this—"

"I must have cut quite a swath to be remembered fifteen years."

Frailey said scornfully, "How long has this amnesia been bothering you?"

Marratt shook his head.

"Have you forgotten telling round how you were going to put a window through Clem Ryerson's skull?"

"So I killed this big mogul and dug for the tules, eh?"

"You never went near him—never even waited for your old man's funeral!"

Marratt's look turned thoughtful. "You know," he said, "Frailey, you *could* be mistaken."

"Hell, I'm not passing judgment. You asked and I told you."

"You haven't yet told how you got onto me so quick."

"It wasn't quick," Frailey sighed. "I had a look at you, of course, soon's I got out of the buggy. Knew

I'd seen you before but it was finding you there, not forty yards from this house, that finally put my wheels to churning. Time I'd got you inside and scraped off some of the muck I was pretty damned sure. The picture cinched it."

Marratt's eyes narrowed. "Picture?"

"Old Jake's. Above the couch. You can't miss the resemblance."

Marratt was willing, for the moment, to take his word for it. He went over and sat down. He laid the gun on the chair beside the water glass and pitcher.

"Feeling shakey?" Frailey asked.

"It ain't so much that; I just can't seem . . . " He scrubbed a hand across his eyes. "How bad's this hole in my side?"

"Cracked rib. You'll get over it."

"Why do you reckon I've come back?"

The tall man looked at him sharply, then he glanced at his watch and put it back in his pocket. "I don't know—I don't *want* to know. I don't want any part in it."

"Who was Ryerson? Why did I threaten to kill him?"

The doc studied him quite awhile. "I'd rather you found those things out from someone else—"

"My God," Marratt said, "I've already been shot once! If you didn't think I was in danger why'd you leave me that gun?"

"The gun was here. It belonged to your father."

Marratt, eyeing it, said slowly, "It's been well taken care of."

Frailey shook his head and waved a hand at the wall. "It was hanging in that gun belt. I took it apart. I cleaned it and oiled it." He said on an irritable gust of breath: "Don't ask me why—I just did, that's all!"

A meager smile tugged the corners of Marratt's mouth. "Why hide your light under a bushel, Doc? It was a generous impulse; particularly in a man who thinks as poorly of me as you do."

"I wasn't thinking about you!"

"You must have thought a good deal of Jake Usher then. Did Ryerson kill him?"

Frailey opened his mouth, changed his mind and strode doorward. But halfway there he spun around and came back. "All right, I'll tell you. When you were tanked up on rotgut, and it was doing your talking, you *claimed* Clem Ryerson killed Jake. You were in the Red Horse Bar, yowling what you would do to him. But when they got you sober enough to know wild honey from cow flops you got right into a saddle and commenced laying farapart tracks for the border."

Marratt sighed.

"You had folks on your side up till then," Frailey grumbled. "Now the boot's on the other foot and you're a fool twice over." He puckered his lips up irascibly and spat. "What the hell good did you think coming back would do?"

"Ryerson still alive, isn't he?"

There was a long instant of silence then Frailey said explosively: "You damn well better believe he's alive! His outfit covers almost half of this county—goes clear around you. What Wineglass says is same as law in these sandhills; the marshal's his man just as much as Churk Crafkin."

"Must be a comfortable feeling," Marratt observed, and then asked abruptly: "What am I supposed to do about clothes?"

"I took those old rags of yours out and buried them."

"I'll make quite a hit going around in a blanket."

"There's some of your old things hanging in the closet. Probably be a mite tight—"

"Would you mind fetching a few of them in here? I'll need a pair of boots, too, and a hat while you're at it."

The moment the doctor's back was out of sight Marratt got up and took a look at that picture. He'd been prepared to find a vague likeness in it; a shade of eye, perhaps, a not dissimilar nose. But, staring into that gilt-framed ferrotype, he was almost too astonished to breathe. The pictured face of Jake Usher so closely resembled his own that, except for the sideburns and chin tuft, he might have been looking at a photograph of himself.

He got off weak knees and sagged against the couch's rest with the damndest feeling he had ever experienced. But his mind was made up. There'd be some risk, all right; in fact there'd probably be fireworks—but where better could he hide until the law quit looking than in the clothes and behind the problems Luke Usher had run away from?

Frailey came back with an armful of range clothes which he dumped, with boots and hat, on the couch beside Marratt. "If these don't fit maybe some of Jake's will."

Marratt tried on the boots; a little tight across the sole but he reckoned he could stand it. "How much land have I got here?"

"It's kind of late in the day to start reaching for a halo."

Marratt kept staring till Frailey said testily, "You haven't got a damn inch without Wineglass says so."

"Never mind that. How much was Jake holding onto?"

"Twenty-four thousand acres."

"How come Wineglass didn't take the spread over?"

"They been using it."

"But the books still show it as owned by Usher?"

"Ryerson likes it better that way; he gets the good

of it without so much squawk. He don't give a damn who owns it on paper so long as its grass goes into his cattle."

"Then it's legally mine," Marratt said. "Tomorrow—"

"There'll be no tomorrow for you around here. You better take my advice and get out while you're able."

CHAPTER 3

After Frailey departed, Marratt got himself dressed in an assortment of Usher clothing and scraped together a meal from the staples the doctor had left on the table. He had plenty to think about and he gave the bulk of the evening to it.

One thing he'd probably ought to do right away was to let it be known he'd not returned—in his character of Luke—to make trouble. He was perfectly willing to let sleeping dogs lay and hoped Ryerson might hold a similar conviction.

After all, Marratt argued, it didn't have to be Wineglass that had triggered that shot at him. It

29

could be the cook from the Lone Star Grub, or some-one the cook had set onto him. He had no way of guessing what antagonism Luke had kicked up be-fore cold feet had hustled him out of the country.

One thing, however, could almost certainly be banked on: Whoever had tried to cut him down with those bullets was pretty near bound to have another whack at it.

But there were several different ways of looking at this business. And the more Marratt prodded it around in his mind the less inclined he became to feel sure the answer was Wineglass.

On the face of such facts as had been supplied by Doc Frailey certainly Ryerson stood to gain the most by getting rid of Luke Usher. Luke's bolt on the heels of his father's death had already given Wineglass fifteen crops of Usher grass, not to mention the pro-fitable revenue from fifteen crops of abandoned cattle which Ryerson's men had probably branded with impunity. One could not readily imagine Ryer-son being willing to abandon the source of such pro-fits.

On the other hand, however, if Wineglass had be-come as powerful as Frailey's talk had indicated, why should Ryerson have tried to pot his duck from ambush? Why go out on a limb when the obvious thing would have been to laugh in Usher's face?

Bushwhacking, generally, was the resort of a

frightened man. What had Ryerson to be afraid of? Why should the owner of Wineglass, controlling local law and presumably backed by a crew of hard-riding rannies, be even mildly perturbed by the return of a man he'd already run out of this country once?

Marratt shook his head. It just didn't make sense. Even assuming Ryerson to be a bit disconcerted by the apparent return of old Jake's spineless son, there would seem little occasion for such drastic measures. Much, of course, might depend on the two men's characters and Marratt realized he knew precious little about either of them—and who was this fellow Doc had called Churk Crafkin? The answer to that attempted drygulching might well lie in the relationship of Usher to Crafkin.

Marratt, scowling into the fire, was uncomfortably aware of the risks he was taking. But better a feud than the steel bars of Yuma. Better the dangers which he saw piled around him than the certainties he'd be facing if he let opportunity's knock go unheeded. He had no horse and damned little money yet, here in Bella Loma in the guise of Luke Usher, he need only face the perils inherent in Usher's name and past entanglements. On the dodge as a fugitive, every man's hand would be turned against him. Here he faced only the threat of individuals; in flight he'd be surrounded by all the multiple and ever-vigilant resources of the law.

All his thoughts in prison had been concentrated on escape, on getting outside where he could search for Clagg's partner. Now, having escaped and re-acquainted himself with liberty, life had become suddenly dear to him again and the likelihood of coming across the man he was hunting almost hopeless. Clagg's partner—like Clagg himself—had been a stranger to the country around Prescott. Marratt had no means of knowing where the man had come from and those five years he'd spent at Yuma had not freshened the trail up any. The description he'd gotten of the fellow's appearance indicated a certain prosperity and his horse had been rigged in the manner of desert travel; beyond this all Marratt had as clues to work with were the few things Charlie had mentioned—that three-fingered hand, an uptilted nose and the knife scar across a left temple. Not much to go on with the hounds of the law in full cry all about him. But if he could stick it out here until the law became engrossed in matters more urgent and he had got himself accepted indisputably as Luke Usher, why then he might be able to go after that guy in earnest.

He got up and turned around and had another long look at Jake Usher's pictured features. The resemblance was uncanny. Usher had the same stubborn sweep of jaw, the same sandy hair, dark inscrutable eyes and lean gash of a mouth which had looked back at Marratt from countless fords and mountain pools while the horse had been dropping its head to water.

And speaking of horses, Marratt reflected, he had better put his brain to the task of promoting one. He certainly hadn't the price in his pocket and a fellow caught afoot in cow country was uncommon likely to be regarded askance.

His mind had just winged back to that corral he'd seen in town when he suddenly tensed, hand dropping to gun butt, as hard knuckles pounded the outside of the door. He cleared the gun for action, got back to the couch and called: "Come in."

The man who shoved open the door was a study in contradictions.

Marratt had been halfway expecting to see the face of that cook or the short and broad shape of the one who had tried to cut him down the other night. This bird was a stranger. He was garbed in a blue-and-white striped shirt, open at the throat, and the bottoms of his corduroy trousers were thrust into fancy-topped Hyer boots—which don't grow on bushes. A black curly-brimmed Stetson was shoved back off the forehead of a long narrow face that, from the nose on down, was sheathed in black beard.

But no beard was going to conceal his pleasure in greeting a friend he hadn't seen in fifteen years. He came in like a wriggling collie with hand outstretched and teeth shooting splinters of light through the bristle. "How are you, son—"

His voice suddenly forgot the good will it was building and went into a bleat as he caught sight of the snout of that motionless pistol. "Great Gawd a'-mighty, Luke! Put that dratted thing away—you ain't forgot Clint Gainor, hev you? Ol' Clint that learned you how to set a buckin' bronc—Gee-rusalem! I—"

"Close the door," Marratt said without change of expression. "Now come around here into the light where I can see you and don't make no sudden passes."

Gainor followed instructions, sideling into the downturned glow from the lamp like a drunk on a chalkline. There was something strangely ineffectual about his big-bellied shape, a suggestion of timidity he'd probably hoped to hide—and maybe generally did—behind that bluff hail-fellow-well-met air of heartiness he'd been so busily exuding as he'd stepped over the threshold.

Marratt put up his gun but kept a hand close beside it. "How'd you know I was here?"

"Perkins—he cooks for the Lone Star—was tellin' me he seen you and then, about a hour ago, I run into Doc—Hell's fire, boy! Don't you remember Ol' Clint what wrassled steers for your pappy down to Keeler's Crossin' that time the Mesca—"

34

"Sure. Vaguely," Marratt decided. "But I can't seem to recollect us ever getting so close for you to come busting a gut to get over here the minute you learn I'm back in the country. And so spider-footed quiet—"

"I kin tell you about that—"

"What'd you do with your horse?"

Gainor licked his lips while a slow flush spread through his haired-over jowls. "I'm goin' to tell you about that—it's all part of the same thing, of the reason for my bein' here. I guess maybe you got some call to be wonderin', but it sure ain't what you think. I've had to play my cards mighty close these last years. You don't want to believe more'n half of what you hear—"

"All right," Marratt said. "I've got the salt box handy. Get down to brass tacks."

Gainor stared. He said defensively, "I dunno what you've heard but what I've done's been 'cause I've had to. It ain't been easy to live around here I kin tell you with Wineglass knockin' right ag'in my east fence. Let Clem Ryerson hev his way an' he'll glom onto this whole country from the Sierra Estrellas clean to Pozo Redondo—an' don't you never think he won't!"

"We'll let that stand as said, for the moment. Let's hear about the reason you came hiking over here. And why you didn't ride up like a neighbor."

Gainor's look turned reproachful. "You know mighty well I can't afford to neighbor with Ushers. Now don't get me wrong! You might not hev guessed it but I've always kinda nourished a secret likin' for you, boy. I'm one of the few around this patch of cactus that never figured you pulled out account of bein' scairt o' Wineglass."

"That so?" Marratt allowed himself to unbend a little. "Why did you think I pulled my freight?"

"'Cause you was too damn smart to go ag'in a stacked deck."

"The line separatin' smartness from cowardice ain't much easier to latch hold of than the hair on a frog. You must have a good pair of eyes."

"I got 'em," Gainor nodded, "an I kin put two an' two together. Lots of guys—most all of 'em—what heard them cracks you made in the Red Horse Bar that night figured it was the whisky talkin', but I knowed better. I knowed you meant every dad-gummed word of it—an' that's what's fetched me over here now. I knowed damn well you was aimin' to come back an' I've been buildin' toward that time."

He grinned felinely through the brush of his whiskers. "I kin see you think I'm just butterin' you up. Don't you believe it, boy. I'm here to do my Christian duty an' you a good turn at the same time mebbe."

Marratt watched the sly eyes go from himself to

Jake's picture. "Put your cards on the table."

But it wasn't in Gainor's roundabout nature to travel the shortest way if he could avoid it. "How much dough hev you got?" he asked.

"Do I look like a bake shop?"

"I mean money—hard cash."

"I couldn't stake you to a hairpin."

"What I figured," Gainor nodded. "You ain't even got a horse. Doc said the clothes you was wearin'—"

"You come over here to crow at me?"

"Just pointin' out where you stand is all. Matter of fact, I'm here to help you—"

"You reckon you'll get round to it before morning?"

Gainor managed a parched smile. "You hadn't oughta begrudge me a little mite of time; you're in a bad hole, boy, an' I'm fixin' to pull you out. I'll give you six thousand dollars for the title to this ranch."

Marratt looked at the man and grinned without speaking.

Gainor squirmed around inside his clothes and looked flustered. "All right—I'll give you eight!"

"Eight thousand dollars for twenty-four thousand acres. You call that pulling me out of a hole?"

"You ain't got no twenty-four thousand acres; all you've got's the goddam title!"

"What about Jake's cattle?"

"How many can you produce?"

"That remains to be seen. I can always send Ryerson a bill for what's missing."

Gainor snorted. "You kin fly a kite, too, but what good'll it do you? Way things stand right now you couldn't get six cents on the dollar for this place with Wineglass riders workin' four sides of it an' Winglass cattle gobblin' up the grass! For Chrissake talk sense!"

Marratt said coldly, "The only way it makes sense you'd give me eight thousand dollars for the deed to this spread presupposes you're convinced I've come back to kill Ryerson. I haven't; but on that basis—and providing I was able to get the job done— you'd have title to a property worth around eight times what it cost you. Not to mention any cattle you might be able to round up."

Angry color jumped into Gainor's scowling cheeks. "So what if I did figure it that way?" he blustered. "No skin off your nose! You can't use the place anyway. You got no money to stock it—no way of gettin' Ryerson's stock off. Even with the cash to do it you couldn't get a crew that would go up ag'in' Wineglass. If you funk killin' Ryerson he'll run you outa the country. If you avenge your pappy, like any guy with a lick o' gumption *would* do, you'll still hev to run. So what good's this place to you?"

His eyes ran over Marratt shrewdly. "Be reasonable, Luke. If I'm willin' to take the gamble you oughta be glad to hev me do it. A guy can't pick that kinda money off the bushes." He said persuasively, "Once you're across the border a stake like that'll set you up like a king. Think of the women it'll buy—the whisky—the *mozos*. Christ, I'm almost tempted to go down there myself!"

He got out a roll of banknotes and counted eight thousand down onto the table, stood peering at Marratt smugly. "There it is. All I want is your name on a quitclaim."

"Yes," Marratt thought, that was really all he wanted. He didn't give a damn what Luke decided to do afterwards.

Gainor, obviously knowing more about Luke than Marratt had, produced a flask from his pocket and set it down on the table beside that thick sheaf of currency. "Reckoned you might like a nip—"

The oily smile suddenly whisked out of sight in Gainor's whiskers as he fell back in alarm before the look of Marratt's eyes.

"Pick up your bottle and your money," Marratt said, coming off the couch, "and get outside that door before my temper gets away from me."

Several afternoons later Marratt, getting out of the saddle before the administration offices at the Malicora agency, left the horse Doc Frailey had hired for him on grounded reins beside a similarly anchored head-tossing bay filly. Stepping onto the porch he slanched a casual glance at the silent Indian solemnly squatted behind the sweltering folds of a red wool blanket. "Agent in?"

The Maricopa's eyes rolled up at him indifferently and as indifferently returned to contemplation of the faroff mountains.

Marratt pulled open the screen door and stood

a moment just inside accustoming his eyes to the drawn-blind dimness by which the agent was attempting to modify the heat. There was no one in this cramped waiting room but a shadowy corridor, leading off to the left, revealed a door standing open. Marratt, gravitating toward it, heard a fluttering of papers.

The cavity beyond the door turned out to be a quite spacious office. Dust-covered Indian artifacts were arranged on boards hung about the walls and products of Indian industry, equally dusty, were heaped on tables below them and stacked without care in obscure corners. A comely squaw in a beaded headband looked up from a desk to say "Yes?" and Marratt told her that, if possible, he'd like to have a talk with the agent.

"Stanley Beckwith," she said. "He'll be back in a moment," and, extricating several slips from the sheaf she'd been going through, rubber-banded the rest and dropped them into a drawer which she closed. Picking up the others she went off down the hallway.

Pretty efficient, Marratt thought, and wondered where Beckwith had found himself a squaw with sufficient education to serve as office help.

He dropped into a chair and sat with his thoughts picking over other talks he'd recently had with Indian agents and hoping, by God, this one was going to be different. Leather heels coming down the corridor drew him out of this thinking and pulled his eyes toward the door.

The man who came in was stoop-shouldered, tall, and so thin he'd have to stand twice to cast a shadow. The skin of his face was like yellowed parchment in the blind-filtered light coming in through the window as, with a querulous glance, he gave Marratt a nod and said, "Well? What is it?"

Marratt kept his seat. "I'm looking for Stanley Beckwith, the agent."

"You've found him," the tall man grunted, gingerly lowering his bones into the padded desk chair. "I've no range to lease if that's what you're here for."

"Thought, perhaps," Marratt said, "you might be needing some beef."

The agent looked as though he were about to say no but, as his mouth came open, something changed his mind. He picked up a penknife and got to work on his nails. "What . . . ah . . . kind of beef?"

"Cheap," Marratt growled, and Beckwith turned that over awhile but instead of asking *how* cheap he said without glancing up from his nail job; "Anyone suggest this agency to you?"

"Just occurred to me you might need some."

"Customarily we purchase beef supplies by contract—"

"I know all that. I've sold beef to Indian agencies before."

"In that case you'll understand our funds are rather limited. Which reservations have you been doing business with?"

Marratt said, fed up with this fencing, "This beef is priced right. Can you use it now or can't you?"

He knew as soon as the words were spoken he'd used the wrong tone with this fellow.

Beckwith's look turned cagey. "Where are you getting this beef?"

"Where do you suppose I'm getting it? From my own spread, naturally."

"Naturally." Beckwith smiled. "Now suppose you tell me with what iron it is branded."

"Do you find certain brands to be more palatable than others?"

Beckwith managed a rusty chuckle. He laid aside the penknife and pyramided his fingers into the shape of a steeple. "We are forced to be very careful what kind of beef we feed to the Indians. Our buying powers are fenced with restrictions. It might be, however, that at some later date—"

"Look," Marratt said, "I've got some beef to sell now; I don't know what I'll have later. I might close out this ranch and go somewhere else. I'm not trying to hurry you into a deal but if you can't use this stuff just say so."

43

Beckwith peered at him uncertainly, wanting the cattle but scared to stick his neck out. Marratt understood the man's dilemma. The Indian Service was notoriously underpaid; if he could get these cattle cheap enough he could pad out his income by putting the difference in his pocket. He wanted like hell to do it but he had to be sure there wouldn't be any comeback. "Are you willing to guarantee—I mean to put it down in writing—you're the sole and legal owner of every steer you're offering to sell me?"

"I'm putting nothing on paper. On the other hand," Marratt said, "I'm willing to produce local residents who have known me for upwards of twenty years and will verify my right to dispose of the beef in question."

"Reputable residents?"

"That will be for you to say. I'll name them when you agree to do business."

"What do you call 'cheap'?"

"Will you pay seven dollars a head?"

Beckwith's eyes gleamed. Sweat broke through the skin of his face and he was starting to get up when worry dropped him back again. The price was too low. Beckwith said suspiciously, "You couldn't afford to sell steers of your own raising—"

"I never said they were of my raising. As a matter of fact I have just come into them. The reason I'm practically giving you these cattle is because without your help I couldn't round them up nor attempt to make delivery. I'd have to borrow some of your Indians—"

"I couldn't let you do that. I'm not permitted—"

"Why couldn't we work it out this way? You send a crew down there and hold your own roundup. I'll be available to identify the cattle. When you've made your gather, drift them up here and pay me seven bucks a head for whatever you arrive with. That's fair enough, ain't it?"

The agent said with a fishy stare, "Why can't you—"

"Because I haven't any crew."

"Then how do you know you've anything to sell?" Marratt got up. "Hell with you," he said.

He was partway through the door when Beckwith's discontented voice plowed after him. "Wait—"

Marratt wheeled.

"I might take them at five."

"You're not the only flower on this dunghill. There are other agencies," Marratt reminded him.

Greed in Beckwith was still clawed by fear but you could see Marratt's price making weight in the balance. The man couldn't bear to think of losing such profit. He stood squirming and trembling on the verge of acceptance when a last jab from caution prodded him into asking, "Where do I go for these cattle?"

"Vekol Wash, south and east of Bella Loma."

Beckwith looked like a sledge had struck him. His face turned green. His eyes bugged like they would roll off his cheekbones. "That's Wineglass range!"

"They can't stop you from picking up Usher cattle."

"Ush—*Merciful God!*" Beckwith collapsed like a ruptured sack.

Marratt returned.

The agent cringed. He flung up an arm. "Go away —go away," he gasped, whimpering.

"For Christ's sake, what ails you?"

Beckwith moaned. When Marratt stepped nearer he ground bony shoulders into the chair back.

Marratt, fastening a hand in the front of his shirt, hauled him onto his feet. "Answer me, damn you!" He cuffed Beckwith's face until some of the crazed terror fell out of the agent's stare. "Start working your jaws!"

"There—" Beckwith shuddered. "There ain't no Usher cattle."

"Why not?"

But Marratt already knew without Beckwith telling him that what hadn't died from natural causes had sure as hell gone to stuff Indian bellies out of contracts filled by Clem Ryerson's Wineglass.

With a snort of disgust he flung the agent away from him.

How long he'd been riding or how far he had come to where he was now Marratt had no idea when the dog's growl riveted his horse in its tracks. They'd been about to move into a thick growth of willow and the dog stood before it, growling through the folds of what he held in his teeth.

Marratt's horse blew a gusty breath through its nostrils. It danced to one side and the dog growled again. He was just a big overgrown shaggy-haired pup, a typical Indian cur by the look of him. Marratt spoke to him softly and the dog wagged his tail. Just a little, that is. He kept watching them belligerently, not moving from his tracks.

Marratt stared a bit more carefully at what the pup was holding. It seemed to be some kind of buckskin shirt. "Your boss," Marratt said, "is going to whale the hair off you." Alert for a rush he swung out of the saddle. "Where'd you get that?" he asked, holding out his hand.

The dog loosed another growl and stood bristling. But when Marratt squatted down, not going any closer, the big pup let go of the beautifully tanned leather and with a tentative tail wag proceeded cautiously to approach.

Marratt remained still while the dog sniffed over him. Then the pup put his panting face on Marratt's knee and, receiving the pleasurable touch of friendly fingers, rolled over to let the man scratch his chest.

Marratt did, and picked up the shirt as he got to his feet. The dog jumped to grab it but flattened, tail thumping weeds, when Marratt ordered him down. "I think," Marratt said, "we'd best take this thing back before somebody gets into trouble."

That suited the pup. He darted off through the trees. Marratt, following, let his mind slide back to his talk with Clint Gainor. He was unprepared for the blue-gray look of the gleaming dug tank which suddenly confronted him. He was even less prepared for the lovely naked figure that abruptly went splashing into it.

When she again broke surface she was out in the middle and not in any mood to be reserving her opinions. She still had the beaded headband around her dripping hair and her eyes—brown or black— were flashing with bitter outrage. "What do you think you're doing around here?"

Marratt felt like a fool. It was the girl from Beckwith's office. "I—I wasn't figuring to spy on you. I—"

"Not much, you weren't! You despicable polecat!"

"Lordy, ma'am, I had no idea—"

"Then why did you follow me? Let go of my dress, you grinning hyena, and start making tracks before I—"

"Dress!" Marratt stared blankly at the fringed piece of buckskin. He was utterly astounded. He supposed it *could* be a dress at that, now she'd mentioned it. "Golly," he said, "I—"

"Spare me your lies. Just put it down and go away."

"But I thought it was a shirt—a man's hunting shirt," he explained. "The dog—"

"*What* dog!"

Marratt, to his considerable consternation, discovered the pup had vanished. He peered helplessly about, feeling and probably looking as big a hypocrite as she thought him. He even loosed a couple of half-hearted calls, hoping the dog might put in an appearance, while the girl's scathing eyes stared with angry contempt.

Finally, in desperation, he told her how he'd encountered the dog and how he'd happened to arrive in this clearing, but he could see she wasn't believing a word of it.

"All right," she said when he'd finished, "what are you hanging around for now?" Are you intending to wait till I come out of the water?"

"Christ, no!" Marratt gasped with cheeks flaming. He whirled in confusion, made a dive for the trees, and heard a tremendous splashing behind him. Sweat poured through the pores of his skin. Was that damned girl actually coming out of the tank?

He risked a look, found she was, and broke into a run.

"Come back here, you dadburned lowdown hypothecator!"

But Marratt wasn't wanting any more of her tongue. He redoubled his efforts and came out of the trees panting to find his horse looking at him with a palpable astonishment. It wasn't till he started to swing into the saddle that he realized he still had her dress in his hand.

He stared at it blankly and then with a curse flung it down and got out of there. He had troubles enough without getting tangled in any squabbles with Indians! He hoped she would find it but he'd be damned if he was going to wait around to make sure.

5

All the way home Marratt angrily tried to concentrate his mind on the talk he'd had with that conniving agent but his exasperating thoughts kept sneaking off to the girl he had found in Beckwith's office. Mostly his recollections were of how she had looked going into that tank; though there was one part, too, about the look of her coming out that persisted in taking up a lot of his attention.

Her voice, he remembered, had been unexpectedly deep, not mannish at all but a kind of bright contralto that would have made a carven image turn around for another look. She had the blackest hair he had ever encountered; the whitest teeth, most eloquent eyes, the longest legs and captivatingest pair of—

"Hell!" he snarled through a growl of disgust, and tried again, scowling fiercely, to cuff his thoughts back to Beckwith.

She probably wasn't, he decided, more than seventeen or eighteen, but if you cared for Indian models she'd come off the topmost shelf. And she hadn't been hid in any hogan when the brains were being passed out or Beckwith wouldn't have had her working around his office.

Something queer about that deal anyway because, generally, white collar jobs around an agency were given to widows or elderly spinsters when the Service didn't have any spare males available.

He had never heard of the government hiring squaws in any capacity and you'd have thought that rabbity agent would have been a heap too careful to go hiring one on his own hook—even so delectable a one as he appeared to have latched onto. It got Marratt to wondering all over again how they had managed to get acquainted and if there might not be something more between them than was immediately apparent.

He found this notion strangely repugnant and sought uncomfortably to find out why it should bother him. Beckwith's morals—or hers, for that matter—

were certainly no concern of Grete Marratt's. It surely wasn't an interest in the girl herself that was prodding him . . . or was it?

Thoroughly disquieted he scowled at the horn of his saddle.

He had never considered himself to be much different from the average run of fellows brought up in cow country. He had known a few women, two or three of them intimately, but when he'd driven that slug between Clagg's bulging eyes he'd renounced further right to normal relationships. And he sure wasn't about to set up as a squaw man.

So far as that went—and he was positive of this much—he had no right to the regard of any woman. Not with the law trying to pick up his trail.

He was able on that thought to put her out of his mind for the moment and to go over somewhat sketchily the gist of his conversation with Beckwith.

The man was a puling self-confessed crook who had knowingly bought Usher cattle from Wineglass, secure in the presumption of Ryerson's local influence.

Marratt, with customary thoroughness, had already tackled the other roundabout agencies without discovering any interest in stock which could be had on terms substantially beneath the current market value. Wineglass contracts, he'd been pointedly informed, were amply taking care of all the beef their

53

money was able legally to purchase.

He had never seriously intended trying to unload Usher cattle although he had, to be sure, briefly pondered the possibilities. What he had been after was the knowledge just uncovered, an Indian Agent's duplicity which he could, if he were forced to, hold over Ryerson's head.

He hadn't, of course, any proof that would stand up if it came to a lawsuit, nor did he imagine such proof existed, but he was strongly inclined to doubt that Wineglass would court a public inquiry. His obvious course should things start getting rough would be to have a talk with Ryerson and give the man to understand he'd placed written particulars in other folks' hands to be examined in the event he happened to turn up dead or missing.

It wasn't the best defense in the world because a bullet might catch him before he ever got to Ryerson. It might be smarter, he decided, to seek out Ryerson right away; the only trouble with this idea was that it might take a deal of doing. Undoubtedly Ryerson had heard Luke Usher was back and it seemed equally believable he would have taken precautions to make sure the fellow had no chance to get near him.

The girl swung Marratt's thoughts once again in the direction of Beckwith and on a sudden hunch he stopped his horse and devoted several moments to a frowning speculation. Moved by the result of this thinking he sent the horse obliquely north and after twenty minutes of hard-pushed riding he pulled the gelding into a more comfortable lope and commenced to look round for sign.

He could be entirely wrong but, considering the man's character and the jolt he'd received, it appeared to Marratt quite likely that at the earliest opportunity the jittery agent would light out by the shortest route for Wineglass.

Through careful questioning of Frailey, Marratt had a pretty good idea of the approximate location of Ryerson's headquarters. This was the knowledge which had hurried him north hoping to intersect the line of Beckwith's probable travel. After another fifteen minutes he discovered a trail that looked likely and when he came onto it he found ample evidence that someone had used it within the last hour. Someone headed west and in a hell of a hurry.

He had no reason to doubt this was Beckwith. The man was in a sweat to reach Ryerson and Marratt didn't know if he'd best follow him or not, finally deciding to follow him far enough to make certain this hunch was paying bonafide dividends and not sidetracking him down some blind alley.

If these tracks were made by a horse packing Beckwith and the agent was actually making for Wineglass it behooved Grete Marratt to find a hole to crawl into until he could arrange to have that talk with the cow king. It wasn't hard at all to imagine Ryerson's reactions once he learned the supposed Usher was on the trail of those vanished cattle.

Marratt took a quick look at his shadow, rapidly calculated how much longer he could expect to have daylight, and set out on the trail of the hurrying hooftracks.

He rode leisurely now, giving himself time for thought, seriously wondering if he had made the right choice in deciding to pass himself off for Luke Usher. There was so much he didn't know. . . .

He might have dug some of these things out of Beckwith if he'd thought of it—he might still. But further thought tended to persuade him it would be too risky to overtake the agent within striking distance of Ryerson's headquarters. They'd have the whole crew out hunting him and, with superior knowledge of the country, would have him bottled up in no time. No, his best bet now was simply to make sure the agent was carrying his story to Ryerson.

Marratt had concluded there would no longer be any proof of what had happened to the Usher cattle; now he was inclined to question this assumption. Some of the Wineglass crew who had been in on the drives which had taken that beef to Beckwith might still be around.

He wished the hell he knew more about Luke's character, about the fellow's habits and personal mannerisms. By the way he had run you might suspect him of a broad stripe of yellow where he should have had a backbone, but Marratt dared not depend even on this. This drygulcher evidently hadn't considered Luke a coward. By Doc Frailey's telling, however, Luke had got blind drunk after his father's killing and had then pulled his freight without even attempting to make good on his brags.

Marratt stopped his horse of a sudden, eyes narrowing. The plain trail he'd been following had just come over a section of ledgerock which in turn had given way to a stretch of loose shale as it left the dry bed of a once-a-year river. He was still on the trail but the fresh tracks had vanished. He scanned the line of old willows bordering each bank and then glanced back at the ford, not liking this a little bit.

Why had Beckwith quit the trail? Where was he now? In those willows someplace watching Marratt across a rifle?

Marratt's frowning stare angled back across the wash to where the trail curled down off the flank of a ridge, striving to recall if Beckwith's tracks had come down also. But they must have else Marratt would not have entered the wash himself. They must have quit the trail as it crossed that ledge.

If somehow Beckwith had discovered he was

being followed and was now concealed and watching within the cover of those willows it would be the height of folly to show an interest in his tracks. To cast around for sign would almost certainly fetch a bullet; even now the flesh was cringing between Grete Marratt's shoulders.

He swung down, pretending to be tightening the girth of his saddle. He stretched then and yawned and took a cursory glance at the lowering sun which seemed about to drop behind the Maricopa Mountains. The feel of eyes was strong in Marratt as he climbed back into his saddle and sent the gelding foxtrotting forward into the unscuffed trail.

He did not look back but kept his glance unostentatiously employed with scanning the landscape ahead of him, seeking to find a place where he could leave the trail himself. There very obviously wasn't any, not in the next couple of miles which stretched before him flat as a table. A number of big boulders farther along constricted his vision and there was a scattering of gnarled mesquites but nothing which might serve as a competent screen for departure.

It seemed impossible Beckwith could have discovered him for at no time had he caught sight of the man or even heard sound of his travel. It seemed a deal more likely the harried agent had simply got off the trail at the best opportunity, hoping thus to outfox any possible pursuit.

He must be getting, Marratt decided, uncomfortably close to Ryerson's headquarters. Another three or four miles should be giving him sight of the buildings. The sun was gone, dropped behind those purple crags, and dusk would soon be unrolling its sables. He resolved to cut south as soon as he could.

He reached the first boulder and put it behind him. He passed several others and was rounding the last of these miniature buttes, observing how the land dipped beyond into greasewood, when he discovered fresh tracks beneath the gelding's feet. These curled in from the right and were without question the ones he'd been following and lost at the river.

So Beckwith *had* been attempting to mislead pursuit. And he was still bound for Wineglass.

Marratt, bending from the saddle to closer scrutinize the sign, was suddenly frozen in the posture when a lifting breeze fetched the sound of a hard-pushed horse from behind him. The dim clatter of shod hoofs on that ledge was unmistakable.

He was out of the saddle in the flash of an eye, leaving the gelding rooted on dropped reins. Snatching off Usher's hat he ducked round the butte until, down on his belly, he could catch the dark line of the willows and a low-crouched rider coming pell-mell out of them.

He watched the oncoming animal for several wondering moments, seeing the shape of it grow and become clearer. Though he could not make out the rider it was apparent the man was traveling this trail and that, before very long, he was going to come tearing around this butte.

Wriggling cautiously backward Marratt got to his feet. He resumed Usher's hat and, not drawing his gun but regathering the reins, held his horse by its cheekstrap, his free hand lightly placed across its quivering nostrils.

A man didn't usually travel hellity larrup without he was hunting a sawbones or doing his damndest to outride a sheriff. Marratt did not know what was driving this fellow but he had no intention of being seen if he could help it. Not by anybody bound for Ryerson's Wineglass.

A small stand of salt cedar fringed the butte's right flank and when the pounding hoofs of the rocketing rider reached the zenith of that building crescendo of sound Marratt led his horse into these and, swiftly turning, got one quick look as the man flashed past.

He stared incredulously after him, jaw sagging in astonishment. He said, "I'll be damned!" for the man on that foam-flecked arrow of horseflesh was Stanley Beckwith, the Indian Agent!

It didn't seem possible Marratt could have been overtaken by the man whose sign he'd been all this while following. When he got over his surprise Marratt knew it wasn't. He had just seen Beckwith—that much he was sure of. Whose, then, were the tracks he had spent so much time on?

It didn't, perhaps, make so very much difference but Marratt's penchant for thoroughness wouldn't accept such an answer. He'd roughly an hour left of daylight and if it lay within his power he meant to find out.

When he had rammed his feet into Luke Usher's

boots he had assumed, along with the identity, all the consequences attendant on Usher's past entanglements. He felt certain it was no coincidence that two separate riders in so short a time should have come this way in such a hell of a hurry. There had to be a connection of some sort between them and, caught up in this now, Marratt had to see it through. Waiting only until Beckwith's shape was lost in the tossing sea of that windwaved greasewood, he came back into the trail and carefully examined the two sets of tracks; the only similarity was that both had been made by fast-moving horses. Speed had gouged them deep into the earth and the ones he'd been following were smaller than the agent's—narrower, probably made by a number 2 shoe.

This, in Marratt's experience, was plain indication of a cleaner-bred mount. The sign left by Beckwith's were the tracks of a puddingfoot.

When he'd first come onto them Marratt hadn't thought of back-tracking this smaller set; he'd been too sure he was on Beckwith's trail to see any point in it. Now he wished he had done so, at least for a way; because, all things considered, he was pretty well convinced he'd been observed by that fellow—that it was this which had occasioned the man's desire for haste. That business at the river practically clinched this assumption and the two, taken together, strongly suggested Marratt had been recognized.

He swung into the saddle and, despite an increasing feeling of uneasiness, again took up the trail. Why had that fellow been so anxious to avoid him?

Forty rods from the butte the small tracks quit the trail and went digging off toward a low ridge adorned with the flaming blossoms of wolf's candle. Marratt, scowling goodbye to Beckwith, followed.

The man had gotten too much of a start by now for there to be any chance of Marratt overtaking him, but there was a slim possibility that he might, with good luck, catch sight of him. Failing that, by grab, Marratt was determined to discover the fellow's destination.

He lifted the big gelding into a run. These tracks weren't over twenty minutes old, grass in some places was just beginning to straighten; and he still had a good bit of fair light left. When he'd first reached that butte where he'd picked up the sign again he must have been right on that jasper's heels. The guy had lost time fooling around in that wash.

They crested the ridge and went down into a trough that was cross-hatched with timber. The tracks slowed here as though the fellow had been aware of Marratt's nearness and had been scared to push his horse lest Marratt hear.

Marratt sailed right along with the gelding wide open. If he could just see this hombre he might learn a lot of things. The guy was parallelling the trail taken by Beckwith or appeared to be, at least, until he reached the valley's end. Then his tracks dived into a kind of shallow canyon whose floor was grown to prickly pear and mounded with the burrows of gophers. These had slowed the fellow further but Marratt didn't let them interfere a bit with his own pace.

He was having more luck than he had imagined possible. That rannyhan couldn't be more than ten minutes ahead of him; they were cutting down his lead with every thud of the gelding's hoofs.

The canyon walls fell away. They crossed a stretch of dwarf cedar, followed the small shoes' sign through a brush-choked ravine which gave onto a darkening gulch angling west in the direction of Wineglass.

Marratt pulled up in the thickening shadows, dubious about going nearer to Ryerson's. If that were this rider's destination after all it might be smarter to let the son-of-a-gun go than risk bumping into the Wineglass crew.

It was while he was stopped, thus considering, Marratt caught the low growl of an angry voice.

Eyes narrowing, he came out of the saddle. They—for a fellow wouldn't be likely to waste that tone on himself—were in this gulch and not far ahead of him. If the man he'd been trailing had come here to meet someone, and Marratt were able to make out their faces and possibly overhear a little, he believed it might strengthen his hand immeasurably.

It was worth a try anyhow!

So, leaving the gelding, he commenced snaking forward, ears cocked and eyes wary, through the green sheen of oak brush, making all the haste possible commensurate with caution.

He didn't know whom he was expecting to encounter but the long narrow face and sly eyes of Clint Gainor weren't far from his thinking as he followed the gulch's inconsistent convolutions, skirting old rock slides and keeping off the direct trail as much as he was able.

He hadn't caught any talk for the last several moments and worried they might have heard him; this being the only explanation he could find for such quiet without they'd finished their business and gone off entirely.

Grown reckless with this last thought, and with no sound for guidance, he shoved through a ten-foot stand of brush and, without warning, was upon them. They stood caught together—one lithely slender, the other short and chunky—before the farther-off shapes of their ground-hitched horses. In the apparent ardor of their embrace the nearer, chunky hombre almost wholly concealed his companion and it wasn't until, with a desperate wrench of slim shoulders, she got one hand loose and tried to get at his

65

pistol that Marratt realized the brawny one had hold of a woman.

Neither one had heard him. The shadows were deepening and Marratt hung there uncertainly a couple of heartbeats before the true significance of their postures registered. It took him that long to untrack his mind from the accepted misconception that, because she must have been awaiting him, she welcomed the man's attentions. But when he saw the fellow, growling, cuff her hand away from his belt gun, Marratt flung himself forward.

Through a red fog of anger he caught the man by the nearest shoulder and spun him around with a berserk fury. His sledging right fist exploded against the man's jaw, sending him crazily staggering slanchways as though he'd crashed into the end of a maul.

It wasn't till then Marratt saw the girl fully, the torn buckskin dress, the dusky pallor of frightened features framed by jet braids as she involuntarily clutched the ripped leather against the pale gleam of an uncovered breast.

He stood rooted in the astonishment of complete incredulity, knowing her now for the girl of the tank —for the Circe of Beckwith's office. A clamor of questions hammered his mind and his churning thoughts failed entirely to comprehend the utter urgency of the occasion until the girl's cry snatched his glance from her face to pick up the tag end of the man's blurred reach for gun butt.

Marratt threw himself toward him and a bit to the right, at the same time dropping his chest toward his knees as the whistle of lead screamed above his left shoulder. With the man's wrist flexing to shake out another shot Marratt's lifting boot tore the gun from his fingers. He was reeling, half upright, when Marratt's fist landed with the sound of a pile-driver just below his left ear. He went spread-eagled and skidding across the clatterous shale.

When Marratt looked for the girl she was gone with both horses, the hard-drumming impact of their hoofs tumbling off the gulch walls in brittle shatters of sound.

Marratt, rubbing the knuckles of his bruised fist, went over and stood awhile considering the now slack-jawed features of the slugged squaw molester. He had burnt-dark cheeks that were highboned and solid as the muscles that bulged the whole short and broad shape of him. His hat lay brim-up against the base of a juniper and his black hair was straight as a Papago Indian's.

But this was no Indian, Papago or other kind. He looked like a transplanted Texican to Marratt with his lowslung shell belt and grease-grimed open-topped thong-fastened holster. Scowling down at the man Marratt was almighty glad those big knobs of

67

hands hadn't managed to lay hold of him. Strength enough there to snap bones like pipestems.

On a random thought he bent and picked up the man's crown-dented headgear. He hadn't reckoned there'd be one chance in a thousand the battered felt would reward him, but it did. There, burned into the gommy-feeling sweatband with a bit of hot wire, was the bravo's handle: Churk Crafkin. A monicker Marratt had come across before.

Was it Gainor who'd spoke it—Clint with tongue-oil enough to run a whole fleet of windmills? Or was it that cook at the Lone Star Grub?

No, by God, it was Frailey; and Marratt suddenly remembered how the old doc had used it. They'd been talking about Ryerson and Frailey had advised, "What Wineglass says is same as law in these sandhills—the marshal's his man just as much as Churk Crafkin."

So this bullypuss baiter of defenseless squaws was one of Ryerson's crowd. A hired gun thrower probably. The notion didn't raise the cow king much in Marratt's opinion; it fit snug enough though with the rest he'd learned about him.

Marratt dropped Crafkin's hat and reckoned he'd better cut a shuck toward Usher's before some more of Ryerson's range-roughing maverick makers got wind of him. Next time, like enough, the breaks would be with Wineglass and this gulch wasn't Marratt's idea of the kind of a place a man would want to be trapped in.

He made slow work of getting back through the brush to where he'd left the rented gelding. His gymnastics with Crafkin hadn't helped the convalescing of that bullet track any and his cracked rib was aching like an ulcerated tooth. It wouldn't endure any further sudden bendings but it didn't keep his thinking away from that dratted squaw.

She certainly had Marratt fighting his hat and he admitted it. He couldn't think why he'd gone and stuck his crazy neck out. Some bulls, people claimed, couldn't stand a red rag and maybe he was like that when it came to baiting women—like that poor sap, Don Quixote, who couldn't pass a goddam windmill.

Any kid in three-cornered pants would have known better than to go ramming into a play the girl had patently invited. If she hadn't wanted Crafkin's attentions why had she come there to wait for him?

Why, indeed, Marratt wondered, abruptly remembering some other things. The first time he'd seen her she had been in Beckwith's office. Then he'd found her at that tank. How the hell had she got to this gulch to be waiting for Ryerson's man in the first place?

That had taken some traveling; Churk Crafkin himself hadn't picked any daisies once he'd discovered the supposed Luke on his trail.

Marratt swore irritably. The whole thing was such a damned mixed-up tangle a man couldn't hardly tell straight-up from down. Only one thing looked certain: There was some sort of tie-up between Beckwith, that squaw and Churk Crafkin. There was another—or was it the same?—between Beckwith, Ryerson and Crafkin. And where did Clint Gainor come into this deal?

On the theory of first things first Marratt tried to work it out on the basis of time but was distracted from that when another thought hit him. This conception was so cogent it turned him clear around and sent him back toward the scene of his encounter with Crafkin. He hated bitterly to waste further time that might prove precious but he'd come here for information and even one concrete fact could be a damned sight more valuable than the mess of loose ends he now had hold of. It might turn out to be the key which would put sense into all he'd discovered.

He moved fast as he dared but kept his gun in hand just in case that fellow Crafkin should be up and about again. The girl had gone off with the burly gun fighter's horse. He might be in a mood to do murder if he'd recovered that pistol.

But there was no sign of Crafkin when Marratt came into the clearing. Apparently the guy had found his gun and struck out afoot to get back to ranch headquarters; he wouldn't waste any time and, once he got to Ryerson, they'd have the whole crew out scouring this country.

It was horse tracks Marratt had returned for a look at and when he found them he had his fact. It was the girl, not Crafkin, he'd trailed into this gulch. She hadn't been waiting for Crafkin. He'd been waiting here for her!

It was after ten when Marratt rode into the Usher yard. Moonglow dappled the buildings with silver but Marratt right then had no eye peeled for beauty. He was weary in mind as well as in body and had to just about pry himself out of the saddle; but he was too much a cowman not to care for his horse.

He pulled off the gear and spread the damp blanket where the wind could get at it. He rubbed the gelding down thoroughly with wisps of old straw from the leaky barn and then staked him out where he could fill up on grass. He fetched him a pail of water and finally headed for the house.

That cracked rib was giving him hell in good measure but he forgot all about it when he stepped onto the stoop. In the center of the door there was a fluttering square of paleness that made a sound like flapping paper.

Marratt's bleak eyes narrowed and he stood there several moments before he at last pulled it loose and

went inside and eased the door shut. Only then did
he strike a match for there was that much caution
left in him.

Two lines of block letters had been inscribed with
a pencil.

USHER: KEEP RIDING IF
YOU WANT TO KEEP BREATHING

He was still staring at it when he realized he
wasn't alone.

CHAPTER 7

He was tempted—urged by every instinct of self-preservation—to let go of the match and grab for his gun, but common sense kept him motionless. If whoever was watching had wanted to kill him they'd have done so the moment flame had leaped from that matchstick.

He said, "Well?"

"Put that light to a lamp."

"What about the windows?"

"They're all taken care of."

Marratt crossed to the wall and lifted the lamp's chimney. He rubbed the flame across the wick, watched it take hold and flare orange and smoky, and set the glass back on. Only then did he face the sound of the voice to find Gainor eyeing him across a cocked pistol.

The man motioned toward a chair. "Take the load off your feet. We've got some rag-chewin' to do—"

"You put this thing on the door?"

Gainor grinned. "Not me. That was one of your other friends. You know—" his sly eyes brightened with a secret amusement, "you're lucky, at that. Mostly, around here, they just hang up the crepe."

"You're wasting your time," Marratt told him. "You made me your offer and—"

"I made you *an* offer," Gainor remarked pointedly. "Nothin' to keep me from makin' you another."

Marratt said flatly, "I'm not selling this place. And if I was you'd be the last guy I'd consider."

"A man can talk too brash for his own good, my friend."

"Go on—say the rest of it."

"What took you over to the Malicora agency?"

"I don't consider that any of your business."

Anger's roan stain crept through the black of Gainor's whiskers. Resentment plowed through his tone. "You better take another squint at your hole-card! You're playin' a wolf's game that's goin' to get rougher an' you're like to hev need of all the help you can get here."

"I'll pick my own help, thank you."

"Why, you goddam fool . . ."

"Yes?"

Gainor got hold of himself with an effort. "Now see here, Luke," he wheedled, "we got too much in common, you an' me, to go flyin' at each other like a couple of trollops. Let's chew this over calm-like an' see—"

"You talk a lot," Marratt said, "but you don't say anything. What the hell are you holding that gun for?"

Gainor grinned through his tangle of whiskers. "Let's just say for the good o' my soul," he said, chuckling. Then his look turned cunning. "I got a stake in this business myself; I got my back ag'in' the same wall you hev. That should make us compadres if nothin' else would. Ryerson's usin' this place an', one way or another, he means to hev mine. So the natural thing—"

"I don't see it," Marratt said. "I've been given to understand Ryerson's got pretty powerful. If he wants your place why doesn't he grab it?"

"You mean same's he grabbed this one? It ain't quite that simple. Situations are different. I ain't got no ol' man to be killed like Jake Usher; an' I'm still squattin' on mine. I ain't aimin' to skip out."

He let that sink in, his eyes watching Marratt blandly. "Besides," he said abruptly, "he's buildin' a loop for the legislature. He kinda fancies droppin' his butt in the governor's chair an', till Murphey's term's up, he'd prefer to slide around the strong-arm stuff an' let things simmer in the status quo."

"You think that's why someone tried to drygulch me?"

Gainor's hooded eyes widened. But he said coolly enough, "You kin see for yourself he wouldn't want no old scandals bein' dug up around here now. I tell you, Luke, we're in this together an' if you aim to stick it out here you're goin' to need help. You won't get no more warnin's."

"Suppose you come to the point."

Gainor peered at him, frowning. "Well," he said gruffly, "I'd like to hev this spread outright, but if you're bound to hang onto it I'll buy in as pardner. That's fair enough, ain't it?"

Marratt studied him thoughtfully. He guessed perhaps Gainor'd said a bit more than he'd aimed to. If Ryerson didn't want trouble right now there was a fair to middling chance he wouldn't buck too strenuously any move on Marratt's part to rid Usher range of Wineglass cattle. Gainor, he reckoned, would be counting on that. He wasn't exactly figuring to throw his money away.

"But why," Marratt asked, "would you want to buy into it? We could still be allies—"

"You'd be more apt to consider my end of this

stick if I had a sizeable stake in your outfit. There's nothin' wrong with your spread a little money wouldn't cure."

"You keep talking around things. If you want to do business fetch it out in the open. Just what do you propose?"

"A fifty-fifty interest with you continuing to manage the ranch."

"As presumptive owner?"

"That's correct," Gainor grinned. "Because if anything goes wrong I ain't honin' to have Ryerson camped in my hair any more'n he is already—for as long, anyway, as I am able to prevent it. You'll be the big cheese; I'll be your silent pardner."

"And you'll expect me to use the price of your half to stock it?"

"No," Gainor said, "I'll pay my share toward puttin' stock on it."

"What's the amount of your offer for this proposed half interest?"

"Six thousand dollars."

"I'll think it over," Marratt said.

Gainor sidled around him, still with his gun out. At the door, he said, "I'll want your answer tomorrow. It could be damn unfortunate for both of us if Ryerson should discover we're havin' any dealin's. There's a can of white paint in the barn. If the answer's yes, put a coat of it on your chimney."

77

Marratt was too bone weary after Gainor's departure to think any further about anything. He pulled off Luke's boots and old Jake's gun belt, wedged a chair beneath the knob of the door which had held the warning and dropped exhausted across the couch.

The sun was high when he awoke the next morning. The first thing he did after a hasty splash was to soothe the pangs of his growling stomach. Then, with Jake's artillery once again strapped about him and a fourth steaming cup of black coffee before him, he sat down to some serious thinking.

Though Gainor's talk last night had held a reasonable sound, going over it step by step convinced Marratt it was geared to a pattern reminiscent of that which had fetched the man out to see him that first time. Gainor had an axe he was bent on grinding and was craftily hoping to maneuver the supposed Luke into turning the stone. Gainor wanted the ranch but deep in his scheming was some festering sore that was not to be healed short of Ryerson's death. This was the core of Marratt's impression.

How much of the man's talk had been built from whole cloth was debatable, but the ring of sincerity had marked his voice when he'd declared all he wanted was Usher's signature on a quitclaim. Failing to get it he'd come round with this new deal.

Marratt felt pretty sure if he had signed away the

ownership of Usher's grass Ryerson would now be dead and Luke saddled with the killing—the supposed Luke, of course. And even granting as true all of Gainor's talk last night, the net result of teaming up with him would likely still be the same. A dead man at Wineglass and Marratt on the run.

There might be other things mixed into Clint Gainor's thinking which impelled the man to such antigodlin tactics as concealing his horse and coming only after dark; as suggesting Marratt show his choice by painting a chimney and holding a loaded gun on him while offering a partnership. But there wasn't any doubt in Marratt's mind the main goal of Gainor's endeavoring was Ryerson's death.

And what of the girl from Beckwith's office? Where did she fit into what was going on around here?

He cursed the persistence with which his thoughts kept harking back to that brown-eyed squaw. Light complexioned she might be, and pretty as a speckled pup under a red wagon, but she was still a squaw so far as Marratt was concerned. Those black braids told the story, and the quickening suspicion that some of her folks might not have worn mocassins did little to make her more acceptable. She was still a woman, and there was no place for women—red, black, white or yellow—in the plans which had dug Grete Marratt out of Yuma.

79

He scowled bleakly at the steam curling up off his coffee.

Like it or not, she was going to have to be considered. She was part and parcel of whatever was going on or she would not have slipped her tether to keep a rendezvous with Crafkin. Well . . . *would* she? If that meeting had been simply an affair of the heart would she have been trying to fight Ryerson's understrapper off? What story had she concocted to explain her absence to Beckwith?

Every angle he sought to follow dead-ended against the inescapable fact of Crafkin's presence in that gulch. He'd been waiting there for her and if she hadn't been aware of it why had she gone there?

The only alternative a quarter hour of thinking was able to dredge up was that she'd been heading for Wineglass and Crafkin had intercepted her. How would Crafkin have known this? How could he have guessed at what time she would appear or that she'd have left the regular trail to take so roundabout a route? And, assuming these things could be answered, why would he want to stop her?

It was palpably too far-fetched to be given credence. Was it less far-fetched to assume the government had hired her to take care of Beckwith's paper work? Yet, if she were Beckwith's wife or Beckwith's woman, would a man of the agent's puling character have dared thus to flaunt her in the faces of his underpaid white-collar help?

She didn't make sense no matter what role he gave her and he finally tramped outside to put the gelding under gear.

He was going to someway have to get his hands on a chunk of money. He needed more groceries and owed the doc a bill for those he'd already eaten; and he reckoned his hair had grown out enough now to chance the attentions of a barber. His whiskers, too, could stand a trim and he was anxious to see Frailey though he doubted that he would catch him this late in the day.

As things turned out he didn't even have to hunt. The doc came driving into the yard just as Marratt was lifting his left foot to stirrup.

"Fetched you out some more vittles. How's that side coming along?" he hailed, pulling up. "Better let me have another look at it."

Marratt brushed that aside. "It's getting along well enough. I'm glad you came by though. I want to know what I owe you. There's the wound and the grub and this horse you hired for me. I can't keep piling up expenses—"

"You've got to live, haven't you?"

"I don't have to live off your generosity."

Frailey showed a mild surprise. "Well, we can figure it out, I reckon. What are you going to do?

Not thinking of working the Half Circle U, are you?"

Marratt assumed that by that Frailey was referring to the Usher ranch. He said, "Any reason why I shouldn't?"

"I understood you'd been warned to clear out of the country."

"Where'd you hear that?"

"It's all over town."

Marratt's solid lips twisted. His big shoulders stirred restively. "If I'd been figuring to leave I wouldn't have come back in the first place. I can't do anything without money—any chance of the Casa Grande bank putting up some?"

Frailey shook his head. "Phelps is in too thick with Ryerson." He considered Marratt narrowly a couple of moments. "You've stayed away too long. Why start something you know will be bound to end in bloodshed?"

"I'm not looking for a fight or aiming to tear any scars off old wounds but—"

"You won't be able to help yourself. If you stay there'll be trouble—don't that damned warning prove it?"

"I'm staying," Marratt said with his jaws tightening grimly. "What do you know about a fellow that calls himself Clint Gainor?"

Frailey said without expression, "He owns the Boxed Triangle. A not too-important spread bordering Wineglass on the west." He sat watching Marratt for a couple of heartbeats. "Well, let's get this grub put away," he said, getting out of the buggy. "Your dad left a will with myself as administrator. Now that you've returned we can put it through probate; I've been keeping the back taxes paid up for you. There's about $3500 cash, banked in Chandler. You won't be able to draw on that yet but I can let you have a couple of hundred if you'd like."

Marratt said stiffly, "If it wouldn't inconvenience you I'd be glad of the difference between that and what I owe you."

After they'd come back from packing in the groceries Frailey said, "I suppose you'd like it right away? We'll have to go to town then. I ought to be getting back anyway. Hitch your horse on behind and ride up here with me."

"No point rubbing some of the smell off on you."

"Nonsense!" Frailey snapped. "I may not perhaps be able to prevent your making a fool of yourself, but—"

"I'll ride the horse," Marratt said, and climbed on him.

It wasn't that he didn't like Doc, because he did; but there was no use compromising the old man more than he had to. And if trouble came up he wanted to be in a position to get hold of his gun.

Also there was this matter of pride. He reckoned

he owed something to the man whose name and clothes he was wearing. He didn't want folks who might see them to say he'd come into Bella Loma trying to hide behind Frailey.

He thought of Clint Gainor bellied down someplace waiting for him to daub white paint on a chimney. Recalling the way the man had kept that gun on him he remembered the odd expression he had several times trapped in the fellow's too-bright eyes. It were as though the joker had been steeling himself to the unburdening of something he couldn't cut loose of; every time he'd get that look he'd kind of take hold of his gun a little tighter.

The doc was pulling up before Danvers' General Store. Reining his gelding over to the tie rack Marratt got down and joined Frailey on the porch. "We'll step in here," the latter said quietly. "I'll get a check cashed and give you that money—"

"Just the difference," Marratt nodded, "between what you've offered and what I already owe you. Two hundred is all I can afford to be in debt."

As they were about to move inside, a deeply bronzed goddess in starched gingham, arms stacked with bundles and black hair piled against the flash of a Spanish comb, twisted gracefully through the door with a quick smile as her eyes met Frailey's.

The doctor removed his hat. "Naome," he said, "I

would like for you to meet Luke Usher. Luke, this is Clem Ryerson's daughter."

Marratt started, features frozen, stopping dead in his tracks. It was the willowy 'squaw' he had rescued from Crafkin—the girl of the tank and Beckwith's office!

CHAPTER **8**

Churk Crafkin, by the time he came limping into Wineglass headquarters, was in the sod-pawing mood of an affronted bull moose. He went storming through the house banging doors like a twister and if he'd gotten his hands on Naome right then there'd have been a sure understanding of who was boss around here. He didn't find her, of course, because she'd fled to Bella Loma.

Grinding his teeth he came back into the yard and that was when he noticed the lamplit window of his shanty. Highboned cheeks still stiff with anger, he veered away from the course that would have taken him to the bunkhouse. He'd told the crew more than once to stay out of his diggings and if he found one of them in there now he was minded to break the snoopy bastard's neck.

He came into the place like a wet-footed cat and the hooded look of his eyes turned black as obsidian when he observed the gaunt shape which came out of his rocker. "What the hell," he said roughly, "are you doin' here, Beckwith?"

Beckwith quailed from his look, thrust a hand out placatingly. "I—know you told me never to come here," he gulped, "but something terrible has happened! Where is Mr. Ryerson?"

"What do you want with Ryerson?"

"I've got to see him right—"

"You *can't* see him. He's off on one of his trips, pullin' strings to get that appointment. Now quit that damn shakin' and tell me what's got your bowels in an uproar."

"It's those wretched Usher cattle!" Beckwith blurted. "Some fellow came into my office this mor—"

"Hold it," growled Crafkin, and swung around and very carefully closed the door. Then he went to the windows and pulled both shades. When he came back his cheeks were like slabs of granite. "Now let's have it," he said, "and keep your goddam voice down."

The perspiring agent, with many lip-chewing pauses, nervously sketched in the salient features of Marratt's visit while Crafkin's eyes turned blacker and blacker. With the skin stretched tight across the jut of his cheekbones Crafkin finally asked, "You see Naome today?"

"Naome?" Beckwith stared at him stupidly.

"All right," Crafkin growled. "What'd this guy look like?"

"The fellow was obviously Usher—"

"You never saw Usher; he left before you come here—"

"But I told you—"

"Never mind what you told me. Describe him."

Beckwith stammeringly did so and the Wineglass ramrod reluctantly nodded. "It was him, right enough," he said, as though to himself, "but what I can't understand is—"

"You haven't heard the worst of it. I'd been outside talking with a couple of Indians. When I came in he was already there—in my office, I mean. In a chair," Beckwith said, swallowing hard, "by the desk. I hadn't any reason right then to be suspicious—like you said, I'd never met up with either of the Ushers. And I was—I'll admit it—pretty shaken up by the time he'd gone stamping out of there. Coming at me that way right out of the blue . . . but—"

"For Chrissake," Crafkin snarled, "get on with it!"

Beckwith mopped his face. "After—after I'd got my mind squared around to it, I got to thinking about those cancelled checks—"

"You goddam fool! Mean to say you been keepin'—"

"Yes. Of course." A faint surprise flittered through Beckwith's frightened stare. "Naturally, I've been keeping them—it would have looked rather odd, don't you think, if I hadn't?—I had them filed by date with all the rest of our beef checks—"

"And now they're gone?"

Beckwith licked his parched lips. "I can't find them."

Ryerson's range boss glared. He hulked above Beckwith like an outraged orangoutang; but, strangely enough, he didn't strike him, didn't curse.

"All right," he said at last. "I'll take care of this. Clear out of here now and keep your mouth shut."

Crafkin, as soon as Beckwith had gone, went back to the house with pulses racing. Here, if he could just get his hands on them, was the best possible weapon he could get for his purpose. That bungled attempt he'd made to compromise Naome—even had it been successful—would never have given him one-tenth the shocking power he'd be able to wring from those cancelled checks.

Not for an instant did he believe Luke had gotten them—it was that damned brat of Ryerson's. She'd been a heap too elaborate in her departure this morning, babbling to cookie how she was figuring to visit that sick nester woman over on Breakneck Creek, then dawdling around until the crew had been dispatched before setting off in that outlandish getup.

If she'd been any kin of his, Crafkin would have taken a rope's end to her before he'd have let her flaunt her old man's shame all over the goddam cactus. But it wasn't her costume which had sharpened his suspicions. Always—ever since she had been grown enough to get into them—she'd taken a bastardly delight larruping around in them trifling gewgaws. That crap had been her mother's and, like her blank-faced Injun stubbornness, had become familiar enough by this time to go unnoticed. It was her un-Injunlike chatter, her shining up to the cook, which had caught at Crafkin's attention. He had let her get a couple of hours' start, then had tracked her long enough to make sure she'd been bound for Beckwith's.

He had angrily supposed she was having an affair with the agent and it was this which, having watched for her return, had decided him not to wait any longer and launched the savage coup brought to naught by that dog of an Usher.

Too long and much too carefully had Crafkin been

at pains to insure this big spread's future to be cheated of his intention at this late date. All through the years—even before that day at the Half Circle U—he'd been working to bring about Ryerson's sudden death or downfall in such fashion as would give himself complete control of Wineglass—if not outright possession. By patient and crafty maneuvering he had made Clem Ryerson into a feared and hated cattle king; it was Crafkin, not Ryerson, who had made Wineglass all-powerful. It was a tribute to the ramrod's genius that not even Ryerson suspected this.

But patience was a thing any man could get fed up with and Usher's return had badly jolted Crafkin; he couldn't understand how he had gone so astray in his judgment.

Ryerson had been out of town at the time, away on this string-pulling trip he'd arranged for him; and the range boss, dangerously rattled, had attempted to gun Usher down from ambush. Poor light and distance had played hob with his marksmanship, but he had certainly expected Usher to panic. Instead of hauling his freight as he had that other time, the crazy fool had moved into his abandoned ranch house and gone snooping around that chiseling agent's office.

Crafkin's black orbs winnowed down to glittering slits every time he recalled facing Usher in that gulch; but those cancelled checks were the important things right now. The problem of Usher and where he'd gotten such courage could wait, like Naome, till he got hold of those three-by-eight pieces of paper. Once those were in his hands he'd have a real whip to work with; his mind would be unfettered to put the screws on all of them.

Through the rage churning through him came one lancing streak of caution that swung him completely around on the porch and sent his bull voice over the yard. "Tularosa!"

Into the glow of the lamp he'd left burning came a bony breed with forward-hunched shoulders who was clad in a dirty pair of cotton *pantalones* and a dirtier cotton shirt gaping open to his navel. A club foot gave him a crablike motion which was no more repulsive than the rabbit's pink eyes in the pockmarked face upturned to await Crafkin's orders.

"Mount the crew and put them to combing the flats and gulches for sign of Luke Usher—I run onto him down by Snake Canyon shining up to Naome. He's probably dug for the tules but tell 'em to make sure. Then come back here and sit on this porch till I call you."

He didn't wait for an answer but, turning, tramped inside, picking up the lamp and going into the girl's bedroom. He personally hired every man in this outfit, inconspicuously replacing those who'd been on the place when he had come here to manage it so that Ryerson could spend more time prospecting around for that goldmine he'd used to be hipped on. But Tularosa was the only one he put any trust in. Marihuana was the key to the warped and twisted gunman; Crafkin kept the halfwit in smoking and got in turn a doglike devotion which he'd found extremely useful on more than one occasion. He had sometimes toyed with the thought of using him on Ryerson, and he might even yet if he couldn't hit on anything better.

Now for those checks!

First he examined the flooring. When he'd convinced himself there were no loose boards he started on the bed, running every inch of the quilt through careful fingers before dropping it into a heap on the floor. Kicking it out of his way he stripped off the sheets and, with his knife, got to work on the mattress.

He wasn't worried about her squawking. She had too much Injun to go tattling to Ryerson.

While he worked his thoughts slipped back seventeen years and he was remembering the towering rage he'd been in when Ryerson, lank and drawn and looking bleached as a cadaver, had come back from one of his mine-hunting trips with the goddam squaw who had been Naome's mother. She had found him delirious and dying from snakebite at the edge of a waterhole and nursed him back to health.

She'd been a good-looking wench—even Crafkin had been willing to concede that much—and he could have understood Ryerson keeping her around —at least for a little while. But marrying her! And publicly!

He had come almighty near throwing up the job until he'd sensed the effect it was having on Ryerson's neighbors. Then the big idea had hit him. If Ryerson was dope enough to get hitched up to a redskinned squaw he might be fool enough to let Churk Crafkin take this spread away from him.

It was worth a little thought and he had given it plenty. It was after the squaw had found Ryerson a papoose that Crafkin decided he had better get rid of her. A girl he could handle; he didn't want no fool boys.

He didn't have Tularosa on the payroll in those days and there was no hemlock handy, so he'd introduced a handful of chopped-up oleander into the mustard greens she'd been boiling one day while Ryerson was over to the county seat. It hadn't worked quite as rapid as he had reckoned it would but it had finally taken care of her in spite of old Frailey's efforts.

He'd thought for awhile the boss would go off his rocker, and he had been kind of worried because he hadn't been ready to discard Ryerson then; he'd needed a front for the steals he'd been planning.

But it had worked out all right because the chump had gone off on a mine-hunting bender, clean out of this world, away back of beyond. Months he'd been gone, trying to turn up that bonanza he had used to talk so much about. He hadn't ever found it but he'd kept right on hunting, along the border, deep into the Saucedas—once he'd even been sighted as far north as Humboldt, and another time over along the Santa Maria River, west of Skull Valley. He was a traveling fool if Churk had ever seen one.

Of course he was back off and on and every once in a while he'd be seen around long enough to give folks the notion he was passing out the orders. Crafkin managed with considerable ingenuity to let Ryerson have all the credit for his skullduggery. He always publicly regretted the things he was forced to do; and whenever he was about to clamp down on some outfit he would always fetch Clem Ryerson around beforehand, adroitly fostering the impression he was there himself only because the cattle king had ordered him to be.

He remembered the first time Ryerson had taken Naome with him. She hadn't been over three or four at the time but "She's got to learn self-reliance," the boss had explained. "Some day she's going to be the owner of this spread and I aim for her to know what the score is when she gets it. When she's older you can teach her all you know about the cow business. She's got some hard knocks ahead of her, people bein' what they are. She can best be got ready to meet them by a thorough acquaintance with nature."

It had been evident to Crafkin right then he had a screw loose. It had been evident before but, if further proof were needed, that kind of talk supplied it. The guy was loco as a hootowl. When she'd fallen off her horse he'd picked her up and set her on again, never paying no more attention to her tears than Crafkin would have paid to a horned toad. When they'd rode off into the shimmering desert he had reckoned he'd seen the last of her and didn't much care one way or the other.

It was when she was nine and beginning to bud out that he'd finally made up his mind he would marry her as the easiest way of making sure he got Wineglass. Strangely enough she had never taken to him, always meeting cold-eyed his most artful advances. Two years ago he'd quit bothering his head with her, telling himself that when the sign was right she would be damned glad to hitch up with him.

He'd have had her dead to rights today if that dog of an Usher hadn't come riding into it.

Usher's presence had stimulated one idea though. He would see that folks were reminded of the threats Luke had made after old Jake's killing. Then, if Ryerson turned up with a hole through his skull, this country'd have no trouble knowing where to place the blame.

He had mattress stuffing strewn all over the floor and still no sign of those goddam checks. He pulled her clothes off their hooks and began emptying drawers. He tore the pillows apart. He just about turned the place upside down before at last he faced the fact she must have taken the checks with her.

He dropped the knife back into his boot and slammed the door shut behind him. His eyes were like agate as he headed for the porch. There was just one place she could reasonably have gone. Ryerson kept a year-around room at the Buffalo Bull, Bella Loma's only rooming house with any pretentions to grandeur. That was where he would find her.

"Get your horse," he told Tularosa. "I've an idea Miss Naome will be needing your attentions."

Marratt was still staring, still locked tight in the grip of his astonishment, when the girl said, "How do you do?"

Her contralto voice was cool as fresh spring water. Her eyes behind black lashes were as gravely polite and impersonal as though she were considering an utter stranger. And yet he sensed behind this show of mild interest an on-guard sort of feeling that made him say perversely, "Haven't I come across you someplace before, Miss Ryerson?"

Her eyes regarded his with a not too-interested curiosity. "I can't seem to recall the occasion. Perhaps you have me mixed up with some other girl you've met during the course of your extended travels."

He felt a stir of admiration for the quick-thinking smoothness with which she'd turned the talk back on him. He guessed she must have done a bit of traveling herself to have acquired such a nonchalant facility with words.

As though divining his thought, she said smiling, "I've never been outside Arizona, Mr. Usher, and all the schooling I've had I got from my dad during trips we used to take when we were hunting the foot of the rainbow. Of course," she added reflectively, "I've done a little reading . . . Walter Scott, some Dickens and Thackeray."

Marratt reckoned to know when he was being made fun of. "And do you add swimming, Miss Ryerson, to your other accomplishments?"

Her eyes returned his look demurely. "A girl doesn't have many chances around here—"

"I suppose working for one's living does take up a deal of one's time?"

"She doesn't work," Frailey said, looking curiously from one to the other of them.

"Then what was she doing at the Malicora Agency, got up like an Indian, when I saw her yesterday morning?"

Naome laughed. "I'm afraid Mr. Usher's a rather imaginative person," she told Frailey. "And now, if you'll excuse me, I think I'd better go see if Dad came in on the stage."

"I'll go with you," Marratt said quickly. "I've been meaning to have a—"

"Daddy!" the girl cried; and Marratt swung round as a spare sunbronzed man with white hair and blue store clothes stepped onto the porch and came toward them. Tired eyes smiled at Naome and then looked closely at Marratt. "How are you, Usher?" he said quietly, and reached out a hand.

Frailey slanched a nervous glance at Usher's belted gun; but Marratt never noticed.

His stare leaped from the three fingers of that outstretched hand to the uptilted nose and jagged track of a knife scar lividly marking Ryerson's left temple.

Naome screamed.

CHAPTER 9

Thirty years of patching bones and stitching hides for the folks who ranched the Bella Loma country had given Doc Frailey a considerable insight into the foibles and follies of a matured humanity. He had come to believe he could pretty well predict how the most of them would react to any given set of circumstances; yet the returned Luke Usher was continually amazing him, so unlike was the man to Frailey's preconceived notions.

He remembered Luke well as a gawky lad of sixteen, loud of mouth, always complaining and given to violent rages when things didn't go the way his

99

mind was bent on having them. Clumsy as a colt and never knowing what to do with his hands when they weren't wrapped about some firearm, he'd been considerably taken up with his own importance and over-ready to resent the least infringement of his imagined due. Half Circle U had been the most prosperous spread at this end of the cactus and Luke had been very determined folks should keep that fact well in mind.

And, mostly, they had while in Luke Usher's presence; because, in addition to his irascible temper, he was known far and wide as a red striped whizzer when it came to putting a belt gun in action. He was also known for his love of the bottle, and this combination was not of a kind many married men cared to shove out their jaws at. They'd been made too aware of Luke's homicidal tendencies to cherish any illusions regarding their own rights and privileges.

Thus had talk roundabout been stirred to a fever heat when, after Jake's killing and Luke's subsequent brags, the local champion of six-shooter justice had cravenly tucked tail and proceeded to roll his twine. Doc Frailey, however, had not been noticeably surprised, his friendship with Jake having privately convinced him Luke's bark had been infinitely more lethal than his bite.

He had always been prepared to concede the boy dangerous, but mainly where circumstances were arranged to his advantage. With better opportunity than most to observe him Frailey had personally considered Usher's son to be a bully battening on a gratuitous rep he hadn't any right to. He had made his brags that night while drunk and obviously forgetful of the man who didn't have to brag—Churk Crafkin, Ryerson's range boss.

An outlander hired two years before to ramrod Wineglass, Churk Crafkin was believed to hail from Texas where, it was clandestinely rumored, he'd gutshot several men in a feud before seeking greener pastures to preserve his continued health. According to the way Frailey'd viewed the matter Luke, when he had got sufficiently sober to recall the frozenfaced Texican, had made up his mind in a hurry which part of valor was like to return the greatest dividends. He had flown the coop exactly as the doctor would have expected him to.

Frailey *had* been surprised to stumble onto Luke in the rain that night he had encountered him in the road out front of the old Usher ranch house. He'd thought at first his eyes had been playing him tricks, that the fancied resemblance to the blustering Luke was simply the result of imagination on proximity. But when he'd carried him inside and got him stripped beneath Jake's picture their alikeness had been too apparent for him to entertain further doubt.

Incredible as it might appear to him, and contrary

101

to all his most cherished predictions, Luke had come back to the obligations he'd run out on. Or, at least, he'd come back. And characteristically broke.

It had not astonished Frailey to discover he'd been shot, things being the way they were, but he'd been definitely astonished when Luke had failed to enlarge on the subject, and even more so when, during their first exchange of words, he'd volunteered no explanation. This wasn't much like the Luke doc remembered.

Nor was his voice, nor his mannerisms, nor the direct challenging way in which those inscrutable eyes regarded you. Beyond the matter of looks there was practically nothing discernible about the fellow which reminded Frailey of the Luke he had known in the old days—the loud-mouthed Luke who had pulled his freight after telling the town what he would do to Clem Ryerson.

Frailey'd never believed in leopards changing their spots, but he hadn't believed Luke would come back, either, so perhaps after all he'd been wrong about leopards. After ten days of Usher he'd begun to believe so and to even look forward to having the man around again. He'd begun to find in Luke traits he'd known in his father and these in turn had engendered hopes he might be able to talk Luke out of any notions he might have of kicking sleeping dogs awake.

Whatever the man had in mind regarding Wineglass, it was plainly no concern of Frailey's. Wineglass was able to look out for itself. The big trouble with that line of reasoning was that it presupposed the outfit and its owner to be synonymous— a probability the doctor wasn't ready to accept. He knew Ryerson's neighbors had never questioned this assumption but the doctor wasn't the sort to let popular beliefs lead astray his own conclusions. He was still far from satisfied Ryerson fit the local conception.

Frailey had fetched Naome into this world and, because of her mixed blood, had done considerable thinking about her, carefully watching the result of Ryerson's influence. She'd been much away on long trips with her father and had herself told the doctor a great deal about these without realizing she was doing so. It had been good medicine, he thought.

Under Ryerson's guidance she had learned about life from nature, from the observance of birds and animals and the study of their ways with each other; a hard school, perhaps but thorough. Nor had the man neglected the more formal aspects of her education; he had taught her to read and write along with self-reliance and grounded her in the more useful other things she might have learned had he sent her away to school.

Frailey felt pretty sure he understood why Ryerson hadn't.

The girl's thinking was direct and wholesome, no vicious misconceptions or evil gossip had unbalanced it. Her mind was clean, graceful and attractive as her body; and for these things the old man respected Ryerson.

Whether or not the rancher had killed Jake Usher —as Luke had proclaimed—he had no means of knowing, but he did not believe the man deliberately had planned to put his neighbors out of business for the benefit of Wineglass; that kind of man would never have established the rapport Ryerson enjoyed with Naome.

The doctor could not brush away the fact that several smaller outfits had been absorbed into Ryerson's holdings; but a lot might depend on how much rope he'd given his ramrod. On how much of the rancher's authority the man had taken on himself.

Clem Ryerson was Naome's father and what hurt Ryerson was bound also to hurt Ryerson's daughter. In direct proportion to the tie between them.

This was the fact which had influenced Frailey's hope that he might steer Luke away from any further trouble with Wineglass. And, knowing from past experience how stubborn an Usher could be, he had welcomed this chance of introducing Luke to Naome.

He'd been totally unprepared for the turn Luke's talk had taken. He'd been a lot more disconcerted than the girl appeared to be but he had glimpsed one thing which had given him cause for renewed hope. Whether or not he yet realized it the girl's appeal had got under Luke's hide pretty deeply. Given a little time such magic might well work wonders.

It was therefore with considerable misgivings that Frailey watched Clem Ryerson round the store's north corner and step onto the porch. The rancher's glance found them instantly. The doctor stood with caught breath as Ryerson came up to them and, putting out his hand, said quietly, "How are you, Usher?"

It was not the remark or manner of a man laboring under a guilty conscience but the doctor could not help looking nervously at the belted gun riding Usher's right thigh. It was while he was looking that Naome screamed.

Frailey's glance jerked up. The look in Luke's face made his guts turn cold and crawl. He could not blame the girl for crying out or for the frantic way she'd flung herself, arms spread, between that vision and her father.

Ryerson's own cheeks were gray but his eyes never wavered. He said, "Keep out of this, Naome," and put her gently aside. "If you've come back," he told

105

Luke, "to wind up any unfinished business, don't let a child's hysteria stand in your way."

Frailey's jaws ached with strain. He could see and he could hear but he was powerless to move. The words he would have spoken were all piled up and clogged in his throat. He was like a man in the path of a rampaging cyclone, immobilized by his grasp of impending disaster.

For the space of ten heartbeats there was no sound whatever. Then, immeasurably, so slightly as only to be sensed rather than seen, the frozen stillness of Usher's stance became again imbued with breathing. The killer look leached out of his stare and he stepped back half a pace to say with bitter clarity: "Next time your tracks cross mine have a gun on you."

He swung round on his heel and stepped off the porch.

CHAPTER 10

It was late, close to one, when Tularosa reached town. The only lights still showing came with a lemon effulgence through the dust-grimed windows of the Red Horse Bar. He didn't care about that; light, at this stage, not being essential to his purpose. He had been given by Crafkin, before taking off, just enough of his favorite poison to see him through his present chore and fetch him back for refueling.

Crafkin had told him where to find the girl and what manner of things he was to look for in the event she refused to hand them over. Four little pieces of pale green paper measuring three-by-eight with writing and numbers on them.

He pulled up his horse and scrabbled a hand across his bristled face. The lemon glow from the Red Horse Bar looked a million miles away and about as fat as the top of a pin's head. He felt unutterably lonely but he wasn't shaking and he knew what he was here for. The black haired girl had Churk's little green papers and when he fetched them home he would get another smoke.

He sat his saddle awhile pleasantly dreaming about it when, with a renewed depression brought about by his aloneness, he was reminded of what that smoke depended on and his eyes raked the shadows with a mounting fright. He knew from Crafkin where to find the girl but he couldn't think where he was in relation to it.

He kicked the horse into movement that seemed slow as a snail's pace. The Buffalo Bull, Churk Crafkin had said. First room off the right of the second floor hall.

He found the place finally, drenched with sweat. He got out of the saddle and pulled the horse around back where he tied it in the gloom of an ancient pepper tree. Then he retraced his steps to the front and went in. Churk had said, "Be quiet about it," and when he found the banister he went up the stairs with all the stealth of a spider.

First door on the right.

The place was darker than a wolf den but his clammy fingers felt their way across the door till they closed on the smooth metallic feel of the knob and cautiously turned until it would go no farther. His heart was thumping like the pounding of a stamp mill but he pushed infinitesimally and knew it wasn't locked. Lifting up on the knob then to circumvent squeaks he edged it slowly open till he could slip inside after which he quietly edged it shut.

The room was totally black. But night's coolness came from an opened window and gradually his eyes made out the shape of the bed.

He stood perfectly still for a long while remembering the black haired girl in a hundred poses. He swallowed uncomfortably and licked his cracked lips. He dilated his nostrils trying to catch the clean smell of her and lewdly imagined how she'd look without clothes on. If she didn't tell him right away about those papers he'd find out.

Excited by the prospect he moved toward the bed warily. A groping hand touched the near edge and with the stealth of a stalking cat he was crouched at its head, breathing raggedly. Swiftly bending then, cracked lips pulled back from his stumps of teeth, he put out his left, nervously feeling for her body while his spraddle-fingered right, poised hawklike, hung ready to be clapped across her mouth if she sought to holla.

But that creeping left hand couldn't find her.

With a frustrated snarl he raked both hands across the bed savagely, still not finding her. But she *had* to be in this room—Churk had said she was!

She must be hiding!

Voice turned wheedling, he called to her softly, cunningly coaxing her to show herself quickly lest she be done out of this treasure he had fetched her. When it seemed these blandishments were going to be ignored he crawled under the bed, thrashing about like a snake with its head off. He went into the closet but she wasn't there, either.

He sank onto the bed, hardly able to believe it. His frantic stare raked the intolerable blackness and he got down on all fours, creeping twice around the walls, muttering cajoleries and curses. He got up, soaked with sweat, and thrust his head out the window. A terrible sense of isolation oppressed him and he commenced to shake, feeling hot and cold together. He shook worse when he thought of going back empty-handed.

What he needed was a smoke—but there would be no more smokes without he got Churk those papers.

The girl must have holed up someplace else for the night. It was too frilling early to make a hunt for her now—be quiet, Churk had said. He whimpered like a dog that has been forced to sleep outside.

Because he didn't know what else to do he remained where he was until the sun's yellow disc proclaimed another day was starting, then he crouched behind the window, anchoring his attention on the Lone Star Grub. At eight fifteen this vigil was rewarded when he saw the black haired girl go through the warped screen of its door.

Ten minutes later he was sitting his horse by the tie rack fronting the general store, a gaunt ungainly shape with hunched shoulders. His lips peeled back in bitter outrage when the girl left the hash house with Ives Hanna, the marshal.

He climbed off his horse and went into the store, watched them stand awhile, talking, through the dust-grimed window. He commenced shaking again and, when a clerk stepped over to see what he wanted, the look he gave the fellow would have withered a white oak post. The man scuttled away but the damage was done. Naome had vanished.

He limped outside and got aboard his horse and rode it scowlingly over to Hamp Isham's corral. The girl's bay mare was inside the enclosure, eating hay off the ground with the other nags.

He left his gelding there, telling Isham to feed it, and set off in his crablike motion up the shady side of the street. He loitered across from the marshal's office till he made sure the girl wasn't in there. Something warned him not to ask around for the girl. He finally went and hunkered down outside the blacksmith shop in the shade of a gnarled mesquite, white-ringed stare unswervingly fixed on the mare Ryerson's daughter had left in Isham's corral. When she was minded to leave she would come for it, and when she came for it he meant to be ready.

Marratt, the jingle and scrape of his big-roweled spurs sounding loud in the stillness, stepped off the store's porch and swung into the saddle.

He sat woodenly a moment, hung up in his thoughts, the savage impulse he'd mastered still brightly reflected in the unseeing look he flung over the street. Then he pulled his big shoulders together and sent the hired gelding quartering over the dust on a tangent that would fetch him past Isham's corral. He never noticed the shape squatted by the smith's wall, nor saw how men's heads turned to follow his progress.

He reined in by the twenty-foot mound of baled hay stacked windbreak fashion to the right of the enclosure. Isham, quitting a conversation with one of his helpers, came over. "How'd you find him, Mr. Usher?"

He meant, of course, the horse; and Marratt said after a moment, "He's got plenty of speed but I'd like to get something with a little more bottom and I'm going to tell you right now I haven't got any cash. If you want to make me a deal I'd like that gotch-eared gray yonder. What do you want for him?"

Isham looked at the horse. It was a big rawboned stallion he had paid too much for considering its temperament and the amount of use he had for it. He told Marratt so. He said, "I'll have to get a hundred dollars for that hide. What bank was you figurin' to give me a check on?"

Marratt hadn't been figuring to give him any check but now he turned the thought over. He still had fifteen thousand in the bank at Prescott. If he drew on that money the law would probably hear of it but he might have ten days before the check could be cleared and traced to Bella Loma. Ten days, with Clagg's partner right here, should give him all the time he would have any need for.

But as he was opening his mouth to name the bank's title and address he suddenly realized the folly of handing Isham any check that didn't carry Usher's signature. In the first place the corral man probably wouldn't take it and, if he did, there'd be talk.

Marratt said, "I was aiming to ask you to wait a couple days till I can get hold of some cash."

"I guess that will be all right, Mr. Usher. We all know you around here—ain't like as if you was a stranger. You want to use the gear you've got on that geldin'?"

"If you don't mind," Marratt said, and stepped across to a pen that was holding some she stuff. This was not so idle a move as he managed to make it appear. He waved one of the animals around a few paces, admiring its action, covertly noting the comparative size of its tracks. And all the while one part of his mind was still exploring the possibilities of cashing a check.

He needed money—and might be needing it worse before he wound up his score with Clagg's partner. He'd have had his showdown with the skunk right then except for the conditions under which he had met him. When he gunned Clem Ryerson he wanted the man to know why he was being cut down and he couldn't very well state the facts in front of Naome. This was how his mind tried to rationalize the matter but something beyond his mind stood off and jeered at such paltry subterfuge; he wouldn't let himself examine it closer. He had dug his way out of Yuma to kill Clagg's partner and he wasn't about to let anything stop him.

That fifteen thousand was no good to him in Prescott. He couldn't afford to put his name on a check in a region where everyone knew him as Usher. He couldn't do it in Casa Grande but he thought, if he could make the trip quick enough, he might risk going to Ajo or Chandler and, closing out that account, there open a new one under the name of Luke Usher.

There'd be plenty of risk but the most of it, he thought, would be wrapped up in the time element, the margin he'd have after passing the check before it could be traced back to him.

Ajo would seem to be the best place to chance it, being the only large town in that end of the Territory. Two horses with plenty of bottom, used in relay, should get him there and back in under twenty-four hours. The thing to do now was cancel the proposed loan and get a blank check from Frailey. Signed by Marratt and made out to Usher, he could. . . .

He said, "What are you asking for this snip-nosed bay?"

"Not mine to sell." Isham shrugged. "That mare belongs to Ryerson's daughter. You want I should throw this hull on that gray?"

"I think," Marratt nodded, "if you're willing to trust me I'd like to have that apron-faced roan yonder also."

Ten minutes later, riding the one and leading the other, he was on his way out of town, headed for Usher's Half Circle U. Not having noticed the squatted shape by the smithy he had no reason for missing it now. The bay mare he'd just seen in the pen at Isham's convinced him that Naome, if she hadn't lied outright, had made a mighty good stab at confusing the issue; for the bay was the same he'd seen hitched outside Beckwith's, the same whose tracked sign had led him to Crafkin. Regardless of the cause or true significance of what he had witnessed, the fact remained that he had found Ryerson's daughter with the fellow, and if it wasn't by her choice then how could it have happened? Why had she been to the agency? Why had she pretended to be working in Beckwith's office and what were those slips—

Marratt suddenly swore. Of course! Those were the checks paid out by Beckwith for the vanished Usher cattle!

He'd been a fool not to realize it sooner.

The first chance she'd got, after learning Luke was back in this country, she'd gone after those checks and gotten away with them. If more proof were needed of Ryerson's involvement than he'd already pried out of Beckwith, she had certainly given it to him. For she would never have taken them without—

"That's right, Usher; glad to see you actin' sensible. Just stop right there an' watch those hands if you don't want to catch a blue whistler," Gainor said, edging out of the brush on a mouse-colored dun, a leveled rifle resting lightly across the pommel of his saddle. "You're a kinda hard man to do business with."

"I've decided," Marratt said, "to play a lone hand—"

116

"What you've decided ain't the point," said Gainor, brushing that aside. "I'm all done with fiddlin' around. You had your chance an' passed it up, so now I'm tellin' you the way it's goin' to be around here. You'll put your name to a paper givin' me—an' I said *givin'*—a full half interest in the Half Circle U. As of right now."

"I guess not."

"Then guess again. Furthermore you'll stock it an' hire a crew out of your own pocket, an' you'll get busy right away pushin' Ryerson's cattle out of there."

"You been too long in the sun—"

"I expect," Gainor said, "it's about time I was refreshin' your mem'ry." He gave him a prolonged scrutiny, obviously savoring the situation. "Why do you suppose—"

"You talk too much. Make your point," Marratt told him, "or get out of the way."

A sudden rage seized Gainor and for a moment his eyes showed a blazing malevolence. "You've treated me like dirt for the last time, you bastard! From here on out the shoe'll be on the other foot—"

"You got to make a speech every time you open your trap?"

"That's all right—I kin make your epitaph too, boy. I ain't forgot how you come runnin' around that house with a pistol right after Jake was killed! It was you, not Ryerson, that murdered your ol' man—an' you'll do what I tell you or I'll see you hung for it!"

After Ryerson left for the ranch with her bundles Naome'd hurried back to Smith's Rooms and hastily changed into her buckskin and squaw boots. She'd wanted mightily to go with her father but hadn't yet found a safe place for those checks so had put him off with the pretended need of visiting that nester's wife out on Breakneck. She'd felt a little uncomfortable about deceiving him, but disliked even more the thought of telling him the truth.

She was sure it had never occurred to him that his range boss could be unfaithful. Her dad in so many ways was like a little boy, living in an imagined world of his own, seeing nothing but good in the people around him, closing his eyes to ugliness and greed. This was weakness, of course, but it was beautiful and she had never been able to bring herself to point out the snake in his garden of Eden.

She had recognized this for weakness, too, but by using her eyes and her ears she had come to have a pretty bleak conception of their ramrod's real character. She'd unearthed those old rumors concerning why he'd left Texas and had recently talked with a freighter who had known him at Tombstone where Crafkin for awhile had been connected with the Clantons. "That feller's plumb cultus," this old-timer had told her, "an' if he's prowlin' this country I don't want no part of it."

That had started her wondering about the killing of Jake Usher and she'd got hold of the remarks Luke had made while he was drunk, and the story of how he had afterwards vanished—some seemed of the opinion old Jake's son had been bushwhacked.

She knew Wineglass had been using the Usher range for years and that her father and his range boss very seldom discussed ranch business, Ryerson seeming content to leave the spread's management almost entirely in Crafkin's hands. She'd once taxed him with this and he'd said with a laugh, "Naome, honey, that's what I hired the man for, to take all that stuff off my shoulders. Churk's doing all right, don't bother your head with it. He couldn't do better if the place were his own."

He couldn't indeed, she'd thought grimly when, appalled, she had discovered how many smaller spreads had gone into it. She began to notice little things which had escaped her attention before, began to have some understanding of many things which had previously puzzled her such as the attitude of other people's relations with the ranch and with her father. People looked on him as a range hog, on the outfit as though it were some kind of monstrous octopus.

Gradually, insidiously, the notion took hold of her that whenever her dad chanced to visit some other man's holding, this was taken by their neighbors to indicate the approaching end of that spread's independence. And, to her horror, she'd suddenly realized that invariably it had. Within a few weeks or months that place became a part of Wineglass.

With apprehensions mounting Naome had sought to find out whether, previous to old Jake's killing, her father had visited Half Circle U. She found that he had. With Churk Crafkin. She did not know they'd been there together the afternoon the old man died but she began very strongly to suspect it.

Thoroughly alarmed, she got to wondering what had happened to the Usher cattle. She couldn't turn up one steer marked with Usher's iron and this seemed to her to be uncommonly peculiar. Nesters and maverickers—even, perhaps, a few Indians—might well have accounted for much of this stock, but certainly not for all of it.

She finally went to Frailey. Despite her careful approach to the subject the old doc glanced at her sharply. After a deal of harrumphing he'd made out to allow they'd likely all died off the year of the big blow.

From her father Naome had found out which that was but couldn't bring herself to go further. She ached to get this thing talked out with him but a belated awareness of something glimpsed in his look that time she had taxed him with permitting Churk Crafkin too free a hand sealed her lips. She was suddenly afraid. Afraid, with a terrible dread, of the future.

This was why, at last, she'd gone to Beckwith's office, driven by the reported return of Jake's son to discovering some part of the truth. And there she had found the cancelled checks which had rid the range of Usher's brand.

Fright moved cheek by jowl with her now. She did not dare destroy them—did not dare tell her father. She was afraid, after that clash with Crafkin, to stay at the ranch any longer. She was trapped in a nightmare, scared even to stay at the Buffalo Bull. She was like a man with a bear by the tail, envisioning the awful price of her knowledge. The masks had slipped; there'd be no backing out now. The pattern had almost reached full circle.

Meeting the marshal, Ives Hanna, at breakfast she'd been mightily tempted to put the checks in his care, sealed of course, till she could find a way out of this. If she might only have been sure whose man he was . . . But on the verge of decision she'd seen the ungainly shape of Tularosa entering the store and had fled in blind panic.

Back in her room, badly shaken, she'd gone over what she knew and those things she suspected while mending the leather Churk Crafkin had torn. There'd be no quarter in this, no chance for retrenchment. The stakes were too high. The first false step would fetch death, swift and final.

She must someway get hold of Luke Usher. Even this might not help but it was the only course she could see at the moment. She must talk with him quickly. And it would have to be private.

She went to the window, keeping far enough back to insure her concealment, eyes anxiously searching what she could see of the street. After awhile she saw Tularosa, aboard his horse, ride toward Isham's.

The stage would be coming into town very shortly; she knew her dad might be on it. She left her room, hurrying down Smith's stairs and out into the hot bright smash of the sun. She slipped around to the back, went down a bottle-strewn alley and into the general store by the rear. There was only one clerk in view and he was busy with a customer.

She fingered some yard goods, percale, taffeta, calico. "I'll take some of these, George," she said, "when you're not busy—about eight yards of each. Please wrap them separate."

She picked her way through a clutter of sacked potatoes, barreled flour, crated eggs and stacked tarps, the topmost of which had been recently unfolded and then thrown carelessly back on the pile. Rounding a display of racked rifles she came to where, through a web streaked window, she could see a portion of the street.

She did not locate Tularosa but was satisfied he hadn't departed. He hadn't come to Bella Loma after any load of groceries. She didn't believe he was here to keep an eye out for her father. He'd come after those checks and the knowledge made her desperate.

Two ranch wives with baskets came into the store, their heads sheathed in bonnets, while the clerk was wrapping her cloth up. "You want these charged to the ranch?" he called, and Naome nodded. Then she saw doc's buggy wheel in to the hitch rack and her heart gave a leap when she beheld Luke Usher reining in behind him.

It was like a great load had been lifted from her shoulders; just the sight of him made her almost light

123

headed. There was a strength in this man that you could feel and rely on.

After that scene with her father she was far from sure Usher's strength was going to help her, but she had to make the try. There was no one else she could turn to. It was more imperative than ever that she talk with him now. He must be made to see the truth and there was no time to lose.

She'd given the bundles to her father, said she'd try to be home tomorrow unless Baisy really needed her, and gone hurrying back to her room at Smith's. She'd take those checks to Usher's ranch. No matter what Luke thought now, once she'd told him her story she should have raised enough doubts to make him want to know more before he unleashed the fury that had been in his eyes when he had looked at her father.

Clad again as he'd first seen her in buckskin and squaw boots, black braids confined in gleaming circlet of wampum, she hurried back to the street and was just about to leave the protection of the buildings when she saw Tularosa. He made a deeper and motionless kind of crouched shadow in the smoky shade flung down by the mesquite whose branches overhung the pingpanging clamor being beaten from Rubelcaba's anvil.

By the slant of his hat she knew the gun fighter's

glance was pinned on Isham's in an unswerving stare. He was obviously waiting for her to go fetch her mare.

She drew hesitantly back, but she hadn't much choice. She had to leave town without that leather slapper seeing her and she couldn't afford to risk any further delay.

Predicating all subsequent actions on the presumption Luke Usher had already gone home—which he hadn't—she moved casually forward and, with her heart banging wildly, unloosed the nearest mount from the handiest tie rail. She hauled it into the alley and swung into the saddle. Carefully guiding it through the debris behind buildings, believing she'd eluded Tularosa's vigilance, she sent it into the brush on a shortcut for Usher's.

Marratt never was afterwards able to recall what notion he was worrying when he came into sight of the old Usher ranch house. His mind had been filled with thoughts aroused by Clint Gainor. But the moment he saw the pair of hard-breathing horses standing spraddle-legged before the front porch all the hardness ground into him by experience was apparent. His eyes turned bleak, all the bones of his face standing out like castings.

Those broncs had been pushed and, though grass stood hock deep all over the yard, neither one of the pair had dropped its head to start browsing. If this visit were hostile it didn't look like they'd have left those horses in plain sight. But the men weren't in view and, at this stage of the game, one wrong move could put him out of it for keeps. If these were hirelings of Ryerson . . .

Leaving his animals in the brush at the side of the road, Marratt drew old Jake's pistol and cut around to the barn, moving silently and swiftly. He came in from the rear and moved through it warily without discovering anyone.

Thirty yards of grass-covered open lay between the barn and Jake's back door and he was crouched outside it within twenty seconds, glad he'd forgotten to shut it when he went off with Frailey.

Easing off his boots he stepped into the kitchen. They were in the front room, two open doors beyond and, while he couldn't yet see them because of the angles, he caught the sound of ragged breathing.

"Give 'em here!" growled a voice; and there was a quick rush of bootsteps punctuated by a gasp and the sound of something ripping. He caught the slap of hands against flesh and panting—a sudden curse. Spur rowels rattled above another rush of feet.

Marratt was at the hall door half crouched to go through it when a black-haired girl with the dress half torn off her caromed into his arms, knocking the legs out from under him. He went down hard. His gun flew skittering across the floor. He felt warm flesh against his cheek and shoved her off him, rolling to hands and knees just as the man in pursuit of her, unable to stop, crashed into him.

It fortunately wasn't his bad side which sent the fellow sprawling, but it was plenty bad enough. It knocked him halfway around and left him gagging for air. "Look out—" the girl cried, and the desperation in her voice cut through Marratt's stupor.

He pulled the chin off his chest and saw the fellow unscrambling himself from a wrecked chair. They reeled to their feet at about the same time and the man brought around what was left of the chair in a whistling arc that only missed braining Marratt by inches.

He came alive fast then, sensing the murderous urge that was pushing this fellow, and swaying forward in the whooshing wake of those rungs struck hard as he could at the man's right shoulderblade.

The chair spilled out of Tularosa's grasp. He staggered, striving frantically to keep his balance. Before he could get his feet planted under him Marratt slugged him again, at the point of the left shoulder.

Tularosa slammed into the wall. Something on its far side hit the floor with a crash. But Marratt was too anxious to get his hands on the man. With the wall for leverage Tularosa's brought-up boot took

127

Marratt in the chest and flung him half across the room.

Those shoulder blows had slowed the man up but he came within an ace of getting his gun out of leather before Marratt got back to him. Marratt got hold of that wrist just in time. Even so the gun came out; all Marratt could manage was to deflect the man's aim. That first slug, grazing Marratt's shoulder, brought down the stovepipe in a cloud of soot. The second plowed into the ceiling, but Marratt knew his luck wasn't going to last forever.

He couldn't break the man's hold, couldn't wrest the weapon away from him—the bony gun fighter seemed to have the strength of a tiger and his pistoning left kept battering Marratt's head with a punishment that was reducing Marratt's vision to red fog. There was a ringing in his ears. There were butterflies in his stomach. He finally got his left fist wrapped around that six-inch barrel and, forcing Tularosa's gun arm above his head, attempted to drive the man wallward.

Only then did he commence fully to realize the real nature of what he was up against. It wasn't just that his fellow appeared to have anchored himself to the floor like a leech or that he seemed endowed with three times the strength any man so built could normally count on. A foul stench came out of him, sour with the acrid reek of marihuana—it rose from his sweat like the fumes off a bog; and Marratt began desperately to wonder what chance he stood of coming out of this alive.

His skin started to crawl. He wasn't able during those first harried moments, with all his weight thrown into the struggle, to rock the man from his tracks by one inch. Those crazed white-ringed eyes glaring into his own were filled with the fury of a man gone berserk.

For the first time in his life Marratt experienced the bitter knowledge of fright in all its aspects. His belly trembled, the hinges of his knees seemed on the verge of collapsing; he thought for a moment he was going to throw up.

His grip, rimed with sweat, was beginning to slip and the clubfooted gunman, suddenly abandoning those bludgeoning blows at Marratt's head, directed all his monstrous energy into a series of maneuvers designed to break Marratt's hold on that gun-weighted wrist. He writhed and twisted like a sackful of snakes but, with his arm above his head, he couldn't get enough leverage. He gave backward a step and was carried back another by the thrust of Marratt's weight. He lost his balance and went over, taking Marratt with him, throwing a knee up as he fell.

Marratt thought that knee had gone through his guts, that he was impaled upon the thing with his backbone folded down across it like a dish cloth.

Waves of nausea racked him and he retched, never knowing the fellow's wrist had twisted free of fingers that were no longer part of him.

He wanted only to die. Merciful and quick like. There was a brimstone taste to his rag-dry mouth and all the fires of hell were hurling flames across his loins. Yet when he saw the glint of that gun barrel coming he had sense enough left to try and roll away from it.

The blow missed his head but almost took an arm off. He could feel the cold shock all the way to his toenails. Through a haze like spun glass he could see the blue green of the sunlit tamarisks and the curl-patched trunk of the long-leafed eucalyptus beyond the rear door's bright oblong, and down by its threshold the shine of Jake's pistol.

He let go of his belly and began to crawl toward it.

Something charged across his vision and plowed into something behind him. He heard the gun fighter curse, the scuff of struggling bodies. He didn't stop to look. He locked his eyes straight ahead and kept crawling.

It wasnt till he heard the ragged jump of Naome's breath hit high C in a scream that Marratt jerked his head around. There was blood on Tularosa's gun barrel. Blood's crimson was lacing through the blue welt beneath the girl's breasts; and it was this which pulled Marratt onto his feet through the reedy crackle of the gunhawk's laughter and slammed him, snarling, at that grotesque shape.

He saw the crazy eyes turn, saw the gunmuzzle lift, saw the flame gouting out of that blood-spattered barrel. He didn't feel the slug's impact. The only thing he had room for was the satisfaction of seeing that pockmarked face rocking backward, eyes enormous, from the force with which he'd hit it.

The bony arms flapped outward as the man tried to catch his balance. Sight of the gun still clenched in one fist brought all Marratt's rage boiling up from his bowels. His right caught the barrel, his left grabbed the arm, and he slammed the man's wrist hard against the door's casing. Even through that wild screech he could hear the bones snap. He spun the man around and broke his other wrist also. "Go show those to Bella Loma!"

Then he flung him through the door.

CHAPTER 12

Naome was watching him when Marratt passed out. He'd retrieved the pistol lost at the outset and, crossing to the door letting into the hall, had been stooping to pick up the one the man had struck her with when the hinges of his knees let go and dropped him, limp, across the boards of the floor.

She did not cry out. She did none of the things a lady would have done, though the memory of Tularosa firing at him point-blank was the most vivid recollection in her mind at that moment. She stepped around Marratt and picked up Tularosa's gun, glad

132

to find when she broke it open its chambered cylinder still held two unfired cartridges.

She went onto the back stoop with the heavy pistol in her hand and looked around for Tularosa without seeing him. Her narrowed glance raked the tamarisks and went ahead of her into the barn without finding any sign of movement. She went on around the house and still could not find him. The borrowed horses were browsing, proof he hadn't gone near them.

Returning, she saw Marratt's boots on the stoop and took them inside. She rolled him carefully over. Tularosa had missed. There was torn cloth edged with blood high up on his left shoulder but examination revealed this to be little more than the track of a powder blast. His collapse had been the result of exhaustion.

She found needle and thread and repaired her appearance as best she was able. She fetched some rags from a cupboard and the half-full bottle of turpentine she'd found while hunting the needle and thread. Unbuttoning Marratt's torn shirt she did what she could for the powder burn and, soaking two of the rags with turpentine, bound them over his chest and stomach just tightly enough to keep them in place.

She righted his overturned table, put the groceries away that were still fit to put away and swept up the rest, including twelve broken eggs it made her sick just to think of. Then she sat down with Tularosa's gun in her lap and waited for the man on the floor to come round.

So this was Luke Usher.

With the chance now to really study his features she tried to find in their lines some indication of the character local repute had ascribed to him. It wasn't the kind of face she would expect to have found on the man who had done what he had fifteen years ago; nor could she make his performance in the Red Horse Bar gee at all with the one she'd just witnessed.

It was all so confusing, so mixed up in her mind. Especially the way her rebellious emotions continually disregarded what her thinking considered irrefutable logic. This man had threatened her father—she had heard him herself this very morning in town. How *could* she—how could any decent girl—feel so drawn toward such a man after remembering the way he had looked on that store porch?

He groaned and she got up and went over to him. "You're all right," she said, "just take it easy." She helped him onto his feet.

"Close that back door," he grumbled. "Did you take care of my horses?"

She looked surprised. "I didn't see any horses but those two in the yard."

He told her where he'd left them and while she was gone he got into his boots. When she came back he was in the front room stretched out on the couch underneath Jake's picture. The resemblance was startling. "Is that old Jake?" she asked.

Marratt nodded.

"I shouldn't think, after what I said to your father—"

"We'll talk of that later."

She went back to the kitchen, put the stovepipe together, swept the place out again and went outside and washed up. She built up a fire and while she worked she went over in her mind what she would say to him. She was not shocked by what he had done to Tularosa; all her thoughts were concerned with what he might do to her father if she failed to convince him. She looked in on him once while the meal was cooking and found him asleep.

When she had everything on the table she called him. He came in from the back, having detoured to wash and slick back his hair with his fingers, cowpuncher fashion. He surprised her by returning thanks and still further astonished her by passing everything her way before helping himself.

When they were finished Marratt pushed back his plate. Their eyes met and locked and something stronger than themselves pulled them onto their feet and his hands gripped her shoulders. They stared at one another, Naome's eyes frightened, questioning; Marratt's hungrily demanding. Their lips met and clung and then she pushed him away and Marratt said, inexplicably bitter: "You came out here because of what I said to your father?"

"Of course. You're wrong about Dad—terribly wrong."

"Did you fetch that gun fighter along to persuade me?"

"I didn't fetch him. I came to give you those checks I took from Beckwith's office. Tularosa came out hoping to get them away from me."

"And succeeded, of course, so that—"

"No. I still have them."

Marratt looked at her awhile, his bearded cheeks inscrutable.

"I find that somewhat hard to follow. The cattle those checks paid for were stolen by Wineglass. Ryerson owns Wineglass; Jake Usher owned those cattle. You took the checks to protect your father, yet you claim to've come out here to give them to me. It doesn't make sense."

"I think it will if you'll listen—"

"You could have given them to me yesterday."

"I didn't know you yesterday."

"You knew who I was this morning."

"But I hadn't decided then what to do with them. It was what you said to Dad that—"

"Does your father know you've got them?"

"He doesn't even dream they exist."

"Yet he sends this gunhawk—"

"If anyone sent Tularosa it was Crafkin—"

"Crafkin. Tularosa." Marratt's smile was starved and wintry. "What difference does it make? They both draw their pay and get their orders from Ryerson."

She considered him a moment. "I'm going to show you where you're wrong," she said. "While they both get their pay out of Wineglass, neither of them takes any orders from Dad. For a proper slant on what has happened around here you must understand, in the first place, that my father has spent half his life on a dream. On a quest for the pot at the foot of the rainbow."

"A romantic notion," Marratt said. He fished out the makings.

Naome's chin came up. "Call it foolish if you want to. The essential fact is still true. In the last seventeen years he's been around Bella Loma very little. He's never cared for ranching; always he's been sure he's going to uncover some lost bonanza." She brushed a strand of black hair back away from her cheek. "You must have known people like that."

Marratt didn't say whether he had or he hadn't. He lighted his cigarette, lifting and lowering his shoulders, his attention seeming more absorbed with the girl herself than with the thoughts she was attempting to put into words.

"You've got to listen to me, Luke," she said half-angrily. "That's the way my father *is*—it's part of the explanation of how things around us here came to be as we find them. He has never cared a snap of his fingers for ranching. Because he loved her my father married an Indian woman who was able to share his nomadic life happily. To allow him more time to do as he wanted he hired Churk Crafkin to manage the ranch. He literally turned it over to him lock, stock and barrel."

Marratt still didn't speak but she could see that he was thinking.

"I don't want to labor the point, but you have to believe that to understand what's been happening. He has never, to my knowledge, demanded any accounting or asked one question of Crafkin. The man's like a king; he does just as he pleases—in the name of Clem Ryerson. And my father reaps the blame!"

She went on then to tell him of the things she'd discovered, concluding with the story of her visit to Beckwith's office, her finding of the checks, her waylayal by Crafkin and subsequent flight to town. She told how, badly frightened, she had taken the room at Smith's and of, this morning, seeing Tularosa. "Beckwith must have looked for those checks and sent word right away to Crafkin."

"But when he stopped you in that gulch I don't see how he could have known—"

"He didn't, of course; he wasn't after the checks then. He was trying," she said, flushing, "to put me in the right frame of mind to accept him for a husband—can't you see what he's been up to? what his goal's been all along? He's after Wineglass! If he can't get it by forcing me into a marriage—I know it sounds incredible but the man's an incredible person. He's utterly ruthless, and I think he suspects—"

"But the only real evidence you've got is those checks," Marratt said. "It just doesn't make sense. If he's the kind of a two-legged polecat you're painting he'd have himself so protected on that deal with Beckwith that the only one those checks could incriminate would be your father. They'd be made out to Wineglass."

"They are," Naome said.

"So you're presuming a kickback that can't be proved. If it ever came to court it'd be his word against Ryerson's—"

"Now you've arrived at my own conviction, the thought which sent me after them. Since they'd almost certainly be made out to Wineglass and would therefore convict my father, whom everyone around here considers an unprincipled range hog, I knew, when I heard you'd come back, I'd have to destroy them. What I had overlooked—what you and Churk Crafkin have, too, for that matter—is the character

139

of the man who was buying those cattle." She came back and dropped into her chair.

"What about it?"

"Ask yourself—you talked to him."

Marratt nodded. The lids of his eyes squeezed down a little.

"I see what you mean. The man's a born double-crosser whose every instinct would be to protect himself. So he marked them when they came back from the bank."

Naome pulled off one of her boots and passed them over.

But after studying them awhile Marratt shook his head. "This might tend to show Stanley Beckwith's good faith. It won't help your father."

"With those notations?" Naome said uneasily, "Why won't it?"

"Because even though this shows they were Usher cattle Beckwith bought from your range boss, Crafkin will say he was only following instructions and delivered them to Beckwith on Ryerson's orders. Things being as they are, no matter what your father says folks are going to take Crafkin's word—"

"The *bank* won't take it," Naome broke in heatedly, "and when the bank's records are fetched into court no one else in his right mind is going to take it either. Churk Crafkin endorsed every one of those checks and not a penny of that money ever went into the ranch accounts!"

"If you can prove that it may get your father off, but—"

"You still think he was back of it?" Naome's glance locked with Marratt's incredulously. "After all I've told you and—"

"I'll give him the benefit of the doubt on the cow deal, but you've said yourself he was on this ranch the day old Jake—"

"So was Crafkin! Can't you see how it all hangs together?"

"I can see how you'd like it to," Marratt conceded. "I'm not blaming you. If I were you I'd feel the same. You've built up a good case but that's all it is—theory. Just a lot of slick guesswork—"

"And what do you call what you've built up against my father? Did you actually see him *shoot* Jake Usher?"

Marratt stared at her a moment. "No. I didn't see him shoot Jake—"

"But you told everyone he did it! If I'd maligned anybody the way you have him I'd certainly feel responsible for finding out the truth! Or are you," she said bitterly, "afraid to find out—afraid to go up against a man who's made a career of killing?"

Marratt's eyes turned bleak. But before he could answer they heard the sound of a buggy coming into the yard. Naome jumped up. She leaned across the table and snatched up the checks. She said suddenly, fiercely: "If you go on with your intentions with regard to my father I'll see you in hell if it's the last thing I do!"

Hoof sound and buggy wheels stopped outside the door. Brown eyes still showing the seething violence of her emotions, Naome jerked it open. Frailey's face appeared, surprised, hung indecisively there a moment and looked about to be withdrawn when Marratt growled, "We ain't got nothing that's catching."

The old medico looked uncomfortable. "I could just as well come back later, Luke . . ."

"No need to do that. Miss Ryerson's about to leave anyway. Would you care for a cup of java?"

Naome thrust the checks at the doctor. "I wonder if you'd mind keeping these for me?"

As Frailey reached to take them Marratt said, stubbing out his smoke, "Never heard you express your convictions on the subjects of life and death, Doc, but if you ain't in no hurry to meet your Maker I'd suggest you stick to rolling pills."

The girl's face turned, threw an irritated glance at him.

Marratt said, ignoring its message, "You should know what you're getting into. Those pretty green papers are coffin bait, Doc. They're the checks paid by Beckwith for stolen Usher cattle."

Frailey's wrinkled cheeks sagged with a variety of emotions, the most discernible of which appeared to be shock. He seemed to be having a little trouble with his breathing if one could judge by the way he tugged at his collar.

Marratt said to Naome, "Don't ask him to go into a thing like that blind. Tell him what you told me and let him do his own thinking."

As she told him the story the doctor's countenance, schooled by many a crisis, revealed nothing of his thoughts but grew steadily more grave, particularly when she came to Marratt's fight with Tularosa.

When she was done he did not speak at once but appeared to be turning it over. He said at last, "I've long suspected that fellow Crafkin had a pretty free hand in the things that have made your father unpopular—"

"Then you believe I'm right?" Naome asked breathlessly. "You think, as I do, it was Crafkin who really killed Luke's father?"

Frailey hesitated. "I believe it was Crafkin who pushed Wineglass expansion, who built the spread up to its present size and power, and I believe he did this with the intention of eventually taking it over. But—"

"If you concede that much you've got to admit he killed Luke's father—it's all of a pattern. And he was here that day. He had the opportunity."

The doctor said, frowning, "We have only your conviction on that point, Naome. I happen to know your father made several offers for this property—"

"Dad? Or Wineglass?"

Frailey looked uncomfortable. "The most of them may have come through Crafkin, but your father made at least one of them because I was here myself and heard him. He offered Jake ten thousand dollars for the place without the stock."

"There was nothing wrong with that price or with him offering it," Naome countered.

"It suggests he was determined to have it—"

"Not necessarily. It borders our ranch on this side and if Crafkin persuaded Dad we might have trouble over the boundaries . . . You've got to realize that Dad took Crafkin's word unreservedly on anything having to do with the running of Wineglass. If Crafkin said we had to have this place Dad probably thought it would avoid ill feeling if he offered Jake more than the ranch was worth. Jake Usher's stubbornness was proverbial from what I've been told. They say he was very hot-headed and very—"

"Yes, he was proud and hot-headed, and he was stubborn," Frailey said, "and if your father and Crafkin did come over here that day, there might very well have been trouble."

His frowning eyes touched Marratt's face. "You made some pretty wild statements that day yourself, Luke. Has your memory been able to dig up the sight of Ryerson shooting—"

"No," Marratt said.

"Did you see Ryerson or Crafkin here that day?"

"I have no recollection of it."

"Were you here when your father was shot?"

"I—" Marratt said instead, "It seems to me to be highly suggestive that, if Ryerson and Crafkin were here when Jake was killed, neither one of them has ever seen fit to admit it."

"It seems suggestive to *me*," Naome came back sharply, "that you've never said why you accused Dad—never offered the least evidence in support of your charge!"

Frailey's eyes, too, looked the question.

Marratt's cheeks remained inscrutable.

Frailey said to Naome, "I'd like to make it plain—"

Marratt lifted a hand. "Somebody coming."

Naome's face twisted doorward. The doctor looked that way, too. The sound of a walking horse rounded the house and stopped in the back yard and a man's voice called: "Anybody home?"

Marratt stepped around Frailey and went out on the stoop. The man on the horse said, "Your name Usher?"

"What's on your mind?"

"Heard you might be figurin' to open up again so I reckoned I'd drop by an' test the chances of a job." He sat his horse like a man who'd been born to the saddle but his long-fingered hands showed little acquaintance with a rope and were too well kept to belong to a range hand. He wore benchmade boots and blue serge pants that were powdered with dust and showed the glint of long usage. The coat to the pants was on his back, hanging open to reveal a shirt designed for a stiff collar which he had apparently discarded. He had straw-colored hair and a straw colored mustache; but it was the bone-handled gun that Marratt looked at the longest. That, and the half-amused slanch of green stare.

"Gainor send you?"

"Don't know any Gainor. Do I have to get the okey from him to get a job here?"

"Mostly," Marratt said, "you've got to be able to work a gun." He was conscious of the girl stepping out of the door behind him and of the bold and lecherous way those arrogant eyes assessed her figure. "On the barn door behind you there's a piece of strap iron that gets by for a hasp—"

The report of the pistol jumped through his words. Sixty feet away the hasp banged round on its swivel and the richocheting slug screamed to silence over the tamarisks. Smooth and swift as had been its drawing the fellow's gun was snugged in leather.

"Try it again," Marratt said and, ignoring the coatwearer's look, watched carefully. He saw no more than before, a mere blur of motion culminating in thunder. The hasp remained static but the hole the slug drilled wasn't two inches from it.

He watched the empties punched out and replaced with live cartridges. "You been long around here?"

The green eyes grinned. "Not long enough to get in no trouble."

Marratt's sinews pulled tight as a shaggy-haired pup came around the barn's side and, answering the man's whistle, trotted over and sat down, ears pricked and tongue lolling.

"Is that your dog?" Naome asked.

"Never saw him before."

"He seemed to know your whistle."

"Looks to me like anybody's dog that'll call him."

Marratt whistled. The dog came over and sat down with his tail happily thumping the stoop.

147

"Just dog," the stranger said in a tone bordering smugness. "Do I get that job or don't I?"

"For as long as it lasts," Marratt said, "you've got it." He scowled at the discoloring knuckles of his hands. "Turn your cayuse in with those others and stash your truck in the old man's bedroom." About to start off he swung back, saying sourly, "What name do you want burnt onto your headboard?"

The green eyes laughed. "Kid Boots will look good as anything, I reckon. But don't get me planted till I been cut down."

Marratt strode past the girl and went into the house. He didn't care what label a drifting slug-slammer gave himself; it was the tail-wagging part of the yard's assemblage he was scowling about. That dog might come to anyone's call but it was still the same pup he'd seen by that tank when he'd come onto Naome swimming in the raw.

At Wineglass Clem Ryerson, in his room with the door shut, was squatted before a cast-iron safe sifting through a batch of reports and clippings having mainly to do with folks who'd once lived in Texas. He leafed through them again with a nervous care.

Frowning, he thrust them back in their envelope, dropping it into a metal drawer which he carefully closed and locked. Methodically, then, he started through the safe's pigeonholes, finally with a grunt going back to his desk with a yellowing page of newsprint carrying a five-year-old Prescott dateline. Smoothing this out he stared a long while at the pair of cuts accompanying a two-column item headed: U. S. MARSHAL VICTIM OF LOCAL RANCHER.

Rummaging his desk he produced a partly-filled bottle of ancient ink, a screaky-nibbed pen and several sheets of blank paper and, with a bleak expression, wrote in a crabbed left-handed scrawl for upwards of ten minutes. He then folded the sheet of newsprint and put it with his writing in an envelope which, after considerable thought, he addressed to the governor.

Thrusting this envelope into his pocket Ryerson closed the safe, gave the knob a quick flip, and picked up his hat. He hadn't seen a soul since he'd got back to the ranch and, just at the moment, he didn't want to see anyone. He went out the back way and climbed onto his horse. He stared a moment or two in the direction of Bella Loma, then reversed the long-limbed speedy looking grulla and took off for Casa Grande.

On the kitchen table beside his pushed-back plate Marratt saw a sheaf of banknotes which he picked up with some surprise. But as he stared at the crisp new bills in his hands his thoughts left the dog and his new serge-suited employee. "Hey, Doc!" he called, hurrying into the front room; but Frailey had gone.

He thrust the currency into his pocket. It was the loan they'd gone to town for. The old medico had left him the whole two hundred.

Naome came into the room. She said, "I wouldn't put too much trust in that fellow."

"Did you give Frailey those checks?"

Her look met his defiantly. "I don't think, Luke Usher, you have any right to ask."

Marratt's lips pulled in a bit tighter at their corners but he couldn't leave it there. "At least take my advice and get rid of them. Don't keep them on you. If Crafkin was back of Tularosa he's not going to—"

"Then you *do* believe—"

"Look," Marratt said. "No matter what's the straight of that deal in Usher cattle, those cattle were stolen and Beckwith's checks prove it. You might just as well lug around a live rattler—"

"That wasn't the impression you gave me a little while ago."

"I'm getting a wider look at this now. I believe you're right about Crafkin rigging that cow steal. If you should also be right about him figuring to take the spread over, the smartest thing you could do from here on out is to stay plumb away from there."

Some of the tightness went out of Naome's cheeks. Something changed in her eyes and she said with a shy impulsiveness, "You mean—you want me to stay here?"

"Lord, no! Stay in town where you'll have some protection. You must know *someone* you could stay with."

"Well, there's Clint Gainor's wife . . . "

Marratt stared like he couldn't believe he was hearing it.

"Of course," Naome said, "she's not in town exactly, but—"

"Go to Chandler or Casa Grande. Get put up in a room at some prominent hotel and stay out of sight until this thing's been ironed out."

She considered him carefully. "You mean to go after Crafkin?"

"I can't tell," he said flatly, "what I'm going to do. But if I've got to be watching out for you all the time—"

"You won't," Naome said with her chin coming up. "My place is with my father and I shall stay right with him until I know where you stand on the matter of Jake Usher."

He was too goaded, too harried by the hell of his thoughts, to give any proper care to his words. "You'll be with him on a slab at some undertakin' parlor if you don't stop getting in Churk Crafkin's hair!" He glared at her angrily. "Can't you get it through your head that going out there now you'll

151

be playing right into that bastard's hands?"

"I can see that the things I've told you about him haven't made the least difference in your attitude toward Dad!"

Something warned him to go easy but the bit was in his teeth now and his tongue was in top gear. With a kind of shocked horror he heard his fool mouth telling her, "What's between your father and me ain't got nothing to do with Jake Usher or Crafkin or anything else that's happened around here. Go tell him that if you want to—and you can tell him from me that the next time we meet he better come a-smokin'!"

Long after the girl had gone Marratt sat in the darkening front of Jake's house and bitterly thought how right Doc had been when the old man had prophesied there would be no tomorrow in this country for him.

The cards had been stacked from the very beginning, from the moment he'd walked in on Charlie and found her—from the moment he'd lined his sights on that marshal. He'd been licked right then and he'd known it. But what choice had he had? Could any man who called himself one have done different?

He'd been over this before and he still had to shake his head.

Perhaps he needn't have got into this mess at Bella Loma. But that had looked like the hand of Providence then, a good chance to hide out from the law till he could pick up the trail of Clagg's partner. And if he hadn't stepped into the boots of Luke Usher he might have gone straight away, never guessing his quarry was the big mogul round here.

In some ways, he thought, it was too bad he hadn't.

But that was weakness, the natural wish to see shifted to other shoulders the awful responsibility which the luck of discovery had shoved on his own. For the law would never worry Hugh Clagg—he'd seen that much. It would have been Marratt's word, and unsupported at that, against the say of a federal marshal. The girl was dying when he found her, dying of her own hand because . . . You couldn't take a thing like that into court. No one could. No one decent.

And so he'd hunted Clagg down and killed him, shot him just the way he would have shot a mad dog.

Could he do less to Naome's father?

There was no use thinking he might have gotten Charlie's words wrong. She had described them both while she'd lain sobbing in his arms; the three-fingered man, she'd said, had been Clagg's partner.

When you were dealing with facts you had to look

them in the face. If anything Clem Ryerson, with a daughter like Naome, had less excuse than Clagg.

Maybe Ryerson hadn't touched her. If he'd been framed in the Bella Loma deal—and it looked as though he had been—might he not also have been framed in this? But Charlie had described him; and there was a sameness to the pattern. If you believed the one could you deny the other?

Ryerson had gone with his range boss to visit old Jake who had subsequently died with a slug through his skull. But had Ryerson come forward? No, he'd kept his mouth shut. Just as he had kept his mouth shut at Prescott.

Across the screen of Marratt's mind flashed the remembered look of Ryerson's daughter as they'd got up from the table and he had gripped her shoulders. There'd been a kind of shining compulsion about her and he realized now that she had wanted him to kiss her, welcoming his passion and wanting him· to know how much she had to offer. The wild shock of that embrace, the solid feel of her against him . . .

There was a time for thinking and a time for action, and the time when thought could help was gone beyond recall.

He heard Kid Boots come into the house and carry his belongings into Jake's bedroom and go back to the porch; and he heard the dry screak of his weight in Jake's rocker.

Marratt sighed in the darkness and reluctantly got up. He rolled big shoulders together, clamped jaws on his resolve and, putting behind him the things he could not change, dragged his big-roweled spurs to the porch's screen door. "Is there a horse still browsing the grass out yonder?"

"If there is he's bein' damn quiet about it." Kid Boots said after a moment, "That girl, when she left, took an extra bronc with her. You want me to go after it?"

"No," Marratt said, "I want you to stay right where you're at."

"That's the kind of a job I can stand a whole lot of. Rockin' my time away an' bein' paid for it. You must be well heeled."

"I'm riding into Bella Loma. Any visitors you may get while I'm gone will be trespassers to be dealt with according to the degree of their hostility. And don't be surprised unless you're hankering to get planted."

Going back through the house Marratt crossed to the corrals and, getting down his rope, put a loop on the apron-faced roan he'd got from Isham. After cinching on his rig and climbing into the saddle, he took a moment to examine the loads in Jake's pistol. Then he walked the horse around to the front.

156

Kid Boots' guarded hail came out of the porch shadows. "Expectin' anyone special?"

"Fellow named Gainor might decide to pay us a call. I think he kind of imagines he's got an interest in this outfit."

"He just imagines it, eh?"

"I'm keeping this place unencumbered."

"What about Wineglass?"

Marratt said, very soft, "What about it?"

"From the talk I've picked up they been usin' this spread. That all right with you?"

"When it isn't," Marratt said, "I'll make sure you're informed."

The lights of Bella Loma threw a lonesome shine across the dust of its single street when Marratt rode in and pulled up near the general store. Frailey's second-floor office and dispensary were reached by an uncovered outside staircase. Marratt observed a number of still-saddled horses dozing hipshot before the town's four saloons and, above the dark store, a reading lamp's golden circle made a halo of brightness behind a drawn shade.

He took the stairs quietly, having no way of knowing what he might be about to run into. But the doctor was alone. He came to the door with a book in his hand, seemed a bit surprised but invited him in.

When the door was closed he said, "Nothing wrong, is there?"

"Nothing a couple lead pills won't cure. I came after those checks."

Frailey, in shirtsleeves, went over and got a cigar from a case in his coat. With a sharp little knife he amputated the end he planned to put in his mouth. "Air in this country plays hell with these things," he growled, carefully licking frayed edges of wrapper. "Naome tell you I had them?"

"I don't want to get rough but if you make me I'll take 'em."

"Reckon at that I'd fare better than I would with Churk Crafkin." Frailey handed them over. "Mind saying what you want with them?"

"I'd like, if I can, to pull some of the heat off Naome. She's let me believe she's on her way back to Wineglass."

Frailey lowered his cigar. "Do you consider that wise?"

"Of course it ain't wise. It's about the dumbest damn thing she could do; but she's stubborn." He looked about to say more, but he didn't.

Frailey said, "And where do the checks—"

"Crafkin, naturally, is wild to get his hands on them."

"You think he knows about Beckwith's notations?"

"He's going to know about them," Marratt said

158

grimly, "and he's going to know I've got them just as quick as some bar fly can fetch him the news. You got any mucilage? You got a sheet of white paper?"

Frailey produced them.

Marratt picked out the check that was for the greatest amount of money and, careful to leave the end free which showed Crafkin's endorsement, stuck the other end of it to one side of the paper, lengthwise. "Now, if you've got a marking crayon . . ."

The doctor got one off his desk and Marratt, making his letters big and black, printed beneath it: A WARNING TO SKUNKS.

"That won't scare him off," Frailey said. "Put that up in the Red Horse Bar and you've shown this country he's a crook all right but you've lost any chance of ever getting a conviction. You're selling Crafkin short. He'll tear it up and laugh in your face."

"He'll tear it up," Marratt nodded, "but he won't do no laughing till he's torn up the rest of them. And while he's trying to do that he won't be bothering Naome."

"He'll be bothering *you*. He'll come down on you like the side of a mountain. Every hired gun on his payroll will be after your scalp. You understand that, don't you?"

"You worry too much, Doc," Marratt said, getting up.

159

"Don't imagine," Frailey said, "I think you're reaching for any halo. Sticking out your own neck isn't diminishing by a particle the mental anguish you're inflicting on that girl. What have you got against her father? Why are you so obsessed—"

"Aren't you forgetting old Jake?"

"You don't care two hoots whether he killed Jake or not. You haven't made the slightest effort—"

"Maybe you know what you're talking about—"

"You better believe that," Frailey said gruffly. "You're no more Luke Usher than I am."

Marratt went still with his throat dry as cotton; and then, bleakly, he grinned. He lowered a hip to the desk and met Frailey's eyes straightly. "That's right. I'm Grete Marratt."

Frailey's eyes narrowed slightly. "The Prescott marshal-killer?"

"Right again."

"Seems to me I did hear something about you breaking out of Yuma. You came through, I presume, hoping to strike some section of border where the authorities wouldn't expect your appearance. You looked about half starved the night I found you; so I imagine you must have stopped for grub and someone, obviously thinking you were Luke, tried to kill you. After I came along and made the same mistake—"

"I figured," Marratt nodded, "I might just as well

160

be Luke. I needed a place to hole up and being Luke Usher seemed a lot less dangerous than—"

"I can understand that," Frailey said. "The thing I don't get is your attitude toward Ryerson."

Marratt's look turned bleak. But the doctor, watching with eyes that had diagnosed many ailments, sensed the terrible pressure behind those locked jaws. Wisely he waited and Marratt suddenly rasped harshly, "Did you follow the trial? Did you wonder why I'd killed Clagg—why I made no defense?"

"I thought perhaps there was a woman—"

"It was a girl. Just a kid—a fourteen-year-old orphan girl whose folks had been neighbors of mine till some half-drunk Pimas came onto them one night and rubbed them out, scalping both of them. The girl was away, visiting an aunt at the time; and when she got back I helped her bury them. She was a pretty little trick, big for her age and plucky—they don't come more plucky than that girl was. I had tried to get her to go live with her aunt but she said no, she would be all right there. She went ahead by herself and put in a planting, forty acres of alfalfa which I'd agreed to buy from her; had it just about ready for cutting when this Clagg come along.'"

Marratt stopped for a moment. Frailey, watching with gray cheeks, saw the way the big bones shone through the skin of his fists. He didn't speak and Marratt said, "After Clagg left she'd tried to shoot herself. She hadn't done a good job but even a poor one will serve if enough blood is spilled."

He swallowed hard a couple of times. "She was on her last gasp when I found her. There'd been two of them, this badge-packer and an older skunk which she said was his partner. I got their descriptions. After she'd slipped away and I had fixed her up as good as I could, I fetched a couple of my men and a sodbuster she'd known and we buried her.

"The boys thought it was an accident and I never said no different. I knew this marshal was in the country. I let a couple of weeks slide by so there wouldn't be no talk, then I went after him."

Frailey said at last, and his voice sounded like he might have got smoke up his windpipe, "Man, you didn't have to go to Yuma for that. They'd have—"

"Would you have dragged her shame through all of those papers? through all those weeks of ranting and jawing?"

Marratt pulled his hip off the desk and took a turn about the room. "All the time I was in prison I kept thinking about that other guy, that older devil that had got clean away. And I watched my chance. I knew from the girl's description of his rig that he had come from the south, from the desert country. I didn't know until this morning, when you introduced him to me—"

"But a *description*," Frailey growled. "That's a

hell of a thing to stake a man's life on!"

"I've been over it a hundred times in my mind since I ran into him on that store porch this morning. The description fits. She said he was older than the one with the badge. She said 'a three-fingered man with an uptilted nose and the track of a scar across his left temple'."

"Just the same, you're not God. You don't know that he—"

"Could she have described him, do you think, if he hadn't been there? She called him the marshal's partner."

Frailey shook his head. "I've known Clem Ryerson for thirty years and I tell you, frankly, I can't believe it. Consider Naome. She was left without a mother before she was hardly out of swaddling clothes; her whole outlook is the result of Ryerson's companionship and guidance. If the man had that kind of quirk in his character—"

"Does one person ever truly understand completely the hidden depths of another's nature? How do you explain Usher's killing?"

Frailey chewed on his cigar. "I have never believed Ryerson killed Jake Usher; nor do I now. I'll admit he might conceivably have done so. Given the right set of conditions almost any man will kill. Circumstances or Crafkin—perhaps even Jake himself, may have backed Ryerson into a corner. Jake was my friend but he was proud and sometimes arrogant; his temper was notorious. If Ryerson happened to be around that day—"

"He was there. The girl admits it."

"Then, as I say, he *might* have shot Jake. But there's no parallel, Marratt, between a man in a corner shooting himself out of it and the picture you've painted of him aiding and abetting the molestation of a child."

"I think there is," Marratt said. "In the two situations we have an identical set of facts. In the first we have Ryerson going with Crafkin to Usher's house, and Usher's subsequent death. In the second we have Ryerson going with Clagg to the house of a girl who is subsequently shamed into taking her own life. In each situation we have Ryerson's stated presence and Ryerson's complete unprincipled silence. I would call that quite a parallel."

Frailey was shaken. His face showed it. But he could be stubborn too, and he growled, "I still say you're not God, Marratt. You've no right to take over His province. Even if you've hit on the truth of this matter there is still Ryerson's daughter—have you thought about her?"

"Why do you think," Marratt snarled, "I'm going to put up this paper? I'll take care of Crafkin—"

"Do you imagine 'taking care' of Crafkin will be adequate compensation for what you plan to do to her father? That girl's in love with you, Marratt—"

He broke off, eyes staring, as feet drummed sound from the outside stairs. A voice cried: *"Luke!"* and they stood as though frozen while the door burst open to disclose Naome, the black mop of her hair tumbled about by the wind, the whole look of her telling how near she'd come to hysteria.

"They've got him!"

CHAPTER 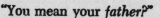 **15**

"You mean your *father?*"

Marratt stared at the girl with disbelieving eyes. It seemed incredible that Crafkin, before getting hold of those checks, would risk the whole structure of all he had schemed for by laying violent hands on the man who had made it all possible. He said as much and Frailey, intent on reassuring her, nodded. "He's probably gone off on another prospecting trip."

"In his good clothes? Without a word?" Her probing stare searched their faces. "I don't believe it. Luke coming home and then those checks right on top of it and Tularosa crippled . . . I tell you Crafkin's frightened! There wasn't a soul at the ranch and Dad's safe's been broken open—there were papers all over the floor!"

"It don't make sense," Marratt grumbled, picking up the surprise he'd got ready for Crafkin and thrusting the three loose checks in his pocket. "But if you'll stay here with Doc I'll go out there—"

"And get Dad away from them?"

Frailey said hurriedly, "He can't answer that until he finds what he's up against. The whole thing may be a ruse . . ."

Naome, still with her face watching Marratt's, said: "Will you?"

She has him over a barrel, Frailey thought; and the torment, the anguished gleam of Marratt's eyes confirmed it.

With a strangled cry he incontinently fled, recklessly plunging down the dark stairs.

But at their bottom he pulled up, his mind taking hold of the doctor's words. It *could* be a ruse; yet even as he conceded this he discovered the flaw in such an assumption. Crafkin, if he had been trying to trap Usher, would have used the girl—not her father.

Irascibly Marratt shoved a hand through his hair, and wondered what the hell had become of his hat. It was one of those irrelevancies which sometimes seem so important in a crisis though you know all the time they have no right usurping thought so direly needed elsewhere.

He struck out toward the lights of the Red Horse Bar, deciding he had probably left it at Doc's.

But if the girl had been right about them grabbing her father Crafkin would have had no reason to break open that safe. Someone else, of course, might have done it. Someone, like Naome, who had gone out there and found the place deserted.

Gainor?

In the press of other things he had forgotten Clint Gainor with his sly little eyes and his gun-backed demand to be taken into partnership as pay for his silence. His greed might be due for a considerable shock when and if he got around to checking up on Usher's signature.

Shoving through the saloon's batwings he looked the place over with a hard wintry stare which failed to discover the least sign of anything hostile among the assembled half dozen who were bellying the bar.

He could not fail to note the sudden way they quit talking but, ignoring this and them along with it, he approached the scarred oak and beckoned the apron.

The man's spraddled lips showed a parched kind of smiling. "H'are you, Mr. Usher? We heard you was back. Figurin' to put the old place on its feet again?"

167

"I'd like to borrow a knife," Marratt said—"a good sharp one."

"You want to pare your nails, maybe?"

"A skinning knife, I think, would be nearer what I'm after."

The bartender's eyes turned a little apprehensive. He slanched a look at the wholly-still wooden-faced customers. "Any you boys got a skinnin' knife on you?"

Someone produced one. He shuffled off to get it. The gleam of sweat was on his cheeks and damply beading his flaccid jowls as he came back and reluctantly laid it down before Marratt.

Marratt got out his *warning to skunks* and, with the knife, silently skewered it to one of the posts holding up the tin ceiling. With a final inscrutable glance he walked out.

He got aboard his roan horse and stepped it past the saloon which the town marshal favored without seeing the man. He was wheeling the horse around, about to strike out for Wineglass, when a small dark man came up out of the shadows. "Your name Usher?"

"And if it is?" Marratt said.

"I been asked to tell you your crew'll show up tomorrow forenoon. You better lay in some grub and a couple dozen gross of boxed cartridges—"

"Just a minute," Marratt called. "I'm not expecting any crew."

"You are now," the man grinned.

Marratt dropped folded hands across the pommel of his saddle. "Who put you up to this?"

"I guess you know who's holdin' your paper. Grub he said get, an' a wagonload of cartridges."

"All right," Marratt scowled—"now you high-tail it back to him. You tell him I said his cinch is getting frayed and without he's craving to get a leg tied up he better make a wide loop around my spread in the future."

"I'll tell him," the man nodded, "but you better be expecting them boys tomorrow mornin'."

"If they come out," Marratt promised, "it'll be to stay permanent."

He set out for Wineglass at a ground-eating canter. There was no moon riding herd on the range but a sky full of stars gave him all the light he needed to pick out a trail by. He still could not convince himself Churk Crafkin was responsible for Ryerson's reported absence. If the man was really gone it seemed a heap more likely he'd taken fright from Marratt's remarks and decided to pull a bolt.

This thought caused Marratt to grit his teeth, but he was not too taken up with thinking about Ryerson to overlook the possible consequences of running onto Crafkin. He fully shared Naome's conviction that the Wineglass segundo was the man to be reckoned with. No one with the perseverence of Crafkin was going to take all this meddling without retaliation; and he was inclined to lay the reputed absence of the crew more to some new move on the part of its ramrod than to any connection it might have with Clagg's partner.

One thing he could bank on. If Tularosa had fetched his broken wrists back to Crafkin, the man wouldn't be in any mood to yell boo at. He'd be out for blood and no mistake about that.

Marratt tried for awhile to think which way the cat would jump. While he could not pin anything down for certain, it seemed increasingly evident that before he was much older he'd be facing Ives Hanna, the Wineglass-owned town marshal.

Time was running out.

Marratt had no way of guessing how many miles he'd put behind him when he became acutely conscious of the smell of risen dust. Casting back he felt sure he'd caught whiffs of it before and, while the fact itself did not unduly perturb him, he was alarmed to discover he could so long have ignored it. Carelessness of that sort could get a man rubbed out.

There was another rider ahead of him someplace.

Since the fellow was patently bound in the same direction it was probably someone who'd quit town just ahead of him. Someone packing the news from the Red Horse Bar.

He hauled the roan down to an easier gait. He had no desire to interfere with this traveler. The whole purpose of that *warning to skunks* he'd hung up had been to channel Crafkin's rage away from Naome. That it would center on himself was a foregone conclusion and exactly what he'd aimed for. Taking care of Churk Crafkin was the least he could do, considering the fate he had in mind for Clem Ryerson.

Once again Frailey's words grimly tramped through his thinking and Marratt bitterly cursed.

He had increasingly to buttress his resolve with visions of Charlie and not even the ghastliness of these could wholly purge his thoughts of Naome. She, too, had a claim and honesty forced him to acknowledge that hers might be the greater; but this in no way lessened the ugly fact of Ryerson's guilt.

Every trail Marratt's conjectures so hopefully embarked on angled inevitably back to that. Ryerson had been there else how could the girl have described him? She had called him the badge-packer's partner, and thus was his guilt established. He did not need to have touched her; he'd been there and hadn't stopped Clagg. More damning still was his

171

subsequent silence. Those locked lips were the proof of his complicity.

For twenty minutes after climbing out of timber Marratt's roan had been following the convolutions of a bluff, picking its way between pear and cholla. Now, abruptly rounding its western flank, Marratt thought, a bit startled, to catch the rumor of gunfire. He pulled up and sat listening without hearing anything further.

Naome'd been wrong—he knew that—in assuming because she'd found the ranch deserted her father's foreman had turned wolf. He would turn wolf all right but when he did, Marratt thought, it wouldn't be to run down game as puny as the man he'd used for camouflage all these years.

Just the same, suddenly worried, Marratt sent the roan forward. That rider whose discovered dust had caused him to drop back need not, because he'd thought it was, be a currier from the Red Horse Bar—it could have been Naome! She'd had ample time to leave town ahead of him; he hadn't noticed her horse when he'd gone back to get his own.

He used his spurs on the roan, unaccountably disquieted. They swept around a tangle of chaparral and up a clatterous slope grotesquely sentineled by the night-blackened shapes of motionless saguaros. Past thickets of squatting cedar they tore and up the high arch of a talus-littered hogback which connected this bench with the vast expanse of grease-wood flats surrounding Ryerson's headquarters.

They crested the ridge and the compression of Marratt's knees, together with the savage grip of the yanked-tight reins, set the big roan back on its haunches. Marratt's widened stare held the shock of complete astonishment.

He'd expected to see Ryerson's buildings down there but he hadn't been prepared to see them going up in flames.

CHAPTER 16

It wasn't the sort of fire which could have caught by itself or have been set off by carelessness. The main house was ablaze from end to end, the big barn was going—the bunkhouse, too. It seemed incredible that anyone should deliberately have intended this; yet he was dealing, Marratt reminded himself, with at least three persons made incalculable by obsessions.

If Crafkin, turned jittery by things he'd not allowed for, had decided the time had come to get rid of Ryerson he might have fired these buildings himself. He might have done it in the hope of drawing Ryerson out of hiding, or be using this means for the disposal of Ryerson's body or to incriminate some-one else. He had the greatest opportunity so far as could be figured.

Ryerson also might have set it, or this could have been the work of Gainor whose reasons were not so easily guessed but who obviously had some kind of ax he was bent on sharpening. And there was also that business of Ryerson's safe which, according to Naome, had been smashed open; the smasher may have come back and done this. The Indian Agent could have been back of it.

The place apparently was still deserted. Marratt could see no evidence of human presence.

A great pall of smoke hung over the flat, writhing and twisting in the glow of the flames. The yard down there looked as bright as day and he could see the panicked broncs of the remuda, squealing and pitching in the clutch of terror, as they tore around and around the smoking logs of their enclosure.

No man who loved horses could long watch that, yet Marratt hesitated, bothered by his inability to find any sign of the rider who had traveled this trail just ahead of him. Of course the fellow could be sitting, much as Marratt was himself, a fascinated spectator of the conflagration which must soon reduce those costly buildings to ashes. Just the same, Marratt didn't like it. The man should be in sight if he weren't hiding.

175

And why should he be hiding? Did he know that Marratt was following him? But that didn't make sense—how could he?

The rider wasn't Naome; she'd have made straight for those buildings. Unless of course she had been grabbed by somebody lurking in ambush . . .

Marratt snorted. Not even Crafkin could have set that fire in the expectation of getting his hands on Naome. He'd better loose those horses and get the hell out of here before Churk Crafkin *did* come along.

He couldn't think why he should feel so reluctant about going down there. It didn't look like, from here, the flat afforded enough cover in the light of those flames to rig an effective trap even were somebody minded to do it. He tried to rationalize this foreboding and nothing he hit upon could rid his mind of worry. With a disgusted grimace he kneed the big roan forward across the downward sweep of the hogback's arch.

They had not moved ten lengths from the jut of its crest when the trail dropped to a hidden hollow which, now opening up, disclosed a black tangle of mixed oak and sycamore and, above and beyond these, the waiting shape of a motionless horseman.

Marratt, instantly alert, scanned the pooled gloom below the man with lifted hackles. He felt certain that fellow didn't just happen to be posted there.

He wished with bitter anger he'd had the wit to fetch a rifle. But, satisfied at last there was nobody else between them, he said sharply: "Move up, friend. I want to see what you look like."

The man had his legs straight down in the stirrups and he kept them that way, making no move at all. "You'd need a light to do that and if you scratch a match we're done for."

"Mister," Marratt said, "I won't be telling you again."

The man held a hand up like an Indian signaling silence. Then he moved it again, like a cowbird intent on yanking a worm from the ground. Only, this time, its gesture was downward.

Marratt swiveled a look toward the burning buildings. The barn's roof had fallen in and a part of the house roof. There wasn't much left of the bunkhouse and one end of the corral was beginning to take fire. The horses against the far end were plunging like mad but he couldn't pick out any other changes.

The hollow or swale—which in truth it more nearly resembled with its rank growth thrusting ragged tops up out of the darkness—was roughly shaped like a fish hook, about a quarter of a mile long by possibly seventy feet wide at the point where its crescent slashed the path of Marratt's travel. The shank or stem of this depression flanked the left of the hogback while the burning buildings of Ryerson's headquarters were considerably forward and to the right of Marratt's position, with the unidentified horseman just across the hook's curve on high ground directly ahead of him. It was a natural assumption the man's attention was fixed on something which Marratt himself could not see.

Cold slivers of disquiet still scratched at his nerve-ends, but a strengthening curiosity and the plight of those penned-up horses were rapidly fraying the stays of his caution when the man on the point began wickedly to curse.

"What's the rub?" Marratt called.

"Can't you *see* them? It's the girl! That dirty dog of a Crafkin's going to— *Merciful God!*" the man cried and, dragging his rifle, piled out of the saddle.

Even as his shape disappeared in the shadows, Marratt slashed his horse with the knotted reins.

Down into the dank chill of that brush-choked declivity Marratt slammed the big roan with all the power it could muster. He had no thought of traps now, his every faculty was straining to come to grips with Churk Crafkin, to feel the jolting satisfaction of doubled fists pounding flesh. There was a shame in him, too—the shame of having put off for so long a chore which he'd known from the first he'd have eventually to tackle. He should have gone after Crafkin as soon as he'd finished with Tularosa; he had seen the man's danger to Naome right then.

He drove the roan through the brush and between trees hardly seen and was flinging him at the opposite slope, aimed toward where that guy had jumped from the saddle, when the first hint of his folly came racketing out of the swale's leftward bend. That hard rush of horse sound rocketing toward him told him plain as plowed ground how that fellow's slick acting had suckered him into this.

He heard Crafkin's shout above the rataplan thunder of galloping hoofs. Muzzle lights, winking, laced the roaring gloom with the hard clapclapping of high-powered rifles. He whirled his horse off the slope as the now hidden decoy, having gauged the range, commenced a grim search with a pattern of slugs.

Bullets tunneled the shadows, striking trees, clipping branches. Ricochets screamed off the slants of rock surfaces and, throwing a look back across his shoulder, Marratt saw the black shapes of Ryerson's crew tear from cover. He whirled again, spurring the roan toward the ranchward end of the depression's crescent. He didn't need any crystal ball to grasp the full notion of what they were up to, but there wasn't anything he could do about it.

Crafkin hammered his shouts through the din like fists. "Keep him goin'! Keep him goin'!"

Marratt felt no desire to tarry. Not with all that lead whistling round. He was devoting all his energies toward utilizing every last ounce of speed the powerful gelding was able to generate, aware that he was playing into their hands but knowing, too, that nothing save distance could spell survival once they got him lined against the light from those buildings.

And then he felt his horse stumble and the guns slacked off as the hard-hit roan careened round the bend that opened onto the flats. And now he could see them, red as blood in the dying glow of the flames, and he could hear the bleak rasp of the gelding's breathing like the wheeze of a punctured bellows.

He had no choice. He dropped off, landing on skidding bootheels and praying the roan would stay on his feet, at least till those feet carried him out of this ravine.

Not waiting to see, he ran straight at the slope of the hogback's flank, doubled over and spurred to an all-out effort by the ground-shaking rumble of thundering hoofs. It was not too light here but not dark enough for that bunch to miss him without he could get well above eye level.

Twelve feet up he was forced to start climbing and twice he very near started an avalanche when rocks he laid hold of came away in his hands. He made another ten feet of straight-up progress before the Wineglass crew came quirting and spurring round the bulge of the bend. There was nothing he could do then but plaster himself like a fly against that wall and hope like hell there wouldn't none of them look upward.

A sudden shout tore out of that confused mass of riders and Marratt almost lost his grip as shoulder muscles cringed in expectation of impact. But no bullet struck him. No bullet was fired though he heard them pull up in a ragged burst of swearing.

Crafkin's bull-throated bellow flailed into them, furious. "Get after him, you fools! He's on that flat someplace! Get out there and find him!"

The whole bunch churned into motion. But where the ravine debouched onto the open plain they pulled up again and, by their sudden wild uproar, Marratt knew they had sighted the capsized roan.

He dared not wait any longer. With all his back muscles quivering he started climbing again, well knowing the danger in movement but desperately aware, too, of his probable fate should one of that crew happen to glance up and see him. There was no possibility of concealment, no hope of getting beyond range of a bullet so long as he remained on this cliff face. And there were still sixty feet of it between him and the rim.

There seemed to be, however, and just a little way above him, a kind of inverted fold or crevice which he thought, if he could reach it, would facilitate

181

progress immensely. It appeared to bear toward the rim at a decidedly healthier angle than the straight-up contour he was currently encountering.

He was above shale now, on the face of the open stone, finding it increasingly hard to secure hand holds and harder still to find holds for his feet. His whole body ached from the unaccustomed exertion, there was a wheeze in his breathing and he was high enough now that if he fell it would go hard with him.

He did not look toward the fire but he could guess by the amount of light refracted against the cliff that it was about burned out. It was more a red stain than a brightening and fading flicker of flames, but there was still too much of it for him to feel any confidence his shape would not be visible should one of those cursing searchers chance to look in his direction.

He paused to rest a moment, fearing the danger of overtaxing his strength. The nearest portion of the crevice was hardly four feet above his head when, taking new hope from this proximity, he prepared to resume his upward crawl.

He raised his right boot to a new position, tested it cautiously and then, putting weight on it, slid his left hand up to clamp cramping fingers about a bit of rock shelving some eight inches higher. But when he went to pull his left foot onto a new location his gun belt wouldn't let him; it was caught on some kind of projection.

He felt cold sweat creeping out all over him and events long forgotten unreeled irrelevant details across the throbbing screen of his harrowed mind. He tried to pull in his belly but the belt wouldn't budge. He couldn't drop his hips enough to do any good without taking his lifted hand from its hold and working them sideways didn't free the belt, either. But these gyrations, while not helping him, thrust too much of his weight and its accompanying strain on the embedded niggerhead supporting that newly anchored right boot.

He felt the rock give and every screaming nerve telegraphed its panic to a mind already on the brink of desperation.

He did not hear the growled reports of the disgruntled greasewood beaters or know they had reassembled for further orders where Crafkin sat his chocolate dun hardly a stone's throw away from the wall on which Marratt's belt had so bitterly trapped him. He did not realize the quiet in which they awaited the ramrod's decision. Fright had dug its hooks in him and the roar of his churning emotions turned him blind and deaf to everything but the terrible need for getting instantly off of that loosening boulder.

He didn't think but, acting purely from instinct,

dropped his left hand to its former hold, resettled his left foot and his weight along with it and, releasing his right hand, unbuckled the damned belt and let go of it. The gun, sliding free, struck rock—struck again and went off with a blast that ripped the night wide open.

The walls flung back a wild clamor of shouting. Several other guns went off and through this uproar Marratt, not yet discovered, found new grips for his fingers and started rimward again, frantic to get himself into that crevice before one of Crafkin's whippoorwills spotted him.

Had that unseated niggerhead remained in place he might have done so. But no sooner had his lifted foot relinquished its pressure than the boulder tore loose and fell crashing.

CHAPTER **17**

He didn't need Crafkin's shout to know they'd seen him. The sharp *crack-crack* of a fast-firing saddle gun would have told him if the splatter of rock chips and the ricochets hadn't. Discarding the last drag of caution he hauled himself into the water crack barely in time to avoid being riddled in the belated blast from the Wineglass riders.

He didn't stop to catch his breath but shoved everything he had into reaching the rim. What little shelter this crevice afforded was made possible only by the matter of angles which would be no good once that bunch got below him. The upward pitch of the crack—roughly seventy degrees—gave him enough traction to make his efforts count double in the matter of speed.

Even so, his hatless head still lacked five feet of reaching safety when the gunslingers fetched by the Wineglass ramrod started pounding the face of the cliff into rock dust. The crevice was fogged with this curtain of grit and nothing, it seemed, could survive such a hammering, but poor light and hurry combined to save Marratt's bacon.

He got over the rim.

Teeth on edge and half blinded he crawled away from the racket and dropped flat, exhausted. Blood seeped from a score of shallow wounds cut by rock chips and every muscle, every tendon, quivered with the wrenching strain put on it. But reactions were a luxury Grete Marratt couldn't afford.

He reeled onto his feet, still groggy but knowing how brief was the time he could count on before Crafkin's crew would break out of the shadows hellbent on finishing the job they had started. Already he could hear the clatter of shod hoofs winging out of that tangle of oak brush and sycamore.

He scrubbed a hand across his jaws and knuckled the sweat from bloodshot eyes. Back away from the rim was the crest of the hogback and scattered thickets of cedar which they'd search straightaway. And back of these the ground dropped through that stand of saguaros into chaparral which was too far away to be of any use to him. Afoot and without any kind of a weapon his only possible chance of escaping destruction was to get back into that swale he'd come out of.

He stumbled toward the steep trail down which the killed roan had taken him, hearing with an alarming increase in loudness the racket of the Wineglass riders coming up it. He thought it must have been Gainor who had fired those buildings but he hadn't any time to pursue that line now.

With Ryerson's headquarters reduced to glowing embers it was much darker up here than it had been. The night swam around him in thick whorls of blackness and, near the head of the trail, he blundered into a rock which knocked the legs out from under him and flung him heavily, gasping, down across its farther side. And none too soon!

Hardly had he hauled his battered body down behind it than Crafkin's crowd came boiling up out of the murk. Creak of leather, clank of metal and the restive stamping of excited panting horses, told Marratt they had stopped short yards away from his concealment.

"He can't of got far," the ramrod's voice abruptly grumbled. "Tracy, you an' Chuck hike along the west flank of this ridge an' keep your eyes peeled. Gimpy an' Gainor will stay here with me in case he tried to double back. Rest of you boys spread out an' comb this hogback an' them cedars off beyond it an' be goddam sure you don't let him get away!"

Marratt sucked in his breath at that mention of Gainor. If the fellow was here with Crafkin it didn't seem too likely he could have had a hand in setting that fire—not at first, that is. But the more he mulled over the implications, the more Marratt was convinced it was exactly what he had done. Listening to the rant of his obsequious whine Marratt could see very plain what that two-faced skunk was up to.

Playing in with Crafkin openly Gainor had spared himself the fate of his more forthright neighbors. He'd been allowed to keep his spread throughout the course of Wineglass expansion. But when Marratt had come into this country and been commonly mistaken for Luke Usher, the man had seen what he considered a good chance to turn the tables.

With what he supposed was Usher's signature on a paper giving him a secret half interest in the patented holdings which the court would be shortly turning over to Luke in compliance with the terms of old Jake's will, Gainor figured he had the whip hand in this deal.

There were plenty of ways he could deal with Luke Usher. What he wanted, of course, was a full scale range war; but whether the supposed Luke gunned Ryerson or not, in the turmoil of such a conflict Gainor could always have both Wineglass principals put out of the way—if he would pay enough for it—knowing the blame would roost right on Luke's doorstep.

Since Luke had failed thus far to become entangled with Wineglass, Gainor had fired Ryerson's buildings to make sure the needed war got properly under way. To anyone familiar with Crafkin's arrogance it was a pretty safe bet that long before this time tomorrow Ryerson's crew, loaded for bear, would be on their way to the Half Circle U.

This was what Gainor was counting on. It was why he had imported that bunch of hired guns which his man had told Marratt to expect in the morning. He had a brand new deck all rigged for slaughter and it was plainly his intention, when the smoke cleared away, to be top dog in this country.

Marratt came out of this thinking to discover they were talking.

"You reckon," Gainor asked, "it was Usher set that fire?"

"You take me for a fool?" Crafkin demanded with a curse.

It was apparent from Gainor's silence he didn't quite know how to take him. Marratt suspected the fat-bellied man was a bit startled and probably nervous besides. If this were so, Crafkin's next words must have just about turned him inside out. Even

Marratt's jaw dropped when Ryerson's ramrod said: "That whopperjawed bastard's no more Usher than you are."

"N-Not Usher?"

Had Crafkin been less ingrained in the habit of considering those about him to be either jerks or morons, he must have been struck by the shocked and rageful cadence of a voice which had for once forgotten to employ its unctuous whine.

But if the ramrod noticed he gave no sign of having done so. Hauling up burly shoulders he spat and said as one scattering his pearls before swine, "If Luke Usher had run into what this guy did that first night he'd have been gone before sun-up. Luke—the *real* Luke—never had the kind of nerve that goes with the things this bird has been pulling. Moreover Krantz came out from the Red Horse, just before you rode up, with a sample of this jasper's signature; he spells it the same but it ain't Luke's writing. Luke Usher's hair wasn't sandy. It was the color of his guts and—"

"Churk! You up there, Churk?"

"Ryerson," Crafkin muttered; and the hidden man saw his short and broad shape wheel its horse toward the rim to call, "Yes, sir. You had better come up."

Marratt didn't wait to hear anything further. He knew if he were ever to get away from here alive, now was the time to make his try while the sounds of

Ryerson's approach could help to cover his departure.

He slipped off his spurs and left them, moving cautiously down the ink-black slope, the progress of Ryerson's climbing horse serving to keep him headed in the right direction. Once he tripped and came within an ace of stumbling but met and passed the Wineglass owner without discovery. It made his neck hair bristle to see the vague outline of Clagg's partner within six feet of him and, despite his ultimatums, not be able to raise a hand. A more religiously inclined person might have taken it as a sign, but Marratt's thoughts at the moment were a considerable way from heaven. He had got to thinking, crazily, about that mongrelly pup turning up again . . .

His ears began to ache with the strain of listening and it was hard to be careful when you had to test your footing for every stride before you took it. He longed to run like a deer but he continued his snail-like advance toward the place where the hollow's crescent gave onto the open flats facing Wineglass, sometimes creeping and crawling where the brush made progress difficult. And in the end it paid off.

He found out he wasn't alone when an unseen thorny branch, raking him painfully across the face, dragged a curse from his throat and a challenging

191

"*Quien es?*" jumped out of the darkness ahead of him.

Cold sweat beaded Marratt's cheeks as flame leaped out of the same place and gun sound belted the walls with its clamor. He was on hands and knees and the lead went whistling over him but he'd have been a cooked goose if he had been on his feet.

Crafkin's voice roared angrily down from the rim and the man who had fired said he'd thought he'd heard something. "Thought?" Crafkin snarled. "You ain't got the equipment! You do what you're told and leave the thinking to me!" And then three more shots banged out and there were shouts made thin by distance and a racket of hoofs told the ground-hugging Marratt Crafkin's group had left the rim.

While the echoes were still slamming sound through the hollow he went forward in a catfooting crouch until he saw the head and shoulders of the Wineglass *vaquero* against the distant shine of stars. The man was mounted, staring upward, obviously absorbed with the receding commotion above.

Then, before Marratt could gain a position from which a leap would hold out any chance of success, the man's chin came down and he got out of the saddle.

Marratt could not see him now but he could see the saddled back of the man's horse coming toward him. The animal sensed his presence and, suddenly planting its feet, set back on the reins and would not come any nearer. The man growled a curse in Spanish and abruptly went still as though listening and staring. Marratt kept still, too, hardly daring to breathe, until he heard the man start to back off with his horse; then he lunged for him.

The man's shoulder hooked him hard in the chest. The horse snorted and Marratt slugged the man with a rock-weighted fist and grabbed the reins from his hand as the fellow went down. The horse tried to jerk free but Marratt dug in his heels. When the horse quit fighting Marratt swiftly stooped and got the man's gun and shell belt, buckled the latter around him and, catching up the fellow's chin-strapped sombrero, thrust a foot in the stirrup and swung aboard.

Seldom had he experienced such a beautiful feeling; but there was too much at stake for any carelessness now and he held the horse down to a moderate walk until he was absolutely certain Crafkin's crowd could not hear them.

The first gray pallor of false dawn was in the air when Marratt's appropriated Wineglass gelding brought him, via Jake's south forty, into sight of the dilapidated Usher headquarters. The dark huddle of buildings showed no glimmer of light. Nor could he observe any sign of human presence though, from

193

the corrals, a horse nickered and the bronc he was forking gave tired reply. Kid Boots, of the saturnine eyes and fast pistol, was being awfully damned quiet. Playing cagey, Marratt imagined until he recalled the inclination of Indian curs toward barking.

He remembered then with an irascible dissatisfaction several other things; the way Boots had targeted that strap iron hasp and the quietness with which he'd put his things in Jake's bedroom. A really smart man would have been a little more careful. He'd not have lied about the dog which Boots had said looked to him like anyone's pooch that would call it. Sure enough, he had come straightaway to Marratt's whistle; but he hadn't that first time. He hadn't come at the tank when the girl had asked, "*What* dog!" And there were Crafkin's remarks to clinch it.

He turned the Wineglass bronc toward the nearest of the pole enclosures and swung down when he reached it for a look through the bars. The hired man's horse was there but the uncut gray he'd got from Isham was gone.

He dropped the reins and turned around and rummaged the yard with a probing stare. Common sense told him he was acting like a fool. He didn't see anything to get his hackles up. Far away to the south a coyote's yammer made a solitary sound in the immensity of space, and the forlornness of it seemed immeasurably to emphasize the untenable bleakness of Marratt's position. But the fellow was gone or that dog would be barking.

The prod of frayed nerves promptly jeered at such logic. The pup could be trained to keep still . . .

Marratt, silently cursing, moved across the gray gloom. Partway to the back door he swung left on a hunch around the side of the house, impelled by something stronger than reason to have another look at that front porch.

But again the cold jitters inside him howled protest and his feet slowed and stopped in the sound-muffling grass thirty feet from the edge of its weather-warped planks.

"Come on. Don't stop there." The voice, smoothly ominous, came out of the shadows where he'd left Boots sitting. Only it wasn't Boots' voice.

18

It was a voice he'd never heard before, and it directed implacably: "Move up. Move up or you're a dead duck, hombre."

Marratt, in extreme disgust, scanned his chances and growled resignedly, "All right." There was no percentage in trying to beat the drop of an unseen firearm and the man's hands held one or he'd have played this different. "Keep your shirt on," Marratt grumbled, and stepped bitterly forward until the voice bade, "Far enough. Now turn around and shuck that gun belt."

This wasn't Crafkin. It wasn't Gainor, though it

might very well be one of the latter's imported slug-slammers. An angry urge rushed through Marratt to spin and grab, gunfighter fashion; but while he'd frequently been foolish he was not a fool.

He did as he'd been told and, when the gun-weighted belt hit the ground, his captor ordered, "Strike a match, mount the steps and go inside and get a lamp lit."

"Would you mind," Marratt asked, "telling me what you think you're about to do?"

"We'll get to that. Meantime just remember if you drop that match, or if it should happen to go out, you're going to pass out right along with it. Get up here now and step lively."

Because he hadn't much choice Marratt, rasping a match across the hip of his Levis, climbed onto the porch and moved into the house. He found the lamp, dragged flame over the wick and replaced the chimney. He didn't hear the man follow but, when he turned, there he was, spare and florid in a pair of wool socks.

It wasn't the gun which caught Marratt's stare but the bright flash of metal on the pocket of his shirt. That, and the triangular eyes above it so balefully filled with a beady satisfaction.

"A real pleasure, Mister Usher," declared Bella Loma's marshal, a mocking grin pulling back the leathery lips from mossy teeth. "That Mex headgear

197

nearly throwed me but, like I always say, you don't have to be right to be President. Jump first—"

"All right," Marratt said, "you've jumped. What's the next move?"

"Jail for you, boy; an' my advice to you is make a clean breast of everything. Tell the truth an' shame the devil, as my mother used to say. If you've got what these shysters call—"

"I think you've treed the wrong coon, Hanna."

"It don't cost nothin' to think. But I'll tell you right now that kinda talk ain't going to help you. I been marshalin' towns for the past twenty years an' never once saw no guy, wrapped up like you are, beat the rope without help."

Marratt, with no means of knowing what was in the marshal's craw but imagining the man had got onto his identity, said: "What's the price of your help and what will it amount to?"

"Now you're talkin' my language," the marshal nodded. "A man's got to look out for Number One in this world. So here's the way we'll do it. On receipt of your signed confession an' a bonafide quitclaim deed to this spread I'll put the chance in your way to make a run for the border."

"And if the confession and deed aren't forthcoming?"

"You don't look," Hanna said, "like a guy that would very much enjoy a hemp necktie. Let's cut out the bull. You got a pen an' some paper?"

Behind inscrutable cheeks Grete Marratt was finding this mighty queer talk. The man must still think him Usher and, if he did, this was a frame. But if it was that fire they were fixing to charge him with, why this talk about hanging? Had Gainor accused him of killing Luke's father?"

Hanna said, "Well—what you waitin' on?"

"I was trying to figure out what I'm supposed to confess to."

"Beckwith's killin', of course. You needn't put on with me."

"I didn't kill Beckwith—"

"Makes no difference to me if you did or you didn't. You're goin' to hang for it, boy, if you don't write me them papers. You went down there two days ago an' had a row with the feller. Now he turns up dead in his office which looks like a cyclone went through it, an' your hat's on the floor. On top of that you put a check that come out of Beckwith's files—"

"That's not proof—"

"It's a jury you got to convince, not me." Hanna picked up the gun belt he'd fetched in from outside and broke open the pistol he pulled from its holster. "One shot fired. One chunk of lead the doc dug out of Beckwith. An' you think any jury's goin' to listen to you?"

"It won't come to no jury," Kid Boots drawled

from the doorway. "You won't, either, without you drop them guns pronto."

There was a ludicrous look on the marshal's face. "Pick 'em up, boss," Kid Boots said, and Marratt lifted the guns from Ives Hanna's lax fingers.

The marshal came to life then. "You're makin' a mistake—"

"It won't be the first," said Kid Boots, unconcerned. His green eyes grinned derisively. "You want I should knock off this sidewinder now or—"

"I think," Marratt said, "we'd better tie him up. I'll keep him covered. Get the rope off your saddle—"

"You can't get away with this!" Hanna shouted. He glared at them wildly, a man clearly beside himself with rage and balked greed. "I'll hunt you two down if—"

"You won't have to hunt far then. We're not going anyplace," Marratt told him—"not before Churk Crafkin and your sidekick, Ryerson, have paid up for the misery they've caused on this range. Get that rope, Boots."

While the man was gone Marratt, ignoring the marshal's bluster and ranting, sat watching him with thoughts that seemed to have flown well beyond the confines of this room. At last he said, cutting into the lawman's invective, "You're wasting your breath. There's a new day in store for this Bella Loma country and it's time you took a long look at your

200

hole card. Some time this morning there's apt to be quite a ruckus here and if you want to try dealing from the top for a change I might give you the same chance you just offered me. The chance to get across the border when the payoff comes."

Hanna told him what he could do with it, and when Kid Boots came back with the rope Marratt said, "I guess you better swear me in as a special deputy."

"I can see myself!"

Marratt nodded to Kid Boots. "See what a few swipes with that pistol will do."

"Hey! Wait! Hold on; you can't—I'll do it," gulped the marshal, hurriedly capitulating when the yellow-haired man, grinning, spat on his gun barrel. "I'll do it, but we got to have a—"

"Bible?" asked Boots, and produced one from a dusty stack of books piled behind a horsehair rocker. When the ceremony was over Marratt, unpinning Hanna's badge, refastened it to his own shirt and, considering the marshal sadly, told Kid Boots to tie and gag him.

"Now," said Marratt, when this had been accomplished, "take him out to the barn and drop him in a feed rack and pull enough hay down to make sure he won't be noticed. Time you get back I'll have breakfast ready."

And he just about did.

While they were lighting smokes and sitting back with third cups of coffee, Marratt said: "Where were you last night when Hanna came touring onto the place? And don't bother thinking up any tall stories. Just give me the truth, Usher, and give it to me straight."

The green eyes gleamed and Kid Boots showed his crooked teeth, but he said, apparently more relieved than bothered about it, "How did you catch on?"

"I wasn't sure," Marratt answered, "until you dug up that Bible, but I was pretty well convinced when I overheard Crafkin telling Gainor I wasn't Usher. He said the real Luke had yellow hair, or words to that effect."

"I can imagine," Usher nodded, "the words that bird would use to describe me. What other slips did I make?"

"You should never have turned up with that dog. I had already seen him on the reservation; I knew he wasn't anyone's dog that would call him because I'd already tried. I got to wondering what you'd been doing around Beckwith's office, and why you'd bother to deny ownership of a dog that was obviously yours. I was bound to conclude you didn't want me to know you'd been over there."

"But that didn't tell you I was Luke Usher."

"No, but it made a couple of other things seem a

lot more significant. I knew the real Luke Usher was considered fast with a gun. When I told you to demonstrate on that strap iron hasp, the way you drew and fired without hardly looking showed you knew more about it than any stranger would be likely to. You smacked it first crack but when I asked you to repeat you deliberately missed it, proving you'd seen the error of having hit it the first time. You were hoping I would pass that shot off as luck. All and all, you see, you were giving me quite a bit to think about. Your next mistake, much worse than all the others, was in putting your belongings where I'd told you in Jake's bedroom. No one unfamiliar with the house would have known where that was, or that the bedroom you went into had been Jake's rather than Luke's. You didn't hunt around. You went straight to it, left your stuff, and came out again."

"Still the fool," Usher grunted. "How come you didn't slug me?"

"Same reason, I suppose, you haven't ventilated me. Wanted to see what you were up to."

Usher's lips pulled back in a twisted grin. "I wasn't being crowded like you are, Marratt."

In his chair Marratt's shape went uncomfortably still. "So you know who I am."

"I've seen the reward bills; they don't half do you justice, no idea of your coloring, your real personality. I was over in the barn the night Frailey brought you in. I took a squint after he left. You look more like Jake's son than I do. Did you kill that damn agent?"

"No." Marratt said, "Did you kill Jake?"

Usher came half out of his chair, eyes like gun steel. Then a sick, shamed expression writhed through them and he shook his head, hating himself. "If I'd had any guts I'd have evened the score, though. I'd ridden into the yard, had just got off my horse when I heard the shot. I ran around the house. Dad was down on the ground, Ryerson standing over him with a smoking pistol. I saw Crafkin gettin' set to crack down on me." His eyes filled with an indescribable anguish. "I cut my stick—turned tail and bolted like a goddam rabbit!"

"I've been tempted to bolt a few times myself—"

"But this wasn't your fight. Why should you stick your neck out?"

"It's more my fight than you'd be likely to guess. If you've seen the reward bills you know why they sent me to Yuma."

"I've wondered about that. Read a little, back along, in the papers. Figured maybe you was framed—"

"No, I killed him. There were two of them . . . and a girl. Ryerson was Clagg's partner."

"So that was why you took up my quarrel—"

"No," Marratt said, "I'll not fool you. I didn't know when I stepped into your boots what his name was, or that I'd find him in this country. I broke jail to find him and I had to stay clear long enough to get a line on him. The guy in the Lone Star called me Luke; and then Frailey, making the same mistake, supplied a little of your background. I saw a chance to keep the law off my neck."

"You took a damn long chance—"

"But it payed off," Marratt nodded. "Frailey introduced me to Naome and, while we were talking, Ryerson came up—"

"He wouldn't rest after that, not with you free to call him. Why didn't you drop him right then?"

"He didn't have a gun on him—"

"Neither did my Dad; though they said afterwards he had." Usher got up, tramping round the room restively. "What are we going to do?"

"I don't think—"

"Don't count me out of this. I'm through with running!"

Marratt gave him a searching scrutiny. "All right. You'll need to understand what I've discovered, what's happening." He roughed it in for him, concluding gruffly, "So you can see the whole thing is going to come to a boil right here on this spread within the next three-four hours. It's not going to be any Sunday school picnic."

Usher said grimly, "I didn't come back figurin' it was going to be easy." He stopped across from Marratt and stood a moment, scowlingly silent. He dug out a four-bits piece. "You want to toss for Ryerson?"

"There's a chance," Marratt said, "he never killed old Jake—"

"He kep' his mouth shut, didn't he?"

Marratt said with an air of discovering something: "That isn't quite the same." Then, flushed and resentful of the embarrassment occasioned by Usher's sharp look, he growled, "Not that I'm wanting to defend him. But fear can play hell with any man's thinking and, for whatever it's worth, I feel bound to tell you Frailey doesn't believe Ryerson killed your father."

Usher said gruffly, "You're lettin' that girl run away with your judgment. I know what I saw—"

He broke off, reaching for his gun as, green eyes bleak, he jumped for the door.

CHAPTER 19

Though still dark and with the tatters of night blackly piled in the hollows and wreathed like widows' veils about the lost shapes of trees, dawn was definitely on the upswing when Ryerson's range boss finally quit and called his crew off the hunt. He found it hard to believe the pseudo Usher had escaped him yet the man very obviously had.

Nor was Crafkin's frame of mind at all improved when the Mexican left in the ravine turned up missing. Neither Galardo nor his horse responded to Crafkin's cursing; and hard on the heels of this he made a further, more jolting discovery when a swift count of noses revealed that Ryerson, too, had hauled his freight.

"Probably back at the ranch," offered Gainor; but a subsequent search of the gutted Wineglass headquarters failed completely to yield any sign of the ranch owner's whereabouts.

The last lingering of shadows were pretty well scattered by that time. "The old woman," said Gainor, elaborately yawning and stretching, "will be thinkin' I've fell in a boghole. I reckon, Churk, I better be gettin' along home."

It was like a spark hitting powder the way Crafkin whirled on him, catching Gainor's shirtfront in a grip of steel. "You ain't wrigglin' out of my sight till I say so! If that guy wants fire we'll give him fire, an' when I get done there won't nobody else ever dare stand against me!"

"Hell, man, I'm for it," bleated Gainor with his cheeks suddenly quivering, "but you won't be needin' *me—*"

"I'll be needin' all my friends."

"But what could *I* do?" Gainor quavered, his desperation close to panic as he thought of the trap he'd ordered rigged for this guy's welcome. "You know I'm no good for that kind of thing. Can't hit a barn door—can't stand the sound of—"

"You can sit a horse, by God, an' you'll be sittin'

one today when we ride in to settle accounts with that Paul Pry that calls himself Usher!"

"Horse comin'," Luke said tersely, with a narrowed eye squinting out through the door crack; and then, with less tolerance: "Ryerson's daughter."

"Where's the dog?" Marratt asked.

"Tied him up in the barn to keep him clear of blue whistlers. You want him?"

Marratt stood undecided a moment, seemingly weighing the merits of some considered course of action and looking none too pleased with the results of this cogitation. They heard the saddle creak as the girl swung down, heard her crossing the porch. "Let her in," Marratt said, and Luke pulled open the door.

She was still in her squaw boots and buckskin and her dark eyes, wide and round, found Marratt's face and clung to it; and she put out her hands. "Is Dad all right?"

Marratt nodded. "I left him riding with the crew."

Relief swept through her glance then it got dark again with worry and with something which caused Usher, noticing, to go out, quietly pulling the door shut behind him.

Marratt, seeing too, crucified by his thoughts and by the unwanted remembrance of Frailey's parting words, stood for what seemed an eternity without speaking. *That girl*, Frailey'd said, *is in love with you;* and the truth of this statement lay plain and afraid in the eyes searching his.

"I thought," he said harshly, "you were staying in town."

"But I couldn't." She put a lifted hand against her left breast. "I had a terrible feeling—like a knife twisting in me; and then I realized what Crafkin would do when he learned—"

"I'm man grown, Naome."

"But it won't be just him. He'll throw the whole weight of Wineglass against you! What chance will you have? Oh, Luke . . . I couldn't bear—"

"Naome, I must tell you I am not Luke Usher. I'm—"

She put a hand across his mouth. "As if that could matter so long as—"

"But it does . . . it matters terribly. I—" He squared his shoulders. "I'm Grete Marratt."

No look of shock went through her, no dawning horror turned away her eyes. They continued—filled unbearably with trust and love, with all the things she was offering—to gaze deep into his own tortured gray ones. The name meant nothing at all to her.

"I'm a convict." He swallowed hard. "A killer escaped from Yuma!"

"What does that change?"

Marratt broke. He pulled her to him with a kind of sob; and as they clung together the porch door was shoved open and Luke's twisted face said: "They're comin'! Get her out of there!"

Marratt, stumbling off the porch, caught the reins of her horse from Luke's clenched hand. He saw the dust, like smoke, boiling over the trees that obscured the road.

Luke's hand grabbed his shoulder. "What's she waitin' on?"

"She's staying—"

"Stayin'!" Luke's eyes blazed. "An' you're *lettin'* her?"

Marratt squeezed the sweat off his bearded cheeks.

With an outraged expression Usher drew back a fist, then with a snarl let it fall. "Why don't you get the hell out of this country?"

Marratt shook his head. "There are things a man has to do in this world—"

"Like killin' a fine sweet girl off by inches? Damn you, Marratt! If you got one grain of decency—"

"I'm seeing this through." He drew Naome's rifle from beneath the stirrup fender and his jaw was like granite. He thrust the black's reins at Usher. "Take the horse in the house and keep out of sight." He shoved him roughly. "Get in there and keep me covered!"

Wheeling then, with the rifle loose-slanting from the crook of an elbow, he took a few careless strides in the direction of the men riding into the yard and stopped, implacably waiting for Gainor's bunch to come up.

They were five, varying in the details of their physical appearance but cut to a pattern; bleak hard-eyed men with the gunsmoke smell saturating their clothing along with the sweat and steamy pungence of horseflesh.

They hauled their mounts up before him in a loose half-circle, the small and dark man who had accosted him in town allowing lean shaved lips to curl with an obvious amusement.

"Mornin' . . . boss. My name is Green and this is your crew, delivered as advertised. You want to say a few words before the boys go to work?"

"Might save them a little grief," Marratt nodded. "You fellows were hired by Clint Gainor to come over here this morning and, in the guise of being this spread's paid employees, to blast hell out of Wineglass. I think you ought to know before you start burning powder Gainor slipped a couple of cogs in sizing up this situation."

Green's eyes were still amused. "I guess the size of this crew will take up any slack."

"The mistakes Gainor made could get you boys in a lot of trouble. In the first place Gainor's orders were given on the erroneous assumption he had acquired a half interest in this ranch. At the point of a gun he got me to give him a paper to that effect which doesn't happen to be worth the time it took to write it."

"How do you get hold of that notion?"

"Gainor's paper is worthless," Marratt said, "because the man who owns this property never so much as saw it."

"What kind of guff you tryin' to hand us?"

"If he takes it to court I'll prove that signature's a forgery."

"You made it," Green said skeptically.

"But it happens I'm not Luke Usher." Marratt's smile loosed the gleam of hard white teeth. "You boys might as well turn around and ride home."

There was no amusement in Green's stare now. He said, softly wicked, "Who the blue blazes *are* you?"

"The name is Grete Marratt and for this day, at least, I'm packin' just about all the law there is in these parts. As special deputy," he drawled, tapping Hanna's badge with the back of a thumbnail, "you might say I've been sent in here to iron out this trouble."

Green's eyes considered him narrowly. "What about Ives Hanna?"

"My warrant exceeds Mr. Hanna's authority. I'll have to write you boys down as trespassers. Of course, if you want to ride out—"

"We're stickin'," Green said.

"Then you're taking my orders!"

"Let's hear 'em."

Marratt, hiding his frustration behind inscrutable cheeks, said, "Take your horses over back of those trees to the left and tie them there somewhere where they'll not be seen."

Green hoisted a leg across the horn and swung down. The rest followed suit. Flicking a nod at one of the others the dark man grunted, "That's a job for you, Curly," and the man so-selected started their mounts toward the trees.

Too late Marratt discovered that, in sliding from their saddles, Gainor's crew had so maneuvered things he was now caught fast between them.

"I guess you're through with giving orders for awhile," Green jeered; and something hard crashed down across the top of Marratt's head.

Crafkin, riding in the van of a handpicked Wineglass crew, had no reason to believe he'd any need of such a force to put this pseudo Usher where cold weather wouldn't bother him. But he was all done taking chances. He meant to catch him dead to rights and snuff his light for sure this time.

In all their previous encounters the man had appeared to be playing a lone hand. He probably still was; but if he'd smuggled in some help or enlisted aid in the vicinity, the twelve men Crafkin was fetching to this chore should prove ample to get the job done. Then he would tend to Ryerson and that slick piece of baggage Ryerson's squaw had whelped.

He wasn't anticipating any trouble but, this time, he was allowing for it. He stopped the crew two miles west of Usher's headquarters and, splitting the bunch into two groups, told Gainor: "You'll take these five and ride straight in. He may not be there, but if he is he'll see you comin' and fort-up in the house or the barn, most likely. Your job's to smoke him out of there. I'll take the rest and come up through the trees. That way, no matter what he does, we'll have him. Understand?"

Gainor, green about the gills, looked ready to collapse. He had to try three times before his tongue could scrape up enough moisture for sound, and even then it was more like the skreak of a gate hinge. "Wh-Wh-What if he's g-got help?"

"An' where would he be gettin' help around here?" Crafkin grinned derisively. "You talk like a guy that hasn't got all his buttons. Pull yourself together! An' just remember, Mister Gainor, if you try to pull a bolt and slope, these boys has got orders to drop you."

Green deployed his crew with the aplomb of a master strategist. Not guessing there was anybody hidden in the house, and assuming it would draw the bulk of Crafkin's fire-power, he kept his bunch away from it. One man he bedded beneath the sun-curled slats of a rickety wagon that was falling apart across the yard from the barn. Another was sent into the saddle shed which flanked the same side of the house as the wagon. A third took up his stand in the bunkhouse and the last he fetched into the barn with himself.

"Let them get right into the yard," he called, "then give it to 'em proper."

From the house Usher, hugging his rifle, had seen and heard everything which had happened in the yard. When he saw how Marratt was trapped by the way Green's bunch had got out of their saddles, his jaws locked hard against the accusing outraged look flung his way by the girl who was crouched just across the room from him. But he didn't let her words stampede him into firing. Not even when Marratt suddenly folded and pitched groundward under the bludgeoning impact of a swung pistol barrel did Luke put finger to trigger.

"You despicable coward!" Naome lashed at him fiercely, and would have snatched the Colt's .45

from his holster had he not slapped her hand away and, whirling, roughly grabbed her.

"You tryin' to get him killed? Then don't be a fool!" he growled. "He knew what chance he was taking when he went out there—"

"He told you to cover him. I heard him. Let me go!" she cried, her voice choked with anger. "Take your hands off me!"

"I will when you show enough sense to behave. He's got a chance so long as they don't know we're here. They'll tie him up and dump him out of sight someplace till they get done with what they came to do—"

"They came to kill him!"

"On the contrary." Luke said with tired patience, "They came here on Gainor's orders to blast hell out of Crafkin's outfit which, by the simple expedient of last night burning all your dad's fancy buildings, Gainor—"

"He burned Wineglass?"

"Sure, but he made Crafkin think it was Marratt that did it. So now Crafkin's hog-wild to stop Marratt's clock. He'll be showin' up with all the toughs he can gather. Soon as the guns start to crackin'—if you'll promise to do as I tell you—I'll slip out and get Marratt loose."

She didn't reply right away but she quit struggling. After a moment he let her go and stepped back, being careful to stay out of line with the window.

"Who is he?" she asked.

"Who you talkin' about now?"

"Luke—I mean Marratt."

"He's a guy with one chip in a no-limit game. Hold my rifle," he growled and, when she took it, went off through the hall, coming back with an armful of pillows and bedclothes which he dropped on the sofa. There was an extra shell belt and pistol strapped about his lean hips now.

"They've carried him into the barn," Naome whispered.

"What I figured." He took back his rifle. "You can help us both by gettin' down on that sofa. Wad all that stuff I brought between you and the back of it; this is like to be rough when that lead gets to flyin'. An' while—"

"But if he's not Jake's son why would he let people think he is? And why," she asked desperately, "would he be carrying on Luke's crazy feud with my father?"

"He ain't."

She looked up at him queerly. "But he said—"

"I can't help that. The trouble between him and your old man hasn't anything to do with this ranch. Nor with its owners."

Something about his way of saying that caught at her notice and she looked at him oddly, searching his face with a kind of baffled wonder. And then, again taken up in her own worries: "Do you suppose Dad would possibly decide to ride over here with Crafkin?"

"Not a chance! He's too—" Usher broke it off, listening. "They're coming'," he said. "Get onto that sofa and don't budge an inch till I get back here with Marratt!"

CHAPTER **20**

It was the pounding of the guns which battered Marratt back to consciousness. He imagined the tumultuous crash-crashing must take the top of his head off surely; and then the black rage that was bottled inside him began to make itself manifest, clawing his shuddering mind from its hiding. He opened his eyes and the cares of the past became again present problems.

He'd been dumped on the floor of a cobwebby box stall, trussed like a plucked fowl ready for the basting. From the bend of their knees his legs were drawn taut behind him with a length of rope passed

219

around his windpipe. The least pressure on this arrangement fetched excruciating pain. To prevent any chance of an outcry he'd been gagged. Green had been thorough. He had had Marratt's wrists yanked around behind him and securely lashed across the arch of his insteps. There was no possibility of Marratt freeing himself.

The gun racket which had roused him seemed about to have spent itself and was now dwindled away to the random noise of snipers. A man's voice near the front of the barn said jubilantly, "Reckon that about does her, Gus—ain't a one of that bunch even wrigglin'."

Green's voice, nearer Marratt, cautioned, "Stay where you are. Don't go out in that yard yet."

"Hell! There ain't none of them fellers playin' possum."

"You don't know that. Give the sun a quarter hour to get in its licks then we'll go and have a look at 'em."

In his need to get loose Marratt thought of the dog which, according to Usher, had been tied up in this barn. But he couldn't hear any sound of it, not even the stertorous sound of its panting.

As though great minds were frequenting the same channel, the fellow up front said, " 'F you hadn't bashed that dog's head in we could send him out there."

Green merely grunted.

Time commenced most abominably to drag.

Marratt's mouth, parched and miserable with the gag they'd crammed in it, longed for water. His whole racked body cried out for it and a pair of buzzing flies, playing tag through the dust motes, abruptly settled on his face and commenced to crawl over it, pausing now and then to lick a leg or scrape a whisker.

Marratt presently got the feeling there was somebody watching him. It bothered him almost as much as the flies did, and he wondered if it were Green making up his mind what to do with him. No matter what role Gainor's scheming had assigned him they had no real reason for keeping him alive now. They could knock him off any time and be rid of the risk his tongue represented. It was their obvious course now they'd got rid of Crafkin.

Green could pin on Hanna's badge and tell any tale he wanted; always providing, of course, they'd found and liquidated Hanna. Or he could leave it where it was and spin a mighty fancy story of how Usher, saying his name was Marratt and calling himself the law in these parts, had deputized Green's outfit, ordering them to wipe out the Wineglass invaders. He could say Usher, unfortunately, had been killed in the fighting, and show his dead body to prove it.

Who would call him a liar? Not Ryerson or Gainor.

There was Naome, of course, and Luke—the real Usher; but Marratt wasn't pinning any shining hope on that lad. Luke had run out once and had probably sloped again. Or, if he'd fired on this bunch when that gun barrel had knocked Marratt loose of his intentions, he was probably dead—and the girl along with him. For Gainor, no less than Churk Crafkin, had been playing a desperate game here of late and would be extremely unlikely to let the life of any woman stand between himself and the spoils he was after.

Green said, "Give it five more minutes an' we'll go strip off those masks and see what kind of ducks you boys potted."

"Reckon Crafkin was with 'em?"

"Clint aimed to make sure of that. Said he figured the Big Mogul would likely be along, too."

"Crew seemed kinda light. I'd of thought he'd have fetched his whole crowd in for this trick."

"No reason why he should. He wasn't lookin' to find anyone here but Luke Usher—"

"Gus!" the man up front cried excitedly. "Git up here an' grab a eyeful of this!"

Marratt heard somebody high-heel it doorward. Green's low voice rasped furiously, "Where the hell did *she* come from?"

"Come outa the house," the other guy said; and

222

abruptly Grete Marratt had something else on his mind.

A sharp knife had slashed the rope passed round his neck and was severing the knotted turns wrapped about his wrists and ankles. Feeling churned through him in nauseous waves as cramped limbs fell free and released blood roared through his near atrophied arteries. Sweat broke coldly out of his body. Bursts of light warped his vision laced with fragments of blackness and the sides of the stall rocked about him like planks in the grip of a raging sea.

Then his eyes swam back to a normal focus. Surrounding sounds were picked up and Usher's face, thrust close to his own, admonished, "They're still here. Take it easy."

He felt Usher massaging the numbness from legs and ankles and he commenced awkwardly chafing pins and needles into the corrugations of his lacerated wrists. He heard Green say: "She's headin' straight for us!" And Green's trigger-tripper said, "I ain't never had no Inj—"

"Christ a'mighty!" Green roared. "Let her in and get that door shut—"

Whatever else Green may have said was lost in a sudden wild banging of Winchesters. Crafkin's bull-throated shout rolled out of the trees and off somewhere in the direction of the harness shed one man's yell climbed higher than hearing. Lead hammered

223

the front and left sides of the barn and two slugs, tearing through, kicked twin boards off the far wall's studding, letting in bright oblongs of the outside glare.

"Crafkin played it foxy," Usher muttered with his mouth almost brushing Marratt's ear—"biggest half of his bunch are in them box elders and Green's already give his hand away. Here—" He shoved the extra belt and gun he had fetched into Marratt's still awkward fingers.

Buckling the leather about his waist, Marratt tried the weapon for heft and reeled out of the stall without bothering to learn whether Usher was following. He directed his shambling pace toward the front where he could see Green crouched behind the not-quite-shut door coolly waiting for something to throw down on.

Green's companion was stuffing fresh cartridges into a rifle some twelve strides to Green's right where a broken-out piece of the rotten planking provided a circumscribed view of the yard. Naome lay midway between the two Gainor men, uncaringly sprawled on the straw littered floor where a bullet or one of their fists had dropped her.

Sight of that pitifully still, disheveled shape did something to Marratt. A monstrous rage beat and tore at him as his jerked-away stare settled wickedly on Green; and he went lurching toward him, the racket of the guns obscuring any sound kicked up by his advance.

Green's bent back made a slight turn in shifting as he tried for a clearer look at something outside; Green's man yelled "Gus—" and died, still whirling, in the blast from Usher's pistol.

Green's head twisted around and wide-sprung eyes, peering over his shoulder, caught Marratt in their focus. He tried to bring up his gun, pivoting as he did so, a touch of craziness in the grin that showed his broken teeth. His gun and Marratt's spoke almost in unison, the breath of that slug fanning Marratt's shirt. But Green was all done with breathing. He was down on his back with no more use for a pistol.

Marratt tore it out of the man's lax fingers and with a gun in each fist heard Luke cry, "Wait—" but he was through with waiting. Naome also lifted a yell at him but, pausing only to accustom his eyes to the glare, he stepped full into the smash of the sun.

The yard was a shambles. The only one of Green's men still working a trigger was forted-up in the bunkhouse and, even as Marratt moved into the open, this one's rifle quit barking.

Crafkin, with three of his Wineglass crew, catapulted from cover in a dive for the bunkhouse, unconscious of Marratt's appearance behind them, bent on nailing Gainor's man before the fellow could reload. Marratt, hurrying after them, was partway across the barn's broad front when Usher's voice, coming around its far side through the forty-foot alley between barn and bunkhouse, called: "Rack up the balls, boys."

It stopped Crafkin's crew like a rope stretched before them.

But only for a moment. Ryerson's range boss, bellowing, flung his shape to one side and chopped down with his belt gun, firing from the hip. A man beside him, caught in the blast from Luke's rifle, doubled over; another spun and pitched headlong. "Hold it!" Marratt yelled; but Crafkin, whirling, loosed every bean he had in the cylinder.

The shell belt was torn from about Marratt's middle. Something hammered his chest and he went staggering backward, feeling his legs suddenly folding up under him. He felt grass against his dust-streaked face. He pushed his chest off the ground, got an elbow braced under him and finally, carefully, squeezed out two shots at Crafkin and saw the Wineglass ramrod go down.

CHAPTER 21

Luke, propped up under Frailey's care on Jake's front-room sofa and still swathed in bandages five days after the Green-Crafkin battle, declared irritably, "And I tell you again I don't know *where* he is!"

Naome's eyes searched his face. "Did you give him my notes?"

" 'Course I never give 'em to him—how the hell *could* I? Like I keep tryin' to tell you, right after you lit out for town to fetch Frailey he saddled up that big gray studhorse he brought an' took off, headin' south."

"But he was in no condition to ride!"

"I won't argue about that. All I know is he rode. An' he sure didn't waste no time gettin' started."

"But why?" she asked despairingly. "Why would he ride off like that without a word?"

Luke, who had advocated this very course of action, didn't believe there was anything else Marratt could have done, feeling the way he did about the girl. Luke privately considered him one of the whitest men he'd known but this did not alter the fact of his being a killer, a man convicted of what amounted to murder and sentenced to Yuma for the rest of his natural. No, the clean break was best and swiftest mended.

"I reckon he likely had his reasons," he answered, and was debating the therapy of giving her the whole damned guts of the matter when the sound of doc's buggy rolled into the yard.

That the old man had news was obvious as soon as he came into the room. "Your deciding to give Ives Hanna another chance has paid off," he told Luke, setting down his bag and dropping his hat to haul up a chair. "Marratt, as you know, smashed both Crafkin's shoulders. Under the impression last night he wasn't long for this world, the man was persuaded by Hanna to make a complete confession. In this statement, being taken down now in front of witnesses for signing, Crafkin has admitted," Frailey told Naome, "to most of the skullduggery laid locally

228

to your father. He has delivered himself of a terrible account in which he admits poisoning your mother and accepts full responsibility for the deaths of Jake Usher and Stanley Beckwith."

"About Dad's killing," Luke said—"did he mention why Ryerson all this time kept his mouth shut?"

"He didn't say in so many words," Frailey answered, "but the reason is plain enough from what he did say. Ryerson, so far as ranching is concerned, has always been a square peg in a round hole. Never cared about the business or been willing to assume the least interest in its details; a man of Crafkin's caliber would naturally take advantage of this. I think Ryerson must have been more than a bit uneasy now and again, but I believe we can safely assume from the record that he preferred to ignore such things as he discovered to facing the unpleasantness of putting his foot down. When at last he realized the trend events were taking Crafkin killed Jake, I'm sure, deliberately to compromise him.

"Here, according to Crafkin's statement, is what happened. The pair of them went to see Jake about acquiring this property. During the resultant conversation Jake, by Crafkin's tell of it, became extremely abusive, suddenly dropping a hand toward the butt of his pistol. Crafkin, snatching Ryerson's, fired on the instant. As Jake was falling, Crafkin, hearing the sounds of somebody coming, thrust the smoking belt gun into Ryerson's hands. You came on the scene, Luke, to see him standing with it over your father; and from that day on Crafkin has done as he pleased."

They sat quiet for awhile and presently Usher asked somewhat querulously, "When are you figurin' to let me out of this bed?"

"Isn't that woman I sent over to take care of you satisfactory?"

"I want to make a goin' concern of this spread."

"Then you'd better stay where you're at till those wounds heal. And, by the way, if Marratt should happen to drop around—"

"No danger of that. He's probably halfway to the bananas by this time."

Frailey picked up his bag. "Nevertheless, if you should happen to see him, I think you'd better tell him there's a Ranger looking this country over for him. . . ."

Marratt, after five days of living off sourdough and whatever he'd been able to knock over with a pistol, was still prowling the hills above Bella Loma, hollow-eyed, gaunt and no nearer solving his problems than he'd been the day Gainor had got his come-uppance.

The long-buried side of his nature—the part of him that cared for Naome and was willing to acknow-

230

ledge this love and its indebtedness—understood Frailey and Luke Usher were correct in believing that, for him there could be no tomorrow in the things he had found here. Better for all concerned that he get on his gray horse and either give himself up or get out of the country.

Many times after a stretch of thinking about Naome he had been in the mood to do this, but each time something had stopped him; the habit of playing God, he guessed, or the remembrance of Charlie, demanding for Ryerson the same retribution he had dumped on Hugh Clagg.

Fair was fair. Beckwith, scrambling to get his, had got a harp for his trouble. Gainor, with the example of Crafkin's steals to egg him on, had staked his whole future—and his life, as it happened—on the glimpsed possibility of breaking Wineglass and becoming top dog in the process. Their misdeeds had caught up with both of them, and with Crafkin. Did Ryerson deserve to get off scot-free with his?

Marratt's mind, sitting in judgment, rebelled against the irony of spending his life in prison for what he had done to Hugh Clagg because of Charlie while Clagg's partner, meriting a like fate, went his way untouched and unrepentant because he happened to be the father of Naome. It was too much to ask of human nature.

Marratt's mind, sitting in judgment, rebelled

away with him and, crouching beside the spring where he was camped, proceeded to clean his face of whiskers. He left only the roan patch of a mustache, having generally worn one before his trouble with Clagg.

While he was hunting his pockets for the rest of the checks assembled by Naome from the reservation files he came across the badge he had taken off Hanna; and he held quiet for an interval morosely considering it. Only this bent piece of metal had stood between himself and a hole in the ground when Crafkin's lead had hammered him into the grass of Jake's dooryard. Spared by the grace of God, some would say—but why had God bothered? Had He saved him to settle Charlie's score against Ryerson?

Better, Marratt thought bitterly, to have croaked then and there than be faced with a future cursed with memories of a girl who could never be more to him than she had. For, no matter what course he finally took with her father, he could not ask Naome to share the fate of a brush-running fugitive. And there was nothing else in the cards for Grete Marratt but Yuma.

He cocked a look at the sky and loosed a long breath that must have come pretty near up from his bootheels. He checked over the loads in his pistol, reckoning he might just as well get about it.

He knew where to find Ryerson, had been nursing

this knowledge for the past thirty hours. Before he'd turned south away from Usher's that day he had lifted a pair of high-powered binoculars from Crafkin's saddle, and with these he had kept Naome's movements under constant surveillance till he'd found the man holed-up at Straddle Bug, one of the spreads which Ryerson, through Crafkin, had taken over. No crew was being maintained there and Naome herself had ridden off about an hour ago.

He cinched the hull on the gray and thrust a boot in the stirrup. Funny he mused, how things kept coming back to you; little things, insignificant trifles which a man ought long ago to have forgotten. The weary lift of tired eyes across the length of a store porch . . . the tremulous shape of a girl's twisted smile.

Marratt, cursing, ground his teeth and slammed the horse into motion.

Raising a spurless heel above the horn of his saddle Marratt dropped to earth with eyes bleak as a gun fighter's. He loosened the weight that was sagging his shell belt and stepped onto the verandah, hollow sound rumbling out of the planks as he moved doorward—sound which fled into the hard stillness around him.

The paintless door was pulled open with a groan from dry hinges and Ryerson's face was staring into his own. The man had aged ten years since that day on the store porch. "You needn't worry," Marratt said. "I didn't come here to kill you."

The ranchman's eyes smiled tiredly. "I didn't suppose you had." He stepped back from the door. "Come in, Marratt. I've been expecting you."

Marratt looked at him suspiciously. "I imagine so," he said grimly, and raked his glance about warily as he followed the man down an uncarpeted hall.

Turning into what had evidently been the ranch office, Ryerson motioned to a chair and dropped into another behind a desk that was cluttered with papers. "You didn't hear from my daughter?"

"I've been camped in the hills ever since that fight."

"She left a couple notes at Usher's asking you to come here—"

"Did she tell you my name was Marratt?"

Ryerson nodded. "But I had already placed you. You'll remember I called you 'Luke' that day in town. I supposed you *were* Luke; as such I could understand your refusal to shake and the terrible look which flashed out of your eyes when you advised me the next time we met to be armed. Riding home, however, I recalled a picture I had once come across in a Prescott paper—"

"Then you admit to having been there?"

The ranchman stared at him curiously. "Of course I've been to Prescott. As it happens, I was there just before you came to trial . . . Now you're looking," Ryerson said, voice and features expressing bewilderment, "very much as you did that day in Bella Loma—"

Marratt snarled, "How the hell did you expect me to look?"

"I don't get it," Ryerson said. "You're not Luke Usher. I don't understand why you should look as though killing me would give you a great deal of pleasure."

"Perhaps," Marratt drawled, "this will freshen up your memory," and recounted the story as he had gotten it from Charlie.

"Merciful God," Ryerson whispered when Marratt stopped speaking. "So that was the way of it . . . I don't wonder you killed him. Why didn't you tell the judge—"

"And publish her shame?"

"But to spend five years in Yuma . . . " He shook his head, swearing huskily. "And all this time you've been imagining I—"

"Do you deny it?"

"Certainly. Most vigorously. I wasn't within miles of the place when that happened."

"The girl described you."

"Of course she did—"

"And called you his partner!"

"She would have, naturally," Ryerson nodded.

235

"We'd stopped at her place that morning to get water—"

"You and Clagg?"

"I didn't know the fellow's name. He'd ridden into my camp the night before—"

"He must have given you some kind of name."

"Yes. 'Gunderson', I believe—anyway something Scandinavian. It wasn't his right one, you may be sure of that. He showed considerable curiosity concerning the packs on my burros; since they held nothing of value I let him paw through them. I am convinced, however, that if I'd had any dust I would never have left that place alive—"

"Are you talking about Clagg?"

Ryerson showed his tired smile. "Let me finish. As I was saying, we'd stopped at this girl's place that morning for water. A couple hours after we'd left I was glad to hear him say he had decided to turn off for Skull Valley. He said, 'If I was you I wouldn't be doin' no lingerin' around here.' You may be sure I had no intention of lingering; I was too glad to be rid of him to risk a change of mind. I spent that afternoon and evening with an old friend of mine— Joe Guthrie—at his horse ranch—"

"You can prove that?"

"I imagine Joe will vouch for it. If I had thought this fellow as planning to go back to that girl's hay ranch—"

"Why don't you call him Clagg?"

"Because the man you killed wasn't Clagg, Marratt."

Marratt stared at him, speechless.

"Oh, I know," Ryerson said, "he had Clagg's badge and papers, but he was no more a marshal than you are."

Marratt eyed Naome's father an uncomfortable while, at last asking, "What kind of a shine are you trying to cut?" He got his wind back then and said, suddenly furious: "Maybe you've forgotten I was tried, convicted and sentenced to Yuma for killing Hugh Clagg, a deputy U. S. marshal!"

"I *had* forgotten it until I learned the other day of your escape. But I know Clagg, and the fellow who went with me to that girl's place after water was not Clagg—"

"How long have you known this?"

Ryerson shrugged and said tiredly, "The man didn't try to pass himself off as Clagg to me, remember. He gave me to understand he was some kind of agent for the Federal Narcotics Bureau. It wasn't until I saw his picture with yours in that Prescott paper that I realized the supposed Clagg I'd been hearing about was this Gunderson. Joe Guthrie had sent me this paper at the ranch and it was six months old when I came back from a trip and read it.

"I meant to do something about it but someway

or another I became busy with other matters and it completely slipped my mind. You had refused to make any statement at the time of your arrest. Even had I been in the habit of keeping abreast of current events I would have had no reason to connect this man's killing with the girl at whose shack we had stopped that morning for water."

Ryerson sighed. "Since the death of my wife I've been little concerned with the things going on in the world of the present. Too little concerned, a lot of people would say. My coming onto you that day in Bella Loma was quite a shock, particularly when I realized you were Marratt and not Luke Usher. I'm deeding back to their original owners the various properties taken over in my name by Crafkin. I've sent Frailey, for young Usher, a substantial check for the fifteen years I've been told Jake's grass fed my cattle, and another for the stock Naome tells me Crafkin stole.

"I'm not trying to put myself in a better light with anyone; I'm simply trying as best I can to make what amends are possible. After bumping into you with Frailey and my daughter on the porch of Danvers' store, I came home and dug up that paper. I enclosed it with an exhaustive letter of true particulars which I sent posthaste to the Governor. His answer came yesterday."

Ryerson picked up an official envelope which he pushed across the desk toward Marratt who, with no move to touch it, said through the whirl of his churning thoughts, "You've thrown over any chance you ever had of going to Phoenix."

The ranchman smiled his tired smile. "I never wanted to be governor. There again I followed the path of least resistance, letting another man's persuasion urge me into making a not very praiseworthy effort. I told the—But why don't you read that letter?"

Marratt shook his head. "I wouldn't know straight-up from down, right now—"

"Then I must tell you that an investigation, based on the facts revealed in my letter, has proved my contention. The man you killed was not Clagg but a notorious outlaw for whom—"

"I think," declared a voice from the open door back of Marratt, "that what this fellow will most enjoy hearing now is that, to all intents and purposes, he's no longer a fugitive from justice."

Marratt, twisting his head, could only gawk at him stupidly.

"That's right," said Ranger Smith, grinning pleasantly. "I've been instructed to give you notice you'll be expected in the Governor's office on the seventeenth for questioning at one o'clock sharp. You may be held up a week or two, but I guess I can safely prophesy that, once all the official red tape's been unwound, you'll be free as a bird."

"Free!" Marratt said and, then, to Ryerson: "Where's Naome?"

—the end—

HORSES,
WOMEN AND
GUNS

1 YUMA PRISON

Patience was a thing a man was forced to learn in this place. Nights could be long and cold. They had a way in certain seasons of being long and hot. Jim Final could not recall that he had ever found them comfortable.

Actually he hadn't expected to. Rock piles and dungeons, heavy chains and leg irons—indeed the whole complexion of life atop this bald and windswept knob had been conceived and harshly ordered that men outside might change their ways and those condemned regret them.

This was Arizona, lately a part of New Mexico Territory, a sweet and bitter land whose long tradition of wildness had become an intolerable burden. No vigilantes rode its trails but a ranger force was increasingly mentioned as a means of combatting recurrent evils. Meanwhile there was Yuma—as rough on rats as man could make it.

The town, below, was a boisterous place of riverboats and rattling dice. Incredibly crude by cultured standards it held compensations denied the lockstep crew in which Jim Final presently moved. No cribs in stony lonesome, no gambling, no forgiveness.

Everything about the place was there for a particular purpose. Walls high and thick of beaten rock, of puddled mud and tamped *caliche*. Formidable gates and gun tower. Strap iron grills and gun-hung guards as fiercely without scruples as the meanest brute they

243

herded. Yuma was rightly spoken of as "hell without
the music".

Jim Final flexed his lean hard jaws. Staring through
crossed iron at what he could see of the night's dim
splendor he wondered what the chances were of surviv-
ing another seven years of it.

Ten at hard labor was what they had given him; ten
years at Yuma to teach him a proper respect the judge
said, and there were those who thought he had gotten
off light, being caught with five stolen beeves branded
Skillet.

He'd been caught right enough. Caught by Strunk's
foreman, Bill Tapp, and a pair of Squatting 0 hardcases
whose word wouldn't have moved a bluetail fly if the
twelve good men hadn't feared a hereafter.

The desert wind took a sudden shift and its brought-
in scent of resinous greasewood made Final clench
scarred fists. But three years here had taught him much.
He was able now to contain his wrath.

He'd been caged with the incorrigibles, no man
trusting his paraded meekness. He had the hottest cell
of the lot and even by night in this season the winds
seemed to come straight out of a forge. Final was
inured to heat. Bred to the Indian smokes of the lost
lands he'd lived his whole life in such dust-deviled
wastes. Though gaunt by the nature of his tasks and
scant rations he had mesquite's durability, the tough
indestructible fiber of rawhide. He felt a saturnine
contempt for these bullies the law had placed over him
but he did not wear this scorn on his sleeve.

A hacking cough came out of the gloom and Final
wondered how Ruidoso, his cell mate, managed to
support both life and consumption in addition to the
abuse the guards continued to heap upon him. Better
wonder how much he himself could put up with.
These fellows welcomed temper for the license it gave

them and there was no place in Final's plans for a cripple.

Very secret he had braided, strand by strand across the months, a rope of cotton threads which was wrapped about his legs beneath these grimy pants. They were ill fitting, sloppy and coarse, little likely to give the show away so long as he was able to keep the guards' hands off him. The rope was thin but strong as Final's purpose. Many dreary nights had gone into its present eleven-foot length; it had been a thing to fiddle with when sleep wouldn't come and his thoughts inevitably had turned to Strunk.

Wheeling away from the door he picked up his ball and five-foot chain, carrying them to the coverless bunk which was built, like the gratings, of strap iron firmly anchored. The stench of this place was insufferable.

He had schooled himself to lie still, Indian fashion, but he could not control the prowl of thoughts which, grown more savage, continued to gnaw at his memories of home.

Getting out of this place, he understood, was about as likely as heiring great riches. Men had done it but that gun in the tower, a ten-barrel Gatling, was a powerful dissuader—as some had learned to their cost when the wife of Cap Ingalls had quelled a mutiny with a couple of grim-faced twists of the crank. Yet it was still believed a man could get out if he would bide his time and was lucky enough.

During the thirty-nine months Final had been here, four men had made it over the walls. One had got into the river and drowned, sucked under by whirlpools and trapped in the sands. Rifles had accounted for two of the others but the fourth had managed to elude bounty hunters and put twenty miles of desert behind him before hard luck in the shape of a sidewinder had done for him. The four bodies had been recovered and the

245

entire roster of inmates called to view the cost of an all-too-brief freedom.

Christian charity at Yuma was something to make jokes about. Cap Ingalls wasn't running the show any more. The man at the head of things now was a pure-quill s.o.b. and the Cravetts and Harpers did pretty much as they pleased. These were guards who liked a little fun with their labor. The least provocation whistled clubs into motion. Some men, wild with hunger, deliberately invited crippling. At Yuma when a man was badly enough hurt he got three days in hospital where the fare included one boiled egg a day in addition to the mulligan the work crews were fed.

In the black creep of shadows Final saw Quail's face but his thoughts, bleak as always, grimly harked back to Strunk. This, with Final, had become almost a ritual. Until Strunk's skill with cards had taken it away from him, Final had been a rancher, sole owner of Squatting O.

Loss of the place had not too greatly upset him, being mostly a matter he'd charged off to growing up. But there'd been later things he could not shrug aside. Like the job Bentain had given him. The top screw job at Skillet.

Jim had come increasingly back to this favor, uneasily considering the rancher's possible motives. Final's name had never been associated with guns; his brief fling at ranching could hardly have fitted him for so responsible a job. Of course—and he thought of this reluctantly—at the time Bentain had hired him he had been seeing quite a bit of Quail, Bentain's daughter. He didn't particularly like to be brought head-up against that. Bentain, with the most grass and surest water, had been practically a king.

The displaced ramrod, Rockabye, had appeared to accept Final's advent with good grace, even kidding a little about the new "wagon boss"—this being an allusion to Jim's arrival in a buckboard, the only thing salvaged from his tournament with Strunk. If the man had nursed dissatisfaction over his own diminished stature he had been to a lot of trouble hiding it. Only two small things caused Jim to consider the man at all: the shotgun in the barn and the chance remark dropped by Rockabye which had put Jim into that brush back of Black Cross with those misbranded cattle just as Strunk's bunch had come onto them.

It was Strunk Jim's thoughts always came back to.

The prison was still deep in dark when the scuff of boots and metallic clatter of the guards' huge keys jangled nearer. One by one the gratings yawed open. *"Come on, you yardbirds—rustle your butts outa there. Harper—"* Cravett snarled, *"haul that son of a bitch out where I can crack him!"*

Final, ignoring this, shook Ruidoso awake and helped him up. "Old Gruff's in one of his tail-twisting moods. Think you can make it out there?"

Ruidoso's cough was a thing of blood and phlegm. By the time the paroxysm left him, spent and shaking, a guard's gleaming eyes were peering through the squares with a lantern. Final heard the key's rasp, the protesting scrape of the bolt. The ponderous hinges, red with rust, skreaked dismally as the door was pushed back by the rod at its bottom.

Last man out as a matter of course usually felt the guard's spleen. Final's hand, lightly guiding Ruidoso, steered the consumptive ahead. Though Jim knew the rules he was very nearly tempted to pick up and tote the sick man's ball and chain. Not fear but an unwillingness to humble the man's stubborn pride kept Jim's fisted hands at his sides.

When he stepped out, dragging his own, Cravett's night stick caught him in the small of the back. Jim went almost to his knees. A red fog enveloped him, pain splintering through it like the clutchings of delirium. Breath clogged in his throat and he gagged on the sourness of it but managed to catch hold of the wall and stay upright. He kept his face away from Cravett and did not offer any comment.

The head guard grinned. "Don't you hear good this morning? I said 'Close up there.'"

Final, strangling his fury, stumbled over to the end of the forming line. In this pre-dawn chill the assembling shapes, cowering under the monstrous shadows thrown against gypsumed walls by the smoking lanterns, looked like the vomitings of hell. Like hobgoblins they looked in their chains and tattered rags, the older ones so bent and gnarled they could scarcely straighten even in the face of the guards' flourished clubs.

Through the count, which discovered the roll call one man short, Jim thought of the dandified gambler, Strunk, and kept the skin pulled over his teeth. The missing man was Bexby, and now Cravett's growl tuned up like a saw going through inch planks. "Come outa there, you black-bellied bastard! Harper—roust that nigger outa there!"

A brawny black, naked but for filthy dungarees whacked off at the running sores on his knees, shuffled out of his hole sullenly mumbling. "What's that? What's that?" Cravett shouted, infuriated as always by the slightest hint of malingering. "What you snarlin' about?"

"Ah said Ah's sick, Mistuh Cravett, suh—"

"Sick, is it? Well! You're always sick! What do you think this is, a rest home? Give him a pass to the infirmary, Harper."

Harper, licking tobacco stained lips, sidled up. "Handsome Harry" the inmates called him when they weren't slandering his ancestry. A pass to the infirmary was Harper's specialty. He had made a project of it and knew to the inch how far he could go without killing a man or permanently disabling him. Drifting his eyes to catch the glint of covering rifles he grinned with a baleful pleasure, massaged his club and struck. The wheezing grunts of his breath and the thuds of the stick biting into flesh were the only sounds in that shadow-draped yard until the Negro dropped senseless.

Hate was so thick it was like a hand clamping hold of you. Cravett's cat-and-mouse eyes slyly probed Final's cheeks. Finding nothing to fasten on he said, falsely anxious, "You all right, Mister Final? Reckon you'd like to lay off for the day?"

"No sir," Final said, although the words almost choked him.

Cravett turned away. "All right, you scum, fall in!"

The prisoners were marched over to a row of iron buckets, each man taking up one as they filed past to commence the grueling trip to the river.

This was a daily ceremony which the guards in Harper's detail dearly loved. Swinging their wooden billies they swapped coarse jokes in lewd anticipation as they watched the first few shambling shapes begin the perilous descent. There was room on the path for two abreast if the nearer hugged the cliff but it was against regulations for prisoners; there had to be room for Harper's bullies to sprint up and down the line. It was Harper's private ruling (at which Cravett winked) that a man who spilled his water could be rapped by the guard who saw him. It was another of Harry's rules that every bucket come out of the river brimming. It took a lot of water to slosh down those cells, disinfectant at Yuma being reserved for the privileged few.

It was no lark to navigate that goat trace with the ball at the ends of those five-foot chains rolling and banging and bounding like crazy. It was worse coming back. Always the uptrip was hell with the handles off.

In the chill of this morning, bedeviled with river fog, it looked worse than usual. Groans and muffled cursing boiled up through the mist like prayers from the damned and abruptly, just ahead of Jim Final, Ruidoso lost his footing.

Letting go of his bucket Final lurched forward to catch the man's arm and might, despite the sixty-pound drag of ball and chain, have succeeded had Cravett, behind him, stayed out of it. The boss guard had been hunting an excuse to tie into him. As Final surged forward desperately reaching, Cravett swung.

The weighted two-foot length of polished wood cracked Final across the seat with a force that sent him sprawling off balance onto the gray glint of the trail's treacherous surface. The black gurgulous sound of the river rushed up at him and, frantically twisting, slipping in his loose brogans, gouging grit with clawed fingers, he managed to cling to the harsh abrasive of the trail.

The iron ball went over, very nearly carrying him with it. Only the strength of bleeding fingers held him. Tears stung his eyes and through this misty blur, clanking link over link, he hauled the weight back. Breathless he pushed up to peer around for Ruidoso. Locked jaws kept him from retching but these couldn't control the shake of his limbs as with burning eyes he stared toward the fog shrouded rocks below.

"You murderous dog!" Cravett shouted. "Shove a man off the trail, will you? By Christ I'll have your hide for this—Harper!"

Handsome Harry came running with rifle and club. His little pig eyes looked like glass in the lantern flame. They waggled from Final to Cravett as he licked shining lips. "It's the Snake Den for this duck." Cravett's voice was hoarse with passion. "Get him up there on the

double. If he opens his yap you knock his goddam teeth
out!"

He shoved Jim at Harper and the big bruiser started
him uptrail, ramming him through the staring huddle of
convicts who cringed away from the threat of his club.
Some among them growled but none interfered.

2 WALK IN THE DARK

The penal establishment at Yuma, while intentionally
primitive, was not so much Final thought the reflection
of justice as an instrument of vengeance. The territorial
prison had been created on the assumption that crime
did not pay and the sooner this was recognized the
better for all concerned. When a man turned wolf he
would be treated as a wolf. There was never any
thought of reclaiming him; too many had suffered too
much from their kind for the authorities to have any
patience with half measures.

The cells in large measure had been constructed by
men working out their time. Toilet facilities consisted
of a bucket emptied once each day by one of the pair,
or five, or more, who used it. Largest quarters were
about eight by ten, the main cell blocks underneath the
infirmary housing six men per unit.

The cells on Tough Row, intended for incorrigibles,
were hacked out of the granite and *caliche* of the hill—
three-by-five caves with iron gratings, each having a
pair of rings in the floor by which rough customers
could be kept apart when in anger they seemed likely
to incapacitate each other. There were twelve such cells
holding two men each and the women's ward wasn't
much different, the only light being what came in

251

through the strap-ironed front. The snake dens or dungeons were west of Tough Row, quarried from solid stone, little more than burrows. The one Final drew barely allowed him to stand up and hadn't even a bucket. No matter which way he turned with elbows squeezed to his sides his hands came against the jagged edges of rock. It was impossible to sit down.

He watched the river crew shuffle past on their lock-step way to mess hall and chapel. It was not yet quite dawn and in this uncertain light it was like watching a procession of stumbling ghosts. No talk was permitted.

Jim's body still ached from the abuse it had taken, though what he'd got from Harper's stick was as child's play to what he could except when Cravett got around to him. They seldom lashed a man at Yuma but when they did they made it thorough. The last man fed a "taste of the cat" had wound up a jibbering idiot. Sometimes, Final remembered, the howls he loosed would work clean into your bones.

After chow his fellow convicts plodded past again. Sun had brightened the white covering of earth until the glare was enough to put a man's eyes out. Normally now the Super's pets would be paired off to police the grounds. Others would be taken to the shops to spend time on hair bridles and less intricate novelties they were encouraged to make under the improvements inaugurated by old Cap Ingalls—God rest his soul—who no longer had anything to say for "his boys". Wood, silver and onyx was additionally furnished those with work-shop privileges (cost to be recovered from sales). The gang from Tough Row would be herded back to their quarrying—but today of course, in view of Cravett's accusation, this routine would be held up until after Final's punishment.

He felt like a captive tiger staring through the crossed iron straps of the grating. His grip tightened on it as the incorrigibles filed past in the direction of the tool shed. Astonishment wormed its way into Jim's mind as group after group of inmates took off toward the places of their various employment under the watchful scowls of the club-swinging guards.

Although work, apparently, had not been interrupted, Final had witnessed too many examples of management's ire to imagine the death of Ruidoso would be allowed to pass without official cognizance. Jim was not being reprieved; they were letting him stew—letting him sweat awhile.

Exhausted, he sagged against the jagged wall and drifted off into thoughts of Strunk and Bentain, even considering Bentain's daughter and the letters she kept sending—though he'd never answered one.

The scuff of hobnailed shoes moving nearer made him presently aware of the approach of Handsome Harry. The man's ugly face eventually stopped in front of Jim's grating. After about ten minutes of this infuriating scrutiny the brawny guard got out his key and unlocked the strap iron door, passing Final the smaller key to his fetters. "Step outa that now an' don't try nothin' fancy."

Final dropped the chain and returned Harper's key. The temptation had been in him to wrap that chain around Harper's leering face, but there hadn't been enough slack and both of them knew it would have done him no good. Harper, sneering, swung open the grating, alerted his club and stepped back for Jim to pass.

A lot of wild notions scrambled through Final's head when he found they had the yard to themselves. There were guards of course on the walls and in the gun tower but in his desperation it almost seemed to Jim that anything would be better than to accept like a dog whatever they had in store for him.

253

Harper's grin stretched out. "Go ahead. Bust a gut if you wants. You'll never git a better chance."

Final got hold of himself and set off. At Harper's growled order he turned into the mess hall. Through a clatter of dishes coming out of the kitchen Harper laughed. "It's real enough. Set right down an' start stuffin.'"

Jim had an urge to pinch himself. He pulled out a bench and dropped onto it. He kept his hands in plain sight while his disbelieving eyes roved the food set in front of him. Here was one of the things men in this place dreamed about. Oatmeal and a pitcher of cream to go with it. Coffee—real java by the smell. Ham and eggs. A plate heaped with toast and a slab of pure butter, not the hog fat prisoners were accustomed to.

It was real enough. Across the room, behind the same kind of fixings, Cravett sat shooting the breeze with the Super. Except for them, and the convicts on KP, the great hall was empty. Harper growled, "Tie into it."

Like a man in a dream Final did so. The food was good as it looked. Harper settled his butt on the edge of the table and played with his billy until Final got through. Then he tossed Jim the makings.

Final, rolling the smoke, was conscious of the glances of the Super, yonder, and Cravett. Harper passed him a match. "Rules of this place ain't fer fellas like you."

Jim dragged smoke deep into him. After that business of Ruidoso he had nothing to lose. He smoked the quirly right down to his fingers. "All right," Harper said, getting up. "Let's go."

In the hot smash of sunlight Final stopped for further orders. Harper spat and pointed. "Over there," he said, waving Jim on with his night stick.

Over there was a long sort of barracks-like building which housed, so Final had heard, the various shops for prison labor. He had never been near the place and his interest now was strongly tempered with dread and mistrust. Nothing in his experience had prepared him for such a bewildering order and naked fright stirred in him. He hadn't forgot Cravett's anger or the way the man had watched him back there in the mess hall.

He suddenly wanted to run. With an equal abruptness Harper's spurious good will dropped away. "Get movin'."

Final looked at the stick and willed his legs into motion.

As they moved closer he could tell by the signs what each of those doors apparently let into. One said TAILOR. Another was BLACKSMITH. A number of the rooms were given over to the crafts. The sign above one door had a double row of lettering: STEAM BOILER ROOM & LAUNDRY. There was even, by God, a bath house!

It was before this last that Harper stopped and jabbed his stick out. "Git in there an' slosh the stink off yerself. When you git done ask Suds fer a clean set of stripes."

Final went in with his mouth set like iron. All of this fofaraw wasn't fooling him a particle. This was Cravett's cat-and-mouse way of doing everything. If the bastard craved a drink he'd probably have to sneak up on the dipper.

When Jim emerged ten minutes later, grim of face and followed by Suds, he was not surprised to see Harper's eyes pop wide open. "What's this?" Harry said, like rope.was something he had never got acquainted with.

It was all part of the act, even the way Suds coiled and passed it over. "Little present for the Super. This guy," Suds said, jerking a thumb at Jim Final, "had it round him like a corset."

Final passed the rest of that day in the snake den. He

got no more to eat; he couldn't even relieve himself. He had plenty of time to consider what might happen to him.

It must have been close onto nine when they came for him, Harper and two guards armed with rifles. He placed the time by the changed personnel walking sentry-go along the tops of the walls and by the light streaming out of every lantern in the yard. This light discouraged any thought of resistance. The Gatling in the gun tower could tear a man in two.

Final locked his jaws and went where he was told. Across the white *caliche* of the yard, past the tower with the mess hall falling away to the left. Final's face was like a mask. The iron-sheeted main gate skreaked open and, extra watchful now, Final's escort took him through, marching him over to Harper's own quarters in the guards' building north of the gun tower. There, on a chair, neatly laundered and folded, were the clothes he'd been wearing when he'd arrived at this place. "Get 'em on," Harper said, "and pick up the rest of your junk off that table."

Final dressed and, increasingly grim, picked up the things they had taken from his pockets. "Where's the shell belt and gun? If you've got me pegged for chief part in a breakout—"

"Stow the gab," Harper said, and pushed a form across the table. He shoved a pencil after it. "Put your name on that bottom line."

Final picked up the form. "I like to know what I'm signing."

"Haw, haw!" Harper jeered.

It was a receipt for his effects. Final put it back on the table. He didn't for a moment imagine he was getting out of here. "I'm not signing anything till I get back that gun and belt."

"Okay," Harper snarled. "Do everything the hard way."

Under close surveillance Jim was prodded into the night and taken by trim walks to the administration building, also situated outside the walls. They moved down a dingy corridor. Harper pounded on a door and was told to come ahead.

The Old Man was reared back in the shine of a swivel behind the dull gleam of a scarred flat-topped desk. His name was Wiggins. Very tall and sallow-complected, he looked like a plant kept too long in the basement. His eyes were black marbles in puffy pouches of flesh and a scraggle of whiskers stuck out like gray wires from the sag of tired jowls. He'd been paring his nails but broke off to look up when Jim was shoved forward by Harper.

"Says he won't sign till he gits back his pistol."

The Super's nose quivered like a rabbit's. "Take off that hat!"

Final removed it, not looking at Cravett or the fellow who stood beyond him in a clawhammer coat and black stovepipe. You didn't have to look to see the piece of cutup tin throwing back the lamp's glitter above the glint of this citizen's watch chain.

Though as fixed of expression as any redskin passing the peace pipe Final's feeling of confused dread and insecurity hit a new high when Wiggins opened a drawer and pushed a holstered gun across the desk. Jim was reaching to pick it up when the Super, smiling leanly, thwunked something else down beside it. "Better take this along too," Wiggins said; and Jim found himself staring at the rope Suds had come from the bath house with.

Final lifted it off the desk, more convinced than ever these men were playing with him. Tightening the coil he slipped it into his brush jacket and picked up the gun, slipping it out of its leather, rudely jolted by the bright gleam of brass in the cylinder. He felt like a man climbing onto a gallows but thrust the gun into his waistband. He hoped his face was as stiff as it felt.

Harper held out the form and Jim signed it.

Wiggins steepled blunt fingers, eyeing Final across them. "You're going to take a little walk with the marshal here and Cravett. Be entirely up to you as to whether or not you come back." He showed a dry smile.

Cravett touched Final's arm. "Door's right behind you."

They went out with the sound of dead quiet settling after them and up the gray line of closed doors to the steps. The night wind was cold against the sweat that was on him. The Mexicans had a name for turning a prisoner loose with a gun. Jim had no doubt of Cravett's ultimate intention. They'd likely known all the time he'd been planning to break loose. The gun was probably loaded with blanks.

They turned left toward town at the base of the hill. They passed the dark maw of a livery's runway, the acrid whiff of ammonia rising through lesser smells, and Final stared with bleak eyes at the glimmer ahead.

His clothes were damp with his sweat. All his caged instincts were clamoring for action, his nerves tight as fiddle strings. They would look for him to run at some dark place; it was what they were expecting him to do. He kept walking. The only chance he'd get was one that plainly appeared impossible.

Now they were into the lights from the Barrel House, hearing its racket, smelling the stench of it, Jim still wretchedly fighting his silent battle.

Three abreast they came even with the doors of the dive and heard some man curse another, and a woman's high shrill laughter. The night chill tightened around

Final and locked his chattering teeth together. Cravett slowed, peering into the place, obviously thinking about wetting his whistle. "We can stop comin' back," the marshal said, and they went on.

Now the wind came again, dankly stinking of the river, and these rank flavors called up a wildness, and excitement rushed through Final. But he shook his head knowing the time was not yet.

They crossed the shadow-hung street beneath balconies where voices cried down and jeered after them, bars and dapples of light all about them. Two sternwheelers were tied up at a landing. A grunting line of roustabouts were manhandling heavy cargo. Cravett shoved Jim roughly. "You ain't takin' no boat—get a move on, damn you!"

The walks hereabouts were blatant with traffic. More than once Jim was tempted to make his try but each time he felt Cravett's eyes digging into him. He saw a woman go past on the arm of a man and was touched by her fragrance and felt recklessness tugging him. The street up ahead was more heavily crowded, fogged with the lemon dust churned by wagons. There the guns would have a harder time finding him. He rode hard on impatience, putting no trust in any part of this business. The Arizona Hotel thrust its light across the walk and Cravett said, "Turn in."

Final swore under his breath, saw the grin of the marshal.

"Take them stairs beyond the desk," Cravett said.

There were people in this lobby but not any near enough to give him the chance he had figured on. The clerk looked up as Jim approached with his escort. Several heads came around idly curious to watch. "Wind's gittin' downright blowy," someone said.

The marshal gave Jim Final a shove. "Up them stairs."

"Swing right," Cravett said as they came onto the landing. "Third door. Rap."

There was no one else in the corridor. Again Final desperately considered resistance, but there was less chance here than there had been on the street. Disgusted, Jim did as he was told.

A man said, "Come in."

3 THE CARDS ARE DEALT

The room was elegantly furnished. Beneath a crystal chandelier a serge-suited man with the build of a wrestler stood with his hands in the pockets of his coat. "Close the door."

Final stared like a fool at the man's twisted smile.

"Close it, Jim. Your friends will wait at the bottom of the stairs." The man dropped into a damask covered seat as though exhausted.

It was no secret Joe Bob had a bad heart condition. Jamaica rum, black cigars and double-strength creamless coffee were bound to do something to a man's constitution when partaken of in the wholesale fashion the Governor was said to employ them. Red veins were beginning to overlay and coarsen a face that was still undeniably handsome and the fingers he brought out of his pocket showed a noticeable tremor as he picked up and relit a black butt from the table edge. "You're awake," he smiled—"it's no dream, believe me."

The dark, self-mocking eyes considered Final, seeing the stubbornness of jaw, the pinched lines about nose and mouth, the whole brashly taciturn look of him; and the man sighed, thinking back to those days when he too had known something of these qualities before soft living had embezzled them. This fellow would do. Tempered by ill fortune and made dangerous by the toughness three years in that prison had ground deep into him, Jim Final looked desperate enough for anything. The Governor waved him toward a chair.

"Since you've recognized me we can dispense with formalities. How bad do you want to get out of that place?"

"Bad enough," Final said, and the Governor nodded.

He sat engrossed for a moment with the cigar dribbling smoke into a haze that fogged his features. "Understand —I don't want my name to come into this. What I'm going to say is just between the two of us. If you're big enough for this—if you measure up, I'll make it my business to see that you're let off."

Again his glance swept Final, narrower now, less readable, more probing. Whatever he saw appeared to reassure him. "I'm supposed," he grinned, "to be in Ehrenberg; soon as we're through I'll be heading upriver on the *Colorado Queen*. Well—say something, man. Take a chair," he added irritably. "You don't have to stand on ceremony with me." He lifted a liver-spotted hand toward his chest. "Smoke?"

Final, taking the cigar he held out, bit an end off. He accepted a light and did some looking of his own. Joe Bob's lips twitched again in that much-discussed smile which for two terms hand-running had kept his hands on the reins of government. "You didn't come here," Final said, "to waste time listening to anything I'd have to say."

Joe Bob leaned forward. "A cattleman friend of mine's in hot water. He's got a neighbor that's stirring up the Indians. My friend is apt to be in a pretty bad way if those moccasins decide to dig up the hatchet."

When Final said nothing the Governor spoke grimly.

261

"I need a man I can trust to go down and look into this."

Jim grinned bleakly.

"It's not as simple as you might think," Joe Bob growled. "It wouldn't do any good to send star packers down there, the man would pull in his horns and play pious until they left. We know the fellow's getting whisky to those breechclouts but we can't pin it on him. My friend needs help—he's too near the reservation. If the lid comes off his will be the first place hit."

Jim shook his head. "You don't want me."

The Governor brushed that aside. "You'll go out of here on a provisional pardon. Stop this fellow and you can write your own ticket."

"After I'm planted I won't need a ticket."

Joe Bob sighed. "You've had three years of this place. Think you can take another seven? There was a man killed out there this morning wasn't there?"

Final stood perfectly still.

The Governor smiled. "You're the man for this job. You've got all the qualifications. Your father was a friend of that chief down there. You can do it, by God, if anyone can—you've got a personal stake in this. The fellow I want you to stop is Strunk."

Final's eyes turned sharp as glass.

"When Strunk diddled you out of it your place was just one of a dozen shoestring outfits squatted around Bentain; now Strunk's got them all. You owe that old man something, mister. Strunk used you to put him into a corner."

"I never stole those cows—"

"You were caught with them. Your spread gave Strunk a club in that country, your conviction took all the fight out of Skillet. Strunk's chased Bentain back into the brush. Now, by God, he wants those Indian lands! You've got to stop—"

262

"I'm no gun fighter!"

"Every night for three years you've been going through the motions." Joe Bob crushed out his smoke and got up. "I know what's in your head." He took a turn about the room. "Wake up, man, this is what you've been waiting for, a chance to get at him. Anyway, Bentain—"

"You're not crawling out on no limb for Bentain!"

The Governor flushed. He finally nodded. "I want to keep my connections for one more term. I'll be washed out of politics if we have to use cavalry to put down those Apaches. Strunk wants their land—him and that bunch of fool hoemen he's sucked in there. If those tomahawks start killing folks Strunk and his weed-benders can get up enough stink to have those lands thrown open to settlement."

No point in telling this goddam fool he wanted a chunk of those lands himself and had things set up to get the chunk Strunk was counting on. Like Joe Bob had mentioned, Jim had all the qualifications; no need to point out which ones made him so perfect. The Governor wanted Strunk stopped but not too soon. He wanted him deep under ground but first there had to be blood on the range—enough atrocities to call in those soldiers. Pushing Final at Strunk came mighty close to genius. A beautiful thing. A few pieces of silver slid across certain palms should take care of the loose ends nicely.

"Well," Joe Bob said, "that's the story. Are you with me?"

"I don't like—"

"Hell's fire!" the Governor swore impatiently. "I don't like kicking a man when he's down, but I can. You're going to do this, Final."

"I can croak just as easy on Groaner's Hill."

263

"You can croak," Joe Bob said, "but you won't find it easy."

Gray twilight was fading into colder dusk when Jim Final came out of the cedar brakes and got his first look in many months at Bandoleer.

The town hadn't changed much. Jim had used to hunt grouse along these bottoms and over yonder—by the hind side of that tumbledown shack—was where he had dropped his first muletail deer. Been more trees around then—even room for the Apaches, though he could not recall when they'd got anything cheerfully.

The good smell of supper smoke was filtering through the pungence of catclaw and greasewood and the marsh-sprung odors breeze lifted off the river. Alert, he put his horse across, flattening broad lips against the clamor churning through him, anxious to be done with this yet somehow reluctant to put his hand to it. The urge was still there but twisted now like the Governor's smile, crossgrained with mistrust and a suspicion extending even to the boxed loads Joe Bob had given him for his pistol.

Some of that harsh bitterness came back again to slap him. "What d'you want me to do," he'd cried—"kill him?"

The Governor had looked at him fishy eyed. "Do whatever you have to do. I want the man stopped. That's all I'm going to say to you. When he's stopped I'll sign that pardon; I'll clear you of any further trouble you've got into."

And now he was here, gnawed by doubts and fore-boding, plagued like Taunee's Mad Springs Apaches by the ghosts of too many things left undone. He swore at the remembered look of Joe Bob, at the Judas kiss of the man's twisted smile. And there was Quail Bentain that he might have to face, too.

He put his horse into the road, shod feet plopping up a tired grumble of sound snatched away like the dust by the fangs of this gale. It was spring if you could believe it. He shivered and the wind had precious little to do with it.

How did you go about stopping a man like Strunk? Getting at him wouldn't be easy if what he had heard about Strunk was true. The man would not be gambling on saddle blankets now. He was a power in this land, a force to be reckoned with, steel inside a velvet glove.

Jim's narrowed eyes probed the thickening dark, sorting out the vague shapes of roundabout mountains. Lamps shone from small holdings scattered over the slopes and some kid with a stick ran along a picket fence. Several times dogs tore out, barking and snapping at the roan gelding's heels. The sudden swoop of a bughunting nighthawk fetched a curse out of Final when the horse pretended fright. What would the people around here think?

"Folks will think just about whatever you give them cause to." That was Joe Bob's answer. "You're a whipped cur," he'd said, "trying to get back of the stove. Better remember it. If Strunk even begins to suspect you're after him you'll wind up in some gulch and be no good to anyone. Play it smart. You can't just step up and stick a gun into his gut."

It was what Jim Final was tempted to do. A man who chose to act like a cur should have no complaint if he were treated like one; but Jim could understand if the man was a big mogul now getting to him was not likely to be easy. And there were those years at Yuma. The fellow should be made to think about them. He'd come up, bite by bite, through the ranks of his neighbors; he should go that way with plenty of worry at what was happening. This was another of Joe Bob's notions.

A number of early stars broke through but the wind

265

didn't lay. It came through Jim's thin brush jacket that hung loose on him now after three years of Yuma. His feet were numb from the squeeze of his boots.

He passed a couple of arguing cowhands snug in fleece-lined half-coats. He kneed the roan away from these, idly thinking of Chris Stegner who had run the Red Horse livery.

Jim was on Fremont now with the town's multitudinous voices shuttling into buried niches of remembrance. People hurried along the scarred plank walks, chins dug into turned-up collars, hands deep-thrust into the warmth of pockets. Not many were loitering in this weather. "Cold night," someone muttered. An opening door spilled golden light. The laugh of a woman was snatched away by the gusts.

A man stepped with some abruptness, looking backward, out of an open doorway directly into the street so that Final was forced to yank the roan up sharply to avoid running him down. The fellow's face twisted around. It would have been hard to say which was the more astounded, the blond face peering up at him or Jim's. The both of them froze there, Final with a dozen conflicting impulses beating at the confusion which had turned him rigid.

Out of the corners of his eyes he saw a yellow vest checked with lines of black and red. Black coat, gray pants. A silk tile cockily perched above a flash of remembered blonde curl. The man was Strunk, bold, half handsome, recovering quickly, able to push full lips into a sneer. "Well, well!" he exclaimed. "The cinch ring artist from the back of beyond—thought you'd been turned out to pasture."

When Final said nothing the gambler laughed shortly. "There's nothing here for you, kid. Get wise to yourself and clear out—"

"Before your hired guns put the lid on my box?"

Strunk looked at him through ten seconds of silence and stepped back, thinly smiling, coldly sure of himself and of Final's impotence. "It was you that said that. Better hang it up, kid, where you can have a good look at it. Bandoleer's got no use for a con or a cow thief."

Final forgot Joe Bob's advice. For one wild instant every guard he'd put up against anger shriveled; but only a fool would buck the case ace. The man was trying again to push a stacked deck at him and his eyes, when Jim resisted this bait, turned hard. But he managed a laugh and swung around and walked away. Only after he'd disappeared did Jim fully realize how close he'd stood to death. It was there in the shadows, in the wink and glint of a leveled sixshooter.

Strunk didn't walk the streets alone now.

4 FIRST BLOOD

Shadeless windows spilled dapples of brightness across the black tangle of shadows as Final kneed the tired roan past Rankin's Emporium and Hastenfeldter's bakery, the smell of rising bread fragrantly laced with the sharp spice of cooking apples. The teased-high wail of a cater-wauling fiddle sailed above the clamor whooping out of Whisky Row.

Fremont and Main—hub of the universe local yokels liked to figure it, though Jim no longer shared this stiff-necked persuasion. If he cherished any illusions Jim was not aware of it. He sat a moment undecided, but the roan had needs and directly ahead in the night's blustery halflight was the open maw of the Red Horse barn where once Jim had forked for old man Stegner. Some of his happiest days, looking back on them now. Jim's father had been alive then, a town patriarch, and Squatting 0 an inheritance for a boy to look forward to.

He peered again along the street and tried to put Strunk out of his mind. A man needed something besides hate in his gullet. But thoughts you have lived with are hard to get shed of. Chris Stegner had come to the trial, Jim remembered—sat clean through it without opening his mouth. No one else had opened theirs either with Strunk's dogs staring around with fangs showing; not one of those Jim had supposed were his friends.

The roan, about then, sniffed that cured alfalfa and Final, shivering, let him follow his nose. Every bone in Jim ached from all this time in the saddle constantly battered by the pummeling wind. And there was a kind of malicious defiance at work in him, sharpened by that meeting with Strunk.

Swearing under his breath he put the horse up the lane. Hoofs woke a hollow racket from the straw-littered planks and they passed under the lantern. In the gloomy warmth of the stable Jim got stiffly out of the saddle as the office door opened, cracking light down across the long row of stalls. Against this, Stegner's high-chested shape brought the start of a smile to Final's stubbled features.

The man in the doorway stood stiff as a gunstock. The silence piled up and he finally growled, "Just stoppin' by or figurin' to light a spell?"

Chris Stegner, a man Jim had known all his life.

He rasped at the cottony dryness of his throat and ground the palm of one hand against his dust-gritty pantsleg then gave a short laugh that came out like cloth ripping. "It's me, Chris—Jim Final."

"I'm not blind," Stegner said.

Final eyed him, lips thinning. He took hold of his reins and got into the saddle. The gelding whickered a tired sound of protest but Jim pulled its head around and kneed it into the whip of the night. The cutting edge of the wind bit roughly into them but Final's mind was miles away, his hand seemed to have forgotten the roan entirely.

The horse flattened its ears and headed for shelter.

Kelly Kramer, after two and a half years of competing with Stegner, had the look of a hound with its tail in a crack. He got a small share of the transient drummer trade and a few of Chris' regulars when the Red Horse was filled but this wasn't enough to put lard on his ribs.

Tonight was a Friday and he hadn't an outside horse in the place. Had anyone offered him four bits, hard cash, they would probably have found themselves owning his equity. Kramer hadn't sold a ton of hay in six months and was so close to being strapped he'd gone to eating his own cooking.

He was in a mood to have welcomed the devil when a done-in roan stumbled out of the night with a rider he'd never set eyes on before. "Get down, man," Kramer said, moving up. "Stove in the office an' a pot on the back of it."

Fellow sure had a fishy look. Without taking blue hands from their grip on the saddle the stranger said, "Take a good look, mister."

Out in the weather too long, Kramer figured. He flashed a grin but no answering smile cracked the stranger's face as Kramer reached out for the reins. He was a levi-legged jasper in a faded brush jacket that hung loose across his front. His eyes looked hard as the bore of a Greener. Kramer began to feel vaguely uncomfortable.

The stranger finally stepped off the horse. "Go on in," Kramer said. "Java in the pot. You'll find a cup around there someplace."

The stranger was on his second when the stableman

269

came in. "Cold enough to freeze frogs. Set back an' make yourself comfortable mister."

"Name's Final—Jim Final." The man watched him, waiting.

Kramer's brows corrugated. His eyes widened, then he whistled. "The Skillet boss that was sent up for rustlin'!"

Final nodded. "Maybe you'd rather I'd go someplace else?"

"Ain't noplace else you'd be welcome. Settin' right here is the only two livin' specimens in towns that ain't knuckled under to Gideon Strunk. Hell—have some more coffee."

Final said presently, "I don't remember your face."

"Since your time. Kelly Kramer. The fool that tried to buy into this town." Kramer chuckled. "About as popular as you'll be." He commenced rummaging his shelves. "You lookin' for trouble?"

Final's eyes narrowed.

Kramer waved a hand at him. "That's all you'll find here. Man don't spit in this town without Strunk says so. How about a little belly liner? I got these warmed-over whistleberries that ain't been et yet." Kramer pushed a frypan of beans onto the stove.

"How'd you mean, about trouble?"

"Man's born to trouble." Kramer grinned, and then said slyly, "Gid took a ranch away from you once. Might get the idea you're here to take it back." He stared at Jim shrewdly.

Final said, "I better shove on."

"You ain't hurtin' my rep none." Kramer's bright eyes watched with his head on one side as though trying to discover something he so far had not found. Now he said, poking the beans, "Man with a printin' press could make a fortune with all these stages gittin' stopped, army

270

payrolls bein' lifted, Injuns layin' around drunk in the gutters. This sure ain't no place for weak hearts!"

"You figure Strunk's provoking it?"

"What I think don't cut no ice."

"Any proof he's monkeying with our red friends?"

"No more'n there's proof he's had a hand in them stickups an' beatin's that's goin' on all the time."

Final said, "How's Taunee's bunch taking it?"

"Son, them Injuns ain't dancin' for exercise. They're gettin' tired of the hind tit—I mean they're proper boilin'!" He thumped the pan against the top of the stove and dug up a tin plate. "If they ever do come outa them rocks these heroes at Grant is goin' to know they been soldierin'. Bandoleer won't be nothin' but a coup stick to broken promises!"

"Who's in charge now at Grant?"

Kramer spat. "Berkley. Stand ten Injuns in a line he couldn't tell one from the other."

Jim remembered the officer, a stiff-necked major who'd been shunted west from Washington for opening his mouth when he should have been listening. He knew every rule and nothing at all from firsthand experience. He was replacing Royal Whitman. Why was it, Jim wondered, that men who understood and were respected by the Apaches were always found to be needed some other place?

He dropped onto a nail keg and, taking on his knees the tin plate Kramer handed him, said, "What's the matter with Strunk?"

The stableman snorted. "He's got this bee up his ass—got to *own* things. Everythin'! Can't abide to have—"

"Does he own this stable?"

"Stable don't count. Figures I can't hang on much longer anyway."

"Bentain's hung on."

"Ah—" Kramer said, peering down at him. "Bentain."

"I'm talking about the owner of Skillet."

"Yeah. He's back in the brush with what's left of his outfit."

Jim remembered the Governor's words. "What's happened to him? He was the biggest man in this country."

"That was some while ago. Three years can be long as forever sometimes. You oughta know. As for what's happened to him—"

Boots scraped sound from the planks outside. Someone hammered the door with a testy impatience. Kramer pulled it open and a leather-cheeked man shoved him out of the way, moving in with drawn pistol, three also-armed others pressing close on his heels. "Your name Final?"

Jim eyed the badge and, nodding, picked up his fork.

The brawny star packer knocked the tin plate off Jim's lap and yanked him erect with a fistful of brush jacket. "When I talk I aim to hev a man's full attention! What're you doin' with that gun in your pants?"

No one had to tell Jim this fellow came from Strunk. Kelly, looking nervous, shook his head behind the marshal's shoulder.

The marshal slammed Final across the face with his pistol, this ungiving impact spinning Jim sideways. Trying to stay on his feet, half blinded and bloody, the backs of Jim's knees hit the keg, heavily throwing him.

The marshal kicked Final's gun loose. He said, standing over him, "You'll pack no iron in this town!" and backed off a little then, left-handedly motioning Kramer forward. "Hand me that sixshooter."

The stableman, bending, tried to warn Jim with his eyes. He was afraid in Jim's condition the former Skillet ramrod might get himself killed. He knew this marshal, a bootlicking bully that, before Strunk's rise to power, had swamped and run errands at the gambler's Hall of Mirrors. Though Kramer hadn't known the marshal in those days he'd had plenty of opportunity to figure him out since.

Stepping back now, straightening, Kramer handed over Final's pistol. The marshal thrust it into his belt. "I'll give you some advice," he told the man on the floor. "Get out an' keep goin'. I won't tell you again."

Final, pushing himself up, got dizzily onto his feet. His mind bitterly told him to let well enough alone, but this bullypuss treatment on top of everything else was more than he could stomach. He hunted the badge packer through the fog pain put around him.

"He's gone, if it's Dawks you're lookin' for," Kramer told him, guiding Jim over to the edge of the bunk. "You better set—"

"He got a handle?"

"Dawks. Seeb Dawks." Kramer looked worried when he saw the black fury that was in Final's stare. "Lord God," he cried, paling, "don't tangle with that guy! He's a sure-enough killer—plumb cultus!"

"How'd he get to be marshal?"

"Like everyone else gits their jobs around here. Strunk give it to him."

"What about the town council?"

"Some more of Strunk's understrappers." Kramer picked up the bent plate and, scooping up Jim's spilled supper, scrinched his jowls up more than ever. "Look— set down till I fix your face—" He pawed at his whiskers and, mumbling back of them, tramped over to the desk. The stuff in the bottle he came back with considerably resembled indelible ink. He poured some onto a swab and dragged it across the gash. Final swore, lifted onto his toes by the pain. "Any way," Kramer said, it'll keep the flies down. You're lucky to be above ground. Damn lucky."

Final rasped spread hands across the legs of his levis. "Got a gun I can borrow?"

"Gun!" The stableman reared back like a snake had struck at him.

Final eyed him disgustedly. "What's eating you now?"

"You don't want no damn gun—"

"I'll need a horse too." Final said gruffly: "I'm heading for Skillet."

Kramer said testily, "Why don't you just shove your head in a noose! By grannies—"

"You don't think I'll take this lying down, do you?"

5 MAD SPRINGS

Walking Wolf was a stream gurgling two hours north and Jim Final reached it without untoward incident. Twelve miles west, if memory were reliable, this water crossed Fish Creek before dropping into the quivering blue of Canyon Lake. Bentain's home was a bit northwest of that crossing and some ten miles southwest of Apache Lake.

The wind was down now but what light the stars gave did little to help Jim spot half forgotten landmarks. Time, he found, had tricked him and he'd come out west of the ford where rock slants were too steep to let him down to the water. He was forced to swing east, all the while keeping his eyes peeled on the chance Strunk and Dawks may have readied a surprise for him. Strunk probably wouldn't risk moving into the brush to get rid of him, but if the man was half big as folks thought he was he had plenty of guns he could put into the field. Not knowing Jim's status he might hold off for a bit but a man couldn't count on this. Something big was in the wind around here. No doubt about it. Strunk evidently had the buffalo sign on everyone. It was a measure of the man's strength and the gains he had consolidated that Joe Bob, instead of moving against him openly, was forced to depend on a man he'd got out of prison.

Jim found his crossing and, after letting the mare blow, pushed on to the farther-shore. This was Taunee's domain, a part of the reservation which housed the Mad Springs Apaches. Disquieting thoughts of Joe Bob kept gnawing at Jim. What lay between the man and Bentain that he would go to such lengths to pull him out of a jackpot? Or was it the prospect of trouble from the tribe which had brought the Governor into this?

None of Jim's thinking seemed to make any sense. He could understand the Governor wanting to keep his job, it must be worth a good many thousands of dollars a year to him; but was that the whole reason?

The wind got up again. Jim was following the creek west toward Bentain's when he suddenly pulled up, face to face with a new thought. Strunk had wanted him out of town; Strunk's killer-marshal had ordered him out and he'd gone, never thinking to ask himself why.

He gripped the saddle with a tightening fist and wished he'd thought to get a rifle from Kramer. He had the sixshooter the stableman had loaned him but, considering what was shaping up in his mind, he'd have felt a lot more adequate toting something with a little greater reach. It was barely possible Strunk could not afford to have Jim Final loose around here, that in some incomprehensible way it ruined the man's plans. Incredible Jim could stumble onto information which made it imperative he be killed or disappear at the earliest moment; and yet— Sight of him had certainly given Strunk a bitter jolt. Beneath the man's sneering words there'd been fright, or at any rate fury.

Final's thoughts switched back to the Indians. According to Kramer they were stirred up for sure. According to Joe Bob, Strunk wanted them on the warpath. How could Strunk manage this swifter than by provoking the authorities to some further injustice? Eyes thinning, Final nodded. Someplace between town and Bentain's headquarters some of the gambler's outfit could be setting up an ambush.

Jim thought about that and, deciding to take no chances, pointed the mare north. It was better to be sure than to wish he had. Holding the mare to a cautious walk he caught some three miles later the muffled beat of hurrying hoofs and put her into a tangle of mesquite before the unseen riders could discover him.

Peering out of the thicket a few moments later he watched four horsemen cut his trail on a tangent, pushing their horses northwest toward Bentain's.

When they had passed out of hearing he pointed the mare southwest, grimly walking her. He planned now to pick up the Walking Wolf again and follow as long as its brushed banks might serve him; but he ran into more riders before he could reach it and was forced back into the north, really worried.

This bunch detected him and guns started banging even though he felt certain they couldn't know his identity. He put the mare into a hard run and, resorting to guile, finally lost them. But these wastes tonight were acrawl with riders; some of them were almost certain to be hunting him.

He was deep into the reservation now, quartering through a maze of wart-shaped hills and the ravines which ran between them. Ten years ago this region had been considered worthless. Not laying right to catch or hold water, it was too dry even to grow decent grass. Now with little else available there was, according to the Governor, considerable agitation on the part of Strunk's grangers and other late arrivals to have it thrown open. But why would Strunk, now one of the biggest cowmen, ally himself with a class of people who were anathema to folks who made their living off the grass?

He stopped, shocked motionless, ringed by dim shapes. "Where you go?"

Dealing with Apaches a man couldn't afford to get excited or show fear. There was no possibility of escape. Final said grimly, "Mad Springs."

Silence held for several moments. The spokesman said nastily, "Mad Springs that way!" and, thrusting a hand out, pointed behind Jim. The group closed in. A short and stocky man in skin leggings grunted, "What you do on reservation?"

Final took too long. The one in the leggings leaned toward him arrogantly. "You got whusky?"

Jim shook his head. "White Father—"

"White Father make heap wind!" The whole outfit looked at him scornfully. Now the stocky one said, "Why you go to Mad Springs?"

Jim pulled himself straighter. "Me talk with Chief."

"All white mens talk with crooked tongue." The hair of this one was chopped off at the ears. The tails of a dark wool shirt that looked like Cavalry flapped about his breechclout. A hand darted out. "Gimme fire stick."

"Gimme coat!" cried another, pressing forward.

Jim's Dad had been respected by this tribe, had been on visiting terms with Taunee—about as close as any white man, not adopted, could get with an Apache. But Taunee wasn't in this group and Jim knew how little it could take to set them off; yet he had to try. Kramer's pistol was inside his jacket but before he could get at the buttons they were onto him. He kicked one in the chest, heard the fellow grunt, but this was the only forceful blow he struck. Hands sprang from everywhere. In a matter of moments they had him flat on the ground.

The man who had wanted the jacket pulled a knife. The stocky Apache knocked it out of his hand. They hashed up a racket of furious gutturals. The stocky Apache barked loudest and won. He pitched the coat into the snarling pack, interlarding his lingo with threatening flourishes of Kramer's big pistol. They dumped Jim across the saddle and tied him. The man with the pistol caught hold of the mare's bridle and struck off at a trot, the rest following.

The white blaze of the sun was peering over Dog Mountain when they sighted Mad Springs. The mare was dark with sweat but the Apaches weren't even expanding their chests.

Taunee's headquarters was a village of some size, totaling upwards of sixty *wickiups*—pole houses covered with grass and deerskins. A pack of mongrelly dogs came yapping and naked children ran screaming after them as the stocky Apache made the most of his big moment.

An old man sucking a pipe stared after them and squaws looked up from their various occupations. The man with Kramer's pistol seemed not to notice this rising clamor. The little ones spat and shouted insults. Two or three of them picked up rocks but the boss Apache drove them back with a snarl. "*Pinda lick-o-yi!*" they screamed, but careful to keep beyond reach of him now. "Kill! Kill! Kill!"

Final, heavily sweating, kept his mouth shut. Everywhere squaws were hard at work, some in a garden patch close by springs which were hidden behind towering cottonwoods and broom. All the faces Jim saw looked hostile.

The boss Apache stopped before the largest dwelling. He growled a few words and an old man came out, impassively listening, abruptly motioning Final off the mare. Two of the Indians untied him and he got stiffly down. Someone led the animal away. The night's chill had fled before the heat of the sun. Jim wondered if Taunee remembered him.

The Apaches, watchful, were silent now. Several potbellied urchins sidled up in their nakedness. It was plain to Jim whites had worn out their welcome.

The short Apache with the chopped-off hair abruptly spoke too swift for Final to follow, though he was familiar enough with their lingo to catch scattered fragments. The old chief nodded and scratched himself and asked the short one, who appeared to be called Chuleh, what he wanted to do with this White Eyes. After Chuleh had concluded a long-winded harangue embellished with gestures the old man, addressing Final in English, said, "I am Taunee, the chief of this people. I have tried to be friends with the Americans. When Cochise and others in the days of our fathers paint themselves against the White Eyes my warriors work their fields.

"Taunee's heart is sad. The Americans are many and he cannot understand them. How can one believe them? They say that we are brothers yet fight with us as enemies, even though we are at peace."

"If we cannot know we are at peace," the stocky Chuleh rasped, "is it not better to be sure we are at war?" His angry eyes skewered Jim. "Why you here? What you do on reservation?"

Final, uncomfortably aware of his gun-torn cheek, said nothing. Chuleh barked gutturally at the men who stood about them. "War paint!" he snarled, accusingly pointing at the purple stuff Kramer had daubed on Jim.

Final watched Taunee. The chief had greatly aged. His steel-gray hair, like Chuleh's, had been cropped, though it reached almost to his shoulders that looked bonier now, more bent than Jim remembered. The dark face was a network of wrinkles, the plump cheeks of other days drawn closer to the skull. He wore a shirt that had once been white with a beaded collar tightly buttoned. The tails were stuffed into beltless store pants whose lower legs were hidden by crinkled leather leggings. An uncreased straw sombrero was set squarely on his head and a Navajo blanket was folded over his left arm. "Speak," he ordered Final.

"Enemies seek my life," Jim said. "I was hoping to hide behind the shadow of Taunee."

"Lies!" Chuleh shouted. "He was alone. None came after him!"

Final eyed the cartridge belt with its enormous silver buckle that was strapped about the chief's emaciated hips. Jim looked at the man. "You knew my father. We have shared meat."

No change, no flicker of remembrance disturbed the crevices and canyons of the old man's tight-lipped countenance. "He was your friend," Jim said.

"Taunee has no friends. His heart is sick for the wrongs done his people. I think pretty soon we leave this place maybe."

Final's hope fell away. But he drew himself up. "I came as a friend. Now I go," he said.

The old man said, "Go how?" and some of the bucks around them laughed.

"The Long Knives will be very angry."

"They are all the time angry," Chuleh said, and spat. "When the young men get rifles all the soldiers will be dead, I think." He shoved Final roughly. Before Jim could regain his balance two other Apaches caught hold of his arms.

6 HIRED KILLER

The Tucson stage was late again and Strunk, feeding his outrage with the intolerance hoarded for anything which opposed him, furiously cursed the undependability of Butterfield's service. Bill Tapp, who ramrodded the gambler's ranch crew, dug a brassy looking turnip from his vest and declaimed, "Can't never figure what them gut eaters'll do. Chances are—" He let the words trail off. Stuffing the watch back into his pocket he went over to the halfleaf doors of Strunk's ornate Hall of Mirrors, stepping partially through to peer down the street in the direction of the mountains.

"Any sign?" the gambler called.

Tapp, who was stoop-shouldered and wore Texas bullhide chaps even when he went to bed, shook his head. Having those drum beaters take care of Final had been Strunk's inspiration, not his. Tapp had one golden rule which had never let him down—*when you want things done right do it yourself.* His boys had hazed Final into the hands of Chuleh's paleface haters but they still didn't know if this had cooked Jim's goose or not.

Strunk called irritably, "What time is it now?"

Tapp had to have another look before answering. "Ten after."

"Ten after eleven and it was due at ten-fifteen!"

"No use flappin' your fists about it. If there ain't nothin' happened it'll git here. If there has you'll have to find another deuce. Wasn't no sense in sendin' outside anyway."

Strunk went back to the bar and tossed off another drink. "If you had sense enough to see through a knothole you wouldn't be working for what you get out of me."

Tapp pulled up his head and sucked wind but Strunk chopped a hand through the air and Tapp stayed put. This, with Gid Strunk, meant the subject was closed.

The ramrod's cheeks turned a mottled roan. Behind the bar the apron industriously began to polish glasses.

Nursing another drink the gambler considered his reflection in the mirror. Tapp in his own job was admirable. Big and surly, prone to err on the side of violence, he was utterly loyal. He'd been a two-bit rustler nibbling the fringes of Basin beef when Strunk had dealt him in as Squatting O boss. That ranch was Tapp's life; he was proud of what with other spreads he had made of it, and this pride he'd instilled into every man working there. A hardcase crew. This was why he didn't like what Strunk was doing now. There was no situation in Tapp's experience that Squatting O, given the chance, couldn't handle.

But this was different. Final had been sent up for ten years, yet he was loose and back at the end of three. That didn't make sense without the Governor was into it. Bentain had probably yowled for help but he couldn't have got Final without Joe Bob being party to it someplace. Was the Governor putting up the lease money which had let Bentain get onto the reservation? By God, that tied!

Strunk wondered he hadn't thought of this before. With Tapp's hardcase crew he had been hammering unmercifully at Skillet for months and yet Bentain hadn't collapsed. He had lost enough cows and land to ruin him twice over yet was still afloat, hiring grass from Taunee over the sub-chief's protests. That sonofabitchin Joe Bob!

But there was lease money due right now, Strunk remembered. If the Governor was backing Bentain why hadn't he sent it? Still nursing his drink the gambler turned this over, finally nodding. That was Joe Bob for you, slippery as slobbers, never letting the left hand know what the right hand did. The dollar-hungry bastard! Someway he must have got onto Strunk's ace—why else would he have bought into Skillet? Why else would he have been keeping it so quiet? So now, instead of the lease money, he'd sent Jim Final in to check up. Final—the man Strunk had put behind bars!

Strunk downed his drink and poured another stiff one. He'd been right in thinking Final dangerous if, on top of the man's own grudge, Jim had the Governor's go sign! The man was here to start trouble, to get him off Bentain—to sidetrack or wreck completely everything Strunk hoped to accomplish. Jim Final had to go, and quick; but in a way that couldn't pin what happened to him on Strunk. This was more essential now than it had been before. So he'd been right in keeping Tapp out of this. When a man found himself up against Joe Bob he had damn well better keep his nose clean.

Tapp said, "I'm goin' out an' catch a breath of air."

The gambler shrugged, finished his drink and ran a finger around the inside of his collar. The rise in the temperature from last night's 40 was enough to melt the hinges. By God, he wasn't licked yet! Joe Bob wasn't putting money into that lease without some pretty tough strings on it, but Strunk would take care of that when they got to it. Joe Bob, setting in on a land steal, was in no position to heave many bricks. Bentain was wrapped up and everything else was going like clockwork. The only shaky timber in this whole deal was Final and if those Apaches didn't take care of him this fellow, Roup, would. "Wait," Strunk called, "I'll go with you." By the time Joe Bob got another man in here it would be too late for the Governor to interfere.

They went out on the porch. They watched a rig go

by with a couple of johnny-come-latelies who were convinced, once they got the land, they could farm what was now given over to bunch grass and cactus. Strunk lifted a hand, glad to encourage them, not showing the contempt he shared with Bill Tapp. Those fellows were fools but he could use a good many in the plans he had shaped for taking over this country.

Tapp's sudden nudge fetched his face around. A buckboard was coming down the street behind a team of blooded bays that weren't half as pleasing to look at as the girl whose slim hands held the gathered lines. Though somewhat short for Strunk's complete admiration she was certainly exciting; and being away to that school in the East had given her a style Strunk liked in his women.

She looked sixteen though she was closer to twenty; lithe, full bodied, the sort to whet a man's hunger with that bright red-gold hair and those kiss-me-quick eyes behind the cool sheen of her sand-colored lashes.

Strunk watched her swing in and pull up to the front of Rankin's Emporium. Tugging his silk tie to a more rakish angle he struck off across the road's smoky dust, arriving in time to offer his arm. She barely came to his shoulder but, as with each time they'd met, she quickened his pulses immeasurably.

Extricating her hand she laughed up at him, saying, "And how's the boss gambler of Bandoleer this morning? I hope you aren't still trying to put Father out of business."

"Oh, nothing like that, Miz Marcia." He looked at her boldly. "Be a sorry day when Gid Strunk tangles with a man that's—"

"Go away with your blarney. Father's so upset he can't even keep his accounts straight." But she laughed as she said it, red lips making a joke of the matter, blue eyes bright with mischief. "You're a very wicked

man and I must go for a fitting quick as I can get this
shopping out of the way."

He found her voice enormously attractive. When she
would have reached for the weight under the seat he
got it for her, snapping its leather shank to the cheekstrap of the nearest horse. "Don't believe all you hear,"
he said gruffly. "Some people just can't help resenting
success in others."

There was pride in the turn of her lips, in the way she
carried herself, in her gestures. The lingering look of her
eyes turned him brash and he said, intently staring,
"How'd you feel if I was to come out some night?"

Something left its dark track across the wheel of her
glance. She said, plainly frightened, "Oh, no—please
don't. Father would never—I can't talk any more."

She whirled and, gathering her skirts, went hastily up
the Emporium's steps. But at the door she glanced back.
Strunk would have sworn those demure eyes invited him.

He stood a bit after she had gone, staring thoughtfully.
He set his hat on his head and recrossed the street.
There was a kind of a swagger in the spring of his walk.

Tapp's surly glance morosely considered him. Strunk
was not even aware of Tapp's existence. Tapp's voice
rudely fetched him back to reality. Strunk peered
around. "What?" he said, staring.

Tapp pointed. "There's your stage."

"By God," Strunk said, "he better be on it!"

Inside Rankin's Emporium Bentain's youngest daughter continued to watch until the gambler moved away,
and even then her eyes went after him while, uncon-
sciously, she gripped her furled parasol more tightly.
Faint spots of color touched her cheeks when she found
herself the object of Jesse Rankin's avid regard. The
storekeeper, a skinny mouse of a man in gallused trousers
and black satin sleeve guards, let out a little squeak as

his horrified stare leaped incredulously past her. "Them crackers," he said scathingly with the look of a snapping turtle, "were put out there to *sell!*"

Two chewing and smirking ranch hands moved reluctantly away from the barrel and anchored their rumps against the edge of a counter. Working through a series of adjustments then the Rankin mouth managed to dredge up a smile. "And what can we do for you, Miz' Marcia?"

She handed him the list of things her father wanted and, on the chance there might be something of interest in dress goods, wandered over to the yardage counter. She prodded bolts and fingered material with a considering faraway expression in her glance. She even toured indifferently through the stack of enveloped patterns. But the prowl of her thoughts shuttled around Gideon Strunk and the things she had glimpsed behind his brazen stare.

Strunk was very much a man of the world—that gay, fashionable world she had forsaken in departing the Misses Botkins' Academy. He might not, strictly speaking, be a gentleman but he certainly had the looks and ginger. There was a smoldering impetuosity about him, a kind of dark magnetism that made thoughts of him exciting. The bull-voiced Rockabye, by comparison, wasn't even worth remembering. She pushed the Bentain segundo out of her mind in conjectures as to how far the gambler dare to go, creating images from the promise his boldness foreshadowed, a bit fearful yet nervously wondering if he had grasped the implications of her final glance.

Heat stole upward along the curves of her thighs and, preening herself in the visions evoked, she forgot everything else, a part of her glorying in the wrongness of her thoughts, in the perverseness of conjuring such inordinate

delight from the prospective attention of a man so
savagely bent on ruining her father.

Lifting her head she glanced about her covertly, blush-
ing a little when she found herself the focus of the recent
culprits of the cracker barrel and the continuing lecherous
stare of old Rankin. Disengaging her regard she pretended
engrossment in the picked-over patterns. *Oh, I'm bad—
really bad! What makes me do these terrible things?*

She felt genuine shame, shuddering in revulsion—but
not too bitterly, not too long. Following the storekeeper
out to the buckboard with the purchase he'd gathered
she felt a stab of disappointment that the gambler was not
still waiting. But even this was vagrant, passing. She went
to her fitting in the comforting conviction he would
make the opportunity to see how far she'd let him go.

Strunk, in the shimmer and shine of his establishment,
was privily closeted with Tapp and the new man, important behind whisky and rolling a fresh cigar across
his gold-capped teeth.

In a community of big men the gambler had the aplomb
of a banker, a yellow haired man with long curling burn-
sides, immaculately groomed and flamboyantly attired.

"We settled the price, Roup, before you left Tonopah."

The new fellow shrugged. "The price has gone up,"
he said with a grin. "I did a spot of checking after you
got in touch with me. Planting a john that was let out of
Yuma seven years short of the stretch he went in for is
the kind of a job that calls for a bonus. Get someone
else if that's not agreeable."

The man was no fool, nor was Strunk. The gambler
said, keeping his reservations well buried, "We'll let it
ride, but there's to be no doubt whose bullet slaps him.
And if somebody else gets the job done ahead of you
don't expect any more than the thousand I promised."

"Fair enough," Roup said. "I'll take it now."

287

Strunk shrugged and got up and went over to his safe. Returning, he pushed a sheaf of currency across the table, watching the gun fighter count and pocket it. Under a black Texas hat the killer had the narrow wedge-shaped face of a rat. He was built like a keg of powder on stilts and looked as explosive with his cat's yellow stare. He was the best Strunk had been able to catch on short notice but good enough, the gambler thought, if half the stories he had heard were true.

"When you want this done?"

"Sooner the better. Get hold of a horse and go out there to Skillet. That's where you'll find him if he's still taking nourishment. When the job's done you hike."

The gun fighter, grinning, stood up. "I'll hike when I've got that bonus."

"Pick it up at Stegner's livery. Don't come into my place again."

"How do I get it?"

"Just tell the old man you've come after the package he's holding for Skillet. And don't get your horse there."

Tapp said when Roup left, "I wouldn't trust that varmint any further'n I could throw him."

It wasn't just that Strunk wanted Indian land, he wanted those parts of it that Bentain had leased. Bentain had to go as certainly as Final, and if Chuleh's Apaches didn't get him Gid had laid fuse to a trick that would. He winked at Tapp expansively. "Just extra insurance—"

"You'll copper no bets with that bird."

Before Strunk could answer someone scratched on the door. Not the one letting into the bar which Roup had just left by but one giving onto the dive's back alley. Tapp, going over, unbarred it after catching Strunk's nod.

The man who came in was a blanket wrapped Apache. A single feather pointed roofward from the crow's-wing shine of the cloth bound hair. He'd been told never to come to this place after sun-up but the gambler, smothering his irritations, handed the man a fat cigar.

He struck a match and held it out, afterwards lighting another for himself. "I've been pretty busy. That whisky will be out there tomorrow."

7 APACHE JUSTICE

The *wickiup* in which Jim Final was left contained nothing but a lousy buffalo robe so ingrained with dirt it lay as flat to the ground as a last year's leaf. Jim's eyes briefly sharpened when he discovered that one of the hides stretched over these poles had come from a cow, and he stared a long while at the brand without moving.

There was no good in thinking but he could not avoid it. The old chief's words, his refusal to recognize Jim, looked bad. The Taunee Jim remembered had been a kindly man, a leader of long vision coupled with considerable forebearance. The chief had endured over many things which, in another, might have put this people on the warpath. Much indeed must have happened to have altered the man's fundamental beliefs.

The obligations of a friend had been ignored. Had anything else been needed to show Jim how the wind blew he had it in the Skillet mark on that hide, the brand of Bentain who leased grazing rights from this tribe. It looked as though Kramer had called the turn. These Mad Springs Apaches were getting ready for war.

Several parties of riders came and departed while the sun climbed higher and added the burden of heat to Jim's misery. They had not tied him, this being Chuleh's idea of humor. "White man no run far without clothes."

He was eventually fed a gourd of loud-smelling stew which he somehow got down despite suspicions about its ancestry. He wasn't able to sleep.

With dark the drums began to throb. In the creep of apprehension Final bleakly stared at the fires that glowed like cat's eyes through the blue-black carpet of the deepening night. He dug out of memory everything he had heard about men getting away from Indians without finding anything that promised a shred of help. Naked and afoot there was no place he could reach before pursuit caught up with him. He could not steal a horse from the herd with all those miserable curs running loose.

There was a ring of silent squaws about his prison, discernible when someone threw more wood on the nearest fire. He'd as soon be roasted as find himself caught up by them.

He must eventually have dozed. Roughly prodded awake he was yanked to his feet and pushed through the doorhole where he fell and was again hauled erect by waiting hands.

There was no talk. He was hustled to Taunee's *wickiup*. It was easily the largest, eighteen feet from wall to wall. The fire burning at its center lit up the ring of angry faces and patterned the hides with leaping shadows.

"This is the one!" Chuleh cried, letting go of his blanket to describe Final's capture. "He was on the fire-water trail—"

Low growls welled out of that ring of gleaming bodies as another of these head men ennumerated the evils of the white man's whisky and the folly of those who would sell their wives to obtain it. "If this White Eyes had no whisky," said another, "what was he doing there?"

"Let him speak," Taunee said.

It had been long since Final had conversed in their

language. His tongue stumbled rustily as he recalled his father and himself to these men. They had not searched, he said, for the yellow iron. More than just a few times when food was scarce they had driven cows to Mad Springs—

Chuleh waving his arms let out an explosive grunt. He sprang onto his feet and declared contemptuously, "These things of the past are as prattle of old women. Let him say what he was doing here!"

"I understood," Jim said, "the grass was leased to Bentain."

"What has that to do with you?" Chuleh pointed an accusing finger. "Did you not give your father's house to the Devil Man? Let your words walk straight."

"They walk straight. Many moons have I been in the white man's prison because of this one who has my father's house. Bad things have come to pass and the governor, *Nantan* Joe Bob, is sick at heart for his friends the Apaches and for his brother Bentain whose cows and grass have been swallowed by this man of many mirrors. 'Go to the chief,' *Nantan* Joe Bob says, 'and find the truth of what is done that I may right these continued wrongs.'"

Chuleh spat on the ground between Jim's feet. Distrust and suspicion were like hands reaching for him and the actual truth would not help him here. *Stop Strunk*, Joe Bob had told him, and certainly Strunk was stirring up something; but these people were too involved to understand their part in the gambler's schemes if indeed that part was as Joe Bob had indicated. Strunk, by the Governor's say-so, was out to get their lands away from them and figured to do this by prodding them into retributive action, into atrocities which would bring in the soldiers. Then, presumably, the grangers he'd brought in would put up a howl to have these lands thrown open to settlement and, as a punitive measure, the Indians would be moved.

The possibility was not far-fetched. Jim could see any number of ways by which Strunk's goal could be reached if this was what Strunk was after; but where did this tie in with Bentain? Sure, Joe Bob had said Bentain would be the first to be hit if these Apaches took to the warpath; and Strunk, by all tell, was after Bentain. But how could you put all this into words that would make any sense to this primitive people? Perhaps he'd lived with hate of Strunk for so long he couldn't get things clear in his own head—but one thing was certain, providing he lived. Unless Jim stopped Strunk he'd be hauled back to Yuma to serve out the rest of his suspended sentence.

Taunee was haranguing the council of under-chiefs: "In the beginning we were at peace. When the White Eyes came we shared our lands and hunting. Our hearts were glad, but the white man speaks with a crooked tongue. He hides the truth with pretty words. His treaties, made forever, last no longer than a summer frost. If a white man kills one of the people their head men do not see this wrong, but when the people kill a White Eyes bad trouble comes heap pronto.

"In friendship Juan Jose was killed, the great chief of all Apaches. Mangas Colorado is also dead for these pretty words. Some of our people paint their faces but always the Mad Springs Apaches remain in their place along the little river, weaving their baskets, harvesting their corn and pumpkins, still at peace with the White Eyes. Not even bad Mexicans would they fight because Taunee knows that to fight is to perish.

"To preserve that peace we moved to the worthless country high in the barren mountains where Rurales dared not follow. But there are bad Apaches too and some, I think, who are only desperate. These make war and soldiers put up many log fences and say all Apaches must live in these places."

He looked around at the silent faces. "Cochise say 'Do not fight unless you can win.' Paramuca felt as I do that the White Eyes are many as the torches Great Spirit waves in the night. Taunee and Paramuca make new treaty with paleface soldiers but Paramuca is killed by the Long Knives when he comes to put mark on paper.

"We are much concerned. Santo, Chuleh, many others of this Council urge me to avenge Paramuca but I know that for every soldier my people kill two others will come—maybe three or three times three. It is better to move. But afterwards we have no corn. Roots and bark are no defense against the cold and the Americans have driven all the game away. Many of the people die. So we make again a paper, this time with *Nantan* Whitman who has Long Knives at Camp Grant."

Again the old chief paused to scan those gleaming faces. Jim had heard all this before, this father had seen it happen.

"Whitman," Taunee said, "did not speak with forked tongue but he was only a little chief with many other chiefs over him. He call big powwow and the people come in, sixty warriors—all the rest squaws and papooses. Smoke pipe. Whitman our friend, give us meat. The buffalo was gone and we had no horses. Whitman say he cannot make peace that would last until rains wear away the great rock, only a little peace, but we returned to our homes in the Canyon, rebuilt our *wickiups* and got to our planting."

The others grunted but Chuleh glared with fury and would not open his mouth.

"A good time," Taunee said. "Others of our people came from the hills until our number reached five hundred. In the time of the Corn Dance *Nantan* send for me. 'Bring your people. I make big feast on second sun.'

"But the Chiricahua Apaches are still at war because of that bad one, Bascom.* And the Pinal Apaches are painting their faces because of what was done at Bloody Basins. At Tucson there are people who wanted our Canyon land for themselves, bronco Americans and Mexicans; and Pinal Apaches raid the Missions San Xavier, taking four ponies and six cows. One paleface dies and a great cry goes up.

"*Nantan* Whitman told his general we have nothing to do with this thing of San Xavier but the Tucson people would not listen. A great army of Americans, Papagos and Mexicans come without warning and fall upon us. Children and women clubbed to death, twenty-eight little ones taken. One hundred eighteen from our village die—eight men only.

"*Nantan* came too late. But he give us meat and, because he is our friend, we agree to come back and rebuild our homes. Our hearts are sick. 'The peace you have promise,' I tell *Nantan*, 'is twice broken by your people.' Whitman say we must live on reservation where pony soldiers will be guard for us. Taunee not like but he agree for it is better to be at peace than dead. But we are fooled again by pretty words."

A growl ran through the sweaty shapes like wind going through a field of grain. Taunee's voice changed, became more guttural, his eyes were like bright beads of glass. "Whitman say this our place forever but when

---

* Lieut. George M. Bascom (October 1860) ostensibly in an attempt to recover the kidnaped Ward boy, invited Cochise under a flag of truce to come in and discuss the matter. Cochise, accompanied by several lesser chiefs, came in and Bascom accused him of the kidnaping which the chief denied. Bascom, treating Cochise badly, imprisoned him there and them.

we are here a new man comes, *Nantan* Berkley," he said and spat. "To this one we are dogs—beggar dogs. When we go to the town we are beaten and kicked. If we raise our hands we are killed with the fire sticks which bark many times. Now they wish to take this place away from us—even Bentain, I think, who has not paid the lease money he promised. There is too much firewater. When because of this our young men do a badness all are blamed."

In the stillness after the chief sat down the burning wood made loud bursts of sound. There was no room for doubt in Jim's mind now; inevitably they would elect for war. Taunee would go along with this or the tribe would split.

The coals gleamed like hot metal. A kind of moaning swept the circle. Chuleh leaped up, brandishing his hatchet. "It is better to die than live without honor!"

"*Enju!*" they cried. "Death to the palefaces!"

Outside in the blackness others took up the shout. Chuleh barked at Final's guards and flung them a rope. Jim's arms were seized and jerked behind him, bound over a stick placed against his back. Chuleh barked again and Jim was dragged from the *wickiup*, roughly shoved toward one of the cottonwoods which grew about the springs. To this he was tethered with damp rawhide thongs. Jim guessed what was now to transpire. In drying those rawhide thongs would shrink. Chuleh had denied him even the honor of being roasted.

It was this, Jim guessed, which rasped the worst. Yet he reckoned he had it coming. Strunk had outguessed him every step of the way, pushing him right into Chuleh's hands. But it was hard, bitter hard, to realize he was himself to become one of the atrocities, a penciled statistic, which must help to bring about the very thing he'd been turned loose to stop. Jim had held the gambler too lightly, thinking him dependent on ambush when all the while the shadow shapes of Strunk's riders had moved him at will.

What now of Quail and Skillet and the Governor's mission and these redmen whose recited wrongs went back clear past the day of his birth? Strunk would have his way for who would be left to stop him now? Not these Indians—they were his dupes. Never the law because Strunk, in this country, was the law. Not those grangers —he had tricked them too.

Final raged and strained in a fury of desperation, but without avail. He couldn't get enough leeway with that stick at his back to bring any pressure against the damp rawhide which bound him to the tree and even now was grimly tightening. He would have perhaps a handful of hours to go crazy with thinking before his bones began snapping under these thongs' inexorable pressure.

Time went to sleep on its feet, but not Jim.

He watched the wheel of the winking stars, picturing Quail and, more bitterly, Strunk.

No sound alerted him yet suddenly he was rigidly listening, each hair on end, each muscle tensed, knowing he was no longer alone in this grove.

8 A GIRL NAMED QUAIL

Holding the cigar squarely set in his mouth Strunk's visitor produced considerable smoke. "No come about whusky. Come about rifles."

"You'll get them," Strunk said.

"Chuleh say 'wantum now.'"

"That wasn't the deal. Pretty soon, tell Chuleh. That's the best I can do."

The dark face stared unfathomably. The cigar was

fitted into it again and smoke signals climbed above the black eyes. "Squaw hungry. Need beef."

"I'll have the boys drive some over." The gambler sat back and then, aware of Tapp's regard, said casually, "What did Chuleh do about that fellow we chased over there?"

"Chuleh ketchum. Tie um up."

The Apache grinned.

Strunk grinned, too. "Pretty soon kill, eh?"

The Apache puffed, putting a gray fog about him. He put so much of himself into the task the shortening weed became too hot and he suddenly let go of it, setting a moccasined heel on the thing, grinding it into the gambler's carpet.

Strunk, in an excess of good humor now, handed the worrisome guest another. The Indian sniffed suspiciously. He broke it up then and stuffed it into his mouth, pleasurably grinding it into a cud around which he said, "White man heap lucky."

Strunk, taking this as a compliment, chuckled. But Tapp said, "What's the meanin' of that?"

"Chief turnum loose," One Feather said, and departed.

Strunk, after the door slammed behind him, was so thrown out of countenance he took some papers he'd been fingering clear out of his pocket before, catching himself, he quickly concealed them. "Well," Tapp grimaced, as though totally ignorant of assayer's symbols, "looks like you'll have to use Roup after all. Kind of too bad, everythin' considered, we got to shore up the deal with that breed of riffraff."

The gambler glared. Tapp tossed it right back with a belligerent truculence Strunk wouldn't have taken from anyone else. He said with great patience, "If I let you go after him I'd have to get rid of you. We've got to handle this right or the whole thing blows up."

"What's the matter with Cretch?" Cretch was one of the gambler's straw bosses.

"I've told you. We can't *none of us* afford to be traceably connected."

"You got a man planted out there who won't be connected."

Strunk's long face narrowed thoughtfully. "Rockabye?"

"Why not?"

Strunk pushed the idea around and halfway like it. Rockabye had his old job back as ramrod of Skillet. He'd go for it, probably, remembering how Final had been put over him before. And there was no connection, either known or suspected, between himself and Rockabye. The gambler grudgingly admitted the shrewdness of the suggestion, but he had a long-saved use for Rockabye just now and Bentain's crew boss with his cross-grained vanity was a hard man to handle by remote control. Strunk didn't want any ropes snarled.

"I'll think about it," he grunted, and stubbed out his smoke. "Tonight have the boys move some more of Bentain's beef—"

A diffident knock crept through the back door and, no one having thought to bar it after the Indian, Seeb Dawks slipped in looking solemn as Moses handing down the stone tablets. Strunk waved him carelessly over to a chair on which the marshal perched gingerly, balancing his derby on the knobs of his knees.

Seen without its bonnet Dawks' leather-cheeked face lost much of its authority. The varnished gleam of too-thin hair meticulously arranged from a part in the center appeared more to belong on a mixer of drinks than one engaged in dispensing frontier justice—even Strunk's kind. But Seeb knew his place and waited in unshakeable patience for the great man to get around to him.

The gambler finally looked at his watch and frowned. "That deal," he said to the marshal, "fell through."

Dawks stared at the crown of his hat and said nothing. Tapp, scornfully eyeing him, said, "If Final's afoot—"

"He won't be," Strunk growled. "By this time he's probably holed up out at Skillet, getting all set to shove a wrench in the works. I'll drop out there tomorrow and—"

Tapp said dryly, "Think that's smart?"

They were talking over Dawks' head but he couldn't help seeing the hard looks they were exchanging. One of these times Tapp would go too far and a ramrod's job would be looking around for a likely applicant.

"Final," Strunk snarled, "won't be staying at Skillet. No amount of hot air is going to smooth over Bentain stayin' away from that trial. Seeb—" he glared around— "put on a couple more deputies; when I step out of this place I want to know they're around."

Tapp, still sticking with the main issue, said, "That bastard can raise more hell in ten minutes—"

But Strunk chopped a hand down. "Taunee's overplayed his hand, turning Final loose. Strength of that tribe will follow Chuleh now. They're in our hands— we'll get him those rifles. How many boys will you need for that job?"

"I got enough."

"What about ponies? You don't want to use cow horses."

"Don't worry about that. Berkley'll put the blame right where we want it." Tapp shifted his chew and sent a squirt at the cuspidor. "Time we git through rubbin' dirt an' stain on him Cretch will look enough like Chuleh to git into bed with one of his squaws."

Dawks, trying bewilderedly to follow this, said apologetically, "Wouldn't it be simpler to let them Injuns grab them rifles off the wagons theirselfs?"

299

Tapp sneered but Strunk said carefully, "I want this done right. We don't want Berkley bumbling around in it; I want to give him such a fright he's going to have to send for help. Time the government gets around to looking into things, the way I've got it figured, we'll be the only reliable witnesses that's left to tell the story."

Quail saw him first.

She had stepped to the door to shake out a rug and, with an end of it lifted in both upthrust hands, she went rigidly motionless. The fellow was mounted, coming up out of the cedar brakes between the creek's shine and the dark bulk of Horse Mesa. The sun picked out the gleam of naked legs against the white-and-chestnut dapples of the scrawny Indian pony.

She dropped the rug and half turned, startled into putting a hand out for the rifle that, universally these days, stood readily in reach. She stopped with fingers not quite touching it, looking again, more sharply. The man's hair—he was bareheaded—hadn't the look or length of an Indian's. She stared again at those legs and forgot the rifle.

She was tall for a girl, old for an unmarried one, her bones too prominent even where the desert wind pushed against her drab clothing. She had lived all her life on this isolated ranch, imbued with the concepts and a majority of the prejudices common to the relays of dour suspicious men that over the years had accepted Skillet's orders. She wasn't completely convinced, as they'd been, that all live Apaches were necessarily devils, but she knew the same desperations, showed the quiet level-eyed confidence in herself which was the generally accepted hallmark of a hand who had heard the owl hoot.

Much of this dropped away as she stared, one work-roughened hand going up to hold the sun off her face. She could see that the fellow had on a shirt—the cheap

300

fire-colored kind that was stocked by the Agency, but
she couldn't see that he was wearing much else. His
hair had a sandy shade to it now and had been cut on
a bowl. The bare shanks were crisscrossed with marks
from the brush and the shirt showed the signs of rough
passage also. The horse had a rope twisted round its
jaw.

Quail's eyes went wide and were suddenly incredulous.
Her cheeks were the color of the hoof-tracked adobe
when he pulled to a stop scarcely ten feet away with
the horse blowing out a gusty breath. She noticed how
dark with sweat it was, how bitterly bleak was the
rider's stare. "If you were trying to look like an Apache,"
she said, "you should have rubbed mud on those legs and
got enough of that shirt around your head to hide your
hair."

Final dropped off the horse. "Where's the Old Man?"

"He isn't up—he hasn't been well," she cried, redden-
ing, stung to defense by the contempt in Final's look.
She'd been hurt by Jim's failure to answer her letters
and couldn't understand what she saw in him now.
Bitterness, of course, but where was that fairness, that
tolerance she remembered? And his time wasn't up—she
was frightened with the thought of this. She saw the
marks on his wrists and was filled with confusion.

"Fetch him out," Final said. His restless stare swiveled
over the yard. "Where's your crew?"

"Before I answer any more of your questions—"

"I'm not here to swap gab. If you don't want this place
to go up in smoke get Bentain out here and send for
your crew."

There was a driving urgency in the snap of his voice
and the pressure of time swung him toward the corrals.
"I'll want clothes and a gun," he called over his shoulder;
and went into the pen with a rope caught down off a
pole-hung saddle.

After three years away from it his hand lacked much of its former magic but the loop spun true on his second try and a dorsal-striped dun, snared by a forefoot, stopped as though it had come up against a wall.

Final never looked back. He walked down the rope through the churned-up dust and twisted a bight, Indian fashion, around the dun's jaw before shaking off the loop, hauling the horse over dropped bars which he put up. By the time he saw Quail coming out of the house he had the dun saddled. He turned the Indian pony loose and rocked it onto the open range.

The girl came up and held out the clothes. "You can change in the bunkhouse; I'm sending Tom for the crew."

He remembered Tom Connifay, the cook, for his biscuits. 'Saleratus' the boys had called him when they were trying to be especially polite. He said to Quail, "Rockabye still around?"

She bit her lip at the cut of his glance, at the blunt curtness of him and the wall he put between them. Connifay limped from the cook shack strapping a shell belt around his hips. He had no word for Final. "Jim," Quail said, "why didn't you answer my letters?"

Her glance held the awakened puritan passion of the woman he remembered and she still showed the bones. He found it hard to think what color her hair was; mostly it looked brown. Like those too solemn eyes. She wore it severely pulled back from her forehead, twisted into an untidy bun at the back. Her mouth, like the rest of her, looked discouragingly practical. She had never attempted to enhance her appearance as though convinced long ago any leisure she might find could be put to better use. No one had to tell Jim she was all that had kept this damned place going.

Final steeled himself.

"I thought—" she began; and he said with his eyes

like dark pieces of flint, "No use beating a dead dog is there?"

Her hands came slowly to the level of her breasts. There was a lot of character in Quail. Final, remembering, pulled his head around to look at the cook. "Want me to catch one up for you?"

Connifay, with the rope Jim had used, went stony-cheeked past and limped into the pen. Jim's look hardened though he reminded himself the man's attitude was natural. In the old cook's mind Jim was a convicted cow thief. Bentain himself had fostered the man's scorn when he'd publicly washed his hands of Jim by staying away from that trial.

Final picked up his reins. He didn't glance toward Quail nor did he at once climb into leather. The feel of her watching eyes roweled him. Discovering the clothes he stood ridiculously holding he crammed them under an arm and was wheeling to move off when Quail said, "You might at least have let us know you were coming."

"I didn't break out, if that's what you're getting at. Bentain knew I'd be coming; he arranged the whole deal."

She carefully considered his half-turned shape, slowly shaking her head. "You must be mistaken. Dad couldn't believe it when I said you were out here. Jim—" She made a gesture with her hands that was wholly unlike her. "We—we're still engaged, aren't we?"

Final's short laugh held contempt.

Her eyes widened, went dark, but continued to meet that bleak stare without blinking. "Jim, I've prayed every night—"

"I told you once that was finished. Forget it."

"There are some things, Jim, a woman doesn't forget."

"Then she's a fool!" Final snarled, and swung away,

his barefooted stride carrying him over to the bunkhouse.
He went inside, slamming the door.

He pulled off the torn shirt and improvised breech-
clout and got into the clothes he had tossed on a bunk.
He put on the hat and stamped into the boots. These
were some of the things he had left here, the only ones
he had any use for.

Except his rifle. She hadn't fetched that.

When he came out Bentain was beside her. The man
looked twice as old as Jim remembered; the hand the
rancher pushed out trembled. "Good to have you back,
my boy." The false heartiness ran out when Final gave
him·no help. He rubbed the hand against his coat. "It—
it's not like you're thinkin'—"

"What do you know about a jailbird's thoughts?"

When the man's rheumy eyes slid sickly away Final's
stare swiveled around to where the cook sat his horse.
"How long'll it take to get that bunch back here?"

The cook looked at Bentain.

The old man drew a ragged breath and pushed both
hands behind him to hide their uncontrollable trembling.
"Things've changed—" He cleared his throat. "Ain't had
much of a calf crop. We've had to let most of this place
get away—"

"I wasn't asking about that."

Bentain flushed. His watery eyes juned around and
came reluctantly back. "We've only got four men on the
place, countin' Tom here. Two sorry punchers that—"

"Maybe you better hole up in town. I've just been to
Mad Springs. There's almighty apt—" Final stopped
speaking, staring, as a girl came into the open doorway.
Quail, following his gaze, said, "You remember Marcia."

Jim didn't remember anything like this. He recalled
Bentain's youngest as a gangly-legged nuisance in rolled-
up jeans, a mane of rust colored hair and more freckles

to the inch than you'd find holes in a soda cracker. He dragged off his hat.

The only thing she lacked was a parasol. The freckles were gone. Her skin was like ivory, her hair a bright flame. Unruffled, unsmiling, she gave him back look for look. Yet her regard though frank wasn't bold, revealing no more than a girl's natural wonder which she withdrew now, coloring prettily, as Bentain said, "Jim, my dear, used to work on this ranch."

Final's stare toughened up. "Better get her away too. Those Indians are going to get out of hand. May be some on their way."

Bentain managed a shaky laugh. "I can't believe Taunee would—"

"Taunee's not like to have much to say about it. Anyway, these girls ought to mean more to you than what happened to a ramrod that got jugged for stealing cattle."

Some of the whisky floridness fell out of the ruined face. "I—I can—" Bentain's stare pulled away. Marcia's blue-green eyes watched the two men curiously.

Her father made an effort to pull himself together. "I haven't been well," he said, nervously staring past Final at the dust of the departing cook. "Rumors—I seriously doubt if those Apaches will get around to doing more than beat a few drums. Taunee's whole record—"

"Chuleh's the one you're going to be up against."

"Strunk's back of this," Bentain said, his voice shaking. "Strunk and that town crowd and those crazy damn weedbenders! They're trying to get the tribe moved."

"You ever ask yourself why?"

Bentain threw his head back. "Those settlers want land and Strunk is hunting a diversion that'll keep folks busy while he's looting this country."

"And you're still here, thinking that?"

"He ain't runnin' me out!"

"Hear you've got some of that land leased."

"I guess you think I been tradin' 'em whisky. I'll show you—"

Jim, following him into the house, caught hold of him. "Get those girls away from here, man! Can't you realize—"

The rancher shook off Jim's hand, drawing himself up to a pitiful travesty of his former grand manner. "I'll thank you, sir, to let me manage my affairs."

"You're doing real fine. Got that youngest one spoken for?" Jim didn't bother to hide his contempt. "How many ponies you reckon she'll fetch?"

Bentain went livid. "By God, sir, there are limits to what I'll take off you! Bein' engaged to Quail don't—"

"That was all broke off when I took that frame you let Strunk hang onto me. If there's something you've got to show me, get at it; then take those girls and get out of his place."

The damn fool wasn't listening. He'd gone over to a safe and spun the dial and got it open, grumbling under his breath. He twisted about and thrust a paper at Final. "Read that," he snarled, straightening up and shaking it under Jim's nose.

Final skimmed through the stilted phraseology impatiently. "All right. You've got a bona fide lease to Horse Mesa and everything west of its eastern flank, maybe twenty thousand acres. That ain't going to keep. Jesus Christ," he added caustically, "five thousand a year! Where'd you get hold of that kind of money?"

"I'll get it!"

Final stared at the man incredulously. "I should think you'd damn well be fed up with seeing your calf crops go into their bellies."

"They're not stealing my stuff—it's that goddam Strunk!" Bentain shouted. "First thing he done was start workin' on my crew. I damn near went crazy. Money wouldn't move a wheel around here; plenty of grubliners loafin' around but everyone actin' like Skillet was poison. Rockabye an' the cook was all that stuck by me. Last month we managed to sign on these punchers. I *had* to get that grass," he said, glowering. "I figgered gettin' onto the reservation—"

"Why didn't you get in help from outside?"

Bentain dragged a limp hand across his cheeks. "I did. Two was gulched, three was gelded. After that we couldn't get nobody." There were flecks of spittle on his twisted mouth. "You think I sold you out; goddam it, Jim, my hands was tied! Night before your trial I lost three hundred head. I had to think of my girls," he quavered.

"You better think of them now."

"Here—where you goin'?"

"I got to find me a gun. What happened to that repeater I—"

"Rockabye's been usin' it." Bentain dabbed at the shine of his face. "You're not thinkin' straight, Jim. I swear to God—"

"At least I'm not waiting around for those scalp hunters."

Bentain said irritably, "What can they do? Ain't one in ten of them devils got rifles. What few they got is rust-gutted Flintlocks an' mebbe a sprinklin' of Henry percussions."

"Ain't that what Custer said about the Sioux?"

"This ain't no Little Big Horn!"

"No," Final said, "there'll be women and kids in this deal." He struck off down the hall.

Bentain caught up before Jim got to the door. "Long as you're here—"

"You can get that out of your head right now. I wouldn't work again for you if you was the last white alive." Final peered at him bitterly. "That what inspired you to get me out?"

"Honest, Jim, I was meanin' to." Bentain's eyes slewed away. He saw the futility, the uselessness of words. He scowled, half turned, and then swung back. "I hadn't anythin' to do with gettin' you out."

Final stared at the man knowing at last that he was hearing the truth.

"Company coming," Quail called from the yard.

9 HARD CHOICE

With doom, like a Damocles sword, waving over him, it seemed incredible to Final Bentain could think of staying on. The man's ostrich-like tendency to ignore plain facts disgusted Jim. To Final it was plain as fresh paint Gid Strunk would have his way with that tribe. The impetuous Chuleh would win over the hotbloods and fall upon these isolated ranches with all the savage hatred—Pulled up by a sudden thought Jim stopped, narrowed stare on the elongated shadow of Quail's dad. *Of course! Joe Bob was back of Bentain! It was Joe Bob's money that had got Bentain his lease!*

Jim pushed through the door, Bentain crowding after him. He would have clutched Final's arm in his apprehension had Jim's face looked less rocky. He pushed as close as he dared, scowling around Jim's shoulder at the man in the yard.

No one at Skillet had ever seen the fellow before but the horse he rode was one of the broncs the ranch had sold Chris Stegner. The stranger sat anchored under the threat of Quail's rimfire Henry. His affronted glance, ignoring Bentain, fastened bleakly on Final. "What kind of a deal have I rode into here?"

Jim said, "What kind were you looking for?"

The man hooked a leg over the horn of his saddle and put together a smoke with steady fingers, but the prowl of his stare belied this tranquility. Jim noticed other things now and an awareness of danger tightened his cheeks, discounting the smile with which the man drawled, "A ridin' job, friend. Just something to tie to till I can put by enough to take me out of this God-forsook place."

It was too pat, Jim thought, suggestive as those long fingered hands that now rested idle against the pommel, as the dark butt of gun above that cutaway top of scuffed holster. Bentain, pushing forward, cried, "You've hit the right place, man. Get down and come in and—"

"Not so fast," Final growled. "Rockabye—"

"Rockabye will by God do what I tell him! You keep out of this," Bentain glowered.

The stranger, smiling, looked from one to the other but his eyes, Final noticed, hadn't changed in the least. "Use your head," Jim said. "This hardcase didn't show up by accident."

"Name's Roup," the man offered, "and you're right about that. I heard you folks was in the market for gun hands."

"Then I guess," Quail said, "you've heard what we're up against."

The fellow shrugged. "Alls I want is to git me a stake. Makes no difference to me who's footin' the bill. I come where I figured skill would fetch a premium."

"Man, you're hired," Bentain grinned, looking maliciously at Final.

Roup grinned, too. "That bein' the case—" He shook a boot from the stirrup, but before he could swing the

309

leg over his saddle Quail pronounced, "I'll have something to say about that," and lifted her Henry.

Roup went still.

Bentain cried testily, "Don't mix in men's—"

"Ride out," Quail said.

"Now, see here." Bentain wheezed and ineffectually cursed.

A ragged breath whirled through the cavity of Roup's chest. Behind scrinched lids his yellow eyes were like glass.

"Get going," Quail said.

"If I don't git on here I'll have to take up with Strunk."

The girl returned his look coldly. "If this shooter goes off a pine box will take care of you."

The man settled deeper into his collarless shirt. Then he pulled up his chin and stared around at Bentain. "She runnin' this spread?"

Bentain scraped a hand across flushed cheeks. He snarled past Final and stamped into the house. Roup shifted his yellow stare to Jim. "Next time we meet you better dig first because there sure as hell is goin' to be some lead flyin'."

Having said which he clamped his mouth shut and, with a last uncompromising look at the girl, picked up his reins and rode out of the yard. Final swung round as though bound for the dun but Quail said through the fading sound of Roup's pony, "Jim, what's happened to us?"

Jim crossed to the dun, stabbed a toe into the bent wood of a stirrup and swung up. Settling his weight he ground all expression out of his look. "I guess you're just too damned efficient for me."

She regarded him with something like wonder in her glance. She was more gaunt than he remembered but around her mouth was that same driven-in composure which had first attracted him to her. Summer freckles were beginning to show beneath her eyes and the ghost of a sobered smile seemed to hover just back of the bones of her face so that his own mouth had to be whipped into derision to keep back the things that were clawing to be said. But he'd gone over that and over it, the hard finality of his decision admitting no further argument. Until he was clear of Joe Bob and Strunk he had no business—

She said, "Is this what prison has done to you? Crammed you so full of hate you've no room for any thought but vengeance?"

Her sister came out of the harness shed, seemed about to move toward them but stopped to stand watching. Final shifted his reins from right hand to the left, kept his thoughts off his face and kneed the horse into motion.

"Jim, wait!" Quail called.

Final's stare went over the green of scrub cedar to fasten on the blue-gray bulk of Horse Mesa. "I've waited three years too long already." He lifted the big dun into a trot and pointed its head to the shine of Fish Creek.

Quail found her father in the clutter of ranch gear that festooned his office. A cold pipe was held in the curl of tired fingers and the sag of hunched shoulders made the things she'd been going to say unforgivable. Care and the ravages of failure had combined with the weight of his years to give his look that kind of hopeless desperation sometimes glimpsed in a man who has been thinking of putting an end to himself.

But Quail knew better than to put stock in this. He had always been given to dramatizing himself, imagining roles he'd not been equipped to play—like that of the open-handed rancher with which he had put in Jim Final as range boss.

311

Quail hardened her heart. She knew very well Bentain was aware of her, that he would continue making a production of his gloom for as long as he was allowed to.

"Dad!"

He appeared to make a visible effort to recapture some of the pontifical manner he effected in dealings with people outside the family. She had long ago discovered the shoddy compulsions and borrowed dictums by which his ego sought to compensate for things left out of his character. Nor could she be fooled by the tremulous smile with which he put aside things too grave to cope with. In spite of these shams she loved him.

He dragged a hand over his cheeks with a ragged breath. "Really, Quail, you shouldn't have—" He sighed and fingered the wilt of his collar, his eyes slewing away from the probe of her look.

He had never lavished on her the doting which over the years had spoiled Marcia, nor had he sent Quail away to a "finishing" school. Marcia, of course, had the obvious equipment to make such an outlay of cash pay dividends if the goal of these efforts was to trade her off in marriage to a man whose dollars or social standing would enhance Bentain's position. Quail hadn't yet been able to decide whether her father was that cold-blooded or the self-deluded victim of his youngest daughter's vanity. She was not even sure she wanted to be sure.

She came into the room. "What did Jim say?"

The rancher threw up his hands. "He's heard these crazy rumors and got—" He broke off with a snort and banged the desk with his fist. "Taunee's not figuring to dig up the hatchet, what would he fight with? What chance would he have against the Major's new rifles?"

He peered up at her obliquely. "You want to go into town with your sister?"

"I didn't know the garrison had gotten those new Winchesters."

"They'll have 'em soon as that next freight gets in."

"What did Jim say about Yuma?"

"Very little." Bentain, squirming uncomfortably, frowned.

"Didn't he tell you they'd turned him loose?"

"Well, somethin' like that. I wasn't payin' much attention."

"He thought you arranged it."

Bentain heaved himself out of his chair. "Quail, I know you're gone on that feller—"

"He didn't come here on account of me. He must have been told to report to you. Or did he come here because he blames you for what happened?"

"How could he?"

"You made no effort to get him off at the trial—"

"Quail, you know I was warned! Strunk had me hamstrung." He scowled at her nervously but Quail wasn't noticing. She was recalling the hard look of Jim. His wasn't the face of the man she remembered. It wore now the look of a hunter. Implacable. He had lived with thoughts of revenge. Her eyes went back to her father.

A corner of Bentain's mouth twitched. His appearance bred panic; and she cried, "What are you hiding?"

"Nothing—nothing at all," Bentain said, but his eyes belied him, skittering around like bees in a bottle. "My God," he groaned, tugging at his collar, "what's Strunk goin' to think when he finds out? He'll figure I got Jim out sure as shootin'."

"Why didn't you keep him here?"

"How could I? Anyway," Bentain said irritably, "I had to think of you girls. An ex-con—" His glance fled away from the scorn her eyes showed. He shoved the

313

chair from his path, strode about the room. "We've got to do something!" He spun around, blackly staring. "You've no idea how he looked!"

He must think Jim meant to get back at him through Marcia. This was ridiculous, of course. But why was he so afraid?

He started pacing again. "You hitch up the team."

"But you said the Indians—"

"It's not that!" The man drove one fist into the palm of the other, rushed past her then, hurrying off toward the kitchen. "Have you paid that lease money yet?" she called after him. The only answer she got was the slam of a door.

When the team was ready Marcia would not budge. She said reasonably enough if it were dangerous to stay it would be folly to go. Here, at least, they would have walls to fort up behind.

Quail put up the team. She had an idea shelter wasn't it. She kept thinking of Marcia's expression when the girl had been looking at Jim. Bentain, as usual, was putty in her hands. Allowing he guessed she was probably right he went back and shut himself into his office.

But the fright Quail had seen did not leave with his going. It lingered like fog. It made Quail jumpy and restless. What did he know that was being kept from her?

She became so disturbed she went and knocked on his door. His scowling face did not welcome her. She saw a pistol on his desk and the oil and rags he'd been cleaning it with that he'd hastily tried to cover up with some papers.

"Dad! What is it?"

"I don't know what you're talking about."

"If you're afraid of Gid Strunk or those Indians—"

"Why should I be afraid!" he snarled, catching a tighter hold on the door. He tried a parched smile, jiggled the door impatiently. "No need of you worryin.' This'll all blow over. We got powerful friends—"

Final hadn't covered any great amount of distance before recalling the need of the gun he hadn't got. Without a weapon he might as well pitch in his chips. Strunk wouldn't waste much time with him. Jim's mere presence, his return to this country from an unexpired term in the territorial prison, constituted a threat the man couldn't ignore.

Jim didn't know why he hadn't thought of this sooner. It seemed to him now that Joe Bob in sending him down here had tried the worst thing he could if he really wanted peace. He could hardly have made a move more calculated to disturb it, and if he was behind Bentain— if he had made some kind of quiet deal with the man —why hadn't he sent the money that was due on Bentain's lease? Was he deliberately withholding it to embarrass Bentain?

But such a thought was crazy! Failure to pay that grazing fee was enough almost in itself to bring some violent reaction from those much maligned and long suffering Apaches. But this wasn't the only craziness Jim saw. If the Governor was Bentain's partner in the lease the withholding of that money made no sense at all.

His mind prowled back to the start of this business, to things which might be a matter of record. The gambler had framed him on a cooked-up rustling charge as the opening gun in a campaign against Skillet and got Jim sent off for ten years at Yuma. Strunk had then cut down most of the local opposition—at least the other small outfits—and moved onto the best of Bentain's range, crippling Skillet's operation and liquidating the bulk of its crew. This, of course, if you could believe all you heard. Strunk had then proceeded to ply the

Indians with whisky, stirring them up in other ways while bringing in a bunch of dissatisfied weedbenders to set up a howl for the Apache lands, also making himself solid with the new Camp Grant C. O., Major Berkley.

This last was pure guesswork but it had to hit close for Strunk to pull this off, and it certainly fit the picture of conditions as painted for Jim by the Governor himself.

Now if Joe Bob wanted to help Bentain and keep those Indians pacified—if it was peace the man really wanted—he could hardly have managed, sending Jim in here, a thing more calculated to blow the whole mess right up in his face.

By sending Jim he had alerted Strunk who could not afford to lay back with Jim digging. By withholding the money Bentain needed for the lease the Governor was not only aggravating an obvious crisis but was putting his partner in a very good light for getting rubbed out. It was the most mismanaged mess Jim had ever heard tell of!

And what was it all about—what was back of it? Strunk you could tab as greedy and ambitious, scrambling over better men in a vicious drive for empire. But what could the Governor expect to get out of it if the man were as crooked as Jim uneasily suspected? Could Joe Bob really be the fool that he looked?

And now this guy, Roup, showing up out of the blue!

Here, at least, Jim was on firmer ground. The man was a gun shark sent in to make trouble, to wipe out Jim or maybe kill Bentain. He was almost certainly Strunk's man and it came to Jim now they had probably ought to have hung onto him.

Final turned the dun around. He didn't want any more close-ups with Quail but he damned well had to arm himself and there was no place nearer than Skillet.

That shotgun Rockabye had hidden in the barn the day before Jim had been caught with changed brands was little likely to be there now but he would try the barn first; then, if he had to, he'd go on to the house. Quail's blunt talk about revenge still rankled and, no matter that he'd done it for the girl's own good, he felt a natural guilt about the way he was treating her. There just wasn't any place for love in this business and to keep her from getting hurt he had to keep her away from him. With his own prospects dependent on the Governor's good graces—

Jim shook his head. The only plausible likelihood he could pull out of what he knew or grimly suspected was that Joe Bob was backing not a friend but an investment which the gambler's machinations had suddenly placed in jeopardy. Jim couldn't honestly snake much satisfaction from this. Bentain, despite his bluster, was a thoroughly frightened man.

He'd complained he could neither get help nor keep it, yet Rockabye had stayed; Tom Connifay, too. And he had this pair of drifters, but he'd continued to be driven ever farther back into the brush and now Strunk was prodding the Indians and Quail's father had leased reservation grass in an obviously last ditch gamble to keep his cattle out of Strunk's hands.

Or was that why?

Jim didn't know. His mind was weary and he could not seem to jerk his thoughts out of these deepening ruts they'd dropped into. Bitterly he cursed Joe Bob and all his works. Another, perhaps, might have gone his way regardless, concentrating on Strunk because of those months in Yuma, closely following the Governor's instructions because what Joe Bob had told him to do so grimly followed his own inclination. But Jim's dad had been a stickler when it came to responsibilities and Jim

317

was belatedly discovering more of the old gent's views still ruled his ways than he had ever taken time to realize. Maybe he wasn't quite as tough as he'd believed. In any event, with time and his own ignorance both working for strunk there didn't noways seem to be but one course open. Like it or not, it looked almighty like he was going to have to go back to Mad Springs.

10 AMBUSH

Strunk had never made it a habit to stay in the dark about anything. No news might be good news but the gambler was one who liked to copper his bets. Though he knew it was much too early to expect any return from his most recent strategies when Tapp again rode in without definite news from Skillet, Strunk made up his mind to have a look for himself. "We'll go out there tomorrow," he told Tapp impatiently.

"I might not be back from that wagon train stickup."

"Cretch can take care of that."

Tapp straightened bowed shoulders to run the edge of a glance over Strunk's florid features. "Why put yourself in the way of a bullet? The world's full of fillies. You kin find just as good, without risk, over to Benson."

Both of them knew he wasn't talking about Quail.

Beyond a thinning of the lines about his mouth Strunk let this slide. "Give you a chance to pass the news along to Rockabye."

Tapp, always a man for direct action, had small patience with all this stumbling and fumbling with which his boss seemed lately inclined to hedge the smallest move. "You're goin' to a heap of bother over a thing that wouldn't take five minutes of my time."

"Final's the kind we've got to handle with gloves."

"Didn't use gloves on him last time."

"We didn't have Joe Bob breathing down our necks then. Muddle this now and we'll have hell with the hide off."

Tapp shrugged but it was plain he didn't like it. "If that slick-ear throws a slug into you—"

"That's why I'm taking you along." The gambler chuckled. "Jim's going to step mighty soft in front of witnesses. We'll pick up Dawks and work some more on Bentain. Old fool ain't paid that lease money yet. While we're waiting on those rifles we'll get the fix set up. Tell Rockabye the Bishop's going to be riding to-morrow night and to make damn sure he don't miss that stage."

Tapp rose and got into his gauntlets. Knowledge of Strunk's allusion brightened the shine of his lifting stare and crept like a smile along the edges of his mouth. "You tell him," the gambler said, "to make goddam sure he remembers to drop that gun. When I get through with old man Bentain that son of a buck'll never know what hit him!"

The rust and sulphur flanks of Horse Mesa raised starkly back of Final from the curled gray hoops of dead and sunbleached greasewood. South of him the sand lay deep in wrinkled terraces, piled thus by restless winds whose whim tomorrow might change them utterly —even as the drums of Chuleh's bronco Apaches might, unless soon silenced, scald this region in a bath of blood.

North, unglimpsed in the quiet of scrub oak, sang the whispering waters of Canyon Lake and, directly ahead, this ridge he'd been riding dropped into the green of waving grass, a lush meadow where the murmur of

319

insects, the cheerful chirping of birds, broke gradually into Jim's troubled thoughts, reminding him vaguely of brighter days. Without his being consciously aware of it earth and sky were exerting a pull which he only now was beginning to sense in the wistful need of something to tie to, something solid which of late his life had sorely lacked.

His roving glance picked up a covey of quail and saw where a second ridge beyond this meadow climbed into gray rock, blocking off any view he might have of Skillet's buildings. He thought again of Bentain's daughters and the gun in Bentain's barn.

He was partway across the narrow cup of this basin when he noticed cattle browsing the edge of a draw. Sleekly fat they looked compared with others he had seen. There was strength in this grass and Bentain wasn't overgrazing it. Most of the Skillet cows, Jim supposed, had been pushed toward the lake to make it more difficult for Strunk to get at them. He could not find any real hope for Skillet. The only thing likely to deter Strunk was force, the one thing Bentain appeared to have not a bit of. There were tag-ends of things here a man couldn't get hold of. Joe Bob hadn't said he wanted the Indians stopped. Bentain claimed the Apaches had no suitable weapons. But with Strunk's ingenuity—

Jim's mount flinched and stumbled. The horse was going down when Jim flung himself from leather, spurred by the faroff sudden *plop* of a rifle. Belly flat he lay beneath the waving stems of grass, not moving, hardly breathing.

The sun burned into the muscles of his back and the green smell around him became alive with the activities of insects, some of which annoyed him. He caught no further sound from the dun which he knew was off there to the left of him someplace. Time dragged. The bushwhacker, he thought intolerably, would be somewhere up in those rocks along the ridge. With no real accounting for it Final found himself visualizing Roup.

If it was Roup the man would not long be content to remain in such isolation. Experience and the falling dun would already have told him enough to have sent the fellow snaking along to some likelier vantage for another try.

Desperation and anger boiled up in Jim a kind of reckless ferocity. He got up out of the grass. Dropping into a crouch he went up the slope like a scalded cat. The ambusher's rifle did not bark again until the rocks of the crest were but a blurred leap ahead.

The scream of a ricocheting slug drove Jim sprawling. A second and third shot battered the weathered face of the outcrop, showering him with rock chips.

These boulders held the heat of a stove lid but he went deeper into them, preferring discomfort to the slap of a bullet. The man with the Winchester was continuing to use it, the echoes of his fire running all along the rim of this slope. Sweat cracked through the pores of Jim's skin when a slug snapped a stick not two inches from his cheek, but he kept wriggling ahead, now reasonably certain Roup would do about as he'd expected. Already the man had moved, was farther to the right and had probably been in the midst of this when Jim had quit the grass.

It seemed reasonable to assume the man was afoot, that he was hunting some higher, more commanding position from which he might locate Final's changed cover. Jim was after Roup's horse and felt fairly certain he'd be able to spot it if he could keep from getting tagged by one of those blue whistlers.

Reaching a place where the slope leveled off along its crest Jim got up behind a rock and with some caution saw almost immediately the sorrel rump of a horse half hidden in brush along the ridge's farther edge. Barely thirty feet separated Jim from this animal but all of it was open.

Jim didn't hesitate. Roup would be expecting him to try for the horse, would be waiting for it. The fellow might have guessed by now Jim wasn't armed.

He plunged back through the rocks over the course he'd just traveled, making all the racket he could in the process, knowing he'd got to put Roup off balance. When he came out on bare slope Roup drove two shots at him. Doubled over and panting Jim dashed for the end of the ridge farthest removed from where he judged Roup to be. If he guessed wrong he'd be done for. He got into the rocks, hoping the fellow hadn't managed to see enough of his movements to foresee their purpose.

Snatching up a handful of *talus* he threw it rattling and banging into rocks farther on and crouched, mouth open, holding the breath choked in his throat until he heard Roup's booted feet sprint past above him. Grinning tightly, Jim went up through the rockpile with all the haste he dared manage.

He paused once more at the crest, hot and gasping, seeking through a sprangle of catclaw to gauge the man's position. Nothing came out of the land's deep stillness; Roup, evidently, being at the same game.

Jim took off his hat, exposing enough of his head to discover Roup crouched near the end of the ridge about fifty yards distant, watching the rocks and open ground beyond. He must have decided Jim had given up on the horse and was set to cut him down if he tried for the cedars between there and Skillet.

Bentain's headquarters, though not far away, could not be seen because of intervening ridges. Jim hadn't much hope that anyone there might have heard Roup's rifle. The man was still going to see him but fifty yards offered a lot more margin for error than thirty feet. The horse trumpeted as Jim plunged into the open.

Roup yelled. Lead came then, screaming up off the shale, whining, hatefully batting into brush all along the far side of Jim. Roup, caught again between balance and fury, was triggering too fast. Time Jim reached the horse the man was stuck with an empty Winchester.

There wasn't too much daylight left when Jim, recrossing the creek, sighted Skillet's headquarters. Concealing Roup's sorrel in a thicket of cedars he studied the place carefully, finding neither life nor any evidence of violence. Bentain had apparently taken his advice and moved the girls into town. But where was the crew Connifay had gone for? And where was Bentain's ramrod, Rockabye?

Threat of Roup finally prodded Jim into action. Far from satisfied Jim worked south and then cut west to catch a larger view of the yard from the back. He still couldn't determine if the ranch was occupied. All he could be sure of was that the crew hadn't returned unless they'd stabled their horses to make the place seem deserted.

Jim distrusted this quiet, finding in it too much of the impending violence he was trying to avert. He eased back into place a branch he'd been holding, mind moving from Taunee to Chuleh and, inevitably, to Strunk. He reckoned he had better be looking for that gun. It was an English Greener, a sawed-off shotgun belonging to Bentain and normally kept above the livingroom mantel. Why Rockabye ever should have moved it in the first place was something which certainly invited closer scrutiny. The day before Strunk's crew had jumped him at Black Cross Jim had come into the barn after something and seen Rockabye stealthily caching the Greener on the dusty ledge of an eight-by-ten stringer. Jim had backed from the place without disclosing his presence, intending later to discuss the matter with Bentain but had never had the opportunity. Rockabye might have hidden the gun on Bentain's orders but that wasn't the way it looked to Jim. The man might have been acting under Bentain's orders when he dropped the remark which had put Jim under Tapp's guns at Black Cross. Jim hadn't made up his mind about this.

Jim cut over toward the barn on a tangent which put the bunkhouse between himself and the main house's open gallery. The yard was still depressingly quiet. No sound at all came out of the bunkhouse; no smoke showed above the cookshack stovepipe.

As Joe Bob had reminded him, Jim had put in a great deal of practise during the long nights at Yuma trying to give his reach greater speed but this kind of dry run might not mean a thing when it came to lifting a Colt out of leather—providing he ever got hold of one to reach for. He always had been a pretty fair shot but all of his targets had been wild game. He didn't know what he would do with a man in his sights. Miss a mile, maybe.

He made it to the back of the barn, gingerly fingering his gashed cheek while he listened to the restive stamping of a horse and the drone of flies coming off the manure pile. The familiar smells of this place eased off some of the tension but he flinched, involuntarily stiffening, when a door banged over at the house. That sound, in this quiet, was too remindful of Roup's rifle.

Booted feet, plainly audible, crossed the gallery and Jim heard the skreak of the rocker as somebody's weight settled tiredly into it. Time prodded Jim and concern thinned the lines of his mouth with irritation. It looked crazy now after all these months to imagine that shotgun was still on the stringer.

Redoubling caution, he moved around the angle of the wall for a look at the barn's side door. It was closed. He considered again going in through the back but decided against it. The front doors facing the house would be open and if he went in through the rear whoever was holding down that rocker—*and it might be Rockabye*—would be almost sure to see Jim cross light and come tearing over.

He went on along the side of the barn, keeping as far out as he dared from the building so as not to alert the horse he'd heard stamping. It was preposterous, of course, this care he was taking to avoid another run-in with Quail. Made him feel like a damn coyote!

He tried the door nervously, feeling it give. Grasping it firmly, lifting up as he pulled, he drew it open halfway and slipped through, suddenly freezing, staring across ten feet of blurred shadow square into the eyes of a badly scared girl.

She was all set to scream and she clutched a pistol.

11 THE BAITED MAN

It was Marcia, Quail's redheaded sister, and Jim wondered which would come first, the scream or the bullet.

Sweat lay coldly against his skin but she choked back the cry, the pistol's muzzle sagging away from its focus. "I—all I could think about was those horrible Indians." She took a deep breath, exploiting her most prominent measurement, let the air shudder out in the ghost of a smile. "You gave me an awful fright."

"Figured everyone had cleared out," Final said. "I been tryin' to find me a gun."

She was, he noticed, looking him over pretty carefully, the frank interest this implied prodding up feelings he resented and had no patience with. His shoulders stirred and something about her became more direct. "You must be starved."

"I could eat," Jim said, trying to pull his eyes away. The girl laughed, and there was in it, behind the shakiness of nerves, a kind of challenge that made him stare at her more sharply. "What's taking Connifay so long to get back with the crew?"

"I think," she said, "they've been up near the lake. "I've some sandwiches here if—"

One of the horses stamped the floor of its stall and whickered.

Final, shutting her out of his mind, went past the tool closet and crossed to a stanchion that was crossbarred with holds. He climbed up into the dimness of the loft, floundering through hay toward the back where it was deeper. Reaching up he ran searching hands across the top of the remembered stringer.

Marcia said, not far behind him, "Did you expect to find a gun up there?"

He blew dust and cobwebs out of his face and stood still a moment, eyes thoughtfully squinted, uncomfortably aware of the girl's proximity. "Stranger things have happened." He shrugged. "Let's get out of this."

She watched him, not moving. The edge of a smile crept across her red lips. And she touched her tongue to them, head at one side, hands smoothing the dress against the swell of her hips. "There's something about the smell of hay that gets me. Does it effect you that way?"

"No," Final said, and brushed past her, cursing the heat that came into his cheeks. He climbed down from the loft and, brushing chaff from his pantlegs, was staring through the open front when she rejoined him. "Who's on the gallery?"

She said coolly, "Quail, I imagine. How did you get that gash on your face?"

"A little trouble in town." He wiped damp hands on his pants again. "I better get out of here."

They considered each other. She was laughing at him now. "I thought you wanted a gun."

"I'll make out."

She moved nearer. "Take mine," she said, pushing it into his hand. She cut over to the wall and poked around in a saddle bag, graceful as a kitten. Coming back she held out a handful of cartridges. He pocketed them, nodding, pushed the gun between belt and belly. She was a damned handsome female.

She said, briefly amused, "I could talk with Quail while you're making your getaway."

No fool, either, he decided. A sudden thought made him look at her again. "Place must seem strange after being away so long."

"Well, different," she smiled. "It's people, don't you think, who make or spoil an impression? This country seems at war with itself." She pulled another deep breath into her, reaching up to touch her hair. "I feel just two things, violence and security." She watched him gravely. "Before you came all I felt was the wildness." She said, laughing up at him, "Does that sound too terribly confusing?"

She was clever with words. He stirred impatiently and saw her eyes change. She bent over, brushing at her skirt. Her hair against the light looked like strands of burnished copper. Straightening she said, "You don't really think those savages will come do you?"

"I wouldn't be surprised. They've been pushed around enough."

"They're doing all right. Free beef—"

He said, scowling, "They had this whole country. No

one, believe me, wants to have someone else continually telling them what to do."

"Do you honestly condemn Father—"

"I don't condemn anyone," Final said grimly. "People do what they have to do. Or what they think they can get away with."

She nodded, considering that. "An interesting point of view."

But she wasn't getting through to him now. He was far away, lost in dark thoughts of his own. He realized presently she had been saying something. She had her head to one side again as though she were not quite sure what to make of him. He remembered his business and touched a hand to his hat.

"There'll be a moon tonight." She appeared to be listening. With a shrug she turned as though to step out ahead of him. Perhaps she turned her ankle, at least she lurched and swayed. She might have fallen if he had not caught her.

He could feel the yielding swell of her curves. She moaned, twisting against him like a drowning person trying to get above water. Her eyes fluttered up at him. She managed a trembly smile. She murmured something too faint for deciphering. "I'll be all right in a moment."

Someway her arm seemed to have got around his neck. After three years in Yuma the clean woman smell of her came through restraint like the slice of a knife; but Jim was no fool. He tried to step back but she clung to him tightly. She moaned again with her face hard against him, and Jim's wheeling glance found Quail at the door.

"Perhaps you two had better come eat."

Bill Tapp, quitting town after his talk with Strunk, climbed steadily into more broken country, finally reaching a point where the sound of rifle fire stopped him.

After a bit he heard it again. One gun, he decided, probably one of those new Winchesters. This was pretty close to Skillet. Roup had one of those rifles; it had been with the saddle he'd packed over to Stegner's livery. The sound had broken, he guessed, from the other side of that ridge.

He did some cautious maneuvering. At the end of ten minutes he got off and tied his horse. Carrying an old Army Springfield he worked up through the rocks and got a look through the brush at Final cutting for Skillet on a sorrel Tapp immediately recognized. That son of a bitch had set Roup afoot!

He lined his sights on Jim's back and then reluctantly lowered the rifle. Strunk's orders had been definite. Let Roup take care of him.

Tapp suddenly chuckled. There'd been nothing in Strunk's instructions about Tapp staying clear of Roup. With a mean little grin Tapp set out to find him.

12 RENDEZVOUS IN THE HILLS

Final, after a night in the hills, was up in the first gray crack of dawn despite the restless hours he'd put in. He'd left the ranch too late to set out for Mad Springs. The ordeal of that supper lay sour in his thoughts. He got out of Roup's blankets and looked with Marcia—all coyness—and Quail—cool after discovering Jim in his sister's arms—around for Roup's horse.

He found the sorrel still on hobble and cropping grass, shook out the bedding and rolled it for travel. The whole length of Jim ached in the nip of this air. He watched the pale lift of light in the east silhouette a deckle edged skyline, darkly wondering what this day would hold.

Ground fog thinly clung to wet brush. Much of the middle distance was lost in the drift of this vapor as he checked the pistol he had got from Marcia and set out, still frowning, for the emerging scarp of the canyon's left rim. He had purposely camped off here west of Skillet that he might have this last look before taking a trail which—if luck wasn't with him—could put Strunk out of his reach forever.

He had Roup on his mind and Rockabye too, and a flock of unfinished thoughts left to gather. His stomach was beginning to get irritable but more important with Jim right now was the need to learn whether Bentain's ramrod had returned. Though he'd decided temporarily to shelve them he could not forget the grim notions he'd latched onto through the long nights at Yuma. He hadn't realized before how dear these had become; but he was seeing himself a lot clearer this morning and finding some basis for Quail's voiced complaint.

He had certainly fed too long on anger and paid too little notice to what might be left after that last bleak squeeze of a trigger. At least he saw things straight enough now—or did he?

His prowling thoughts kept shuttling back to Joe Bob. On the face of things the Governor's intentions looked to be some different from those he'd declared, almost as though he *wanted* those red men to dig up the hatchet. If this made no sense neither was it probable that Jim, by himself, would be able to stop a Strunk already alerted by his unexplained appearance from an unfinished hitch at Yuma. But supposing the Governor really was Bentain's backer, secretly, well covered but still a partner of record.

Jim scowled around him like a man in a fever. Such a possibility, if Joe Bob wanted those Indians stirred up, made even less sense than anything yet. Still, Jim was free, turned loose by the Governor on a preposterous task. For the man must have known how little likely Jim was, without help, to hamper Strunk. To stop the man he would have to kill him and that, in Jim's present circumstances, would take a mighty lot of doing!

It was like a picture puzzle that didn't have all the pieces.

Jim moved upslope, got over the rim of the wall and began picking his way between a jumble of boulders, moving into thick brush that was beaded with moisture that sparkled in the light of this brightening height. A gray dove in a digger pine, half concealed behind the droop of its needles, went repeatedly through its mournful gamut of calls; and off yonder, below him, at the base of a red fir, a young javelina was rooting and snuffling in search of some tidbit. Jim knew there would be others around, for this wild pig of Sonora was among the most gregarious of animals; but Final's interest was not in animals just now.

Working carefully forward he ascended a slant of rock, wriggling up on his belly to where the high end, masked by the dew-drenched sparkle of branch ends, afforded partial sight of Skillet headquarters.

Less than three miles away, flat roofs a-shine with the touch of the sun, he could make out the barn and more than half of the house with, off to one side, the corrals and dark end of the harness shed.

No horses in sight, no sign of the crew and, though he watched for some while, neither the girls nor Bentain came into view. He didn't see Rockabye, either. Not that he had really expected to. If the man three years ago had set up that frame he would not be wanting to run into Jim now.

Final's shoulders moved, became suddenly still. If Rockabye had set up that frame he was Strunk's man—

or could be! If he were in Strunk's pay that business of hiding Bentain's Greener—

Jim slid down off the rock and started thoughtfully back. There might be no use in this trip to Mad Springs —it might even be the end of him, but it looked the best hope he had of protecting Quail and the only direct chance by which he might bring down Strunk's house of cards. Though it was all still pretty vague in his head, if only Jim could make those Indians see that without their intervention Strunk might be caught out on a limb—

Jim was scarcely a couple of strides from the rim when Roup's horse nickered. It made Final grin a little, thinking how much like people horses were, how upset they became when an established routine was broken off or disrupted. Strunk's pistolman had probably got the horse used to having something done with him at this particular time, and now the animal was fretting to be at it, impatient of the new man's dawdling.

Final stopped again, remembering. The horse belonged to Stegner.

Jim crept to the rim and very cautiously peered over. He saw a skirted shape on a rearing black gelding. The sun hadn't reached that far into the canyon but he could see red hair against the white of her shirtwaist and watched her fight the horse down, appear to study the rolled blankets and then stare toward the sorrel. Marcia's head came around. "Jim—" she called softly, not seeing him. "Jim!"

"All right," he growled. "Stay right where you are."

It sure took a woman to compound confusion. She must have seen he was not pleased. She said a little tartly when he got down and came striding up to her, "You might at least pretend. You don't have to snap my head off!"

"If it would do any good—" He was thoroughly disgusted. "What brought you out?"

332

"Well!" she said, very plainly indignant. But a smile crept over the tempting redness of her mouth. She reached a hand to the parcel lashed back of her cantle. "I tried to catch you last night but you were moving too fast for me." She eyed him steadily a moment. "Aren't you going to help me down?" Jim wondered how she'd known of his decision to camp nearly.

"Look—this is Indian country and right now it wouldn't take more than a snort to set off a full-scale war around here. You ever think how that hair of yours would look folded over some stinking breech-clout?"

The words were brutal, intentionally so, but she only tossed her chin at him, grinning. Like her father, Jim guessed, she would never believe these Mad Springs Apaches might be pushed too far. Her eyes made him nervous and he looked away from them, feeling the pull of her.

She said, "I've brought you some food and, better still, a rifle."

"Thanks." He glanced around at her, frowning. "As it happens I was just about to pull out."

"You were leaving?" She looked startled. "But you *can't* go now! Father's counting—"

"I seem to recollect once having counted on him."

When his glance jerked away the hint of a smile ran over her lips and she swung down, untying the packet of food. "I expect you can wait a few minutes. Build up a fire and I'll fix you some breakfast. If you don't mind eating out of the same plate with me."

Final stamped irritably after Roup's horse, trying to think himself out of whatever she was planning. When he came back with the sorrel she was down on her haunches cracking eggs into a skillet. "You needn't worry about smoke," she said over her shoulder. Rustlers

333

hit us again last night. Rockabye's got the whole crew out."

Jim got a fire going, keeping it small and using only dry twigs, knowing there were others who might investigate smoke. "He go with them?"

Marcia shook her head. "After all that scare you stirred up about Indians, I suppose he thought he'd better stick around. "He was jawing with Father in the office when I left."

"Where was Connifay?"

"Tom—the cook? He went off with the others." She dished up the eggs and filled a tin cup with coffee. Glancing up brightly she patted invitingly the rock she'd sat down on. He came reluctantly over, squatting on the heels of his boots and looking grim. She had the plate on her knees. He didn't want to get that close but the smells of coffee and bacon were than he could stand off. Marcia had handled stubborn males before.

She didn't force him to talk. She could tell she was making progress by the half guilty looks with which he shied away from each contact. She was pleased that her nearness bothered him.

He was bothered all right. He grew acutely conscious of this perilous proximity. He got up as soon as he decently could and moving over to her horse withdrew the rifle from its scabbard. A Sharps in good condition, chambered for the .45-120-550, the caliber most favored by those who had rid the country of buffalo. "Say you fetched this along for me?"

Marcia, poking at her hair, looked up with a smile. "The shells are in my fish." *

While he broke the slicker out and was refastening it to the back of her strap-hung saddle she finished her

* cow-country term for yellow oilskin, so-called from their trademark.

coffee and stood up to stretch, aware of the edgy glance which kept track of her. She watched him dump the rest of the coffee and wipe out the skillet with a twist of yanked grass. He did the same for the plate and for the fork and spoon, afterwards replacing these utensils in the feed sack.

There was a breathlessness about her every contact with this man that gave her a far deeper stimulation than anything she'd known. It was like some rare elixir; and she smiled with a secret, female satisfaction that she was able to bend him to her will. But she was baffled and considerably confused when he began to get Roup's sorrel ready for the trail.

She watched him bit the horse, shake and carefully smooth the blanket, saw him lift the heavy saddle and knee the wind from the animal's belly before jerking up the cinch. She watched through a blur of resentful emotion while he removed the rifle's scabbard and methodically fastened it to Roup's saddle. Her lips turned a little ugly when he picked up his brush jacket and bent to retrieve the boxed loads he'd got from her oilskin. While he was distributing these cartridges about his person she spoke. "I thought you were coming back to the ranch!"

The quick stiffening of those gone-still shoulders compelled her to say more reasonably, "I was counting on it." She walked over to him, laying a hand on his arm, knowing from past experience what power there was in the touch of her hand. "We need you, Jim."

Men found her hard to resist in that tone. She put the need in her eyes and saw a look cross Final's cheeks like doubt. "We really do. Rockabye, of course, is able enough but I would feel," she said with her tone oddly husky, "a whole lot safer if—" and used her eyes to get across the rest.

"We'll ride," Final said, "whenever you're ready."

She studied the look of him, not quite certain, suddenly tingling with this triumph. It gave her a kind of intoxication to have succeeded where Quail had so miserably failed. But it went deeper than that. There was about this bleak and hard-faced man something wild, half Indian compounded of things she had never known. It was oil to the flare of her pride of conquest, presenting him to her as a kind of dare. She was woman incarnate, the eternal huntress.

"I suppose," she murmured, dissembling her excitement, "we had better go." She made it sound intimate, wistfully regretful.

Final moved over to the black, checked the girth and gave her a hand up into the leather, still with that odd tight look on his cheeks. She swung heels with an impatient toss of the head and lined out for headquarters in a challenging way that would have made a race of it. When he held the sorrel down she came back.

"Anything wrong with that crowbait?"

"I don't aim for anything to get wrong with him."
She turned her face away, furious.

They were perhaps a quarter of a mile up-canyon before the significance of his rudeness registered. He was fighting, of course, setting back on the hook, trying to choke down the urges called up by what her nearness was doing. She hugged this to her, presently saying in gentle rebuke, "You're not a great deal of fun this morning."

He continued to scan the surrounding country—almost, she thought resentfully, as though expecting Taunee and all his painted Apaches to come yelling out of the brush any moment. It was enough to give anybody the creeps. She said as much, getting an impatient look from him.

"I don't aim to be taking any foolish chances."

Where the walls dipped they climbed out of the canyon. The day was beginning to get noticeably warm and Marcia, perspiring, commenced to believe she might be thirsty. She twisted around inquiringly when Jim abruptly pulled up his horse. He appeared to be studying the terrain just ahead. This continual devotion to caution angered her. Gid Strunk, had he been with her, she was sure would have found a more agreeable use for such privacy. "For heaven's sake," she cried irritably, "can't you—"

"Let's go," Final said, and put the sorrel into motion.

She followed in sullen silence, filled with the swelling bitterness of outrage. As they came down through the cedars she had a picture of herself tagging along like a squaw and, suddenly furious, she struck her mount with the reins, spurring alongside.

She caught a glimpse of the buildings when Jim stopped to point. "You won't have no trouble getting in from here."

She reared back in her saddle to stare at him blankly. "*You're not coming?*"

"No." The flinty shine of his glance continued quartering the brush and in a pet she almost left him. She swallowed a couple of times and got hold of herself. "You can at least see me over to the edge of the yard."

He eyed her inscrutably. "All right."

They were skirting the corrals, with the barn between them and any view of the yard, when in angry rebellion she hauled up her horse. Deliberately then she reached up and unfastened the second and third hooks in the front of her waist and prodded her mount up even with his. "Don't you think," she said sharply, "we should get rid of Rockabye?"

That fetched him around but his stare went beyond her, narrowing and ominous. There was something so unnervingly implacable about it she was impelled to look too and so discovered the men wheeling in off the wagon road.

13 SHOWDOWN AT SKILLET

Final's hand on the bridle backed her mount out of sight.

Motioning her down, he slid off Roup's horse, dragging both animal's through the barn's side door. An unavoidable racket of whinnying broke out which he hoped the newcomers would believe caused by their own arrival. He looked around for the girl, his whisper savage with impatience. "Keep back out of the light!"

His hand touched the gun he had got from her yesterday. Honed sharp with tension he stepped over against a stall where he could observe developments through the arch of the half-open front. He heard Marcia coming after him, the flap and skreak of her saddle as the black shook himself then nickered at the sound of hoofs in the yard.

Three men out there. Two in a surrey that was stopped, resplendent with yellow wheels and varnish, before the gallery where Quail and her father stood in stiff-cheeked silence. The third was on a horse and this was Bill Tapp, Strunk's riding boss, with his weight cross-armed across the roll of his saddle.

Final said, "Get me that Sharps," without taking his eyes from them.

In the surrey the gambler wrapped the reins about the whip socket and was making quite a thing of fetching fire to his cigar. Sitting beside him was Seeb Dawks, the

Bandoleer marshal, eyes fluttery as candles under the rim of his brown derby.

Strunk tossed away his match and puffed. A grin broke along the ridge of his lips. "Where's that good looking filly," he said, "the educated one with the carroty mane?"

Bentain trembled.

"Well, no matter," Strunk said, stretching the grin across his teeth. "I've come out here this morning to do you a favor." He waved the smoke at his badge toter. "Guess you know our town marshal. Happens Seeb's also sheriff's deputy for these parts."

"Get to the point," Quail said, "if there is one."

A big diamond flashed on the gambler's hand as he massaged a lapel of his steelpen coat. He looked to be thoroughly enjoying himself. "I been trying to get it through Seeb's head your dad's too smart to get taken in twice and not foolish enough to hide out a convict who seems to have turned killer if you can put any stock in the tracks of a horse."

On the gallery Bentain collapsed into a rocker.

Quail's eyes angered Strunk. "Tell 'em, Seeb."

"It's about this guy Final. He's broke outa Yuma—we got the word last night." Dawks grinned ingratiatingly. "Alls I want is the facts. When's the last time you seen him?"

Quail, stiffly still, stared back at them unwinking. When it began to get downright uncomfortable Bentain gasped in a half-strangled squawk: "He was here yesterday evenin'."

"Took supper with us," Quail said. "You sure he broke out?"

"This come straight from the Governor, Joe Bob hisself." The marshal smirked. "Must want that feller bad, they've put twenty-five hundred on him. Dead or alive."

339

"Who is he supposed to have killed?" the girl asked.

"We'll git to that," Dawks said. "What'd he do after supper?"

"Rode away."

"Which direction?"

"West."

"On what color horse?"

"I didn't see—"

"How you know he rode west then?"

"There's nothing wrong with my hearing."

Leather creaked and popped as Tapp shifted around in his saddle. He glanced irascibly at Dawks and then considered Quail. "Had other company yesterday didn't you?"

"One of Strunk's understrappers asked for a job."

"You'd have pretty rough sledding trying to make that stick."

It was Strunk said that. Quail didn't even look at him. Dawks said, scowling, "This feller show up while that jailbird was here?"

"Jim—"

"Not talkin' to you."

Bentain said, "He wasn't here very long."

"You hire him?"

"Jim or this other gent?"

"I reckon you got better sense than to tie up with Final. Roup I'm talkin' about. Did you or didn't you?"

Bentain flushed and squirmed. "I wanted to but—"

"We haven't hired anyone," Quail said for him.

In the barn Final's glance slanched around hunting Marcia. He saw the still shape of her standing just back of him. "*Where's that rifle!*"

"Be sensible, Jim. You don't want—"

"Get it." He stared at her shirtwaist. "And fasten that thing up before you fall out of it."

He looked into the yard again. Nothing appeared to

have changed out there. Strunk, eyeing Bentain, put a hand over, anchoring Dawks. "Some people," he said, "just don't understand kindness. When are you going to get smart, old man?"

Bentain's clothes seemed a little too large for him. The marshal stabbed him with dissatisfied eyes. "It's my notion that jailbird's been put back on your payroll."

"That ain't true!" Bentain quavered.

Jim heard Marcia move toward the horses. She wasn't hurrying none. He'd have gone for the Sharps himself except that just then the marshal said rabidly, "If you ain't hired him you're hidin' him an'—"

"You have a warrant?" Quail asked.

"I wish to hell you'd learn a woman's place!"

"Let's keep this friendly," Strunk put in, and fell silent as a mounted man rounded the house and pulled up. Rockabye, watching Strunk, said, "What's up?"

"We're huntin' a killer," Dawks said maliciously.

"Who's dead?"

"Some drifter who seems to have come here for a job. One of Sawick's riders stumbled onto him last night. Up on that hogback right behind your third meadow."

In the barn Jim Final drew a ragged breath.

Dawks said, "That jailbird—"

"Now see here," Strunk broke in, assuming his role of sympathetic neighbor, "you don't know Final plugged him."

"I got eyes, by God! You seen them tracks where he come up an' worked around through them rocks. And how about that dead dun? Hell, a kid could see where he got onto Roup's horse! I say this bunch—"

"Don't lump me in that," Rockabye grumbled. "I been out all night with the Skillet crew huntin' cattle."

Quail's glance held contempt she made no effort to hide. "What time," Dawks asked, "did that convict ride outa here?"

When the girl refused to answer the badge-packer snarled with considerable malevolence, "I'm goin' to git that feller. Don't make no difference if I kin prove this or not. With Joe Bob payin' twenty-five hundred fer his scalp I aim to shoot that murderin' sidewinder on sight!"

"Tell you what I'll do," Strunk said, eyeing Bentain from the sides of his eyes. "Aiding and abetting can be a pretty serious thing. If you want to get out I'll take this place off your hands—lease and all."

Quail curled her lips.

"By cripes," Dawks snarled, "I'm bettin' that sonofabitch is on the place right now! Climb offa that horse, Tapp, an' 'give me a hand."

Tapp swung down. He looked wickedly pleased. "Where you aim to start, Seeb?"

"I'll take the house. You—"

"He's in the barn!"

Too late, Final saw Quail's redheaded sister dart into the yard and pelt recklessly toward them lugging the Sharps.

14 DOUBLE-CROSS

Jim stared with burning eyes.

Here was what carelessness bought. No one had to tell him she was doing this for spite, for the indifference he'd shown her, for the scorn and contempt she'd read into his voice.

Those in the yard stood like shapes hacked from stone, faces distorted with conflicting emotions. Tapp, straightening first, let out a great yell. Rockabye's cheeks came around bright with sweat. Strunk leaped from the surrey. Dawks threw up his gun. The sound of their boots pounding through Final's head drove him toward Marcia's horse.

In the last fragment of grace Jim veered, catching the reins of Roup's sorrel. Looping these over the pommel Jim belted the horse across the rump with his pistol. The sorrel bolted, squealing, through the open side door. Shouts came from the yard as the horse crashed through the brush.

Jim caught hold of the crossbarred stanchion, flinging himself up it, diving into the loft as booted feet and Dawks' cursing converged on the front. He burrowed into the hay to lie half strangled by the stirred-up chaff. In the contagion of excitement every horse below was now cutting up, some of them by the sound becoming difficult to manage. The marshal swore viciously as one horse broke loose. Short seconds later two others tore off.

Jim waited no longer. Clawing out of the hay he dropped into the stable. Still gagging he ran down the row of stalls until he found the last mount—an apron faced bay—which he led out and swung onto, not bothering with gear. He went out by the front, booting the horse into a run.

He heard Quail's cry as he flashed past the half risen shape of her father. All hell seemed to explode in one convulsion of sound. *The Sharps!* he thought; and dropped Indian fashion along the bay's off flank, hanging on by a heel and his grip on its mane.

Water batted his eyes as they splashed through the creek. Soon as he dared he pulled himself up, knees taking hold again, sending the plunging horse through blurred cedar, thankful to have something as a screen against that rifle. He peered east toward Mad Springs, not forgetting his intention but afraid of Strunk's crew. He cut south, flogging the horse. They wouldn't be looking for him to ride into town.

When Marcia had come running into the yard, betraying Jim, those who heard and saw her could hardly have been more startled. Quail no less than the others had at first thought this a hoax. Then she saw Marcia's open waist and Tapp's enormous grin. As the man went catfooting toward the barn a horse crashed off through the brush to the east of it. Quail heard Dawks curse. "Quick!" Strunk shouted. "After him!"

Tapp whirled toward his mount while the Bandoleer marshal, caught in a funk of conflicting desires, stood frustratedly tangled between excitement and caution. "The barn," Marcia cried, "is filled with fresh horses!"

Quail looked at her sister as though seeing a stranger. Her father looked as though he wanted to weep, futilely twisting the bottom button of his coat. Rockabye, Quail noticed, was not joining the stampede.

She had never had much use for the man but now regarded him with almost open approval. This faded into fright as two other hard-running mounts left the barn. Alarm for Jim grew very real in her now. It was the look on Rockabye's face that brought her back.

Marcia, clutching the Sharps, was watching the barn. Rockabye was almost onto her and the fury Quail saw in his livid cheeks was confirmation of all her secret fears. She had refused to believe her sister could be having an affair with so coarse a man but could no longer doubt. There was something too abysmal—too frighteningly possessive—in that glassy shine of the man's outraged stare. He must have seen at once the condition of Marcia's waist and his pictures of her in that barn with Jim Final appeared to have unhinged his reason. Quail screamed at the girl but the thunder of running horses claimed all of the redhead's attention. Rockabye grabbed hold of her shoulder, spinning her brutally around.

Marcia's eyes were enormous. Quail was starting to run toward them when Final broke out of the gray gloom of the stable. "Jim!" she cried and, frozen, saw Rockabye wrest the Sharps from Marcia's hands. The girl, mouth ugly, tried to snatch it back. Rockabye struck her, knocking her down, whipping the gun's stock into the crotch of his shoulder. Fire gouted out of it and the monstrous report, driven back from the buildings, appeared to sweep Jim bodily off the horse. For a moment Quail swayed, trying to shut out the horror. When she looked again the horse was still going. Splashing out of the creek it plunged into timber, swallowed by rags of green foliage.

Marcia's cry got through to Quail. With muscles blessedly released from their paralysis she swung about to find Rockabye, like some enraged grizzly, grotesquely making for Strunk's surrey. She hadn't the slightest doubt what he was up to. The Morgan horse between the shafts appeared to share her apprehension. Ears laid back and neck stretched snakily, it rolled its eyes at the man's flashing blade.

Quail ran to her father, wrenching the pistol from his pocket. Stiff-cheeked she shot the horse in its tracks.

The Skillet ramrod glared, half lifting his hand as though minded to hurl the glittering knife straight at her. Face bloated with fury he spun toward his own mount. "You're not going anywhere," Quail said. "Stay away from it."

The man looked to be beside himself but Quail's face showed she meant what she said. Snarling, Rockabye stamped off toward the bunkhouse.

Quail did not intend to take chances. The ramrod's horse had been hard used and needed caring for but, tightening her mouth, Quail pulled off the gear and drove it out on the range. She did the same with the horse Tapp had left but didn't bother to remove its saddle.

Bentain was shaking like a man with malaria. She

helped him into the house, Marcia trailing in after them, eyes defiant. "I don't care," she said—"Rockabye's right. That man—I don't see how Quail can bear to have him around."

"You fool!" Bentain cried. "If they get rid of him we're done for!"

Half an hour after they'd entered the house Quail heard horses and knew the gambler was back. She'd returned her father's pocket gun. He'd shut himself up again in his office. Marcia, hating all of them, had gone to her room. Quail picked up her rifle.

Stepping onto the gallery she saw Tapp, on Strunk's orders, hastening barnward. "An' git one fer me, too," Dawks growled after him.

"You're pretty free," Quail said, "with other folks' property. Ever think about asking?"

Tapp's face wheeled. "What've you done with my horse?"

"You won't find it in the barn."

"We'll see." Tapp strode off.

The girl's gun was a 44 caliber rimfire Henry, a lever action repeater. She snugged the stock against her hip and laid a slug between Tapp's legs. The man's whipped-around face showed the blanch of pure shock. Dawks' eyes looked like pin balls.

"You haven't taken over yet," Quail told the gambler. "Until you do, keep your chicken-thieves in hand."

Strunk got a cigar from the breast pocket of his coat and carefully licked the tattered wrapper. "All right," he said. "We'd like to borrow a couple of horses."

"There isn't a fresh horse on this place."

Strunk told Tapp, "Go ahead and take a look."

Tapp eyed the rifle and stayed where he was. Rocka-bye came out of the bunkhouse, his look still wrinkled with fury. He glowered at Quail and stared at the horses the three had come in on. Despite their braced legs and dropped heads the trend of his thinking was plainly apparent. "I would hardly miss," Quail said, "at this distance."

Strunk gave her an affronted look. "Did you kill my Morgan?"

Some pretty sharp feeling got into her voice. "You figuring to leave those horses like that?"

"Where's Bentain?"

"You're dealing with Bentain's other daughter this trip, not that 'educated one with the carroty mane' either. Catch up those reins and cool them out."

Tapp sneered. The marshal, like a trusting hound, looked at Strunk. The gambler folded his arms and anchored his teeth in the tattered cigar. Quail's rifle went off. Strunk staggered sideways with only one heel left.

Quail jacked another cartridge into the breech and Seeb Dawks, not waiting for his turn, caught up the nearest reins and lugged a horse into motion. Strunk looked as though about to burst his surcingle but went limping off with a second horse at tether. The rifle cracked once more and Tapp—who hadn't been about to give in to no woman—tramped after the others.

Quail heard her father come onto the gallery. He mumbled something which the men didn't catch but they had no trouble making out Quail's reply. "It's the first honest work those three crooks have met up with."

"But Strunk—"

"Strunk's no different. He only talks that way."

This was hard for Strunk to take within the hearing of men he had to depend on, but a natural regard for his health held him silent.

Quail said loud enough for all of them to hear, "They're no more to be feared than any other dogs. Any cur will come to heel if you're willing to put your foot down."

She kept them walking the horses till the punished ground puffed dust knee high every time a hoof or foot plopped down. It was a sight for sore eyes though Bentain gave little evidence of enjoying it. If Quail was quaking you couldn't tell it from her look. Off to one side burly Rockabye stood with fists deep in pockets. When he finally took off toward the barn Quail was forced to ignore him. "All right," she called. "You can drop those reins and hit for town."

The men were rumpled, wet with sweat. Dawks' eyes seemed about to roll off his cheekbones. "You mean *walk!*"

"You don't expect to get there by flying do you?"

Strunk's look was the color of murder. His mouth jerked half open, then was clamped shut. He stalked off without a backward glance. While Tapp and the marshal stood stunned in their tracks, Rockabye left by the barn's side door, undiscovered.

He caught up with the hoofers just beyond the second ridge. They appeared to be deep in some kind of argument. Dawks looked as though he had lost his last friend; he had his plaid coat slung over a shoulder and there was a tear in his shirt where the badge had been. Strunk and Tapp were eyeing each other like a pair of riled tigers. "That," Tapp was saying, "ain't the point. She faced you down an' sent us packin'. That's the point, an' every scared rabbit in this country'll hear about it!"

It plainly tore at his loyalty, poisoning his faith in all he had believed. He said bitterly, "What are you figurin' to do?"

The gambler, noticing Rockabye, snarled: "What do you want?"

Skillet's ramrod spat. "There's a little matter of back wages."

"You get fired?"

"Ever try takin' orders from a petticoat?" He jerked

back, nastily startled, from the look on Strunk's face. But Strunk couldn't someway seem to amount to quite as much as he had and, recalling his own size, Rockabye sneered. "I've damn well got a bellyful."

Strunk looked mussed and mean. Dawks pulled off his derby and tried to fan up a little air. "Mean you're quittin'," Tapp said, "pullin' out on us?"

Rockabye said, looking hard at Strunk, "I got a lotta back pay comin'. Before I git in any deeper I want it."

The gambler chewed on his lip. He dug the badge from his pocket and tossed it to Dawks. "Duck on up ahead a bit, Seeb, and keep your eyes peeled."

"Now," he growled when the marshal was out of hearing—"now we'll get right down to cases. Can you still put your hands on that shotgun?"

The burly Skillet man looked surprised. "That Greener? Sure."

"All right. Here's the play." The gambler talked steadily for a couple of minutes and then, very carefully, went over the deal. "You'll have to use one of those broncs we cooled out."

"No trouble there," Bentain's ramrod said. "What about that back pay?"

The gambler, eyeing him, nodded. "He'll be packing five thousand. You can have the whole wad."

"I'll catch a fresh mount when I get to the wagon." The Skillet riding boss grinned. "This is goin' to be good."

"It better be good," Strunk told him. "Don't forget to leave that gun."

Rockabye, chuckling, turned back toward the ranch. He got into the barn as he'd left, through the side. The day was just about shot and someone—Quail probably—had put up the horses. That gray Strunk had used would get him out to the wagon.

He stepped around to the tool closet, easing open the

door. He lifted out shovels, two mattocks and an axe. He put a hand into the cavity, feeling over the dust blurred roughness of the walls and, swearing softly, ran a match across his pantsleg, making a downward cup of his hand. There was no gun in the closet though he'd got it down off the stringer last week, putting it here where on Gid Strunk's orders he would have it in readiness. The match-flame, throwing its oil-yellow shine across the chaff-strewn dust of the closet floor, picked out the track of a woman's boot.

Rockabye snapped the match and straightened, breathing heavily. He left the tools where they were and went down the row of stalls. The gray he had figured on using was gone.

He threw his stare around, scowling. She'd not have got far on a horse tired as these were. He readied a roan, yanking it viciously through the side door. He'd shod that gray himself not three days ago and—though he might have to get down with a match now and again —looked for no trouble in picking up sign. She'd prob-ably headed for town—where else could she go?

He got onto the horse.

15 DUEL WITH A CHIEF

Twice within three miles Jim was compelled to stop and take cover with a hand clamped over the gelding's nostrils while flitting shapes scudded over the ridgetops. Increasingly alarmed by this activity he abandoned his notion of going through town, angling directly now for the Apache *rancheria*. Those bucks he had seen were out on the scout. The sooner Jim got to Taunee the better.

His care increased as he moved deeper into the wilds

of the reservation. He kept to cover where he could, not minded to see his life go for nothing, afraid of the low spots and not brash enough to chance skylining himself where he was able to avoid this. He could have made better time, for the going would have been easier along the hogbacks and rimrock, but he was afraid of these patrols. He'd lived around Apaches too long to regard with anything but sober respect their skill with native weapons. In Jim's father's time survival had frequently depended on a white man's ability to match or excell the red man's wily stratagems. Jim could handle knife or tomahawk, not superbly perhaps, but he could give an account of himself he needn't blush for. He'd spent hundreds of hours unraveling sign. As he rode his eyes were constantly busy, probing, assessing and storing each bit of knowledge this hard land gave up.

He read each darker shading where bent blades of grass no longer caught light and where other grass had been recently bruised. He never passed droppings without determining texture. The rim of a moccasin in sand or dust could reveal as much as a printed page. In his father's day this kind of knowledge was the prerequisite of continued existence and, though rusty, Jim had not forgotten it. Apaches were moving all over this region. Chuleh's eyes and ears.

When full dark came Final took to the ridgetops for safer travel. Although most of the time he could not see a rope's length ahead of him there was still enough light for him to study the ground. He was down, leading the horse now, its shod hoofs muffled with strips from his shirt. Jim's head swung constantly, his glance never still. Though he was going to Taunee's village it made a difference how he got there.

Plagued by doubts, gnawed by worries, he was filled with foreboding each time his thoughts leaped beyond his grasp. What guarantees could he offer these people? What right had he to speak at all?

He remembered Bentain asking *What could they fight with?* But the answer to that was not far to seek. If Strunk could arrange to provide forbidden whiskey he could deliver rifles if he knew where, and if the tribe was expecting them. "When we get rifles—" Chuleh had snarled.

It occurred to Jim he might be doing the smarter thing if he went on to the post for a talk with Major Berkley, yet he knew the futility of attempting to get any help from the Army. Camp Grant was too far away and Berkley would insist on facts. Even if Jim could convince the man Berkley would still have to get the permission of his superiors and these would probably want an okay from Washington. Time wouldn't wait—nor would these Indians once Strunk had armed them.

He was worried about Quail, knowing it was very likely part of Strunk's plans to have the Apaches, once they got started, make Bentain's ranch their first port of call. And there was no good going over that again; if he could not hide his love for Quail from himself he could certainly keep it from involving her further. He was the pawn of Joe Bob in a game played for keeps and as such had decently no right to embroil any woman in the short-term skein of so problematical a future.

Danger was a taste in Jim Final's mouth but his hackles could not tell him whereabouts disaster lurked. His own account with Strunk cried out for settlement but something stronger than desire pushed him through his weird imaginings, his nightmare doubts and anger toward the rendezvous he'd set for himself at Taunee's camp.

Weary and bitter though he was his troubled thoughts would not leave him alone. Why were these Indian lands so important? Strunk was not after them to help those

fool grangers! Normal avarice Jim could understand,
even greed; but was Strunk so blind, so determined, he
could not see that with guns in their hands all whites
would look alike to these outraged Apaches? That he'd
have to pull up stakes himself?

No, the man was playing whole-hog, would never
voluntarily leave the fruits of his plotting for some other
hand to pick. It was Bentain and the lease money which
he still apparently had not paid which dragged the
hardest on Jim's concern. If there was any deal at all
between Joe Bob and Quail's scared father it almost had
to be based on the Governor supplying that money—
there was nowhere else he could raise it. So what was
Joe Bob holding back for? Was he actually, as Jim
more than half suspected, holding it back in deliberate
aggravation, as one more broken promise to skewer
Taunee and prod Chuleh into action? Did the Governor,
too, want those Indians moved?

Out of the blue, sprung from his own desperate thinking, came Jim's answer. Taunee had put the words to
it and Jim, believing that talk pure rhetoric, had failed
to give the lament any value. But it fit all right. Jim's
father had always contended—Jim nodded. This had to
be what Strunk and Joe Bob were after.

Taunee's *rancheria* was not asleep.

Jim heard the drums and the chant of voices before
he glimpsed the wink of their fires. Cold all through,
teeth uncontrollably chattering, he tied the horse where
it could be seen come daylight and warily advanced.

Against the bright leap of wind-fluttered flames the
dappled silhouettes of dancing Apaches invoked deeper
dread than Jim had ever known. Where the light fell
upon them he could see the sweaty gleam of paint-
smeared naked bodies.

He watched for several moments, screened by a tangle

of foliage, then went back for the horse and rode it boldly into the firelight. There was only one way to show up at this dance if you aimed to go off wearing your hair.

They were dancing all right—the real thing this time. The medicine man was shaking his rattle, every warrior in sight was stomping and yelling. The throb of the drums increased its frenzy, gradually falling to a savage whimper. The rhythm became furiously, insufferably provocative, insinuating itself into Final's tissues. His bones ached with the beat of it, its wildness calling to something primitive within him, just as it was calling up the devil in these others.

A goggling child saw Jim first. An old woman screeched but went unheard. Other women sprang up, faces distorted with anger. A pack of curs came at his horse, darting between the legs of the dancers. Two old men wheeled at the edge of the gathering and the drums went still with a breathcatching suddenness.

It was then Jim caught his first look at the captives.

They were obviously bound, huddled off to one side between Taunee's *wickiup* and Chuleh's where shadows lay blue-black as smoke and the leap of flames revealed only brass buttons and, now and again, the bright streak of a saber case.

Cavalry!

Jim swung off the horse. A boy ran up and spat at him. Final pushed his way deeper into the glare. An old man barred his way with a lance. Jim took the thing and, breaking it, tossed both pieces into the flames. It would take big medicine to pull this off.

He stared with scorn into those glowering faces. He saw Taunee's set like stone in its wrinkles; and yonder, making toward him, the hate-twisted expression of the sub-chief, Chuleh.

He shoved others out of his way coming up, planting

himself like a bull about to charge. A wild-eyed Apache, chest draped in charm strings and with a cow's horn sprouting from the bulge of his left temple, popped up at Chuleh's shoulder. A misshapen gnome of a man this was, a gourd vibrating in each fist like a prodded rattler. The sub-chief was making big medicine too.

It was Taunee's right to speak and evidence of his fallen estate that Chuleh took the play away from him. "Bare Chest heap much brave," he growled, "but only fool puts face in fire."

Jim got the makings out of his pants and put a cigarette together, thoughtfully licking it, knowing he'd got to make this good. "Only a child shuts his eyes to the truth." Reaching out he took hold of and scornfully fingered a strand of the horned man's repulsive charms. He let them drop with a grin, ignoring the growls that came out of the man's followers. He brushed the outraged hunchback aside and bending over the nearest fire got himself a cherry-red coal, picking it casually up in left hand.

Smoke made a stinking sickening cloud. The hand smelled like a branding fire. Jim's grin, though ghastly, clung to his face. He touched the coal to his cigarette, drew in deeply and tossed the red ember at Chuleh's gourd rattler.

The medicine man, startled, involuntarily jerked aside. Final, pushing smoke through his nostrils, spoke to Taunee across Chuleh's shoulder. "Tell Man-Afraid-of-Fire to turn those pony soldiers loose. If he's got to show what a big moose he is let him fetch that bringer of whisky and rifles that we may see what tracks his tongue will make when I tear it out of his lying mouth."

Those who think Indians never show emotion should have seen the look on Chuleh's cheeks. With a berserk shout he flung about, so riled every muscle of his squat body appeared to swell. But Jim beat him to the pitch.

355

Snatching the knife from Chuleh's belt he crossed to the prisoners and cut them free.

A growl of angry muttering went up. The sub-chief's partisans, fingering their weapons, sent wondering looks at the man who would lead them. Final came back, cigarette dangling, to face the wrath stirred up by this brashness.

He looked directly at Chuleh. "Give Yellow Legs back their ponies and equipment."

Nobody moved. The stillness pushed against Jim like a hand but you wouldn't have guessed he was scared by the look of him. "Loud Mouth," he said, pointing Chuleh's knife at the sub-chief, "talks of war and paints his face, encouraging the young men to dangerous thoughts and impossible dreams. Taunee knows and has truthfully told you nothing can come of this but death.

"Chuleh has promised you many rifles. Perhaps he can get them. But if you accept these and attempt to use them to bring about these foolish dreams I think pretty soon there'll be no more Apaches. Have you forgotten the great chief Cochise? Can you no longer remember—"

"You make heap big palaver," Chuleh yelled—"now you fight!" He yanked the war axe from his belt and hurled it at Final's feet.

Jim kicked it contemptuously into the fire.

Chuleh's face was livid. He might have flung himself barehanded at Jim had the white man not held up the knife. "If you've got to fight," Final said, "we'll fight with this. Wrist to wrist. And if I win these men go free."

A racket of guttural talk welled up but Jim had forced Chuleh's hand and the sub-chief finally grunted. Two braves ran forward, binding Chuleh's right wrist to Jim's. The knife was thrust into their hands. The braves sprang back. Chuleh instantly tried to rush Jim off his feet.

Final, expecting this, stumbled the man around the braced pivot of his body. Before the sub-chief could recover his balance Jim whirled, slamming Chuleh hard against the bole of a tree. The Apache grunted like a clubbed pig. But the arm whose hand was gripped with Jim's about the half of that wicked blade was like spring steel.

Even with his back being ground against that bark the sub-chief regained control of himself. There was a world of strength in that short stocky shape. Jim had been tired before this got started and now with sweat cracking through the pores of his skin he was beginning to wonder if he'd last the man out.

More wood built up the nearest fires. Chuleh's painted face in this flickering light showed ridges of strain. The muscles in Jim's back and in the calves of his legs set up an anguished throbbing and the scald of burned fingers wasn't helping him any. Now the cords at the back of his knees threatened to pop and a glint of malicious triumph began to show through the hateful shine of Chuleh's eyes. Jim's arm commenced to move toward him from the elbow and the flashing blade jumped at his throat.

The crowd was around them like the roar of distant surf. Change lashed through the howls of Chuleh's followers. Alarm crept into the strained faces of the captured patrol.

Sweat was in Jim's eyes like gritty fingers. He had to give ground to get away from that knife. He gave ground but the knife came after him. With their legs entwined he tried to trip Chuleh up but the Apache, grunting, used the momentum of his weight to grind Jim against the tree. Cold steel scraped the bony top of Final's shoulder. Rough bark gouged his uncovered back. He drove a spiked heel into a moccasined foot, grinding down sav-

357

agely, seeing the thin flash of the Apache's teeth. The pressure eased enough for Jim to force the blade away from him.

Chuleh bent with the thrust of Jim's arm and carried them both away from the tree. He swung clear around, hauling Jim with him; to break the lever this gave to the Apache Final put the drive of his legs into the swing, forcing the man off balance.

They went down, kicking and rolling, their breath coming now in tearing sobs as each furiously fought to keep from being pinned down. A stone dug sharply into Final's side. He thought a rib must surely go. To get away from this he had to turn and Chuleh, grunting, drove him all the way over, dodging the knee Final thrust at his groin, flattening Jim hard against the ground. Jim braced his elbow to keep the knife away from him. Sweat rolling off Chuleh's chin fell into his face.

The groans of the troopers, the swelling shouts of Chuleh's partisans, grew dim behind the roar of blood in Jim's ears. He tried to heave the man off but couldn't get enough purchase. He tried to roll and the Apache blocked him. Chuleh had the advantage of leverage with a knee firmly planted on either side of Jim's chest. Jim's arm began to shake. The shine of steel edged nearer.

Gouging into the ground with the heels of his boots Final tried spasmodically again to get his back up but the dirt kept breaking away. Ignoring the knife Jim went suddenly limp in a desperation trick. Pain splintered through him as the blade sliced into the bulge of a muscle. Before the Apache could whip it clear Jim's legs had come up. He locked his knees around Chuleh's head.

All of Jim's strength went into that hold, inexorably tightening, bending the Indian backward, tearing him away from his leverage. It was the troopers now who were whooping but Jim didn't hear. Every faculty he had, every last bit of strength, was being poured into that terrible scissoring that was dragging the sub-chief up off his knees. As the knees cleared Jim's chest the Apache flung himself sideways, taking Jim with him but not breaking Jim's hold.

Final rolled grinding Chuleh's face into the dirt, grinding the lashed wrist into it also, giving it all the torture he could manage, but the Apache wouldn't quit. His fingers kept their sweaty grip, locked with Jim's about the haft of the knife.

Now he wrenched the blade over, pushing it toward Jim Final's belly. By a sudden switch in direction he shaved two inches of hide off Jim's leg. Jim involuntarily flinched and Chuleh tore his trapped head free, rolling with both lashed wrists hugged against him, trying his best to snap Final's arm.

Breath came through Jim's teeth in a rush but he blocked that try by rolling over. Chuleh's knee slammed into his crotch and everything went black and red. Jim was almost helpless but all of his weight lay across those lashed wrists and Chuleh was not able to get the knife off the ground.

He slugged at Jim's kidney with his free left fist; then, stiffening his fingers, jabbed them into Jim's face. Final, twisting, saved his eyes but the Apache got a finger into the corner of Jim's mouth and forced him to roll, freeing the trapped blade.

Chuleh lunged to his feet dragging Final with him. They were both gagging for breath. Blood was sticky slick against Jim's cut leg and there was blood on his chest from that rip in his shoulder. Chuleh forced the knife up and Final, letting him, suddenly dropped, throwing his whole weight against Chuleh's shins. The Apache went over Jim's back with a yell. He struck hard and went limp with his right arm unhinged.

359

16 THE RIFLES

Quail had been frightened by the gambler's news that Jim had broken out of Yuma and was wanted dead or alive. Twenty-five hundred dollars was a great deal of money. It could fill these hills with bounty hunters and Jim's chances, as she saw them, were not worth a plugged peso. Sooner or later they were bound to get him. Why had he lied to her? What could she do?

She had felt the cold hand of terror when Rockabye had snatched that Sharps from her sister and Jim, at the shot, had seemed to fall off the horse—but this was as nothing to what she felt now. Where would he go? How could she help him?

With the cooled horses put up, sitting here on the gallery with nothing to occupy her mind but dread, she couldn't chain her thoughts and they kept tumbling over each other in bitter repetition of all those recent ghastly sequences. Jim's unexpected appearance. Jim telling her they were through with each other. Jim killing Roup. Jim in the barn with her sister and Marcia running out with her waist— And still she wanted him, wanted him terribly. She could not vision a future without Jim.

Like Rockabye, though she resented the comparison, she was finding Jim's presence in that barn with Marcia assuming an importance she was sure it never had. She could discount what she had seen but she couldn't put down her treacherous doubts. Her thoughts kept picking at them, kept resurrecting them. He was hard now and bitter, angry enough to use a gun on Roup. And if he'd broken out of Yuma only revenge could have fetched him here. Had he sought to revenge himself on Bentain by ruining or trying to ruin Marcia?

She couldn't quite believe that. She kept remembering Rockabye, the wild malevolent look of him as Marcia had run out of the barn with that rifle. The range boss believed she had been shining up to Final—and he'd been right. Quail saw this now. Marcia had tried her wiles on Jim and, stung by his indifference— Yes. That was how it had been.

And Roup—*Dawks had lied!* They'd been trying to pin something on Jim and Roup had been killed before they'd found out about Yuma. They didn't need Roup now. They had Jim dead to rights. An escaped prisoner, wanted! Why had Jim ever been so crazy? How could he have hoped—

Quail got up and looked around, surprised to discover it was almost dark. Twilight's shadows bluely lay across the yard and she thought, looking barnward, to have caught some tag end of motion. Now, looking more carefully, she couldn't find anything and guessed it had been some trick of the light.

If only she knew where Jim had gone off to. She thought of the fright Bentain had shown and was herself more frightened. She needed to talk with Jim, to make sure he understood they were after him; to give himself up if he could be persuaded before this thing got entirely out of hand. Twenty-five hundred!

She shook uncontrollably. It was monstrous, out of all proportion to the crime he'd been charged with; and now, with Roup dead, no one would try to bring Jim in alive. So much money could tempt anyone. The whole country would be after him!

Perhaps she'd better see Marcia. She got up and went inside and, tucking up her hair, with a glance at the mirror went off down the hall. She knocked when she came to her sister's door and then, mouth firming, thumbed back the latch. The door wouldn't budge.

"Marcia!" she cried, and knocked again. When there

361

still was no response she went around through the kitchen and into the rear of the yard. Marcia's window was open but the girl was not in there. Quail couldn't ignore the evidences of flight—the pulled-out drawers, the rumple of discarded clothes. Peering again toward the barn Quail broke into a run.

The roan was gone. The gray as well. Panicked now, without quite knowing why Quail lifted her voice in a tremulous yell. Nothing came back but echoes. With fear like fingers digging into her throat she hurried over to the bunkhouse. The place was empty. She had known it would be. *Had Marcia gone off with Rockabye or had the range boss set out after her?*

Quail ran back to the house. In her distraction she went into her father's office without bothering to knock. The pistol she had glimpsed before lay gleaming and ugly by her father's hand. He was staring at a heap of ore samples he appeared to have tumbled from a buckskin poke. He made no attempt to hide them. "Quail," he groaned from somewhere deep inside him, "what am I going to do?"

It was two hours after dark when Strunk and his tin-badge rode into town on mounts Tapp had got them from Squatting O. They'd traveled mostly in silence, the gambler nursing his fury. Dawks saw huddles of muttering men on the street and the Trail's End saloon was closed, tightly shuttered. Several others were too, he noticed as they passed Whisky Row. More than once men called to them, veering out off the walks, but Strunk went on, ignoring them utterly.

Increasingly worried, the marshal stayed at his heels. It was all well and good for Strunk to say Prektell had to be killed; but Roup had been too, and this guy Prektell was a Mormon Bishop and Dawks was suddenly leery of killing. Final was still loose, maybe waiting here for them, lurking in one of these ink-black alleys behind the snout of a lifted gun.

And those goddam Injuns!

The Arrowhead was shut and all the baled stuff and crates were gone from the loading platform at the side of Rankin's Emporium. And there was that dumb Swede Hastenfeldter boarding up the bake shop. It gave Dawks the creeping willies the way fellows kept twisting their heads to peer after them. He said as much.

Strunk wasn't listening. The double-distilled gall of that girl making fools of them while that slut of a Marcia rolled in the hay with that sonofabitch jailbird kept gouging at his pride till he was at the verge of screaming. He swung up the alley that led behind his Hall of Mirrors, got off his horse and blackly tied it. "Go round up your deputies," he growled at the marshal.

He didn't like the thought of Jim being loose any better than Dawks did but all the rest of the tricks in this deal were good as gathered. Tonight would finish Bentain if not Skillet and tomorrow the Apaches would have those new Army Winchesters. He knew what ailed those fools in the street, that much, at least, had gone off without hitch. A week from now he would own this damned country!

He bolted the door and stepped into his bar to set up more precautions just in case Dawks' deputies should happen to slip up. This was the one place in town that could stand off Indians or anything else. Its windows were slots backed by heavy shutters; its walls, three-foot thick, would stand a heap longer than he would have any need of them. Let Joe Bob rant. He knew all right what Gid was up to but there wasn't one thing he could put his finger on. And Bentain wouldn't be around to help him. When this thing broke Joe Bob was whipped—he couldn't touch Strunk without exposing

himself. It was finders keepers and the first guy there
with the most guns got it!

There was nothing whatever to worry about. The
gambler shut himself up in his office and got the assayer's
reports from his safe.

The whole stinking bunch pressed around them and
Final knew by the look of their faces anything could
happen in the next couple of minutes. On Taunee's
orders a brave cut him loose. While Jim was rubbing
his chafed wrist the lieutenant and a sergeant pushed
nervously up. The officer was green and filled with the
confusions of the inexperienced plus too much stuff he'd
got out of the book. He had his hair on his mind in
addition to other things and likely the hair weighed as
much as all of them. Jim caught hold of the nearest Indian
—a risky thing when he thought back on it later, but
right then he was a little mixed up himself. "Bring up
the pony soldiers' horses. Bring their long knives and
fire sticks too."

The redman glared. Nobody moved. Visibly sweating
the lieutenant said hoarsely, "Maybe we—" but Jim
wheeled down an opening lane and came before the
chief. Taunee's eyes looked flat as stove lids. Jim, steeped
in the dregs of a thousand sleepless nights, caught in
the blind anger of having risked everything to no apparent purpose, cried at the man, "Will you be like fool
whose words wear two faces?"

The heat of the fight still colored Jim's thinking and
all he could fasten on was the total uselessness of what
he had been through if the Apaches refused to release
these troopers. All he would have gained was a small
respite which would count for less than nothing if—
believing this patrol was wiped out—that bullheaded
major stormed into the field.

The chief's look told Jim nothing. The man seemed

to have withdrawn from this place to some level on which Jim's words couldn't find him.

"That devil man, Strunk," Jim tried again, "has pictured a time when, through rifles he has promised, the People shall take back this land for themselves. But you know better than that. Strunk laughs at Chuleh! Not even the great chief Geronimo, mighty in war and wisdom, was able to do this thing—how then can Chuleh?

"It is Strunk who would have the People moved so that he may tear from the ground the Yellow Iron which you have kept hidden. You heard, Great Chief, the bargain Chuleh made. Give these White Eyes what belongs to them that they may speak good words of you to *Nantan* Berkley, the soldier chief at Camp Grant."

Taunee seemed to huddle deeper into his shoulders. When at last he spoke it was to say with quiet dignity, "The pony soldiers can go."

His glance touched a number of the older men. These warriors slipped away and shortly returned with the horses and equipment. When the troopers swung grayfaced into their saddles the lieutenant saluted Taunee with his blade. He glanced around then at Final. "You'd better leave with us."

Jim said grimly. "Extend Major Berkley my compliments. Tell him for God's sake to stay away from this place. The least show of force on his part right now could drive this whole outfit right into Chuleh's camp."

He said louder now and more slowly so that Taunee and any of those others who might savvy plain American could catch the drift. "Say to *Nantan* Berkley the great chief Taunee, whose wisdom and courage is matched only by the trust and friendship he has for his white brothers, has sent you back unharmed after a renegade dog called 'Chuleh' would have roasted you topside down over a fire."

He saw the effect of this through the camp, passed

365

in a mutter from lip to lip. Taunee said, *"Enju—*this is truth," and many a watching brave nodded bleakly.

"Very well," the lieutenant said, "I'll tell him." He shot a baffled, somewhat exasperated look at Jim, fetching the end of that glance back over his men. "In column of twos—" He lifted his saber and the detail moved out.

Final looked for Chuleh but the stocky Apache was gone. No one had needed to draw him a picture of how much face he had lost this night. If he had not already slipped away from the village he soon would. Jim didn't believe he would go alone; there were always plenty of disgruntled men to follow one who promised much for little. Before another sun went down the sub-chief would try, Final thought, to make contact with Strunk—was perhaps even now bitterly bound for some rendezvous. The gambler would find rifles for them.

The departing patrol had ridden into the east. Now, out of the south, other hoofs were lifting. Jim, no less than the redmen around him, tautly stared as the thunder of these hurtled rapidly toward them.

All Jim's anxieties suddenly fused in a frantic unequivocal foretaste of disaster. It was unreasonable, frightening, the way this presentiment hit him when he should have been immune to such foolishness, riding high in the knowledge of his victory over Chuleh which, besides removing Quail and other isolated ranchers from immediate peril, must shake the very mainstay of Strunk's brute drive for empire.

But the old chief felt it too. His eyes were grim as with all the rest he stood tensely listening to the drum of that pony. Now they could hear the labored grunts of its breathing.

The horse burst through the black barrier of night and was hauled to its haunches within six feet of Jim, towering like some rampant monster over the flames of the old chief's fire.

A naked Apache looked down from its back. Fierce
eyes wickedly swept those upturned faces. He loosed
one yell before he let the horse down. He was young
and proud and red-bloodedly savage.

"*The rifles are waiting!*"

17 KRAMER'S BARN

The courier's eyes, discovering Final, went still and
sharp. Danger prodded Jim, opening all the closed doors
of his mind. He understood the grim message the chief
couldn't speak and, wiping the blood-crusted blade on
ripped pantsleg, stepped away from the light.

"Why is this White Eyes here?" cried the horseman.

Guttural voices rose, harsh with excitement while Jim
slipped deeper into the wavering shadows, reached his
horse and swung aboard. He locked his jaws against the
pain clawing through him and with a hand on its neck
sent the gelding angling off through the dark. He
rounded the springs under cover of the cottonwoods and
drifted off through willows whose growth hid the camp
from higher country to the north.

Now he dared push the animal harder, clamped knees
impatiently turning it into a direct crosscut for town.
Bandoleer had to be warned. Strunk would likely be
watching for him, his whole crowd alerted in addition
to deputies sworn in by Seeb Dawks. Between here and
and there the hills could be crawling with patrols put
out by Tapp from Squatting O. Jim had to take these
chances. It wasn't in him to abandon the kids and women
of this country to the savagery Strunk was trying so
hard to unleash.

Taunee, almost certainly now, would hold out for

peace, his authority restored over the older heads. But some would follow Chuleh regardless, the hotbloods and renegades and those wilder untried ones who, to serve their own ends, would take scalps where they could. There didn't have to be many to consummate Strunk's intention.

Jim rode hard, only half conscious of the wind's lonely whine. Once they got their hands on rifles Chuleh's bunch would almost certainly hit the nearest outlying ranches.

It was a terrible thought to ride with, knowing Quail and her sister would be holed up at Skillet, their only defense a half-crazy old man trying to hide from his conscience behind the stuff in a bottle.

Strunk, to Jim now, was little more than a shadow flitting through the dread of this hell he was loosing. Groaning under the weight of his responsibility Jim drove the horse up out of the desert, away from the brooding shapes of yucca into the juniper hills where gray branches kept their trembling vigil. Pressure of time was like a rope snaking after him.

The rank odor of sweat came up from the horse and he could feel the wet hair of its hide like lather against the insides of his knees where he'd torn the ripped legs of his pants away to bind up the cuts Chuleh's knife had inflicted. And he could still feel the fire leaping through his burnt fingers.

Now they were climbing through forests of spruce with the wind's distant wail booming out of high timber. There could be Indians here. Some of Tapp's crew might be prowling this country. The stars looked down palely around a thin slice of moon. Jim kept doggedly on.

He reached the Gap and rode through it with the wind keening weirdly off the immense upthrust rock, around patches of brush that grew precariously out of it. Leaving the gut of the pass, cleaving more to the east though

still generally south, they stayed with the heights
wherever this proved feasible. Watching eyes might
more easily discover them but by keeping to the rimrock
they seemed a lot less likely to encounter an ambush.
That was Jim's dread.

An hour past midnight they picked up the lights of
town. A lot more lights than Jim had been expecting.
The horse was staggering now. Final dropped a com-
passionate hand to its shoulder. A mile farther on he
slid off, abandoning it, still driven by time.

He kept as deep as he could within the blackness of
shadows but there were moments when these were not
as dark as he'd have liked. Every house and most of the
shacks in this place had a lamp lit and, not understanding, he grew more cautious with each step.

There had to be a reason for all these people being up.
He was increasingly tempted to knock and ask what
had happened. He reckoned he'd find out once he got
to Kramer's livery. The stableman could spread the news
of those rifles, freeing Jim to return to Bentain's.

Pinched in on three sides by the bald knobs of mountains the town more resembled something found in lode
country than it did the headquarters of an expanding
cattle industry. Shacks of gray wood interspersed with
Victorian gingerbread flanked narrow twisted streets.
An occasional iron hitching post stood aloof from common cedar rails which guarded carpentered patches of
walk as Jim got nearer to the business district. This was
one crammed block of cheek-by-jowl buildings. Here
the road was wider, almost sixty feet from walk to walk.
There were the twelve saloons of Whisky Row, some
of these combining gambling and women. There were
two general stores, one on each side of the street and
both of them dark. Hastenfeldter's bake shop was also
dark, its windows boarded over like the Arrowhead
yonder and the Trail's End. There was a gun shop, a

saddlemaker's, two pool halls and a furniture store that doubled for a mortuary. At the head of this block where it bisected Cody, Jim saw the open front of Stegner's barn where Roup's horse had come from and where Jim had gone that first night without welcome.

But he wasn't thinking of Stegner. He was thinking he'd better get off this damned street before somebody recognized him. There were not many folks abroad in spite of the lights. The very quietness of the town was disquieting.

He moved into an alley, waiting a moment to see if he were followed. When the way seemed clear he advanced, still watchful, into the deeper dark toward the rear. In spite of this care one boot scuffed a can and the can rolled and rattled. Jim almost stopped breathing. After a bit he went on.

It was not as dark here as he'd hoped for. Shafts of light sliced the shadows from open doors and half a dozen shadeless windows. Brush grew along the slope of these back lots and he watched that too, uneasily aware he might be stepping into a trap. But he dared not squander more time than he had to. He drifted silently through three patches of lamplight, stopping each time just beyond to look and listen. It was while he was sliding through the fourth bar of light that he caught somewhere back of him the gravelly rasp of booted feet.

Final dived into the shadows and dropped. A gun blasted sound against the backs of the buildings. He felt the wind of that shot and wisely stayed where he was.

"Got him, by God! Take a look at him Seeb."

"Look yourself," the marshal's nasal tones came testily out of the blackness ahead of Jim.

The man back of Jim said, "Strike a light. I'll cover you."

Dawks swore. After a moment he moved reluctantly toward Jim. Final, holding his breath, tried to place him by sound. But there wasn't that much. He didn't twist his head. The marshal stopped after a couple of steps. "I don't see him."

"More this way. About three yards farther out."

Dawks, snarling, moved again. "He ain't around here."

"Hell, he can't be more'n three feet away—strike a light an' you'll find him."

"Yeah."

Dawks didn't oblige him. He didn't do any more moving, either. Jim, badly cramped, raised himself onto the balls of his feet. Sweat came out all over him but nothing happened. Dawks started to turn then, eyes probing the shadows. His face came around. He suddenly froze in his tracks.

Jim could see the lips writhe back off his teeth as the marshal pulled air into his lungs for a yell. Jim threw the knife as Dawks' gun whipped around. A grunt leaked out of Dawks, his hand let the gun go. Jim caught and eased his collapsing bulk to the ground.

The other man growled, "What the hell are you doin'?"

Jim cleared his throat in the nervous manner of Dawks. "He ain't here," he said gruffly. "I don't think you got him. He's probably tryin' to squeeze past you."

He bent over, unbuckling the marshal's cartridge belt. He pulled this clear. Strapping it about his own waist Jim freed the pistol pinned down by Dawks' weight and moved with no attempt at stealth toward the end of the alley he had previously been headed for.

The other man swore. "Where you off to?"

"Goin' to get some help," Final mumbled. He paid no attention to the fellow's angry cursing. The rest of his stretch was completely dark, even where it debouched into the lane which went behind the back of Kramer's livery.

Moving into this Jim paused, briefly listening. He could

371

hear Dawks' partner moving around still grumbling, but the man wasn't lighting any matches.

Jim worked to the rear of Kramer's stable. Though he naturally regretted it, killing Dawks had been unavoidable. This was no time for squeamishness. It was Dawks' who'd laid open Jim's cheek with a pistol and the man would have killed him just now if he'd been able.

Jim was deep in the ironwoods back of the livery; he felt his way up against the wall of the stable. The restive stamping of horses came through the warped planks, the rasp of one's teeth scraping wood from a crossbar. It bothered Jim that Kramer wasn't showing any light. Whatever was keeping this town out of bed had surely given it a scare. The sooner he swapped jaw with the stableman the better.

Ducking along the wall he came out of the ironwoods midway between the front and the back. The familiar smells somehow failed to ease him and he grew conscious of his weariness, of the hunger growling through him. His mind caught up that picture again of Marcia busting into the yard with that Sharps. He reckoned his nerves had about reached their limit, and was twisting to catch a better view of the alley when his stare discovered a man's dismounted shape streaking toward the barn's front, trotting up from the lane, and he lifted the marshal's gun, driving two slugs after him.

He didn't hear the man fall. He couldn't cut any sign of that galoot in the alley who by this time ought to have stumbled onto Dawks. Maybe the sight of that knife had stampeded him. Jim, grinning bleakly, went into the barn.

He could hear an excited churning of horses. All his senses were straining, pushing out ahead of him, trying to pin the man down—the one he had fired at—or narrow his whereabouts to one chunk of blackness.

Shadows hung over this place like blankets, the open slot of the runway only faintly suggested, just a gray dab against whatever was flanking it. The barn wasn't floored and the hardpacked ground began to give up dust under the continued movement of nervous horses. This commenced to plague Final's nostrils.

The fellow was obviously waiting for him to move. The horses quieted while Jim was trying to think of some way he might draw the man's fire without disastrous results. The only tossables he could think of were the boots on his feet and he was scared the man would hear if he should try to work one off. He remembered the cartridges Marcia had given him—the ones for the Sharps.

He was tentatively sliding a hand toward his pocket when a voice said back him: "Rattle one spur an' you're a gone goose, feller!"

18 SCALPING PARTY

Caught flat-footed Jim was too disgusted even to grunt. Instead of continuing in the direction he'd been headed the fellow had switched and ducked back when Jim fired. There being nothing he could do about it he said, "Your coon," and heard a shaky laugh.

"Kramer!" Jim swore, and took hold of an upright he was that full of trembles. But even as the stableman started to laugh a yell went up and men plunged from the alley, breaking into the lane.

Kramer slammed the door and twisted a heavy bar into the socket, pushing Jim deeper into the blackness. "Ain't got no damn boots on—got shed of 'em after you—" He stood listening. "Take that horse in the last stall."

"Wait," Jim growled. "Chuleh's bunch have got rifles."

"You don't have to tell *me!*"

"But these women and kids."

"They know all about it. Climb onto that bronc."

"I've got to have two."

"Take ten if you want 'em but get for Pete's sake movin'! Them fellers outside—Here, take this halter shank. Any of them broncs towards the back has got bottom. Allus figgered if I had to light out I wouldn't be stoppin' to pick any daisies."

Kramer worked as he talked; through the sounds of it Jim heard other sounds. Dragging three horses the man went through the back door, was swinging onto a fourth that was already saddled when Jim led his pair into the night's coolness after him. If his mind hadn't been taken up with matters more urgent he might, without shirt, have found it downright chilly. "They'll be figurin' to pinch us off," Kramer muttered. "We better hike up this slope."

"You got no call—"

"Don't tell me what I got!" The stableman snorted. Then a gun by the pens started hammering their eardrums and Kramer, twisting around in the stirrups, squeezed off three slugs at that muzzle flash. "I hope," Final growled, "you know what you're doing."

They could hear bullets whistling and striking all about them, drilling wood and dirt, whining off harder surfaces. Kramer chuckled. "My ol' man fit with Maw the biggest part of their lives without ever winnin' more'n a couple skirmishes. Point is he kep' at it. Man's gotta have principles."

Jim, turning around, swung past the halter-shanked dun he'd been going to mount, thrusting the strap's end to Kramer along with the rope he had put on the other. "I got to have me a hull."

"Righthand wall—I've got 'em on pegs." The stable-man, sighing, drove one low-held shot into a cluster of shadows he didn't think belonged beyond the edge of the pens. Somebody swore over there in a kind of choked whisper and Kramer backed his plunging horses deeper into the lee of a twenty-foot mound of baled alfalfa.

Jim rejoined him with gear and a blanket which he put on the dun—his favorite color of horse—and then reloaded Dawk's pistol. "They've dug in behind that hay!" someone shouted. Off to the left a rifle lifted its clamor.

Final, wheeling, whipped a shot toward the voice but it was wild. The man, belligerently swearing, ducked to one side and laced the night with his fire. Soon as it quit Final climbed into leather, uncovered his lead rope and set after Kramer's batch of towed horses in a scramble for the slope.

Guns cracked spitefully. The night was filled with commotion. Bullets chunked through the brush and the mount Jim was leading went up on its hind legs scream-ing and dropped. "Keep goin'!" Jim yelled. Kramer, muttering, bulled a way through the thorny tangle of branches, dragging the led horses after him.

There was no trail here but the one they were making and if they could not get the horses up they were going to be in a first-class bind. Jim wished for the Sharps Marcia had given and taken away from him, wondering if Kramer had thought to fetch a saddle gun. Somebody back there obviously had one and if anyone got hold of it who knew how to shoot this thing could be finished right here.

Yet Jim knew if he had it to do over he probably wouldn't have done any different. How could he have guessed the town was already warned?

Looking down he could distinguish very little aside from the gun flashes, this poor visibility being mainly the reason he and Kramer were still alive. Someone was shooting from the baled alfalfa now. Two others, alternately firing, were methodically searching the slope with their lead. Another horse screamed and somewhere above fell thrashing. They weren't out of this yet.

There were men in the barn. By the sound they were wrecking it. Jim heard doors go down, the smashing of windows. Flames suddenly burst through the roof and his hopes sank. In a matter of moments it would be bright as day.

He punched the spent shells from Dawk's pistol, reloading. This, with burnt fingers, wasn't easy to do. Already the brush was turning brighter around him. And that fellow with the rifle was getting the range, one slug cutting a gash in the back of Jim's cantle while another jerked wickedly at the brim of his hat.

Final crouched forward, kicking his heels against the dun's ribs. The horse didn't need any urging, it was just as anxious as Jim to get out of this. A slug struck the saddle's brass horn. The dun pitched, squealing, lost its footing among the rocks and went to its knees. Jim quit his seat to yank the horse upright. Miraculously the dun was still able to stumble after him. Bursting through a tangle of catclaw they came onto a shelf that was practically bare rock. They'd got above the guns but it took Jim nearly eight seconds to discover this.

Kramer was waiting in the dark with two spare horses, all that was left of their saddle pool. "I got one of them gun dummies," he snarled, patting the stock of a .44/40. "Might be a smart deal to change off right now."

They made the switch and swung into leather. "Which way?" Kramer growled, passing Jim one of the lead ropes.

"I was aimin' to get back to Skillet but—"

"This ain't no place to be swingin' our jaws!" Kramer put heels to the roan he was forking. Final tagged after him, leading the dun. They rode hard for ten minutes then dropped into a lope. "That town," Kramer said, "is havin' a connipshun."

"How'd you know about those rifles?"

"That's what I'm talkin' about. We got word from Grant. Gov'ment supply train was jumped by them Apaches. Down in the barrens near Lordsburg. Man, we've had it! Brand new Winchester repeaters—but that's only part of it. They got your name plastered all over town! Five hundred bucks for the killin' of some drifter an' twenty-five hundred over the Gov'nor's own John Henry—dead or alive! What'd you do to them fellers?"

Jim pulled up. "You sure about that? Sure it ain't some of Strunk's—"

"Drifter, mebbe, but not this other. Joe Bob's after your hide, man. Them dodgers come in on the stage last night straight from the capital! I've got one right here; you can look for yourself. Signed by the Gov'nor —twenty-five hundred."

Jim, presently shrugging, slapped the scratched calf of a leg with his rein ends. "The old shell game." He grinned toughly. "But which is the distraction?"

"It sure wasn't that coach." Kramer skreaked around in his saddle. "Safford stage was stuck up east of Bowie. Same earmarks as all the rest of these jobs, guy with a Greener. Mormon Bishop got his face blowed off. He was packin' around five thousand in cash."

Jim shook his head. "I'm more interested in—"

"You better git interested. Everybody knows Bentain's present installment on them lands he's been leasin' comes to five thousand an' ain't been paid. Every one of these stickups has been pulled with a double-barreled sawed-off-a Greener, an' you can't hardly git them kind no more. Seems this guy got rattled tonight an' took off without it when he cut for the timber."

"What I want to know—"

"You better know this! Driver found the gun an' turned it over to Dawks. Dawks showed it around. I seen it myself. Three-four of the ranch crowd has tied it to Bentain—claim they've seen it over his mantel. It's got Bentain's initials scratched into it."

Jim understood now much that had puzzled him about Rockabye. "How long has Bentain had that lease?"

"Couple of years, I guess. That guy's a cooked duck."

Jim bitterly scowled. He could clear Bentain, or throw up enough doubt to get him off. He could, that is, if he were allowed to come forward, which he wouldn't be. Even if he gave himself up to do it who would believe him? A convicted rustler broken out of Yuma, stirring things up to get even with Strunk.

"Dawks says that lease money clinches it."

"The gun's his," Jim said, "but it's dollars to doughnuts it was Rockabye used it." He told Kramer about Rockabye hiding the weapon on that stringer in Bentain's barn. "The old man's being jobbed. And by the same combination that put me in Yuma."

"Well," Kramer said, "by now Dawks has likely headed out there with a warrant."

"Not Seeb." Jim told him what the marshal had run into. Kramer whistled.

Jim hitched a boot up. "Tell me some more about those Winchesters."

"Ain't much to tell. Apaches come down on that gov'ment train like hell emigratin' on cartwheels—burnt them wagons plumb to the hubs. Grabbed all the hee-haws an' latched onto them new shootin' irons."

"Notice you're packing one."

In the dark Kramer grinned. "Funny thing about that. I lifted this go-bang outa Strunk's office. Was fixin' to ride the thing over to Grant. Wanted to see what that Major'd make out them letters."

"Letters?"

"That purty US that's burnt into the buttstock."

Jim stared. "You reckon it come off those wagons?"

"I ain't heard of no others floatin' around this country. Like to see Gid talk himself outa this."

"He'd do it," Jim said. "Might come a time when that would be enough, but right now it would just be your word against Strunk's and Strunk holds all the aces. How'd Berkley get wise so quick to what happened?"

"Injuns let one of them drivers git away." Kramer's lip curled. "It's what prodded me into searchin' Gid's office. Sometimes in a raid a feller does git clear but damn uncommon when you're dealin' with Apaches."

Jim frowned at the fist holding onto his reins. "I wish we could use it but I don't see how we can." He kneed the horse into motion. "We better hunt for those Winchesters."

"That ain't all," Kramer said. "Coupla nesters found that youngest Bentain girl not ten minutes from town with her hair tore off an' most of her clothes. You want my notion them guns has been delivered."

Jim was more shocked than he showed about Marcia. He said after a moment, "I suppose she was dead?"

Kramer nodded. "She hadn't been long—that's one of the things that's put the town on its ear. What with them rifles, they figger if Injuns has sneaked in that close—"

But Jim wasn't listening. He had thought to have got the Apache end of Strunk's stick pretty well blunted by that business at Mad Springs—perhaps even gained a little face for Taunee, but this was nothing beside the fact of that wagons raid. Now with a white woman found scalped and near naked—It was a cinch Major Berkley would want a great deal more than Jim and Kramer could give him. Indians had ambushed and wiped out his supplies; he had the word of the lone survivor

379

it was Taunee's Apaches. Nothing short of a direct order from the Department commander was going to save that tribe if Berkley's troopers found one redskin with a Winchester in his fists.

Maybe Berkley wouldn't move till he'd outfitted and got replacements but this would not stop the juggernaut of his reprisal. Another Sand Creek* was clearly in the making.

He told Kramer what had taken place at Mad Springs, about the courier who had brought them news of the missing Winchesters. "We've got to find some way of stopping that damned renegade," he said, but the only way he could think of was to get to the rifles first.

"We don't know where them guns are," Kramer argued.

"We know that raid was the work of Strunk's crowd."

"We'd play hell provin' it if that fathead at Grant won't take my say-so. You can bet Gid Strunk won't be around for delivery!"

"Maybe not," Jim agreed, "but they've got to be handy. They're no good to him till they're in Chuleh's hands. The bunch that hit those wagons has got to put them where Chuleh won't have any trouble getting to them, and that means close to the Reservation. No other locality would back up Berkley's picture of what happened."

Kramer nodded. "I'll go that far with you. But I'd a heap sooner look for a needle in a haystack—"

* A peaceful village of Cheyennes at Sand Creek, Colorado, was attacked without provocation or warning by troops estimated at around 900 under command of Col. J. M. Chivington (November 29, 1864). Almost half of the Cheyennes (variously estimated at between 150 and 500) were slaughtered before the remainder attempted to defend themselves. Chivington's troops killed men, women and children; lost only 12 of their number and looted the village before setting it afire.

"Strunk has got to do that or throw in his hand. They'll be at Skillet," Jim said, and slashed his horse with the rein ends.

The stableman, crowding after him, seemed about half sold, then changed his mind. "It's no good," he called above the clatter of hoofs. "Dawks was goin' to take care of Bentain."

"Strunk always coppers his bets," Jim yelled back. "Always keeps two strings to his bow so if—"

"But with Bentain home how would—"

"They won't care about that. Bentain was figured to be wiped out anyway. The guns won't be at headquarters; nobody'd believe he could be that big a fool. We'll try the linecamp on Horse Mesa."

19 LAST TRUMP

Strunk had moved into the region with no tangible assets and the unalterable conviction the world owed him everything he was able to get his hands on. Though he generally preferred to withhold his presence from the near vicinity of any activity which might later be looked into, it was a foible dictated by prudence and had nothing to do with intestinal fortitude. Strunk wasn't gunshy, just careful; it was the measure of his care that he coppered every bet, insuring success with an alternate means to which he could switch if the method in progress showed indications which worried him. But he could not get rid of his worries about Final.

His first sight of Jim had been a considerable shock. He had supposed the fellow safely locked up in Yuma. the only interpretation he could put on Jim's being here was that Joe Bob had pardoned him. This did nothing to quiet Gid's anxieties.

Final, knowing he'd been framed, could be here for only one purpose—revenge. Retribution with a governor's backing! How like Joe Bob it was to find someone to do his dirty work for him who had personal reason to regard Strunk with hatred. Strunk had long suspected the Governor to be interested in those Indian lands and here was proof of it. The bastard probably knew there was gold in this country and Bentain's lease was almost certain proof Joe Bob knew where it was and had no intention of sharing it with anyone.

Bentain was a credulous fool, and expendable. With Bentain already using the land, if the troops came in and the government later took it away from the Indians as they were sure to do with all these granger votes howling to high heaven to have it thrown open, Skillet would have first choice of the ground with a little string-pulling on the Governor's part. Then if Bentain were killed in an Apache uprising Joe Bob would be left sitting pretty with that lease; Strunk had no doubt Joe Bob had put up the money. The Governor had apparently found out what Strunk was up to. Now it was necessary to have Strunk eliminated and so, instead of more money, he had turned Final loose!

Expecting Final to kill Strunk the Governor now had covered himself with familiar dexterity by proclaiming Jim Final had broken out of Yuma, insuring Jim's silence by twenty-five hundred payable dead or alive. It was the only bright splash in the whole sorry picture, permitting Strunk, as it did, to pull his own crew off the hunt and use them to prod those damned savages to action.

Even that wasn't going as Strunk had planned that it should; he was having to rush things. Rockabye had robbed and killed the Mormon Bishop and that should take care of Bentain if nothing else did. But time was on the side of those crooks at the capital.

The gambler still had a few cards up his sleeve. What would work for Joe Bob was twice as valuable to Gid. The Governor, with that lease, was banking on possession. With Bentain removed Strunk would be on the ground.

He couldn't use Dawks—the fool had got himself killed. Who could he pin the tin on now that would go out there and—Hell!

Strunk swore like a mule skinner. He had Bentain exactly where he wanted him and Seeb, after the way Quail had used them, would have seen this through without a hitch. On the evidence Dawks had assembled it would be no chore finding a man to go out there, but this wasn't enough. Strunk didn't want Bentain arraigned, he wanted him killed while trying to escape. Like Joe Bob figured, dead men tell no tales.

The gambler, snapping his fingers, suddenly jumped to his feet. *Rockabye.* Of course! The man was made for the job. On top of everything else Bentain's riding boss, with his own neck to think of, wouldn't be at all squeamish—nor would anyone be likely to hook him up with Gid Strunk. Bentain's own man! Rockabye, as the law in these parts, would place Gid Strunk above reproach. Only Final, perhaps—

Strunk, irascible again, started pacing, the fine flush of returning confidence shaken. Having been trapped once through the agency of Rockabye, Final would never in this world— The gambler wheeled, went to the desk and poured himself another whisky. He downed one more and, hand still shaking, smashed the bottle against one of the mirrors. Final! Every time it was that goddam Final; *Why the hell hadn't somebody killed him!* Strunk remembered Bill Tapp, the back-shot Roup, the reward bills tacked to every post. He also remembered the gov-

ernment rifles and was thrown into a spasm of pacing and
cursing.

Tapp's crew was in the hills with those Winchesters
waiting for Chuleh to pick them up; but Tapp didn't
know Jim had come into town or that Dawks was dead.
Instead of being reassured by Tapp's recent display of
initiative (in the matter of Roup) Strunk was gripped by
the dread Tapp might improvise again. One miscalcula-
tion, delay or blunder by the crew before they got shed
of those new Army repeaters—

Strunk stopped in his tracks, went cold all over. That
dismantled Winchester Cretch had fetched in. Foolishly,
crazily, still upset by the fiasco of that trip out to
Skillet, he had shoved the damned thing into that drawer
with his bottle.

He ripped the drawer open, pawing wildly.

Gone!

Sick and frightened the gambler straightened. Which
of his men had come in here and taken it? It came to
him now he couldn't trust one of them, Tapp included.

He was too scared to swear now. *He had to get out
there.*

He checked the short-barreled pistol clipped under
his left armpit, thrust it back in its spring. Caught up his
hat, snuffed the lamp and then stood motionless, feeling
the sweat-drenched cling of his clothing.

He went across to the door and very quietly locked
it. Chewed a while on his lip and then, still frowning,
flipped the key back. Relighted the lamp. Making sure
the alley door was still barred he went into the dark
of his sleeping quarters and cautiously let himself out
of a window,

To Quail her father appeared unbelievably fragile and
helpless. Even in the deepening gloom of this room the

sagging skin of his face looked like tired folds of wax.

He said, "I should have taken a gun to him."

"To Jim?" Quail said, startled.

"Rockabye. Rockabye told Jim about those cattle." He dragged a hand across his face, fretfully staring at the sweat that ran off the shaking ends of his fingers. "I should have guessed," he said miserably.

"Why did you put Jim over him? Was it because Jim was seeing me?"

Eyes dull, Bentain shook his head. "Strunk—what I figured Strunk was up to; a grasper. He was always schemin' up ways to get ahead. I was sure he was fixin' to squeeze me out and I thought, after losin' his ranch like he done, your man was the best insurance I could get." He pulled the brown coat tighter over bent shoulders.

Quail said, "Marcia's gone."

She thought for a while he hadn't heard. Then he drew a long breath and some inner leap of bitterness or fury stiffened the cheeks that had sagged and were creviced by drink and defeat. "She made her bed." The fire burned out. "We're done here, girl. I traded your rights for a governor's lies and this is the place where those lies catch up with us."

He scrubbed the hand over his face again and seemed to forget her, pushing around in his chair till he could get shrunken elbows braced on the desk. He seemed to stare long at the gun by his hand, then his face came around. "Pack your stuff an' get out."

"I'm staying," Quail said.

"Like your mother. Like a rock." Bentain looked at her testily. "He won't be back. Strunk'll get him, or one of them bounty hunters."

Final, never putting it into words, was inclined to share that grim opinion. If he'd guessed right and found the cache before Chuleh's bucks latched onto those rifles he would do what he was able. He had no hope beyond this. That twenty-five hundred the Governor had posted didn't leave much future for a man named Jim Final. He wasn't surprised at the Governor's treachery. The dice had been loaded right from the start.

He pushed the pace. When the horses between their legs gave out he and Kramer abandoned them, switching their saddles to the pair they'd been towing.

The moon was down and they were glad to be rid of it but the night was just about gone when they came out of the brush and got into the grasslands surrounding the mesa. The flat-topped mountain loomed stark and still against the fading light of the stars. Jim let the horses blow while he stared apprehensively into the east where already the horizon was beginning to emerge from the dark's loosened grip.

"Reckon they're here?" Kramer asked, keeping his voice down.

"We'll soon know. Trail's over there to the left. We better leave these horses."

"Me an' my bare feet," Kramer groaned.

Jim got down, put his ear to the ground, shaking his head as he pushed erect. He took off his boots, tied them back of his saddle. He filled his right hand with dirt, rubbing chest and left arm with it. Kramer rubbed the other arm and Jim's scratched back. They both stared worriedly toward Mad Springs. "This isn't your fight," Jim said. Kramer snorted.

Jim said, after a moment, "Might've taken Chuleh longer to get moving than we figured. Had to get something done about that shoulder. Maybe he had trouble getting enough bucks to follow him. Fetch the Winchester. If he ain't up there yet—"

"Tapp's crew will be up there. Tapp, too, more'n likely."

"I'm counting on that. If Chuleh hasn't showed we'll try a bluff. You can tell Strunk's crew you're a special agent Joe Bob has commissioned to clean this mess up."

Kramer sniffed. "You think they're gonna fall for that?"

"All I want is a little time." Jim rubbed dirt into his cheeks and forehead, ripped another strip from what was left of his pants and bound it about his head. "Might look more like an Apache if—"

"You look all right. You look half as good when they lay you out you'll hev every woman in hell shinin' up to you." Kramer levered a shell into the breech of his rifle. "Love an' kisses," he said, and stepped after Jim into the trail's curdled dark.

Jim knew that logic didn't always enter into the plans of red men or red-handed ones; the rifles might not be here at all. But if they were he was sure Tapp would have a watch posted. He'd not want to be caught with guns taken by massacre if someone showed up in advance of his customers. Maybe, Jim thought, Tapp had left straightaway, quick as his crew had unloaded the cases. They might all be gone, pulled away by that bounty.

He almost convinced himself; but without those guns the Apaches were whipped, and Strunk with them. The man had to have violence to cover his tracks. Tapp wouldn't have sent word by messenger to Taunee's village that the rifles were ready without there'd be somebody around to deliver them.

Until actually put into the hands of the Indians Strunk would want those guns where if anything went wrong they would damn Bentain and Skillet. But how could they do that if Tapp's crew was with them?

Jim shook his head. There was no use trying to rationalize a hunch. He had a hunch those rifles were up here and another hunch told him Tapp's bunch were with them. Maybe Tapp figured to pull out before Chuleh's gang got their hands on those Winchesters. Tapp would be hard to surprise right now. And he would not be alone.

Final paused where the trail began its climb up the wall. In the old days this had been little better than a goat track but Bentain with picks and powder had gouged out a road you could take a wagon over.

He put his mouth against the liveryman's ear. "Cover me if you're able but don't crowd the play. I'm going to try to get hold of Tapp's lookout but if he spots me first maybe he'll take me for one of Chuleh's bucks. Way the light is I ought to get right up on him before he knows any better. Don't do any shooting without it's a case of have to."

Kramer nodded. Jim pushed ahead. If he'd guessed wrong he would know directly. The rough shale of this climb was hard on bare feet but the things on Jim's mind were what pulled his mouth tight. He might have offered some suggestions for Kramer's guidance in the event this didn't work out, but in this kind of action you had to take what you found and do what you could with it.

Jim knew from the days when he was Skillet's ramrod it was about half a mile from the start of this climb to the brow of the mesa. He could not recall all the bends and windings but there'd be plenty of places for a watcher to hide. He redoubled his caution. Those clouds in the east were noticeably plainer though most of the landscape was still pretty vague. Wind, pulled off the desert by dawn's approach, crept through the brush, chilling his back and the scratched calves of his legs. He felt too edgy, too beset with impatience, pushed and pummeled by anxieties he could neither cope with nor obliterate. He forced himself to pause, breathing deeply.

Though there'd been no sign of Chuleh's band, no

rumor of travel, he was versed enough in the ways of this land to realize such things could not be expected. It was when you didn't see them that Apaches were apt to be nearest.

He moved on.

The lookout probably would be on the rim. Jim, creeping nearer, moved slower and slower. He stopped frequently to listen but the wind was too strong to detect lesser sounds. He hadn't been up here since the linecamp was built but thought he could guess about where the shack and corrals would be located. About a hundred yards from where this road reached the top, well out of the sweep of those desert gales but too near to risk warning Tapp's men with gunplay. Tapp's scout would be expecting some prearranged signal.

Jim, frowning, tried a roadrunner's call but nothing came back. Though he strained his eyes until tears blurred his vision he could not detect any sign of a guard. He stared at the sky; there were still a few stars. He peered again toward the east and saw the gray shapes of mountains. Pushed by his fears he crept forward until his eyes topped the rim.

The shack was about where he'd thought it would be, a more solid dark against the darkness it huddled in, crouched like a toad in the curdle of shadows. Twisting his head Jim could see nothing else. He looked over his shoulder and couldn't find Kramer.

He pursed his lips in an owl call, had about decided there was no one in hearing when a voice snarled less than ten strides away: "Come up slow an' keep them paws out!"

Jim, edging forward, spoke in guttural Apache. The fellow of course couldn't make anything out of this. He was in a dark jumble of rocks, standing up now, holding a rifle. "Why didn't you give the call you was told—" The guard broke off, stiffening, grabbed all his

389

breath to let go of a shout. Jim sprang, the man trying to ward him off with the rifle. Final caught him on the side of the head with Dawks' pistol. He went down without sound but the rifle, striking a rock, blew a hole through the quiet.

Everything seemed to happen at once. A door banged open. Booted feet kicked up sound in a hard run and Jim, snatching up the bastardly weapon, howled angry protest in border Apache. Someone fired from the shack, that bullet screaming viciously off a rock in front of Jim. Jim dropped and the runner, cursing, yelled, "Put down that gun!"

This was Tapp. He was about halfway across from Jim now.

After a moment of quiet he came on, a lot slower, considerably more wary. Jim, grimly anxious to make sure of Tapp, raised the guard's rifle. Left elbow flat against an anchorage of rock, resting the barrel across extended left wrist, he drew a bead on Tapp's belt buckle. When he felt he could score Jim said, "Paleface stop!"

Tapp pulled up. "That was a mistake—damn fool got excited." He tried to put this into understandable Apache, starting forward again, Jim letting him come in the hope of a surer shot. But before he had taken three steps Kramer's voice, somewhere out in the shadows, growled with commendable intent but poorer judgment, "One more inch an' I'm blowin' your jaw off!"

Two shots ripped out of the shack, both muzzle blasts gouting toward that jumpity voice. Kramer's Winchester barked and Jim, bitterly furious, squeezed off a shot but Tapp had already ducked.

"Wait a minute!" he yelled, and then his voice slammed at Kramer: "Who're you?"

Final, changing position under cover of this distraction, called, "Fun's over, Tapp. We've got your bunch surrounded. That's a special investigator sent in by the government."

"What gov'ment?" Tapp snarled, but it was plain that he was upset.

"Territorial. The Right Honorable Joe Bob," Kramer told him. "Throw down your guns."

A stillness closed down, a hush crammed to bursting with distrust and itchy triggers. Tapp was in a bad way caught in the open like he was and caught too, if he could believe it, with those Army rifles from that wagon train wipe-out. He might be in the cleft of something which would prove no stronger than a twig off a branch he could snap in his fingers or it could be a big stick that would squash him if he didn't hold still.

Tension gripped all of them. Final's mouth was so dry he couldn't move his tongue. This was the crux of it, the test which would determine whether or not those Winchesters were used.

It was light enough now to see the shack's open door hole and, off yonder, the twin-peaked top of Tapp's hat where he crouched in grim edginess trying to make up his mind. Then a slap of the wind sent a dust devil racing and Jim knew before Tapp moved that he was finding it too quiet. Perhaps it was the rifles that really tipped the scales.

Tapp came out of his crouch with a high ringing yell, emptying his pistol as ricochets and tunneling whistlers from the shack forced Jim down. Rock chips stung his naked back. Lead shrilled past the dug-in hunch of his shoulders. Dust swirled over him and he caught the pounding drum of hoofs, the wild ululations of hate-crazed Apaches.

The shaft of an arrow suddenly materialized vibrating viciously not ten inches in front of his face, the killing end buried in a crevice between two rocks. These boulders were no good to Jim now with the Indians in back of him. These were the broncos—Chuleh's bunch —come for the promised rifles. He'd be even worse off if Chuleh got hold of him than facing Tapp's crew.

Dust from those racing ponies swirled over the rocks in a lemon fog. There was no place to go but the shack, and Jim ran for it. Visibility with all this dirt in the air was practically zero except where wind tore brief channels through it. Out of one gap a black horse reeled, the bent-forward rider with coat tails flying swinging a blood-darkened quirt at each jump. Dust swept over the ground like a curtain. Jim, breaking clear, saw the shack and the black on its haunches in front of it—saw the man hit the ground in a hard stumbling run.

It was Strunk beating against that jerked-shut door, shouting, clawing frantically. Still running, Jim saw the gambler stagger. Dust swooped down again blanketing everything. When he saw Strunk again the man was a horror without any hair wabbling around in a stumbling circle screaming like a gutted horse, both hands clamped to the dripping shaft that stuck out of his blood-gouting belly.

Jim, hardly ten strides away, felt bile rush into his throat like brass, staring unbelievably at that still-shut door as howling half-glimpsed shapes rushed past. A Winchester cracked spitefully as he attempted to whirl and get away from the place. The trampled ground, weirdly spinning, came up for him like a leaping dog. He threw out his good hand to ward it off, was astounded when the arm crumpled under him.

He felt no impact but remembered to roll. Little geysers of dust spurted up all around him. He felt the slithery stickiness of blood and saw a monstrous shape that was half horse plunging at him.

He saw the point of the feathered lance and made to bring up his rifle, discovering he no longer had it. He tried to reach the butt of Dawks' pistol with his good right hand but the hand wouldn't move. He deflected the thrust of the lance with a foot and with his burnt hand yanked Dawks' pistol and fired.

Chuleh's face with its mouth stretched wide focused briefly and vanished over the rump of the horse. Jim got to his knees and, with the pistol still clutched like a crutch in burnt hand, began to crawl. He couldn't see where he was going because he couldn't seem to lift his head. He guessed the sun must be showing because his skin felt the heat of it and a throbbing rose-tinted glow gilded everything.

He kept doggedly moving until the punch of his hobbling hand stubbed into something that gave and twisted with the weight he put on it; this flung him off balance and one knee buckled under him and again there was the scrape of dirt against his face.

He reckoned his luck had finally run out and fleetingly wondered what had happened to Kramer, but mostly it was the Apaches he thought about, knowing they'd probably finish him before he was able to get under cover. He could hear them larruping around, madly yelling, the cork-stopper popping of their antiquated trade guns, filling the fog with the whir of their arrows; through and above this the *crack-crack* of Winchesters.

But now there was something else being added, some change in tempo, a picked-up pitch to that Indian yelling to which Jim listened in a kind of frozen horror. A wailing, a wavering off-key howl that crept through flesh and got into Jim's bones, a sound like nothing he had ever heard before that set every nerve end vibrating, that choked off breath and put a wordless terror into the bone's very marrow.

He felt compelled to twist his head.

Through tatters of wind-whipped swirling dust the skittering shapes of Chuleh's paint-daubed demons seemed crazily to be scattering, each one driving in some different direction, dropping everything, abandoning all reason in a panic rush to get away from where they were. Jim couldn't believe his eyes. It was incredible, so like some farfetched figment of delirium, that he put down his burnt hand to brace his weight and hauled the other knee up under him and saw the pole roof of the shack brightly blazing. And there was Strunk on his back, all bloody and jerking, making sounds like a cow—but it wasn't these which had spooked those red devils; and Jim himself listening for the call of a trumpet, which was almost as loco. No cavalry was coming, he'd told that lieutenant not to let Berkley move.

Head swimming he pushed himself around a little more and found the rim black with the shapes of horse-backers that seemed twenty feet tall against the bright flood of the lifting sun. *Chuleh's main force moving in for the kill!*

But why were those other fools throwing their weapons down? And why wasn't Tapp's bunch knocking them silly?

All firing had quit. In this unnatural quiet Jim watched the newcomers spill into a great circle. Tapp must have lost his guts, Final thought. It came to him then there hadn't been much firing, not nearly so much as a man would have looked for.

If Tapp had those rifles he must have thousands of cartridges unless—Jim suddenly laughed, laughed until the tears rolled down his cheeks. Tapp's predicament was beautifully clear. That wily bastard, knowing these people had no love for him, for safety's sake had cached those cartridges someplace else. This, in his hurry to get behind walls, Tapp had forgotten and now was caught with Winchesters empty.

The sound of an approaching horse pulled Jim upright and he saw an Apache in a dirty white shirt with its bedraggled tails flapping against bare legs. An uncreased straw sombrero was squarely set on this old head and a Navajo blanket, loosely folded, hung over the hips of his scrawny mount. Jim, grinding knuckles against burning eyes, had to look twice. He was so damned pleased it almost choked him.

Taunee stopped a few yards from the shack and sat his scrawny horse with magnificent disdain, contemptuous of anything its occupants might do. With a great shower of sparks the roof fell in. Barely in time was the door kicked open. Two badly singed men, smoke blackened and coughing, stumbled out with their arms up. Cretch and Rockabye.

The old chief's eyes were glinting like black diamonds. Punching a fist toward Chuleh's dead shape he said, "No damn good. Bad Apache." Then he thrust a rigid finger first at the frightened look of Cretch who had led the attack on the government wagons, then at the glowering man from Skillet. "Bad Americans. Great White Father better hangum."

But Jim, now worriedly watching the shack, reeled abruptly forward. "Drop it, Tapp!"

He was afraid of Dawks' pistol after making a crutch of it. But when Tapp, bringing his gun up, snarled, "No damn Injun's—" Jim fired from the hip—fired again and let go of the gun.

A man could take just about so much and if these Mad Springs Apaches hadn't been all around him Jim reckoned, by God, he might have pitched down himself.

He stumbled over to Taunee. "Those go-bangs and these prisoners—you take 'em to Berkley."

"Yeah, sure," Taunee grunted. He peered down at Jim slyly. "You good man. Good friend my people." Face wrinkling into a grin he dropped off his horse, thrusting the jaw cord into Jim's hand. "White squaw heap worry—all time hurry-hurry."

Following the old chief's glance Jim saw Quail.

395

But what of Joe Bob? What about that advertised jailbreak and the twenty-five hundred they had put on Jim's scalp?

"He can't help himself," Quail said, as though guessing his thoughts. "You've stopped Joe Bob cold."

"Good woman," Taunee chuckled. "Fetch plenty ponies."

Jim eyed her tiredly. "I still don't have one damn thing to offer—"

"Dad has," she said. "He's giving us the ranch."